Secrets

Satisfy your desire for more.

Blood Hunt by Cynthia Eden

Vampiress Nema Alexander has a definite taste for bad boys. Slade Brion, a notorious bounty hunter, has just been charged with tracking her down. He won't stop until he catches her, and Nema won't stop until she claims him, forever.

Scandalous Behavior by Anne Rainey

Tess Marley is tired of her dull life. She wants to take a walk on the wild side. Who better to teach her about carnal pleasures than her intriguing boss, Kevin Haines? Five years of secretly lusting after the man is enough. She wants to see if Kevin is all she's dreamed he would be. But Tess makes a major miscalculation when she crosses the line between lust and love.

Enter the Hero by Sedonia Guillone

Kass and Lian are sentenced to sex slavery in the Confederation's pleasure district. Their only crime was the desire to love each other in freedom. Forced to make love for an audience, their hearts are with each other while their bodies are on display. Now, in the midst of sexual slavery, they have one more chance to escape to Paradise... with each other and with their lives!

Up to No Good by Natasha Moore

Now the owner of a neighborhood bar, former syndicated columnist Simon "Mac" MacKenzie hides a tragic secret. When freelance writer Alison Chandler tracks him down, he knows she's up to no good. Seeking an exclusive interview, she threatens not only his carefully constructed lifestyle, but longstanding ideas of love and trust. Is their attraction merely a distraction or the key to surviving their war of wills?

Cynthia Eden

Anne Rainey

Sedonia Guillone

Natasha Moore

Volume 25

Secrets

Satisfy your desire for more.

SECRETS Volume 25
This is an original publication of Red Sage Publishing and each individual story herein has never before appeared in print. These stories are a collection of fiction and any similarity to actual persons or events is purely coincidental.

Red Sage Publishing, Inc.
P.O. Box 4844
Seminole, FL 33775
727-391-3847
www.redsagepub.com

SECRETS Volume 25
A Red Sage Publishing book
All Rights Reserved/December 2008
Copyright © 2008 by Red Sage Publishing, Inc.

ISBN: 1-60310-005-9 / ISBN 13: 978-1-60310-005-2

Published by arrangement with the authors and copyright holders of the individual works as follows:

BLOOD HUNT
Copyright © 2008 by Cynthia Eden

SCANDALOUS BEHAVIOR
Copyright © 2008 by Anne Rainey

ENTER THE HERO
Copyright © 2008 by Sedonia Guillone

UP TO NO GOOD
Copyright © 2008 by Natasha Moore

Photographs:
Cover © 2008 by Tara Kearney; www.tarakearney.com
Cover Models: Brittany Noles and Jeremy Tirpak
Setback cover © 2000 by Greg P. Willis; GgnYbr@aol.com

Printed in the U.S.A.

Book typesetting by:
Quill & Mouse Studios, Inc.
www.quillandmouse.com

Contents

Blood Hunt

by Cynthia Eden

To My Reader:

I've always had a soft spot for vampires. Sure, they can be the stuff of nightmares, but vampires can also be charming and seductive. When I wrote *Blood Hunt*, I decided I wanted to create a female vampire who was just as strong and seductive as her male counterparts… and Nema Alexander was born. Of course, once I created Nema, I had to make sure I gave her a worthy hero… and in walked Slade Brion.

I hope you enjoy my take on the vampiric world.

Prologue

"Let me get this straight." Slade Brion pressed his palms against the old, scarred surface of his wooden desk and leaned forward, keeping his gaze pinned on the guy dressed in the too-expensive suit. "You're gonna pay me two hundred grand to track down some woman—"

"She's not just some woman." The faint lines around Clayton McDermott's eyes tightened. "Nema Alexander is a killer. Make no mistake about it." He tossed a stack of color photos onto Slade's desk.

Automatically, Slade glanced down. Saw the twisted bodies of the men. Saw the blood that soaked the ground beneath them. He lifted the pictures, studying them, one, then another.

Five pictures total. Five men. All with their throats ripped out.

He reached for the manila file he'd pushed aside moments before. A picture of Nema was inside. She looked delicate, almost fragile. She was a pretty thing, kind of exotic looking, with a long mass of straight black hair, a heart-shaped face and big, golden eyes.

She damn sure didn't look like a monster who could murder five men. Five men who each had to outweigh her by at least a hundred pounds.

A faint whistle slipped past his lips. "You're telling me this woman did that?"

"Nema isn't like other women."

"Um. You don't say." He didn't trust McDermott. Not a damn bit, but the guy reeked of money, and Slade sure as hell could not afford to turn down a meal ticket.

He'd been a bounty hunter for more than two years now. After he'd gotten kicked off the Force, there hadn't been a ton of options for him. He'd managed to keep his office going only by working ninety-hour weeks.

But with two hundred grand... Jesus, his life would change. With that much cash, he could kiss this hellhole office in Houston good-bye and go sun himself on a beach somewhere.

And all he had to do was hunt down this killer.

He stroked the picture of Nema.

"Why me?" He had to ask the question. Normally, he tracked down petty thieves and domestic abusers. Slade didn't want to look a golden gift horse in the mouth, but—

But he wasn't an idiot, either.

Something about this case was off. Way off. "If this Nema has killed all these men, the cops have to be hunting her."

"I don't want the cops to find her."

Ah. Now they were getting to the heart of the matter. "Just what is it that you do want?" He'd heard about McDermott before. Seen the guy's face splashed in all the papers. He was some kind of millionaire, had some hi-tech company that worked with the government. Designing weapons and technology.

So what did a guy like that want with a murderer?

"Nema can't see the inside of a jail."

"You saying you want me to kill her?" Not the first time he'd gotten a request like that, but it still burned in his gut. No matter what the others in his unit had said, he wasn't a cold-blooded killer.

"No!" Real alarm flashed in the depths of McDermott's blue gaze. "The last thing I want is for Nema to be killed."

"Then what do you want?"

"I want to you to bring her to me. To Daylor Labs. I can help her there, I can—"

Slade held up his hand. "If the cops are having such a hard time catching her, what makes you think I'll just be able to find her and bring her to you?" Slade doubted the woman was just going to walk up to him and surrender herself.

A smile curved McDermott's lips. "I know where she is, and you—you're her perfect prey." He pointed to the photos. "You're just like them. You won't have to approach her. When she sees you, she'll make the first move."

He looked back at the photos. Yeah, he'd noticed the resemblance. The guys did all look like him. Same dark hair. Rough features. Muscular build.

His hands clenched into fists. "You setting me up to be her next victim?"

McDermott reached into his jacket and pulled out a thin black vial. "Put this into a syringe. When you get close to her, and I know you will, inject her. She'll be weak then, and you can control her."

Okay. That sounded like a real piss-poor idea. He started to shake his head.

"Two hundred and fifty thousand," McDermott muttered suddenly, as if reading his mind.

Slade hesitated. Sirens echoed in the distance. Two hundred and fifty thousand. To capture a killer.

He drew in a deep breath. There were other questions he should ask. He knew it, but he'd learned that curiosity really didn't pay in his business.

There was an arrest warrant for Nema in the file. The cops thought she'd killed those men. He could track her, turn her over to McDermott, then call the station to let the uniforms know where to find her.

And he could still collect his money.

Provided Nema didn't kill him first.

He licked his lips. "Three hundred grand."

A muscle jerked along McDermott's jaw. "Deal."

For the first time in months, Slade smiled.

And the hot anticipation of the hunt filled him.

Chapter 1

Oh, damn, but she was thirsty. Nema wrapped her fingers around the icy beer bottle in her hand and wished that it would be enough to satisfy her.

But it wouldn't.

There was only one thing that would quench the need tightening her gut and drying her throat.

Only one.

Dammit.

She squeezed her eyes shut, counted to ten and then slowly lifted her lashes. She glanced around the smoky interior of Miguel's. The rundown bar was on the Texas/Mexico border. Filled with drunken cowboys, loud music, and the stench of sweat.

It was the perfect place to find her prey. No one would notice if one of these men disappeared for a bit.

Just long enough to give her a precious drink.

Nema licked her lips. She hated the hunt, but it had become a necessary part of her life. If she could just find someone who was—

The bar's front door was shoved open. A man walked in, tall, midnight black hair, a give-'em-hell attitude stamped on his rough features. His leather jacket was old, scratched, and even in the dim lighting, she could see the swirl of a black tattoo on his neck.

Her spine straightened as sudden interest filled her.

Her heart began to pound hard and fast in anticipation.

Oh, yes. He was perfect. Just perfect.

Nema had a weakness for bad boys. Always had, even in the days before her change. Once upon a time, a wild boy had taken her into the back of his Mustang and showed her just how great it could feel to be bad.

She'd been addicted to the men with a dangerous edge ever since.

Thus her current predicament.

Her love for the wild ones had made her wind up in this godforsaken bar, and she'd wound up, she guessed, godforsaken, too.

Her canines began to burn as she stared at the man. He sauntered up to the bar. Leaned over to speak to the bartender, and then a bottle of beer was pushed toward him.

Her leather-clad stranger turned around, rested his back against the bar. His gaze began to sweep the room.

This way. Look this way.

His stare, a dark, stormy blue, locked on her.

A whip of hunger snapped through her, and Nema quivered as anticipation filled her.

Oh, yes. He'd do nicely.

Nema stretched her lips into a slow smile of invitation, deliberately shielding her growing fangs. Didn't want to scare off the prey.

He didn't smile back, but he did start walking toward her. Not walking. Stalking. Shoulders back, eyes narrowed, hand wrapped loosely around the neck of the beer bottle. He stopped at the edge of her table, staring down at her.

Up close, she could see the faint lines around the edges of his eyes. Nema figured he was probably in his mid to late thirties. His skin was burnished a deep gold—he obviously spent many hours out in the sun, the lucky bastard. He was a tall guy, a couple of inches over six feet, and well-muscled. His jacket was stretched tight across his powerful shoulders.

"You alone?" His voice was rough and deep.

She nodded.

"Wanna stay that way?"

"No." She motioned to the seat beside her. "You're welcome to join me."

His gaze strayed to the seat, but then he shook his head.

Disappointment had her clenching her hands into fists beneath the table.

He said, "Dance with me." Not a question.

"Wh-what?"

He jerked his thumb toward the small, wooden dance floor. Two other couples were out there, swaying slowly to the country western beat.

Dance. He'd have to hold her close. She'd be able to feel that strong body of his against her.

Nema shoved away from the table and rose to her feet. "I'd love to." In fact, at that moment, there was only one thing that she'd love more.

But, well, that would have to wait.

She had to get the guy to trust her first. And then it would be time to attack.

The woman felt good in his arms. Too good. Her body pressed against his, her small breasts teasing his chest. His hands were at the base of her back, just above the soft curve of her ass. He had to fight the temptation to lower his fingers just a few more inches and rub that perfect—

"What's your name?"

He stiffened at the sound of her voice. Jesus. He'd never heard a voice like hers before. Low, husky, so sexy that just the sound of it had his balls tightening and his cock swelling.

Her head lifted from his shoulder and she stared at him. She was a tall woman, just a few inches shorter than he was. Her eyes, dark and molten gold, met his.

"I'm Slade. Slade Brion."

She nodded and curved the full lips that he could already feel on his own. Damn if a dimple didn't flash in her left cheek.

"I'm Nema."

Yeah, he knew that. He also knew he was playing with fire, but he couldn't seem to stop himself. There was something about the woman that was drawing him in. Making him so hungry that his whole body seemed too hot, too tight.

The woman's a killer, dumbass. Keep your control! Don't let a hard-on cost you three hundred grand. Slade drew in a deep breath, and he smelled her. A light, sweet scent. Roses.

Shit.

Her fingers trailed down his neck, hesitated for the briefest of moments over his pulse. Her touch was soft. Light. He wanted to feel those hands of hers all over him.

Time to stop playing before he got in too deep.

Deliberately, he let his fingers drop to her ass. He pulled her closer, letting her feel the hard bulge of his arousal.

She didn't back away or gasp or feign embarrassment when she felt his arousal. Her eyes widened for just a moment and a look of fierce satisfaction flashed across her face.

"You want me."

Hell, he figured every guy in that bar wanted her. Nema oozed sex appeal like no woman he'd ever seen. Sure, she was a looker—he'd noticed that in the picture. But in person, with her shining eyes, wet lips and sexy smile, damn, it was all he could do not to strip her and take her then and there.

Not his usual style.

No wonder the other poor bastards had been easy marks. They'd probably never even seen the killing blow coming.

He wouldn't make that mistake.

The hard weight of his handcuffs pressed against the base of his back.

Time to regain some control of the situation.

He lifted his right hand. Deliberately ran his fingertips over the soft skin of her cheek. Down to her mouth. Pressed against those blood-red lips.

Her eyes widened. Her tongue snaked out, licked the tip of his index finger. Jesus.

His cock pressed against the jagged line of his zipper. But he'd managed to prove a point. The lady wanted him, too.

Slade had seen the lust in her eyes.

Now for step two.

"Let's get out of here." If McDermott had been right, and so far the guy had been, Nema would want to get him out of the bar. Away from any witnesses. And that worked just fine with him.

Provided he could stop his temptress from killing him.

For a moment, he thought of the vial McDermott had given him. But Nema—well, hell, he outweighed her by a good hundred pounds and stretched over her perfect body by several inches. He'd be able to easily control her, even without the damn vial.

The band stopped playing, as if on perfect cue. Slade snagged Nema's wrist and pulled her behind him as he made his way across the bar.

She didn't fight. Didn't struggle in the least. She just followed right behind him, that sweet scent of hers wrapping around him.

His fist shoved into the wooden door, sending it flying open, and he stepped into the night.

There were a few cowboys in the parking lot, smoking, drinking. He turned the corner, keeping his hold on Nema, and he stalked to the side of the building. He'd parked his truck there earlier. Easier for his getaway plans.

Once he was sure they were away from any curious eyes, he pushed her back against the brick wall. She smiled up at him, the corners of her lips tilting and that dimple peeking in the moonlight. He took her hands, pinned them above her and held them tight with his left hand.

Her smile never dimmed. "Controlling type, are you?"

She was about to see just how controlling he could be.

"I like that." Nema licked her lips. Her head tilted back. Her mouth was open. Ready, wet, waiting.

Shit. There was really only so much temptation a man could take.

Her breasts pushed against his chest. Her legs were spread, and his cock pushed hard against the vee of her sex.

"From the moment I saw you," she whispered, her voice a sexy breath of sound, "I've been wanting to taste you."

Then that made two of them.

Slade realized he couldn't look away from her mouth. He wanted to feel her lips beneath his. Wanted to feel her tongue against his.

"What are you waiting for?" she asked.

Damn good question.

The cuffs bit into his back.

His fingers tightened around her wrists.

And his control snapped.

Slade's mouth crashed down onto hers, his tongue driving deep as he gave in to the frantic need to taste her.

His blood was rushing hard and fast through his body. Need burned through him. Nema felt good, too good, in his arms. And she met his kiss, met it head on with a stark hunger he'd never experienced before.

She tasted sweet. Rich. His tongue stroked hers and she moaned softly into his mouth. Her nipples stabbed against his chest. Would they taste as good? He'd bet his life on it. His right hand began to rise toward her breasts.

What in the hell was he doing?

Slade jerked his head up, stared down at her with the drumming sound of his heartbeat filling his ears.

"Why'd you stop?" Her lips tightened for a moment. "I was just getting started."

Her eyes were so gold. Burning bright, shining in the faint glow of the moon.

So gold....

His head lowered toward hers again.

"Better," she whispered. "Much better."

Her nose nuzzled against him and he tilted his neck, liking that soft movement. Then Slade sucked in a sharp breath as Nema's warm, wet tongue lapped against the skin over his throat.

Oh, yeah, that felt damn good.

Her lips closed over the skin and the soft suction of her mouth sent a shaft of pure lust straight to his cock.

Control, he had to hold on to—

Her tongue snaked down the column of his throat. Rubbed against the pulse point that was pounding so frantically.

He fumbled with his right hand, reaching back for the cuffs. If he didn't make his move soon, he'd take the woman right there.

The hard edge of her teeth pressed against him.

Slade shuddered. He'd never really been into the whole biting thing, but Nema could sure make it work.

Her teeth pressed harder and through the haze of his arousal, a faint fear began to stir.

Five men… all with their throats ripped out.

He jerked up the cuffs, reaching for the hands he still held pinned.

And a razor sharp lash of pain sliced across his throat.

"Sonofabitch!" The handcuffs snapped in place and Slade jerked back.

Nema glared up at him, her mouth glistening. "What the hell are you doing?"

He lifted a hand to his throat, touched the wetness that could have come from her mouth… or that could have been blood. Slade stared down at his fingertips. Too dark to tell for certain, but he had a bad feeling he was looking at his own blood.

The lady had almost claimed another victim.

"You've just made a serious mistake." She wasn't smiling at him anymore. No sign of the flashing dimple.

"No, sweetheart, you're the one who picked the wrong prey for the night." He grabbed the cuffs, wrenching her arms down. Time to pack her pretty ass into the truck and go claim his money.

And it was pity. He'd kinda hoped that McDermott had been wrong about her.

But the lady was a murderer. Hell, she'd tried to bite his throat open.

Keeping his hold on the cuffs, he stepped toward his truck, intending to pull her behind him.

But Nema didn't move. Not even when he used all of his strength to jerk against the cuffs.

What the—

"You don't know who you're dealing with," she muttered and with a seemingly casual toss of her hands, she shook him off. Nema glanced down at the cuffs, her lips curling into a sneer. "You have no fucking idea." Then she lifted her hands and jerked the cuffs apart.

Chapter 2

The bloodlust was riding her hard. Her body trembled and her fangs burned in her mouth. The taste of Slade's blood was on her tongue. Warm. Wet. Better than any wine she'd ever tasted.

She wanted more.

And the asshole had just tried to handcuff her.

He'd even succeeded. Too bad for him that the cuffs hadn't held.

He muttered, "What in the hell—"

Nema growled, grabbed him by his throat and turned in a blur, reversing their positions and shoving him up against the hard stone wall.

His blue eyes were narrowed, his mouth open in surprise.

The scent of his blood filled her nostrils, made the beast inside her scream with hunger.

"I tried to do this the easy way with you," she whispered, "but then you had to start screwing with me." The broken handcuffs dangled from her wrists.

Who was this guy anyway? Some bastard who got off on binding women? What would he have done next? For a moment, Nema wished that she had the power of the older vampires. She'd have loved to glance inside this jerk's head to see exactly what he had planned for her.

But a vampire's power emerged over time, and since she was a grand total of six months in vamp life, she was pretty weak. Yeah, physically she was strong. If necessary she could break the guy before her in half. She could run fast. Leap from a two-story window and not get hurt.

But as for the psychic powers that the legendary vampires had, well, she probably wouldn't get so much as a glimmer of those gifts for the next hundred years.

"Your teeth—shit, they're fangs!"

Her lips stretched in a deliberate smile, showcasing her razor sharp canines. "All the better to bite, baby."

And she was most definitely going to bite. She'd drink her fill of him and sate the terrible thirst that had her throat squeezing shut.

"There are two ways to play this game. We can do it nice and easy," she told him, deliberately keeping her voice low and husky. He wasn't struggling within her hold, just staring at her with growing disbelief on that handsome face of his. She dropped her hands, holding him by his shoulders as she stood on tiptoe and licked the drops of blood from his neck.

So good. Her nipples, tight, hard, rubbed against his chest. Her sex tightened as she tasted him.

Nema lifted her head, staring into his eyes. "Or we can do this the hard way." Her teeth came together with a sharp snap.

Slade swallowed. "What are you?"

"Isn't it obvious, handsome?"

The faintest shift of the wind brought their scents to her. Fear. Anticipation.

Nema stilled. The heart that some humans mistakenly thought didn't beat began to drum in a fast, hard rhythm.

Others were out there. Waiting.

Her nostrils flared as she inhaled, trying to determine just who she was up against. At least four men. Armed. She could smell the oil on their weapons. The sweat on their palms.

Not a robbery. Her head tilted to the side. These men were different, they were—

There for her.

Sonofabitch.

Her nails lengthened into claws. "You set me up."

Her prey blinked, shaking his head. "All I wanted was some fun, I don't know what you—"

Bull.

The men in the shadows were advancing. Gravel crunched beneath their boots.

Four men. Plus Slade, who'd now stiffened in her grasp.

Oh, this was not good.

She'd never taken on so many guys at once, and she didn't know exactly what kind of weapons they had.

Damn.

Nema didn't normally like to back down from a fight, but she was blood-low, hungry as hell, and not in the mood to get her ass kicked. And that was a prospect that she couldn't deny right then.

She pressed her claws into the muscled width of Slade's arms. "You wanna live through the next five minutes?"

His jaw clenched. She waited to see fear fill his eyes. Instead, she saw a hot rage.

She licked her lips. She'd sure like a taste of that rage. Another taste of him.

Soon.

His body tensed and she knew that he was planning an attack. Fine. Time to show him how things were going to work between them.

Her hold loosened. He growled, his lip curling, and then he shot forward—

And Nema shoved him back with one hand.

"I don't have a lot of time for this crap," she muttered. The men were getting closer. Their stench filled her nostrils and had her stomach clenching. "You've got a car, right?" He'd had to have used some kind of transportation to get to Miguel's.

Slade grunted.

"Then we're going to use it to get the hell out of here."

"What?"

Nema grabbed his hand, locking her fingers around his wrist. It looked like she was just cuddling him, but the hold was unbreakable. "We're gonna play a little game, Ace. It's called run like hell from the bad guys sneaking up on us. We're getting in your car—" Her gaze locked on the truck—his scent surrounded the vehicle. "Uh, your truck, and we're getting the hell out of here."

Her eyes returned almost helplessly to the small wound on his neck. "Then, once we're safe, you and I will finish what we've started."

Nema Alexander was a vampire.

Slade let her pull him to the truck as he struggled to accept the fact that the woman before him was, well, not human.

The teeth.

The claws.

The amazing strength.

No, Nema wasn't human. She couldn't be.

And the woman had tasted his blood. His neck felt hot, the skin prickling slightly, and it was almost as if he could still feel the wet warmth of her mouth on him.

Damn, but it had felt good. The lock of her lips around his flesh, the bite of her teeth—it should have hurt, should have repulsed him. But his cock had twitched with hunger and he'd wanted nothing more than to shove inside Nema's hot core and thrust deep and hard as she drank from him.

What in the hell was his problem?

He'd never met a vampire before. Hell, he hadn't even thought such creatures were real, but he knew what he was seeing before him and he wasn't about to waste time denying the obvious. Of course, it wasn't like Nema was going to give him any time to waste.

She wrenched open the driver's side of the truck and held out her left hand imperiously. "Keys."

Bossy vampiress. Must be used to ordering the humans around.

Tough. He'd never been the order-taking type. "My truck, baby, I do the driving."

Nema growled low in her throat and jumped into the truck, dragging him in behind her. He jerked the driver's door closed, shoved the key into the ignition and felt the sting of her claws at his throat when she wrapped her hand around his neck.

Those deadly claws of hers dug deeper as she brought her face close to his. "Don't mess with me here, Ace. I know your buddies—"

"I don't have any damned buddies!" Since leaving the Force, he always worked alone. He had no idea what Nema was muttering about. The woman obviously thought she was about to be attacked. Well, once he figured out his next move, he would attack her—but she didn't have to worry about anyone else.

"I know they're coming to get me," she snarled as if he hadn't said a word, "but we're getting the hell out of here now. And you'll do what I say, when I say it, or—"

She stopped, teeth clenched, eyes large and swimming with emotion. With fury. With fear.

"Or you'll what?" Slade asked softly.

Nema swallowed. "Or I'll have to—to kill you." Dangerous words, but they came out in a horrified whisper.

He blinked at her. Not exactly the way he'd expected a cold-blooded killer to sound. The woman who'd savaged five men shouldn't have had a problem telling him she'd rip him apart, but Nema, well, she was looking a little sick now, and he could feel her hand trembling against his throat.

Her slightly pointed chin hitched into the air. "So do things my way, and you'll get to keep livin', Ace." The attitude was back in her voice, but the fear lingered in her eyes.

"Fine." For now, but he'd get his chance to attack soon enough.

"Get us the hell out of here."

Slade jerked the gear shift into reverse, slammed his foot on the gas and shot backwards.

"There they are!" Nema was staring through the driver's window. "The bastards!"

Slade's gaze shot to the left. "Damn." Four armed men erupted from the shadows and ran straight for his truck.

What in the hell was happening?

"Move!"

He shoved the truck into drive and floored the accelerator.

And as they raced out of the lot, he heard the sound of bullets slamming into the back of his truck.

Oh, hell, no. This was definitely not part of the agreement.

McDermott had screwed him. Slade realized that he wasn't just the hunter anymore.

He'd become prey.

They drove without headlights down the old, twisting roads. Nema seemed to be able to see just fine in the dark. Her eyes glowed faintly, kind of like a cat's, and she whispered directions to him even as she kept darting her gaze to the road behind them.

They stopped at a rundown motel. The vacancy sign was blinking and two scantily clad women lounged outside the door.

"Guess you want us to get a room, huh?"

Nema lifted up her hand, flashing the key that was clutched in her fingers. "Already got one."

He parked the truck in the alley behind the motel. Nema grabbed his arm, keeping a death grip around him until they were inside scenic room number nine. Then—

She kicked the door closed and shoved him back against the wall. Her fingers went straight to his groin and at the touch of her hand against him, his semi-hard cock sprang to full arousal.

"Ah, Nema, what are—"

Her hand slipped into his right pocket. Her fingers brushed against the shaft of his arousal. Slade sucked in a sharp breath. He could just see the hint of her fangs, and instead of turning him off, the sight aroused him all the more. He wanted those teeth on his neck and he wanted his cock in her.

The adrenaline rush that had filled him as they raced down the dark roads shifted into a fierce tide of desire. He wanted Nema. Naked. Ready.

He lifted his hips, deliberately shifting so that his cock pushed against her hand. Ah, yeah, that was good.

Then her hand was gone. She reached around him, shoved her fingers into his back pocket and pulled out his wallet.

Realization dawned too late.

Nema flipped open his wallet, her eyes narrowing at the sight of the badge and ID inside. "A cop?"

Well, no, he wasn't a cop anymore. He'd gotten the badge off the Internet and he'd made the ID himself. He'd found that carrying the badge and police identification made things a hell of a lot easier in his new line of work.

But he wasn't gonna tell that to Nema. Not yet. Instead, he exhaled slowly and tried to control the raging hard-on in his jeans.

"Never done a cop before," she muttered and the wallet fell from her hand.

Then she was touching him again, smoothing those soft fingers of hers up his arms and over his chest.

"Ah, Nema—"

"I won't hurt you, Slade," she whispered, "but I've got to taste you again." A shiver worked its way over her body. "I'm just so fucking thirsty."

A vampire had just told him that she was thirsty. Not good. But, damn, the woman felt so soft as she pressed against him. Her breasts rubbed against his chest. Her hips pushed against his. And her mouth opened on his throat.

"Nema."

Her tongue licked his flesh. A long, slow sweep that had him groaning in pleasure and digging his fingers into her hips as he yanked her closer to him.

She's a vampire, for God's sake! The thought flew through his mind, and he tried to fight for his control. He didn't want to end up like those poor dead assholes. And being a meal for a vampiress was a sure-fire way to wind up bleeding out on the floor.

But her mouth was tightening around his flesh and sucking lightly. Her nipples were tight against him, hard, firm peaks that he wanted to feel against his palms. Her teeth raked across his neck. Her sharp canines pressed into his skin.

"Nema." His hands slid around to the curve of her ass. He squeezed the tender flesh, then used his grip to force the vee of her sex straight against the rock-hard length of his cock.

She moaned against his neck, a husky, breathy sound that made the lust flare even hotter inside of him.

Then her teeth pierced his neck, right above his jugular.

Chapter 3

With a growl, Slade shoved Nema away. She wasn't ready for that. The taste of him was on her tongue, rich, warm, wet. She wanted more.

So much more.

She lifted her hand, reaching for him. "Slade, I can—"

"Baby, you might be the sexiest thing I've seen in five years, but no damn way am I about to just close my eyes and become victim number six." He lunged away from the wall, putting the distance of the small motel room between them.

Victim number six. She blinked, having no idea what he was snarling about. The bloodlust was riding her hard. She'd gone too long without feeding and the measly sips she'd taken from Slade just weren't enough for her.

Yet there was more. She had the blood hunger, oh, yeah, she sure had that. But her nipples were tight, heavy, her sex was wet, and she wanted to rub her body against Slade's and feel those big, broad fingers on her ass again.

She wanted him.

She'd been attracted to her prey before—hell, she only picked men she found sexy, but this was different. This was harder and stronger.

Her gaze dropped to his chest. His black t-shirt was stretched taut over the thick muscles. She licked her lips, tasted delicious blood, and let her gaze drop a bit more. Down his tight stomach. To his lean hips. To the thick line of his cock that bulged against the front of his jeans.

A curl of heat spread through her belly. "You want me." Her words were a dare for his denial.

His hands clenched into fists. "And you want to drain me dry, vampire."

She tried not to flinch. Her chin lifted.

"Jesus!" Now he was pacing around the room. "You're a fucking vampire and I let you bring me to this dump like some kind of death-wishing moron."

Vampire. She didn't like the way he snarled the word. It wasn't like she could help what she was.

"Look, Ace, if you don't wanna be here, then don't let the door hit you on the way out." She jerked her thumb toward the peeling motel door.

"My name's not Ace." He stopped pacing and stared at her with blue eyes narrowed to slits. "You're gonna let me go?"

"Uh, yeah." Then she'd barely have an hour to try and find other prey.

"But you kill your victims."

"No, I don't." What was he talking about? It wasn't like she'd had a ton of victims in the grand half a year that she'd been a vampire. She'd managed to stave off the thirst so that she only needed to hunt once a month, and she'd been very careful with the men she'd chosen. And she'd always taken just enough, leaving the men sleeping and safe.

And very much alive.

But Slade was shaking his dark head at her. "You've killed them all. Five men."

I won't be victim number six. Nema stumbled back as his earlier comment blasted through her mind. "Wh-what are you talking about? I haven't killed anyone!"

Hell, it had been all she could do to stay ahead of McDermott and the bastards he'd sent on her trail. She sure hadn't gone out of her way to murder someone as she'd been fleeing for her well, um, not life exactly since she'd technically died already, but—

"There's a warrant out for your arrest, Nema." He was watching her with cold calculation in his eyes now.

And he was a cop. He'd know. Damn. No wonder he'd tried to put the cuffs on her. He thought she was some kind of murdering monster.

"I didn't do it," she told him, her voice soft as she tried to fight the blood hunger and the flood of emotion shooting though her. Five men. "I'm telling you, Slade, I haven't killed anyone."

She was wanted for murder. Slade had come after her because she was a wanted woman.

And then the pieces clicked into place.

Five victims.

She'd fed five times. Five strong, sexy men.

Oh, dear God, no.

"Who?" Her claws dug into the flesh of her palms.

"Trace Guthers, Bryce Phillips, Tony Mag—"

"No." Not Trace. No way. And the others—no. There had to be some mistake. She'd left them alive. *She'd left them alive.*

"I've got pictures."

She met his stare. The cold, level stare that a cop gives a suspect. "I need to see them." Because she had to be certain.

"They're in the truck."

"Go get them. Now."

The woman didn't act like a killer, and, after fifteen years on the force, he'd come to know killers pretty damn well.

He grabbed the data on the murders from the truck, and the small black vial McDermott had given him, and the syringe he'd picked up as a precaution.

No wonder the bastard had directed him to inject Nema. No way would cuffs work on her. The woman had incredible strength, and he wasn't even completely certain that a bullet would be able to keep her down.

But now the scales between them were balanced a bit more, and if he had to, he'd inject her.

He stalked back to the motel room, the photos and case files in a thick manila envelope in his right hand.

Nema paced toward him when he entered the room. Her right hand reached for the envelope, but then she drew back. If possible, her face seemed even paler in the stark fluorescent lighting.

"I-are those the photos?"

He nodded, carefully pulled out the pictures, and handed them to her.

And watched as she shuddered.

For an instant, Slade could have sworn that he saw tears fill her eyes as her fingers lifted toward the photo of Trace Guthers.

A vampire? Crying? In all the movies, vampires were soulless, undead villains who existed to kill and destroy.

But Nema—yes, she was wiping away tears now.

She shoved the pictures back at him. "I didn't do this."

"You were seen with all the victims." Witnesses had placed her at bars with the men. Folks had seen them leave together.

"I was with them, but I didn't kill them!" Her claws were out, full-length, and her razor sharp teeth glinted.

"You sure about that, baby? Cuz you look more than capable of killing to me."

Her golden eyes narrowed. "I drank from them, I won't deny that. I met most of them at the bars, we danced, had some fun, I went back home with the guys—"

"You had sex with them?" Now why did that thought cause a tight knot of rage to burn in him?

She shook her head. "I'm still new to this whole vampire thing," she muttered. "I didn't trust myself to drink and, you know—"

"Fuck?"

Her lips tightened. "I didn't want to risk hurting them, okay? So I just took enough from them to survive and I left them." Her gaze bored into his. "I swear, I left those men alive."

He wanted to believe her. Maybe it was those big eyes of hers with the wet tracks of tears still visible beneath her lashes. Maybe it was that trembling mouth.

Or maybe he was just a horny idiot.

But he really wanted to believe her.

"So what are you telling me? You left these guys all safe and sound, then someone else came in and ripped out their throats? Another vampire maybe?" Hell, he was already in the Twilight Zone. Now that he'd met one vampire, the idea of another one didn't seem so far-fetched.

"I-I don't know."

"Well, you need to figure it out." He lifted the envelope. "I'm not the only one after you, sweetheart. You're a wanted murderer, and the cops aren't gonna stop until they toss your sweet ass in jail."

"I can't go to jail." Her tone was fierce now. "I'd die there."

"Lady, I thought you were already dead." Weren't vampires dead?

"There's being undead," she muttered, "then there's being incinerated by the sun."

Ah, so that old story was true.

Nema stiffened and glanced toward the shade-covered window. "I don't have time for this now."

"You don't have time to convince me you're not a sadistic killer?" He would've thought that ranked pretty high on her to-do list.

Nema glared up at him. She was close to him, less than a foot away. "Look, Ace. I've just found out that all the cops in the state are gonna be on my trail. I've got a rich asshole named McDermott and his idiot patrol after me because the guy thinks he can turn me into some kind of super weapon—"

Ah, so that was why McDermott had hired him, and why he'd been so adamant that Nema be brought in alive.

"—because Trace made the mistake of blabbing about me to the guy, thinking he could make a quick buck off me." Disgust was rich in her voice. "And if I don't go out, right now, and find prey, I'm gonna be too weak to hunt tomorrow."

Trace made the mistake of blabbing about me... Trace. Victim number one. But if the guy had really been her first cold kill, would she have teared up when she saw his crime scene photo?

Things weren't adding up. Slade blinked, shook his head.

"You can't hunt tonight." Not with McDermott out there, not with his small army on her trail.

Her fingers trailed against the sensitive skin of his throat. "Well, you're not going to let me have a taste, so I have to find someone who will." Her gaze darted to the window. "Fast. I haven't fed in a month. So I have to find prey tonight. There isn't a choice for me."

The image of Nema's mouth pressed against another man's throat flashed through his mind. Her body, flush against a stranger's.

His back teeth clenched.

Shit.

The faint mark she'd left on his neck seemed to pulse, and he was acutely aware of the faint weight of the syringe in his pocket. He could use it to sedate her. Or he could give her what she wanted—what she needed.

Could he risk it? Did he trust the woman enough to let her get those teeth of hers near his throat?

She doesn't act like a killer. His instincts were screaming at him. Dammit. His gut told him Nema wasn't the killer. There had been so much shock and pain on her face when she'd seen the photos.

But serial killers could fake emotion. He'd seen it before.

He couldn't let a pair of sexy legs and bedroom eyes get to him.

Besides, he had the vial. If she got out of control, he could inject her. It was his ace in the hole.

Nema tried to step around him. Slade grabbed her arms, pulling her up against his chest.

"What are you—"

"Rules, Nema." God, she smelled good. Weren't vampires supposed to smell like old graves? Rotting flesh? They weren't supposed to smell like sin and roses.

He drew a deep breath, sucking that heady scent straight into his lungs, then he growled, "Rule number one, until we get this mess sorted out, you don't leave my sight." If he was wrong and she was a killer, he wasn't going to have another man's death on his conscience.

"And how are we supposed to sort this shit out?" Her breath huffed against him and her breasts pushed against his chest.

"You say you didn't do it—"

"I didn't!"

"Then we find the real killer." Or, if the suspicions growing in Slade's mind were correct, the killer would find them.

The men in the photos had all died within two days of last being seen in bars with Nema. If someone else was out there, killing the men she tasted, then that bastard would be coming for him, very soon.

Because he was about to give Nema a good, strong taste.

And maybe take a taste of her.

The faint scent of her arousal teased his nostrils. Nema wanted him. Good. He wanted her more than he'd ever wanted anyone in his life. Vampire or human, it really didn't make a difference to his cock. Nema Alexander was the epitome of every wet dream he'd ever had, and he wasn't about to let this opportunity pass him by.

"Rule two, when you need to feed, you're gonna feed from me." Because the idea of her locking those red lips on another bastard's neck pissed him off.

Her eyes widened.

"Rule three." He leaned in close for this. "I'm in charge, baby. You do what I say, when I say it. And if I tell you to stop, then I damn well expect you to withdraw your fangs and not rip my throat out."

She licked her lips. "You seem to like rules...." But her gaze strayed to his throat.

And a lick of hunger fired his groin. He wanted that mouth on him again, because when Nema bit him, it felt damned good. So good that he was afraid he would become addicted to her. To her mouth.

His fingers lifted, buried in her hair, and he brought her face close for a hard, deep kiss. His tongue pushed into her mouth, tasted her.

Ah, yeah, he liked her taste.

She moaned into his mouth, and her lips parted even wider for him. She kissed him back, her tongue moving just as hungrily against his. Her hips began to rock, and Slade pushed one of his legs between hers, deliberately driving his thigh up against her sex.

The rich scent of her arousal grew stronger.

A good cop wouldn't do this, Slade thought. A good cop wouldn't be reveling in Nema's touch like this. Wouldn't be shaking with the hunger to strip her and drive balls deep into her wet sex.

But, hell, being good had never come easy to him.

Maybe he was meant to be the bad guy after all. And being bad with Nema, it sure felt good. He tore his mouth from hers, tangling his fingers in her silky hair and pushing her head toward his throat.

He wanted her bite more than he wanted his next breath.

She licked his neck. Her tongue stroked him slowly, wetting his flesh.

His left hand dropped to her waist. His fingers curled around her, holding her tight.

Her teeth pressed against him, scraped over the flesh—

Then pierced him with a hard bite.

He growled, his fingers digging into her hip. Heat tore through him, blinding, driving heat and hunger. His cock was thick, heavy with arousal. His heart was racing, the drumming filling his ears. Her scent surrounded him. Her taste was on his tongue.

Jesus, but her mouth felt good. Every movement of her lips, every sweet suck, made his cock pulse with need.

He freed her hair and pushed both his hands under the hem of her blouse. Her flesh was like satin beneath his fingers. His hands spanned her midriff, then rose to cup the soft swell of her breasts.

A lacy fabric covered her nipples. His fingers eased under the fabric, touched her breasts. His hands shook as he stroked her, as he plucked her nipples, squeezing them lightly. His head was swimming with lust and hunger.

It wasn't enough.

Another growl rumbled in his throat.

Her mouth fed on his neck, sending a current of heat rippling straight to his groin. He had her supple flesh in his hands, but it wasn't enough.

She'd had a taste of him. Now it was his turn.

Slade released her nipples, dropping his hands to her waist. He fumbled with the snap of her jeans. The button popped loose, and he jerked the zipper down with a soft hiss.

His turn.

And he couldn't wait for his taste of Nema.

Chapter 4

Oh, God. Nema jerked her mouth away from Slade, his taste hot and rich on her tongue. His throat glistened, the faint mark from her bite barely visible just above the curling black tattoo that circled his neck and disappeared beneath his shirt.

His hands were all over her. Jerking open her jeans, smoothing over her belly.

"Slade." The hunger swirling in her wasn't just for his blood. She wanted his touch. Wanted—

Him.

It'd been too long since she'd given into her desires and experienced a man's touch in the darkness of the night. And oh, damn, but Slade knew how to touch.

His fingers pushed aside her jeans and shoved them down her hips. Nema kicked out of her shoes and stumbled out of the denim. Slade caught her, easily steadying her. Then his fingers were between her thighs, rubbing against the crotch of her panties and making a moan tremble on her lips.

"Did you get the taste you needed?" His voice was a hard growl.

She swallowed. She'd taken as much as she dared. Any more, and Slade would start to feel weak. Her head moved in a slow nod and her hands wrapped around his shoulders. Such wide, strong shoulders.

"Then it's my turn."

His fingers eased under the elastic of her black panties, parted her slick folds and stroked her clit. Every muscle in her body grew taut as she rose onto her tiptoes, gasping.

Slade smiled down at her, his cheeks flushed, his eyes glowing with a hunger that matched her own.

His fingers were broad and thick, but his touch was feather-light, caressing, teasing, stroking the tight little peak over and over.

Her nails dug into his arms. "Don't tease me." She needed more than just a light touch. It'd been too long, she needed—

His finger drove deep into her core, a sudden, sharp thrust that had her arching toward him and clenching her thighs.

His blood was pumping through her body, filling her with energy and power, and the sensual hunger that burned within her made her feel almost alive again.

And she'd been so desperate to feel alive. Even if it were just for a few moments. To feel like a normal woman again. She tilted her head. "Kiss me." She wanted to feel his lips again. Wanted the press of his tongue against hers as those strong fingers worked her eager sex.

His mouth crashed down onto hers. His lips were open and wet as they met hers. His tongue thrust into her mouth, a perfect imitation of that strong finger thrusting into her sex.

Her lips closed around him and sucked slowly on his tongue. She loved the feel of him.

When he growled in pleasure, the sound vibrated into her mouth and sent a shiver straight to her heart.

Then his hand was gone. Pulled away just as her peak was building.

Disappointed, she wrenched her mouth free of his. "Slade, why—"

His hand lifted to his lips. His gaze held hers as he slowly licked the glistening cream from his fingers. He seemed to relish her essence, tasting her slowly and then trailing those fingers over her stomach and back to the juncture of her thighs.

His gaze dropped to the small thatch of dark curls. "I think I'd like to taste more."

Then he was pushing her back, and she was sliding, falling down into the worn chair near the TV. Her fingers gripped the faded arms of the chair and she tried to pull her legs closed.

"What are you doing?"

Instead of answering, he shoved her thighs apart and knelt in front of her, using his body to keep her legs spread and open for him. Slade ripped her panties away, and the sound of the delicate fabric tearing seemed unusually loud in the room. He licked his lips as he stared at her exposed mound.

Oh, damn, the way he was looking at her.

His fingers stroked her sex. Parted the plump pink folds and rubbed her clit. Her breath hissed out. "S-Slade." That felt so good.

"I'm gonna taste you," he muttered, lowering his head so that his breath blew over her sensitive flesh as he spoke. "And I'm gonna drink from you until I've had my fill." His eyes lifted, met hers. "Cause it's my turn now, baby."

His mouth claimed her then. His lips sucked her clit, drawing deep on the tight bud as she moaned and jerked beneath him. His hands clamped down on her thighs, holding her in place with a hard grip.

Nema could have marshaled her strength and broken free. She could have but—damn, his mouth was so hot. And his tongue. His tongue was—

Driving into her sex. He plunged his tongue straight into her core, and Nema choked back a scream at the lash of pleasure.

She'd had oral sex before. Even damn good oral sex. But this—

His tongue withdrew, thrust deep.

Her body shuddered. Her fingers locked in his hair and she urged him closer.

He was licking her now, sucking, swirling that tongue over her clit, then thrusting it deep into her sex.

Her head fell back against the chair. Her heart was thundering in her chest. And her teeth were burning with a fierce hunger.

More.

More.

Take.

More.

The bloodlust was pouring through her. She'd just fed, and yet the ravenous hunger consumed her again. She could hear her heartbeat, hear Slade's, and the sound of all his rich, sweet blood flowing through his veins only heightened her arousal.

Take.

More.

"No!" She pushed him away, clenching her teeth against the terrible hunger for his blood and the fierce arousal of her body.

She wanted him.

His blood.

His cock.

But she was terrified the monster inside her would rage out of control.

Take.

The images of the dead men flashed before her eyes.

She wanted him, wanted Slade to bury his cock in her body, but she also wanted to sink her teeth into him again, and drink and drink.

She couldn't take the risk. Feeling human again, feeling alive, wasn't worth the risk to him.

Slade stared up at her, his lips wet with her cream. His cheeks were flushed, his eyes blazing with hunger.

Nema swallowed and managed to whisper, "No, I—we can't." No matter how much she might want him.

It was too dangerous. For both of them.

"Oh, yeah, baby, we most definitely can." No mistaking the hard arousal in his growling voice. His hands were still on her thighs. They tightened with intent.

But Nema shook her head and fought the desire that was clawing through her. "You have to go."

She'd taken enough blood to maintain her strength. The dawn would come soon. She'd rest, the terrible physical need that was clawing her guts apart would end, and she'd awake, normal again.

Or as normal as she could be.

She rose slowly, somewhat unsteadily, and was starkly aware of her partial nudity. She crept around him and reached for her jeans, hurriedly pulling them back up her legs.

Slade rose, following her. He snagged her arm and forced her to face him. A muscle flexed along the hard line of his jaw. "Shame, that," he muttered. "Just when things were getting... hot."

Nema swallowed. Hot was definitely the right word. Every part of her body seemed flushed and the heavy desire she felt for him was burning her from the inside.

Not this time. Her jeans rubbed against her wet sex, making the sensitive flesh ache. Her voice was still husky, but firmer, as she repeated, "You have to go."

He glanced toward the bed. "Seems like there's room for two." Then he reached for the hem of his shirt and yanked it over his head.

Her eyes instantly fell to his chest. To the tight muscles. The faint covering of black hair. The tattoo.

The black swirl of ink that began at his neck, right over his thundering pulse, twisted down his chest, turning, coiling, and forming a fierce black snake that waited, fangs barred, right over his heart.

Oh, she liked that.

Slade turned away from her, showing her the broad expanse of his back as he stalked toward the queen-sized bed.

"Ah, what are you doing?" The man was headed the wrong way.

He paused near the bed, glanced back at her. His hand lifted, rubbed against the faint mark on his neck. "I expected that to hurt more," he murmured.

She hadn't been trying to hurt him. If she'd wanted to give the man pain, she could have. Instead, she'd wanted to give him... pleasure. As much pleasure as he'd given her.

Because the taste of him had filled her with pleasure. Euphoria. Delicious power.

And need.

Slade was watching her, his eyes intent. "You know, I was damn close to coming, just from your bite. And then when I got to taste that sweet cream of yours…." His hand dropped to the front of his jeans, stroked the length of his shaft.

Almost helplessly, her gaze followed the movement of his hand. His cock was fully aroused, rising against the faded denim.

"Ummm…." A rumble of sound that vibrated deep in his throat. "You sure you don't want to finish what we started?"

Hell, yes, she wanted to finish, but she didn't trust herself. The lust burning through her was too strong.

And dawn was coming. The rising was too close. Even if she weren't scared to death of losing control and taking too much from him, she didn't want to risk the sleep claiming her while they were making love.

Having a woman collapse on you in a parody of death wasn't exactly sexy.

"I want you to leave," she told him very clearly—for what now, the third time?

Slade just shook his dark head. "No can do, sweetheart." He climbed into bed, shifted around, then tucked his hands behind his head as he lay propped against the pillows. "From now on, you and I are gonna be inseparable."

No way. Nema considered marching over to the bed and physically yanking the guy up and tossing him outside. She was strong enough to do it. When those assholes of McDermott's had kept her in that lab, she'd hurled two of them through a glass window.

He must have read the intent in her eyes because his body stiffened. "Let me make something clear to you, Nema." He shoved up to a sitting position, no longer relaxed. "You've told me you didn't murder those men."

Her head moved in a jerky nod. The rising sun pulled at her senses and the heavy lethargy of vampire hibernation began to sweep over her, calming the raging arousal in her blood.

Damn, not now. I don't want him to see—

"The men died two days after last being seen with you. So, if you didn't kill them, that means someone else hunted them down, and ripped out their throats, after you'd had your little drink."

Her gaze narrowed at the last words. Why did he sound so pissed off? She had to drink blood to survive. It wasn't like she'd get ticked off at him for eating a Big Mac.

"Until you prove to me that this supposed someone else is real, you don't leave my sight." He held her stare. "If you try, I'll have every cop in the state on your ass before you can so much as blink."

She believed him. Nema took a step toward the bed, feeling the heaviness slip through her limbs. "How do I prove he's real?" And he had to be real. She sure as hell hadn't killed those men.

Although Trace's betrayal had tempted her. She'd known him before her change, and he'd been her first blood taste after her awakening.

Trace had volunteered, saying he wanted to help her.

She'd thought she could trust him—until she'd woken in McDermott's lab, strapped to a table as a white-masked bastard had cut into her with his scalpel.

"Nema?" Slade was frowning at her now and she realized that her body was weaving a bit. Damn. Even the power of the blood she'd taken wouldn't be able to fight off the hibernation. Nothing could stop it.

When the sun rose, she would fall straight onto her face if she didn't hurry up and get in the bed.

She fought to keep her thoughts focused. The present and the past were swirling around her. "How... do we catch him?"

"I think he'll come after us. Or rather me."

"Why you?"

"He comes after the men you drink from."

"No...." She didn't want anyone after Slade, and oh, no, she couldn't feel her right hand anymore. The numbness had started.

"What the hell is wrong with you?"

Slade jumped from the bed, caught her around the waist with his arms just as she began to fall.

"S-sleep." The sun was starting its ascent across the sky. She didn't need to open the blinds to see it. She knew.

He carried her to the bed. "Jesus, you feel cold."

Because her body was shutting down. No, slowing down. And she had to explain to him, fast, just exactly what the hell was happening. She didn't want him to freak on her and think that she'd died.

Once the hibernation began, she'd be helpless.

Shit. She'd have to trust the man with her life. And she didn't have a good track record with trust. But he was a cop. A good guy. She could trust him, couldn't she?

"Nema!" Was that fear in his voice? "Dammit, take more blood, take as much as you need to be—"

"S-sun's rising... body... slows down."

"What? I don't know what the hell you're talking about."

If her would-be hero didn't shut up and let her explain, he wouldn't find out. "Heart... slows. Barely... breathe. Have to... hibernate in... day." A lucky vampire trait that she'd discovered on her first day of undead life. "Sun...

burns... me—" Her tongue was thick. Her lashes had already fallen. There wasn't anymore time.

She just hoped her cop could handle things.

And that she didn't wake up in a jail cell.

"Promise me..." She could barely force the words out. "I can... trust... you...." Then the hibernation claimed her. The last thing she felt before the enveloping sleep swept over her was his hand, gently brushing back a lock of her hair.

If he didn't know better, he'd think she was dead. But then, weren't vampires dead? Slade ran a tired hand over his face as he stared down at Nema's body. He knew piss-little about vampires, and when the lady opened those golden eyes of hers, he was gonna demand a crash course on the undead.

She was breathing, barely. He'd been watching her for the last hour and he'd counted five breaths. Her heart was beating, again, barely. He'd held his hand to her pulse point and had almost given up hope before he'd finally felt one faint beat. An eternity seemed to pass before he felt the second, then the third.

Before, when her hands had run across his body, her flesh had seemed heated, almost feverishly so. But now her skin was cold to the touch.

What had she said? Something about hibernating in the day?

If this happened to her every time the sun rose, then Nema was damn vulnerable. Did McDermott know of her weakness? If so, then why hadn't he just sent his men for her during the daylight hours? And why the hell had the bastard tried to ambush them with those other armed assholes?

Slade crept from the motel room, carefully opening the door just wide enough so that he could squeeze though the entrance. He could still hear Nema's voice as she told him that the sun would burn her.

Not on his watch.

He hurried to his truck, grabbed his cell phone and called the one man he knew could give him answers.

When the phone was answered on the first ring, he didn't waste time identifying himself, just cut to the chase. "McDermott, you bastard, what the hell is going on?"

There was a brief pause, then, "Do you have her?"

Slade's fingers tightened around the thin cell phone. "No." He didn't feel a damn bit bad about lying to McDermott. The bastard had sure as hell not felt bad about lying to him.

McDermott swore. "I was told you could handle this case."

By whom? Since when was Slade supposed to be up to dealing with super-strong vampires? Barely controlling the snarl that sprang to his lips, he snapped, "I am handling the case, and I don't need you sending in some goons to screw things up."

"Ah... I see you've encountered my men."

His men? "What is going on." It wasn't a question, but a roughly gritted demand for answers.

McDermott's sigh carried easily across the line. "I don't understand your anger, Brion. I sent backup. I would have thought you'd be pleased by their arrival, considering the circumstances."

"The circumstances?" He didn't like the sound of those words. A cold fist began to squeeze his gut.

"I was told you were... in some distress."

Shit. They'd watched them in the alley, probably with binoculars equipped with infrared lenses. "I wasn't in distress," he muttered.

"Nema is very strong. When I learned that she had restrained you—"

Yeah, she'd restrained him, all right. Broke his cuffs, then shoved him back against the brick wall in a blink.

"—I had no choice but to give the order to advance."

Time to cut the bullshit. "You know she's a vampire."

"Of course."

The calm answer caught him off-guard. He'd suspected he was bait, but bait for a vampire—not something he'd bargained for. "And you didn't think you should have mentioned that little fact to me?"

McDermott replied, "Would you have believed me, Brion? If I'd told you, would you have believed that Nema Alexander was a vampire?"

Hell, no. Until she'd pinned him to that wall and bared those sharp fangs of hers, he hadn't even considered the existence of vampires. But now that he'd seen Nema in all her glory, no way would he ever deny the existence of the undead again.

"So where is our vampiress?" McDermott asked.

She wasn't "our" anything. Slade inhaled slowly and forced a calmness to his voice that he was far from feeling. "It's daytime. Movies all say the undead go to ground until night."

"So you'll search for her again when the sun sets?"

Not like he'd have to search that hard. "What do you want with her?" He needed to know. McDermott was willing to shell out three hundred grand for her. She had to be important to him.

McDermott didn't answer right away. Then he said, "I believe Nema Alexander is the wave of the future. Her kind—they are the warriors we need out on our front lines. Stronger than humans. Impervious to most wounds and weapons. And immortal. A squad of soldiers like her—they could change the face of wars."

That cold feeling in his gut was just getting worse. "So you wanna use her to make a team of super soldiers?" He could see why Nema wasn't wild about that idea. She didn't strike him as the soldier type, more the leave-me-the-hell-alone type.

"Do you know how much governments would pay for soldiers with her strengths? Do you?" McDermott demanded.

Well, he was getting an idea. "And it doesn't bother you that the woman is a murderer?" He threw the question out deliberately, the suspicion that McDermott knew the truth about the murders heavy in his mind.

Silence.

Slade figured he'd talked to McDermott long enough. The bastard might be running a trace on the call, trying to track the cell phone towers and home in on him.

"Keep your men off my back," he ordered.

"But what if you need them? Nema could overpower you again."

Slade said, "I've got the black vial, remember? I'm the one with the power."

The sharp inhalation was unmistakable, as was McDermott's sudden excitement. "Have you used it on her?"

"Not yet." But he wasn't going to rule out the possibility. "You sure it works?"

"It did before."

He didn't like the implications in that statement, not one damn bit.

"Listen, Brion. Our deal is still good. You bring me Nema, and I'll give you three hundred thousand. And you can walk away, a free and very wealthy man."

He grunted. "I'm beginning to think our deal wasn't that good to begin with, buddy." Not when McDermott had been lying to him, setting him up, setting Nema up.

"Five hundred thousand."

Slade didn't speak.

"Bring me the vampiress. Walk away, and take the five hundred grand with you." A pause. "That's an awful lot of money to a man like you, isn't it, Brion?"

Hell, yes.

McDermott's voice dropped to a murmur. "Enough money to start a new life. To erase the sins of your past and just begin again."

And all he had to do was betray one woman.

"Promise me." Her voice whispered through his mind. *"I can trust you."*

"Think about that half-million, Brion, and then bring her to me."

Slade disconnected the call, his hand clenching around the thin phone so hard that a crack fractured the surface of the cell phone. Sonofabitch.

Now he knew what it was like to be tempted by the devil.

Chapter 5

The sun was setting. Slade stared down at Nema, watching over her as he'd been doing for the last eight hours. Maybe it was just his imagination, but her color seemed better. A faint tint of pink covered her cheeks.

He eased onto the bed next to her, the mattress squeaking softly beneath his weight. He'd been alone with her all day. When the maids didn't come by, he'd called the front desk and learned that Nema had a standing order not to be disturbed during the day. He'd gotten the impression that his vampiress had paid a lot of money to make certain that order was carried out.

Now Nema inhaled deeply and her breathing slowly began to flow in a steady pattern.

He leaned over her, putting his head against her breast so that he could hear the beat of her heart.

Thump.

Thump.

Thump.

Almost normal again.

A heady relief swept through him. Watching her while she'd lain so still, it had frightened him.

And he wasn't afraid of damn much.

But she'd looked so fragile, so helpless.

Because she was helpless. If McDermott or his goons had come in, she wouldn't have been able to fight them off. They could have taken her, and done whatever damn experiments they wanted.

Nema didn't belong in a lab. Didn't deserve to be poked and prodded. She deserved—

Hell, he didn't know what she deserved.

Slade's head lifted slowly and his gaze locked on the curve of her breasts. Her chest was rising and falling now in time with her soft breaths. He was tempted to touch her breast with his hands, or his mouth, and see if her sudden responsiveness would show itself there, too.

Over the hours, as he'd kept careful watch over her, he'd become aware of a curious sense of possessiveness. There was something about Nema that called to him, and he just couldn't shake the feeling growing inside that she was his.

A vampire, belonging to a washed up ex-cop. Crazy.

Slade's fingers traced the line of her cheek. *His.*

He glanced toward the nightstand. The syringe sat on the chipped surface, the dark liquid gleaming faintly in the light. It was his insurance.

Nema moaned faintly and began to shift slightly on the bed. He'd left her in the clothes she'd worn earlier. He'd thought about stripping her, to make her more comfortable, but he hadn't trusted himself enough to do the job.

He'd had a hard-on for most of the day. Just thinking about Nema, the tight clutch of her sex, the feel of her mouth sucking his neck—Jesus, but she made him want.

Never, never had he experienced this tide of hunger for a woman. Was it because she was a vampire? Was she exerting some kind of power over him? He didn't know, didn't really care, he just wanted her.

And as her lashes fluttered open, he decided that he was going to have her.

She awoke to find Slade leaning over her, his expression hard, intent, his eyes filled with a lust that he didn't bother trying to hide.

Nema swallowed, trying to ease the dryness in her throat. Her gaze darted around the room. The motel. She was safe, in her room.

Slade hadn't betrayed her, hadn't taken her into a sterile lab so some sick freaks could start cutting into her.

He'd kept her safe. She'd been right to trust him. Now, if she could just prove to the man that she wasn't a sadistic killer.

"I've got questions for you." His arms caged her, and his warm breath blew over her lips. Oh, damn, she could already taste him.

"Well, good evening to you, too," she muttered, trying for a brazen front. There was just something about the way he was looking at her. *Like he could eat me alive.* Her heart rate seemed to double. Oh, she liked that look. Her sex began to moisten.

"I've been watching you, wanting you, all fucking day, Nema."

She gulped.

"And I'm gonna take you."

Oh, she wished, but it was too dangerous. "No, we can't—"

"Hell, yes, we can." He sounded absolutely determined. His eyes narrowed as he stared down at her. "But first I've got questions, and you're gonna give me the answers I need."

Her breasts were rubbing against his chest. The nipples were sensitive, pebbling at the slight contact. "Ah, if I can."

She hadn't woken to the blood hunger as she'd done every day for the last month, but she had woken to lust, lust for Slade. She'd dreamed of him during her sleep. Dreamed of his strong, tanned body. Dreamed of stroking his skin, stripping him. Of feeling that thick cock in her hands, in her body.

His nostrils flared and his jaw clenched. Then he heaved his body off hers, putting a few precious inches between them. "Have you done something to me?" he snapped. "Made me want you? Put me under some kind of thrall or something?"

Nema shook her head. "I don't know how to do that." Yet. Give her another hundred years, and she'd love to put a guy like him under her thrall.

"Just what can you do?" He was sitting up on the bed. He was glaring down at her with the lust still gleaming in his eyes, and she knew he was fighting to hang onto his control.

And so was she. Nema pushed herself up, tried to rise from the bed, but Slade's arms caught her, holding her in place.

"No, baby, I like you just where you are."

In bed, with him.

She liked it, too. That was the problem. But at least she was sitting up now. Her thigh pressed against his, and the heat from his body burned her even through the barrier of their jeans.

"Tell me," he demanded, loosening his hold so that his fingers wrapped lightly around her arm. "Tell me what makes you different from a human."

She could have gotten away from him if she wanted. Could have crossed the room in a single lunge. Instead, she told him what he wanted to know, and she stayed exactly where she wanted to stay. "I'm strong, strong enough to lift a damn car if I want." Cause she'd experimented in the early days and done just that. "I'm fast, kinda like a human at hyper-speed. My reflexes are better, my vision, smell, and hearing all about ten times stronger than they were before my change."

"And when did you change?"

She didn't want to talk about that. Her lips thinned. "I don't have any extrasensory powers. I can't control minds or any of that stuff. I, uh, ran into another guy, like me, a few months back. We didn't talk long." Cause the guy had been with two other women and she'd seen the bloodlust in his eyes. Not the time for a long heart to heart. "But he told me things change, when a vampire ages. That more powers come." And she'd believed him. Because he'd watched the guy stare into a seven foot two bouncer's eyes and then get the bruiser to do exactly what he'd wanted.

He'd also told her, very clearly as he'd barred his fangs that she needed to "Keep your prey and your pleasure separate."

"When did you change, Nema?"

"Six months ago, all right?" Jeez, the guy was like a freaking bull dog. "And I'm not gonna talk about that anymore now." If he had other damn questions that he wanted her to answer, fine, she'd do it. But she would not talk about that night. Would. Not.

"Fine." The word was a growl and his fingers tightened around her. "Then tell me this, do you know who those bastards were who tried to jump us in the alley?"

Now that she'd tell him. "There's a man in Houston. Name's McDermott. Rich as hell. He knows what I am and he's got it in his head that he can use me to make some kind of vampire army." She shook her head. "The idea is crazy! I mean, I don't even know how to make another vampire!"

That was true. No instruction book had been given to her and she hadn't had the chance to ask Mr. Stud Vampire at the bar. The night she'd been changed, the vampire had bit her neck, taken her blood... and that was it. There'd been no exchange. No you-bite-me, I-bite-you, you-become-undead ritual. The first time she'd fed on Trace, she'd been terrified that she'd convert him just by drinking. If the thirst hadn't been tearing her apart and ripping at her sanity, she never would have risked taking from him.

But her bite hadn't changed Trace. Or any of the others.

"So McDermott wants to catch you?"

Yeah, so he could lock her back up in his mad scientist lab. Not something on her to-do list. "I'm not going to let him take me again," she whispered, her claws starting to lengthen. The claws... another nice vampire side-effect. The first time she'd seen them extend, she'd been terrified, wondering what would happen next. Would she sprout wings? Turn into a vampire bat?

Thankfully, she hadn't.

"Again? You mean the bastard caught you before?"

Nema nodded. McDermott's men had come after him, too. So he deserved to know all about her history with the guy. "Trace, the first guy I bit, turns out, he worked for McDermott. I thought I could trust him. We'd known each other before my change. He agreed to let me drink from him; we went back to his place—"

"You had sex?"

She'd been with Trace before but, "Not that night," she said. Nema swallowed as the memories came rushing back. "He told me to stay there, that he'd take care of me." And she'd been on her own, scared for weeks by then. So the idea of staying with a friend had been too tempting to refuse.

"Trace left, came back just before dawn." She remembered that Trace had been smiling at her, a flush of excitement on his cheeks. "The asshole had something, some kind of black liquid that he injected in me. Knocked me right out. The next thing I knew, I was waking up, naked, strapped down in some lab."

His jaw clenched. "How'd you escape?"

"Broke the straps. Threw two of the bastards who were cutting into me out the window and ran like hell. And I've been running ever since."

"How do you know this McDermott was the guy behind it?"

"Cause the bastard was there, watching, muttering about his army and his plans." And he'd terrified her, watching her with that fanatical gleam in his eyes. The guy was crazy. "He was bragging about how it had only cost him fifty grand to catch me and how he was going to make billions off me."

Slade flinched.

Nema shook her head. "Look, I'm sorry I got you involved in this. I know you thought you were just doing your job, tracking down a killer, but I'm not a killer and things are so screwed up now—"

His finger pressed against her lips. "Stop, Nema."

She stared into his eyes. Saw the hunger that hadn't dimmed. The hunger she knew was in her own stare.

"I don't give a fuck about McDermott. I'm just sorry he hurt you."

"I heal fast," she whispered against that finger, fighting the urge to open her mouth, to press her lips tight against it.

"Good." His finger pushed between her lips and she gave into her hunger, drawing it inside her mouth and sucking as she'd like to suck another part of his body.

And she wasn't thinking about his neck.

"I want you naked," he growled. "I want you spread, and I want you ready to take me. I've held onto my control for as long as I can, but I want you."

Need clawed through her at his stark confession, but Nema shook her head. "We can't. It's too dangerous." The bloodlust and the physical need fed off each other. If they had sex, she'd drink from him. And if she drank from him while they had sex, she wasn't sure she'd be able to stop before she hurt him.

Ah, but she wanted him.

"Don't worry, baby, I've got a backup plan."

She blinked. "What are you thinking?"

He pointed to the nightstand. Nema glanced toward the left and literally felt her body chill. A syringe lay on the table. Filled with an all-too-recognizable black liquid.

Hell, no. "What the hell is going on?"

"I did some reconnaissance work today, managed to catch the men who'd attacked us off guard." His gaze was on the syringe, not her, as he said, "I found that in one of their bags, along with a series of instructions about how it can be used to incapacitate a vampire."

"So you decided to take it?" Incapacitate a vampire. Yeah, it did that. Fast.

"I took it—figured it was better for me to have it than those bastards—and I planned to ask you about it, to see if you'd ever heard of something like that working on your kind." A beat of silence then, "But I guess we've already covered that, huh?"

She couldn't take her gaze off the vial. Fear was pumping through her now, mixing with the lust and making the tension boil inside her.

"What's your plan, Ace?" His backup plan. Nema wasn't sure she was going to like whatever her cop was about to say.

"You don't want have sex with me because you're afraid of hurting me. Well, forget that excuse. If things get out of control, I'll use the vial, you'll go to sleep and that'll be the end of our little experiment."

Little experiment. She shivered. "Is that what I am? An experiment to you?" Screw a vampire and see if you can live. It should be on every guy's top ten list of things to do.

His blue stare locked on her. "No," he said, his voice very, very soft. "You're the woman I've been fantasizing about all damn day. The woman I want more than I want my next breath."

Oh. That was a hell of a lot better than being an experiment.

"But what am I to you, Nema? Prey? The stranger you picked up in a bar because you were thirsty and I was there?"

No. Her hand lifted, stroked the cheek that was covered in a day's worth of dark stubble. "You're the man I want." Had wanted, since the first moment she'd seen him. "You're the man who makes me feel alive." And that was so damn important to her.

"So are you gonna keep being afraid, or are you gonna take a chance with me?"

She didn't look back at the syringe. She knew it was there. And she knew that if he had to, Slade would use it.

Backup plan.

Nema licked her lips, lifted her chin, and said, "I think I'll take that chance."

Chapter 6

He had her stripped in less than a minute. Her jeans landed on the floor. He threw her shirt and her bra across the room.

Then he put his mouth on her.

Nema moaned.

Slade started at her neck. Licking, sucking, making her moan and tremble beneath him. He moved down her throat, slowly, slowly… he kissed his way across her collar bone.

And his hands caught her breasts, squeezing the mounds with slightly calloused fingers.

His head lifted and he stared down at her, watching as his fingers stroked her nipples, teasing the tight peaks. "You've got the most beautiful breasts. Pink and plump. I gotta taste 'em." His head lowered and his mouth opened over her breast. He drew her breast into the warm cavern of his mouth.

Her heels dug into the mattress as she arched toward him. The edge of Slade's teeth pressed against her tender flesh, then he was sucking her nipple, pulling the tight peak past his lips and laving it with his tongue.

Her teeth began to lengthen as the lust built.

Take.

The beast was whispering in her ear.

And Slade was kissing her stomach. His tongue swirled over her belly button, darted inside, then he licked his way down her abdomen.

Nema's body tensed. She wanted him to kiss her sex again. Wanted that wicked tongue on her clit, in her.

Her hands bunched in the fabric of his t-shirt.

"Tell me what you want," he demanded, stopping just over her thighs. His breath blew against the curls guarding her sex. "Tell me."

Damn, it was hard enough to think, let alone talk. "Your… mouth… on me."

"Where, baby? Where do you want my mouth?"

She growled in frustration. Then gazing into his dark blue stare, she whispered the truth, "Everywhere."

"Then that's what you're gonna get." His broad fingers pushed between her thighs, opening her wide for his touch. "Everywhere."

His head lowered and his mouth pressed against the tight bud of her desire.

Nema nearly came off the bed.

Slade's hands flashed out, caught her arms, and pressed her back into the mattress.

Her canines were fully extended now, the fire of her desire and bloodlust pounding through her.

His mouth was working her sex. Licking. Sucking. His tongue swept over her flesh, then drove deep into her quivering opening.

"God, I love the way you taste," he muttered, then drove his tongue deep again.

Nema clenched her teeth, turned her head away from him. Control. *Control.*

"I don't want you in control," he growled, and she realized she must have said the word aloud. "I want you wild."

One finger pushed into her. "Wild."

A second finger worked its way inside her. Thrust gently. Slade put his mouth on her again, licking, using that warm, wet tongue of his against her flesh and driving those fingers in deep.

The knot of tension in her stomach wound tighter. Every muscle in her body seemed to stiffen. She wanted to scream, she wanted to bite him, to drink, to come.

His tongue scraped across her clit. Those fingers thrust one more time and the tension exploded as a wave of white-hot release crashed over her.

Her fingers jerked on his shirt, ripping the material in half.

She felt the rumble of his laughter against her.

"Ah, baby, I wanna see you come again. But this time, I want to be inside you." She heard the hiss of his zipper and her eyes jerked downward.

Slade shoved the jeans down his hips and the engorged head of his cock sprang forward. Thick, dark, glistening faintly with moisture.

She wanted to taste him, as he'd tasted her. But she didn't know if Slade would trust her enough for that.

Maybe next time.

The hunger inside her was coiling again and the sight of his aroused flesh had her sex quivering in anticipation.

Take.

He positioned his cock against her opening, dipping the hard flesh in her cream and shuddering.

She arched beneath him, wanting him to drive that cock inside her. Oh, God, she needed him. Needed—

A slow push inside. One inch.

"Slade." Her mouth was open, her breath panting. More.

His gaze dropped to her mouth and she knew he could see her fangs. "Thirsty, baby? Is the bloodlust driving you?"

A jerky nod. But she wasn't going to bite him, not now—

"What do you want more?" He whispered, his voice little more than a growl. "My blood or my cock?"

Nema moaned and refused to utter the answer that sprang to her lips. Cock. Driving into her, hard, deep. The first orgasm hadn't done anything to satisfy her need. The blood hunger was growing by the moment, twisting with the lust she felt for Slade. Demanding that she taste, take.

"Tell me," he demanded. "What do you want?" Another slow, teasing thrust.

And her control snapped. Nema twisted, grabbed his arms and rolled with him, forcing his body under hers on the soft mattress.

She was on top of him, her legs straddling his hips, that long cock of his pressing into the entrance of her body. Her hands held his arms against the mattress. Her gaze met his and she gave him the only answer she had, "You."

Nema lifted her hips and drove down onto him, taking that full, hard length completely inside her sex.

They both moaned.

Every inch of Nema's sheath felt stretched. His cock was thick, wider than she'd expected, harder—and it felt so damn good.

She wasn't aware that she'd released his arms, but his hands were suddenly around her hips, lifting her, moving her in a fast, driving rhythm. His hips slammed into hers, his cock plunged deep and Nema clung tightly to him, loving the feel of his body beneath her, in her.

Every deep thrust sent a stab of pleasure through her. A second climax was building and her movements sped up, faster, faster....

Her eyes locked on his throat. On the pulse throbbing so frantically.

His blood was calling to her even as his powerful thrusts shook her body.

"Do it." His cheeks were flushed, his eyes stark with hunger. "I want to feel your mouth on me again."

And she wanted to taste him.

Her fingers trailed over that pulse point. Followed the twisting snake down his body. His cock swelled even more within her.

Nema gasped. Her right hand was directly over his heart now. She could feel the vibrations of its beat against her palm.

"Nema." His pupils were so big and dark that his eyes appeared nearly black. "Drink from me!" He drove into her, plunging so deep and hard that his back lifted from the bed.

Nema came, crying out his name, shuddering with the force of the fiery sensations that rippled along her nerve endings.

So good.

Take.

Her head lowered. Her mouth opened.

She licked his skin. Her sex clenched around him, the delicate inner muscles milking his cock as the last waves of her orgasm continued.

Her tongue slipped down his chest, moved below the fierce tattoo, right below his heart.

His body stiffened. His cock jerked within her, and hot semen flooded her depths as Slade climaxed with a ragged shout of release.

Take.

Her teeth pierced his flesh and the sweet flavor of his blood slid over her tongue.

"Nema!" His body bucked beneath hers. His fingers dug into her hips, holding her tighter to him as he continued to thrust. "So fucking good."

She drank from him, drawing out the pleasure, hers, his, with each slow movement of her mouth.

His hands gradually loosened their hold. His heartbeat began to slow, the fierce drumming fading. His cock pulsed inside her and she lifted her hips, rocking slowly as she fed.

He groaned.

Nema licked the small wound. Placed a kiss on his chest and lifted her head. His taste was still in her mouth. His seed between her legs.

Her gaze darted to the syringe.

Elation filled her.

She hadn't gone wild. Hadn't turned into some kind of mindless monster, even when she'd been driven past her control.

Nema didn't try to stop the smile that curled her lips as she turned her attention back to Slade. She was so damn happy, she leaned down and kissed him, a quick, open-mouthed kiss right on those sexy lips of his.

The cock within her began to harden. Nema drew in a surprised breath.

Slade cupped her breast. "Ah, baby, you didn't think I was finished now, did you?" His thickening shaft moved in a slow thrust.

"I, ah, didn't—" Oh, damn. Her inner muscles clamped down him, squeezing.

His nostrils flared and then he moved, jerking upright and holding her tight against his chest.

They were sitting now, face to face, and his sudden move had lodged his cock solidly inside her.

"I've been fantasizing about you for over eight hours," he muttered, dipping his head to lick her throat. "Once isn't gonna be nearly enough for me."

His mouth opened over her throat. Sucked.

The edge of his teeth pressed against her and a dark thrill shot straight to her heart. "Slade…."

He bit her. Locked those strong teeth of his around her flesh and bit down. Not hard enough to break the skin, just enough to have her squirming in pleasure.

Her breasts rubbed against his chest and her legs wrapped completely around his waist.

They began moving together. Slowly at first. His cock grew inside her, stretched until it filled every inch of her sex and pushed against the tip of her womb.

His head lifted. His gaze met hers. The thrusts grew harder. Deeper.

His hands curled around her hips, slipped down to cup the globes of her ass as he lifted her, plunging deeper.

His fingers trailed between her cheeks, and his cock slammed deep.

Harder now. Faster. Faster.

His gaze was still on hers. Blazing with lust and need.

"Come for me," he said, the words a demand. "Squeeze my cock, let me feel you clench around me."

His words sent her over the edge. She climaxed, staring into his eyes and calling his name as the release consumed her.

"Ah, yeah, baby, that's it. I can feel you milking me. So tight…." He shuddered, drove once more into her clinging sex, and came, erupting inside her with a shout of satisfaction.

He held her afterwards, wrapped his arms around her and kept his satiated length inside her.

As she lay there, his heartbeat filling her ears, his scent surrounding her, Nema realized that she'd never felt more alive.

Even in the days before her death.

If he wasn't careful, the woman would turn him into her slave.

Jesus. Sex with Nema had been freaking amazing. The best of his life, and he'd had his fair share of partners.

When she bit him, the sensation was so damn intense, the pleasure singed his nerve endings. But when she bit him *and* squeezed her creamy sex around him, he'd come close to a nuclear meltdown.

The. Best. Of. His. Life.

Nema Alexander had just ruined him for other women, and he couldn't wait for her to do it again.

"Well." He managed to drawl out the word after about twenty minutes of holding her—she just felt right in his arms. Like she was supposed to be there. Bullshit, of course. No man and woman were made for each other. He'd never believed that.

But Nema, she fit him. Eased the ache inside he hadn't even known he'd had.

She turned in his arms, staring up at him with those big, golden eyes of hers. Her fangs were gone now. He'd noticed they grew or retracted depending on her mood, and her arousal. "Thank you," she told him, her voice quite serious.

He blinked. "For what?"

Her fingers stroked over the length of his tattoo. He'd gotten the snake when he'd been undercover in the Narcotics Division. After he'd gotten his "initiation tat", he'd fit right in with the gang of drug runners. He liked it when Nema stroked his skin. Hell, he liked it when she did just about anything to him.

"Thanks for treating me a like a woman, and not a—a—"

Oh, hell, no. "Don't say it," he snapped. "Whatever, you're thinking, don't." Nema was a woman. Beautiful, different. Yeah, so she had a few peculiarities. So she had a yen for blood and a sun allergy.

She wasn't a monster, and she didn't have to say the word for him to know what she meant.

Nema swallowed. Her gaze darted back to the nightstand and to that syringe.

Dammit.

He pulled away from her, for a moment mourning the loss of her smooth body against his, then he rose from the bed. He had to do this now.

Nema tucked the sheet around her body, watching him carefully.

His fingers curled around the syringe. "We don't need this anymore." Every instinct he had screamed that Nema wasn't the cold-blooded killer she'd been described as. Her emotions were too clear, too easy to see and read. No, she wasn't a killer.

So he wouldn't have to use the black liquid to subdue her.

"I'd like that." Her brows were drawn low over her eyes. She held out her left hand, palm up. "Give me the syringe, Slade."

He hesitated only a moment, then handed it to her.

"Thank you." She rose from the bed, one hand holding the sheet to her chest, the other wrapped around the syringe. "I know you wouldn't have used this on me."

He barely controlled a flinch. But, no, he wouldn't have.

"But I'll still feel better once this is destroyed." So saying, she turned on her heel and walked to the bathroom. When she came back, the sheet was wrapped around her, sarong style, and the syringe was gone.

Slade drew in a deep breath. He knew it was time for some honesty between them. Hell, she'd been honest from the beginning, but now she needed to know the truth about him.

"There's something you should know," he began, the words seeming to stick in his throat. He knew he was about to make some of that trust fade from her eyes, and dammit, he liked it when she looked at him with that glow in her gaze.

"I'm not a cop, Nema. Not anymore. I was, but—" Ah, damn, this wasn't gonna be pretty. "I was kicked off the Force two years ago." After giving fifteen years of his life to the shield.

Nema's eyes stayed on him. Still bright. Waiting. "What happened?"

"I was working in Narcotics, with a team I trusted at the time." What a mistake that had been. "I didn't realize those guys were working both sides. Taking a cut of the profits from the traffickers. And when I did realize what was happening, they set me up. Made it look like I'd lost control and wounded an unarmed suspect."

He hadn't. He hadn't been the one to fire at Jose—his partner, Paul, had taken the shot—but he'd used Slade's gun. Slade hadn't even realized that Paul had switched weapons with him until it was too late.

The others in his team had joined in with Paul and spoken against him and, by the time they were finished, Slade's reputation had been shot. No one would listen to his claims about those guys being dirty.

"I was reprimanded for excessive use of force, labeled an overzealous cop and very firmly told to get the hell out of the department." His so-called friends had turned their backs on him in an instant.

And he'd started his bounty-hunting business.

Which brought him to confession number two.

"I'm sorry that happened to you. I'm sure you were actually a very good cop," Nema said softly, and damn if that glow of trust wasn't still in her eyes.

So he'd just confessed to lying to her, admitted that his career as a cop had ended in disgrace, and still she—what?

Looked at him like he was some kind of hero.

A faint line appeared between her brows. "But if you aren't a cop anymore, then why'd you come after me?"

He'd known the question would come. Slade parted his lips to confess. "Nema, I—"

Nema's head jerked to the left, and her gaze locked on the door. "Someone's coming."

He stiffened, but shook his head. "Probably just another guest." They'd been coming and going all day. "Look, I need you to know something. Ah, hell, I was hi—"

Her eyes were narrowed in concentration. "It's a group of men. They're trying to be quiet, to—shit!" She ran across the room, yanked off her sheet and reached for her clothes. "It's McDermott's men!"

Talk about piss-poor timing. Slade jerked on his jeans as fast as he could and reached for the gun that he'd brought in from the truck. He tucked it in the small of his back and demanded, "You sure?"

She nodded. "I can smell 'em. Same stench from last night."

Damn. His confession would have to wait. "Then we need to get the hell out of here."

"Tell me something I don't know, Ace."

"Fast." But not through the front door. They'd probably be waiting for them. There was a window in the bathroom. He grabbed her hand.

And the front door crashed open. Four armed men swept into the room, weapons all pointed straight at Nema.

Slade swore and stepped in front of her.

Her fingers dug into his back. "No, you can't."

McDermott walked into the room, a cold smile on his face. "Hello, Brion. I got tired of waiting on you."

Nema's hands fell away.

"So I sent my men to track you." His beady eyes gleamed. "Took me a bit of time. I'd hoped to be here before sunset."

While Nema was still weak and helpless. The bastard. Slade's hands tightened into fists.

"Slade." Nema's voice. Confused. Angry. "What the hell is going on?"

He shifted slightly, glancing back at her.

McDermott said with a smile, "Ah, hello again, my dear."

Nema bared her fangs at him. "I'm not your dear, you bastard."

McDermott scratched his chin and made a faint humming sound. "You know, you have extremely poor taste in men, Ms. Alexander. This is what, the second gentlemen who has traded your life for a bit of cash?"

"What?" Nema grabbed Slade, using her enhanced strength as she forced him to face her. "What's he talking about Slade?"

There were traces of tears in her eyes. A cold fist squeezed his heart. This wasn't the way it was supposed to go down. "Nema, let me explain." *I wasn't going to betray you.*

"Yes, do explain to her. Tell Nema how I offered you five hundred grand to deliver her to me."

She dropped her hold on him as if she'd been burned.

"Shut up!" Slade snarled. He reached for Nema, but she jerked away from him. "I wasn't going to trade you. Dammit, listen to me!"

But she was shaking her head, inching back, her gaze darting around the room with the desperation of a trapped animal.

"Here's your money, Brion." McDermott kicked a black briefcase across the room. "It's only three hundred thousand, because, well, I did have to do part of the retrieval on my own." He motioned to the men beside him. "Take her down."

"What?" *Take her down.* "No, don't!" Slade lunged, trying to shield Nema, knowing what was coming even before he heard McDermott's cold order to—

"Shoot the bitch."

Slade saw Nema's eyes widen in understanding. A bullet ripped into his upper arm as he threw his body before hers. *Nema, I'm sorry—*

She screamed, a sound of fury and fear. Nema shoved him to the side, and launched across the room. Her claws swiped the chest of the man who'd shot him, leaving blood pouring down his shirt as he fell to his knees.

"Shoot her! Shoot her! Now, get her!" McDermott was yelling orders even as he hid behind his men.

Slade shoved to his feet. He had to help her, he—

A second gunman fired, shooting Nema in the stomach. She grabbed his hand, jerked, and bones crunched.

The blood began to drip down the front of her jeans.

"Again, hit her again—she's getting weak!"

"No!" Slade tried to run for Nema, but it was too late.

Shots exploded, hitting her, one, another, thudding into her soft body. Silence.

She was on the floor, soaked in blood.

No. Not Nema.

"Nema," he whispered her name as he fell to his knees beside her. Her eyes were open, still so gold and beautiful, but blood trickled from the corner of her mouth.

"Bring in the stretcher. Strap her down." McDermott's voice. Barking orders. The sonofabitch.

Slade's fingers trembled as he wiped the blood from her lips. A scream was welling up inside him, a scream of fury, of death. He was going to kill McDermott. Kill all the bastards who'd hurt her.

McDermott ordered, "Get her."

Someone made the mistake of reaching for Nema. Slade turned on him, jerking the bastard down beside him and fighting like a man possessed.

Or a man destroyed.

Bones crunched beneath his fists. He heard the howls of pain from his prey. But he didn't care.

They'd shot Nema.

The cold barrel of a gun pressed against the side of his head.

"Let him go." McDermott.

Very slowly, Slade released him and turned toward his next victim.

McDermott wasn't smiling anymore. His thick face seemed pale but his hold on the gun was steady. He lifted the weapon, aiming it a few inches away from Slade's forehead.

Slade stared at the gun and wondered if he'd be able to kill him before McDermott got the shot off.

"It's not like the vampiress is dead," McDermott muttered, curling his lip. "She's just weak. We'll pump her full of blood when she wakes up, and she'll survive just fine."

Nema moaned then, and Slade's attention snapped back to her. She was on a long, black stretcher, her hands and feet strapped down. Her gaze met his, full of pain. Fear.

Rage.

"The blood flow from the wounds has already stopped." This came from the man in the white coat who was kneeling next to Nema. The guy must've slipped inside while Slade had been doing his level best to beat another man to death. "Her healing speed is nothing short of miraculous."

Thank God. She'd be all right. She just needed blood, and he'd sure as hell be happy to let her drink his.

"Load her into the van."

Unmindful of the gun pointed at him, Slade rose to his feet. "You're not taking her anywhere." And they definitely weren't taking her back to some lab where they could experiment on her like she was some kind of high-priced lab rat.

"You knew what was expected from the beginning," McDermott muttered. "You knew I wanted the woman—"

"I didn't know you were planning to play mad scientist with Nema's life!"

Oh, damn, but he needed to touch her, to hold her. She was too pale, too still, and he wanted to run back to her side and force her to drink.

She needed him.

And, God knew, he needed her. More than he'd ever needed anyone before. "Our agreement's over. Take your damn money and get the hell out of here!" He forced his way to the stretcher, grabbed Nema's cold fingers.

McDermott laughed softly. "Oh, I intend to do just that."

It was Nema's face that warned him. Her eyes widened in alarm and her lips parted as she tried to tell him—

Shit. Slade jerked to the left just as a bullet blasted into his back.

Bastards.

Nema's hand slipped from his fingers. His head slammed into the floor, and he tasted blood on his tongue.

McDermott stood over him, smirking. "Fool. You were just the bait all along. The prey to distract her so that I could get close."

The room was getting dim now. Too dim. He strained, trying to see through the encroaching darkness.

Nema. She was being taken from the room, taken away from him.

No!

It wasn't going to end like this. No damn way. "F-find… you."

But McDermott just shook his head. "Brion, the only thing you're going to find is hell."

Then the bastard turned on his heel and marched from the room, leaving Slade lying in an ever-growing pool of his own blood.

"You need to stay in the hospital overnight, Mr. Brion. Your wounds are—"

"They stopped bleeding, right?"

"Uh, yes," the haggard intern managed, pushing back his glasses, "but you—"

"All the organs working?"

"Uh, yes, but—"

"Then thanks for stitching me up, Doc, but someone's waiting on me, and she's not the kind who likes to wait." Slade grabbed his shirt, managed to pull it on and connect three of the buttons in front.

The intern protested, "You were shot, twice! We have to fill out reports, contact the authorities."

Slade grunted. The authorities. He figured the paramedics who'd found him in that motel room had already called in the boys in blue. That meant he didn't have much time to get out of Mercy General before he found himself surrounded by uniforms who wanted answers—answers he couldn't give.

He took two steps away from the exam table, testing himself. The right side of his back burned like it was on fire, and his head was throbbing with a steady, dull ache, but Slade figured he'd be able to manage the pain.

He wasn't supposed to be alive. He knew that. McDermott had intended to kill him. And if Nema hadn't warned him, the bastard would have succeeded.

But now he was wasting time. There were only a few hours of darkness left, and he would find Nema before the dawn.

He pushed through the swaying emergency room doors and began walking through the hospital corridor. Each step became faster, stronger—

Nema.

"Mr. Brion! Mr. Brion! Wait, you can't—"

The red exit sign glowed up ahead. The entrance automatically opened as he approached. He ignored the doctor's calls from behind him and walked into the waiting night.

Slade figured he'd have to call in a few favors in order to find McDermott, but, luckily, the wrong sort of people owed him.

And they were just the right people he needed now.

Chapter 7

It took him less than an hour to locate the lab. He'd called in his favors and gotten instant results, the address of McDermott's private party lab.

It wasn't Daylor Labs, the big, shining fortress of technology that McDermott had in downtown Houston. Oh, no, this place was a hole in the wall. The lab was hidden in the wilderness, a tall, thick building cloaked by the night. Decrepit. Perfect for McDermott's illegal experiments.

And Slade had learned from his sources that McDermott had a reputation for such experiments.

But not for much longer.

Slade got past the dogs, past the piss-poor patrol and the video cameras. Now, he just had to find his woman.

Slade slipped down the staircase, heading to the basement level. He'd start low and work his way up, and if he had to rip the building apart to find Nema, he would.

He moved carefully, balancing his weight so that the old spiral staircase made no sound beneath him. Dim lighting cast shadows on the walls, on the peeling paint. No high-class lab here. It was a hellhole.

No way did Nema belong here.

A voice spoke out beyond. "None of the five bodies showed any signs of altered tissue."

Slade stiffened at the sound of the voice. He knew that voice. The guy who'd brought the stretcher for Nema, the doctor, the one on in the white lab coat.

"Then they weren't changing?" McDermott sounded pissed. "She didn't infect them?"

Infect them? His hands clenched and he eased down the last few stairs, deliberately sidling around to hide in the shadows.

"I don't know how the virus is transmitted, but I tell you, vampirism *can* be transmitted. She got it, others can, too. We just have to figure out how."

"She drank from all of them," McDermott said. "They should have changed!"

The doctor replied, "It's more than just the blood transfer, it has to be.

Vampirism is a virus, but the mode of infection—that's the mystery." Footsteps echoed. "I haven't been able to determine how the transference occurs."

"Dammit, figure out what it is!" McDermott's voice was furious, and closer. "That woman is the key to the future, my future!"

He was coming this way. Slade took a breath, drew it in deep, and prepared to attack.

"Ms. Alexander, are you with us again?"

His blood chilled at the doctor's question. Nema was there. And now Slade could see McDermott, close enough to grab.

Pity the bastard had two guards flanking him.

Dammit. If he attacked now, the doctor would be alerted.

Slade settled back into the shadows as a blast of fury filled him.

Timing. It was all about timing. He'd get Nema first, then come back for McDermott.

His gaze never left the other man's face as McDermott stalked past him and up the stairs.

Soon.

But first…

Nema.

He crept from the shadows, drawing his weapon.

She was weak. Too weak. An IV tube ran into her right wrist, and the blood pumped into her veins. Nema pulled against the cold, metal bars that locked her against the table. Apparently, the guys had upgraded on their restraints since her last little visit.

Her gaze darted around the dank room. And no windows this time either. Was she even in the same lab? Probably not, it looked like these guys weren't taking any chances this time around.

They'd strapped her down and started the transfusion the minute she was secured by the bars, the better to keep her hale and hearty for their experiments.

"How are you feeling now, Ms. Alexander?" It was the doctor. The one who liked to cut her with his shiny scalpel. O'Donnell or O'Donnelley. She didn't really care. To her, he was just the enemy.

"How am I?" She managed, her voice rasping. "Come closer. I'll show you." Her teeth snapped together in a hard bite.

His muddy brown eyes narrowed. "I think that's enough blood." His gloved hands closed over her wrist and with a jerk, quickly withdrew the IV tubing.

Oh, if only he were a few inches closer….

"You're sick, you know that, don't you, Ms. Alexander?"

She closed her eyes a moment. Where was Slade? Still in that motel room? Slowly bleeding out? He'd betrayed her, but even so, he didn't deserve to be shot in the back. And he'd tried to help her.

Too little, too late.

Nema just couldn't seem to push him from her thoughts. Maybe someone had found him. Somebody had to have heard the gunshots.

"Did you hear me?" the doctor asked, moving around the length of the table.

At least it was just this one man now. She was so glad that prick McDermott had finally left her alone. "Yeah," she muttered, and realized that her voice had grown stronger. "I heard you." He thought she was sick. "Newsflash. I'm not sick. I'm dead."

But he was shaking his head and checking her pulse rate on one of his beeping machines. "No, no, but I think you were *at* death. My theory on vampirism is that you were infected moments before your body would have expired. Instead of dying, the virus changed your cells, altered your system, and made you, well, as you are now."

Great. Not only had they shot her and kidnapped her, now they were forcing her to listen to science lessons.

"Look, jerkoff, I—" She heard a footfall. A faint, close shuffle. Her nostrils twitched.

Slade.

A hot burst of happiness filled her.

He was alive.

Good, because when she got free, she was going to kill him.

"The real mystery," the doctor continued, his voice droning as he talked more to himself than her, "is why your cells changed. So many others haven't." Now he did glance back at her. "We've experimented over the years, you know."

Um, she just bet they had.

Another soft footfall.

Time to keep Mr. Science distracted. "So what's so great about me? Why'd I get to go all uber-vampire while the others didn't?"

"That's what I'm going to find out." His brows drew together. "It's possible there must be more of a mixing of fluids between a vampire and prey to complete the change—"

Her heart began to race faster. A mixing of fluids. Like from drinking blood and having sex.

She'd had sex with Aidan, he'd taken blood from her, a lot of blood, and the next day, she'd woken to discover that he'd buried her in some hole in the woods—and she'd woken as a vampire.

Over the last six months, she'd tasted the other men—Trace, Bryce, Tony, Marc, and Adam—but she hadn't been with them sexually.

Could that be it? Could sex be the key? *Keep your prey and your pleasure separate.* That's what the vampire had said to her at the bar. She'd thought he was warning her about losing control, hurting someone during sex. She hadn't thought, hadn't realized—

Shit.

She'd tasted Slade's blood.

And taken him into her body.

"What's happening?" The doctor stumbled back, staring worriedly at the flickering monitors. "Your heart's accelerating too fast, you're—"

Slade stepped out of the shadows and punched the doctor right in the face. He went down, white coat swirling around him, and didn't get up.

Then Slade was at her side, staring down at her with those dark blue eyes of his and looking so damn good and strong that he made her ache.

"Hold on, baby, I'll get you out of here." Then he was throwing a lever, and the thick bars retracted into the table.

Free.

Nema pushed up and a wave of dizziness made her tremble. Not enough blood.

The good doc had cut off her supply too soon.

"It's all right, I've got you." Slade's arms were around her. Warm. Reassuring.

Her fingers curled into a fist. And she punched him, right in the gut.

Unfortunately, there wasn't much strength behind the blow.

"Bastard," she muttered as his scent teased her nostrils.

The guy never flinched. "Yeah, I am." He lifted her off the table, cradling her against his chest. Her head nestled in the crook of his neck, right next to that tempting pulse point. "But I'm also the bastard who came back to save your ass."

True, and she couldn't deny that she was very, very glad to see him right then.

Even though he'd betrayed her.

His palm cradled the back of her head and urged her mouth closer to him. "Drink."

She hesitated. If her suspicions were true—

"Come on, baby, drink so we can get the hell out of here."

Well, if they were true, then it was already too late.

And she was too thirsty to fight the need. Her teeth pierced his flesh, and the sweet, hot blood flowed down her throat.

Slade shuddered.

The growing bulge of his arousal pressed against her.

"Ah, Nema. That's… ah."

She could feel the curl of heat between her legs, the physical hunger rising to match his.

"Enough!"

She pulled back instantly, blinking up at him. His eyes were narrowed, his lips parted, and for an instant, she could have sworn that she saw a hint of fang.

Then he took a deep breath, and everything appeared normal again. "You strong enough to make it out of here now?"

Nema nodded. If she had to, she'd crawl.

"Then let's go before McDermott and his trigger-happy friends return."

Something was happening in the building. By the time they reached the main level, they could hear men screaming. Flames were burning at the back of the building, people were running.

Slade didn't know what was going on or why it looked like all hell was breaking loose, but it was the perfect escape cover for them.

As they fled, he kept his fingers locked around Nema's wrist. He wasn't about to let her go.

He knew she was pissed at him. He'd have to do a lot of explaining, fast, once they were out of this mess. But he figured there had to be hope. After all, the woman had just punched him, she hadn't tried to kill him.

Yet.

They ran for his truck. One of the goons who'd taken Nema jumped from the darkness at him. Before Slade could attack, Nema swiped out with her claws, and the man jerked away, screaming.

Dogs were howling around them, smoke filling the air. And as they jumped into the truck, there was a strange howl on the wind, a howl that sounded like Nema's name.

Time to get out of there.

Slade slammed his foot down on the gas, spun the truck into reverse and shot out of the covering trees as fast as his trusty ride could go.

He glanced back into the rear-view mirror. Saw a man standing before the fire. Too big for McDermott. The guy was watching the truck, watching them.

Another hired gun?

Too bad.

The truck was edging up to sixty now, and he'd mapped his escape route well.

No way were those jerks going to catch them.

He and Nema were home free.

He drove for miles, keeping a close eye on the rearview mirror to watch for any unexpected company. Nema was quiet beside him. Her hands knotted into fists, her body stiff.

He took the last turn with a screech of his tires, heading down the long dirt road that led to the cabin he planned to use as their temporary safe house.

When he parked the car, Nema still didn't move. His fingers tightened around the steering wheel, knuckles whitening. Facing her then, it was the hardest thing he'd ever had to do.

Slade drew a deep breath and slowly turned his head toward her. "Nema, I'm sorry." For lying to her. For allowing McDermott to hurt her, to take her away.

She looked at him. Shadows fell over her face. "You were just doing what you were paid to do, right?"

Her soft words sliced him worse than her claws ever could. "I wasn't gonna take the money. When I was with you in that motel, it was about me and you." And, God, but he could still feel her body against his. "I wasn't planning to set you up then."

"Right," she drawled out the word. "And all that bullshit about being set up on the Force? What was that? Just some sob story?"

"That was real. Everything I told you about the Force was real. And I was gonna tell you the rest."

"The rest?" she repeated, her voice cold. "I think I've managed to figure that out for myself."

He had to try and explain. Had to try and get past her rage. "I took a job as a bounty hunter, okay? I worked ninety hour weeks for two years, and then McDermott came along."

"And offered you a deal too good to pass up…"

He wouldn't lie anymore. "He offered me a lot of money. Enough to start a new life. I didn't know you." Hadn't seen her smile, seen the fear in her eyes or tasted her lips. "Everything changed when I met you." *Everything.*

In the darkness, her golden eyes gleamed. Her gaze held his, one moment. Two.

"I wasn't going to turn you over to him. Hell, if I'd wanted to do that, I had all day to call him. You were out, hibernating or whatever it is you vampires do. I could have turned you over then, but I didn't. *I didn't.*"

She had to believe him.

"I wasn't going to betray you, Nema."

The tension was too thick, too—

"I believe you."

His breath expelled in a hard rush. Believing wasn't forgiving, but it was better than nothing.

"You didn't have to come back for me," she said, her voice whisper-soft. "You could have left me with him."

Not a chance. "That wasn't an option, baby." He held out his hand to her. *Not even for a minute.*

Faint moonlight spilled into the car, casting just enough of a glow for him to see her fingers slowly lift and reach for his. The soft touch of her hand against his seemed to sear Slade to his very soul.

He'd meant to be gentle with her. Meant to just hold her. The woman had been through hell and he'd planned to show nothing but care.

But then the lust ripped past his good intentions. Her scent surrounded him, stronger, richer than ever before. Every breath he drew tasted of her.

Nema.

His fingers tightened around hers, and Slade pulled her to him. The damn steering wheel was in the way, but he jerked to the side, turning so they faced chest to chest.

And he kissed her. A desperate, deep kiss.

He'd come too close to losing her. Now the need to take her, to reaffirm his claim, was like a fury within him.

Nema's mouth was just as wild upon his. Her lips were parted wide, her tongue thrusting against his. He jerked up her shirt, pushed his hand up the slender expanse of her stomach and cupped the warm weight of her breast.

A moan rumbled in Nema's throat. Low. Hungry. Spurring the need within him ever higher.

His cock was so hard it ached and he wanted to bury himself balls deep in her silken depths. But there wasn't enough damn room in the truck.

With a last, desperate lick, he pulled away from her and shoved open his door. "Come on," he growled, wrapping his fingers around her wrist.

They stumbled from the car. Kissing, touching. Nema threw her shirt to the ground. Slade yanked her bra open, snapping the delicate straps. Her nipples were hard, and with a snarl, he lowered his head and caught one tight peak in his mouth.

He pushed her back against the side of the truck. The moon shone down on them. The whispers of the night surrounded them.

His fingers unsnapped her jeans, shoved down the zipper. He needed to touch her, everywhere.

Her scent was driving him mad. Making a fierce, driving hunger consume him.

Take.

He had to take her. Had to claim—

Nema kicked out of her shoes and jeans. Then her hands reached for the waistband of his pants.

Take.

He could hear her blood pounding. Hear the sweet call of her blood filling his ears. The wounds he'd gotten from the bullets no longer fazed him. All he knew was the hunger.

So much hunger. For her. Only Nema.

Her hands were against his flesh. Stroking down his abdomen. Reaching for the erection that rose, heavy and full, toward her.

A strange ache began to build in his mouth. Almost like a burn, and his hands—

"Slade?" Nema's voice was hesitant as her fingers froze over him.

He grabbed her wrists, pushing them back against the truck, pinning them on either side of her body. He didn't understand what the hell was happening to him, why he felt so damn odd, but he knew one thing. He wanted Nema.

His mouth closed over her neck. Such sweet, tender flesh. His tongue swept over her, tasting, licking. The edge of his teeth pressed into her.

"Slade." Her voice spoke of arousal. Hunger. No more hesitation.

He freed her hands, reached for her legs. "Wrap your legs around me," he ordered, breathing the words against her neck. Her scent was stronger there and that heartbeat, so fast....

Her silken thighs wrapped around his waist. His cock lodged at the tender opening of her body. She wasn't wearing panties. Vaguely, he remembered that he'd ripped them off her the last time they'd been together. Her cream coated him, the wet touch sending a shudder of anticipation down the length of his body.

He drove deep in one long, hard thrust. Her thighs tightened around him as he withdrew. Then he plunged back inside her tight core.

Again.

Again.

Their bodies moved faster, the rhythm a driving fury.

He kissed her throat. Licked.

Take.

The seductive whisper swept through his mind.

Nema was his to take. Always his.

Take.

His mouth opened over her throat. His hips slammed against hers. Her sex squeezed him, sliding over his aroused length and taking his erection deep into her core.

Then she was stiffening against him, her breath choking out and her delicate inner muscles rippling around him as she shuddered with the force of her orgasm.

His fingers sank into her hips as he continued to thrust. So close.

Take.

His teeth opened over her throat.

The most explosive orgasm of his life consumed him, blinding him with pleasure as the waves of release washed over him.

When he finally stopped shaking—it could have been five minutes later, could have been an hour, hell if he knew—Nema's legs had slipped down his hips. Her thighs cradled his and her breasts were cushioned against his chest.

He lifted his head slowly. There was a strange, rich flavor in his mouth.

Nema stared up at him, a faint line between her brows. "Slade."

His lips pressed against hers. It was a soft, gentle kiss when before he'd been savage in his hunger.

He fastened his jeans and helped her to dress. Then he picked her up, cradling her in his arms. Yeah, he knew the woman could probably pick him up, but carrying her inside the cabin seemed like the right the thing to do.

The kind of thing that a real good guy would do.

Just to be extra careful, he made damn sure he locked the door tightly behind them and set the alarm before he strode to the bedroom. Nema seemed light, almost incredibly so, in his arms.

He set her gently on the mattress before moving to draw the blinds and curtains in the room. He'd make certain no sunlight touched her while she rested.

Slade returned to the bed and crawled in beside Nema. She turned toward him, and he pulled her close against his chest. A heavy languor began to seep into his limbs.

"We need to talk." Her words rumbled against his chest.

Yeah, they did. They needed to come up with a serious plan for dealing with McDermott, although the idea of just shooting the guy seemed pretty good to him right then.

"I think something's happening to—"

He didn't hear her last word. Damn, but the day and night were catching up with him. He yawned, feeling a tiredness all the way to his bones.

They were safe, at least for the time being. No one had followed them to the cabin. No one would be able to link him to the place on paper, and even if somehow, somebody did manage to stumble upon them, the place had a state-of-the-art alarm system. Yeah, they were safe. He could rest.

"I didn't mean for this to happen. Not to you."

It was hard to focus on Nema's words. They seemed to be fading in and out. And his eyelashes were heavy, too heavy to stay open.

Perhaps he'd rest a bit. Just for a few moments.

"The sun's coming. Not much time...."

He could feel the rise of the sun. Feel it stretching across the sky. Weird.

He tried to reach for Nema's hand, wanting to wrap his fingers around hers while he slept, but he couldn't seem to get his hand to cooperate. He was just too damned tired.

Slade realized he could hear his heartbeat, thudding in his ears. One beat. Another. The beats were slowing, the time between them stretching ever longer.

What the hell?

"Nema?" A vague alarm sounded in his mind. He struggled, trying to open his eyes, to see her and figure out what was happening.

But his lashes wouldn't lift and he heard her whisper, very softly, "I'm sorry," just before the darkness consumed him.

Chapter 8

He awoke to the feel of her mouth along the tip of his cock.

Wet.

Warm.

His eyes opened, and Slade groaned as he stared down at Nema. Her dark hair was a curtain around her body. Her completely nude body. Her breasts swayed gently as she leaned over him. Her fingers wrapped around the base of his cock and her mouth—oh, Jesus, her mouth—sucked the head of his erection.

For just a moment, he couldn't help but feel a flicker of worry. The woman was a vampire, and she did have some damn sharp teeth next to a very important part of his body and—

She took him deep into her mouth, sucking the length of his aroused flesh all the way to the back of her throat.

Fuck.

His hips arched toward her.

The woman sure as hell knew how to use her mouth. She tasted his length, sucking, licking, pulling back so that she teased the thick head of his cock with her tongue.

He reached for her breasts, wanting to feel her nipples in his hands.

Nema moaned when he touched her, and the vibration worked down the length of his erection. The sweet scent of her cream filled the air around him, driving his lust.

He wanted to taste her.

"Nema—"

She rose above him, her lips gleaming and full. Her fingers stroked his flesh, one long, slow sweep from balls to tip. Then she was straddling him, positioning those sexy as hell legs on either side of his hips. He didn't know how he'd gotten naked, and right then, he didn't really care.

She positioned his cock against her. Rose up, just a few inches, then drove her body down against his, taking his cock deep inside in that one, swift thrust.

His heels dug into the bed and he began to piston his hips against her as he drove for his release.

The rhythm was fast, almost violent. His arms lifted to wrap around her. He wanted to pull her closer, to taste her lips, her neck.

Nema growled and caught his hands, slamming them back against the mattress. Her eyes held a faint glow and her fangs shone behind her red lips. Her hips ground against his as she lifted her body, then plunged down against him. Again, again, again.

Then she was tossing back her head and crying out as her sex contracted around his cock.

He grabbed her, rolling and pinning her beneath him as he kept thrusting. Keep driving deeper and deeper into her warm, wet body.

The waves of her release teased his cock, stroking him into a frenzy of arousal. Slade lifted her legs, forcing them high above his shoulders as he thrust, moving so hard the bed creaked beneath them.

His hands dug into the mattress. A gnawing ache began in his mouth and a raging hunger sprang from his very soul.

"Slade, do it!"

Her throat was so close. He licked her skin, tasted the heat of her passion.

"Do it." Her muscles were tensing again, and he knew a second climax was upon her. His cock shoved deep into her tight depths as she whispered, "Bite me."

His teeth locked on her throat and he came, pumping his seed into her sex and tasting her blood on his tongue.

When the haze of lust and pleasure finally faded, the rich flavor was still in his mouth. And one thought blazed through his mind.

Holy shit. I'm a fucking vampire.

❧⟨☾☉⟩❧

She watched his fangs slowly retract, heard the hard and fast thudding of his heart, and knew the exact moment when realization dawned for Slade.

He shook his head. Swiped his hand across his mouth. Left a faint trail of blood on his cheek.

Then he jumped from the bed. "What the hell is going on, Nema?"

"You know." It wasn't like the signs were easy to miss. The man had just plunged his fangs into her throat and he currently was sporting three-inch long claws.

Not the look of an average human.

He was pacing around the room. His head was still shaking. "No, this can't be."

"You're a vampire now." *You're just like me.*

He couldn't have looked more horrified. "You changed me."

No denying that one. Her head moved in a slow nod even as her hand darted down to pull the sheet over her body. She'd known even before the hibernation sleep had claimed him what was happening. It was impossible to mistake his growing fangs and sudden strength.

She'd woken before him, woken as the faint rays of the sun dipped below the horizon. She'd watched him for a moment, tracing the strong lines of his face with a fingertip.

His first night as a full vampire. She'd wanted him to wake to a new world with her. Wanted his rising to be special.

Not like hers. She'd woken to the taste of dirt in her mouth. In her nose, her eyes, her ears. She'd clawed her way out of that makeshift grave. Spitting, shoving the heavy weight of the earth that just seemed to keep falling onto her no matter how hard she'd pushed.

Buried alive. That had been her first thought, and the screams in her mind had been endless. The bastard who'd changed her had dumped her body in the woods. Covered her up and left her.

"Nema?"

She blinked, realizing that Slade had crossed the room to her side. She stared up at him and saw the banked fires of anger in his eyes.

"I didn't mean for this to happen." But it was her fault, and she wasn't going to pretend otherwise.

Slade held up his hands, staring at the claws. "How?" A growl. The hint of growing fangs showed behind his thin lips.

Her shoulders straightened. Her chin tipped back. "Sex and blood. Apparently, it can be a lethal mix." A lesson learned too late.

She stood, wrapping the sheet around her body. "I didn't know, I swear I didn't. Not until I was in that damn lab and that O'Donnell jerk said something about mixing fluids." Then she'd suspected. "But I still thought I might be wrong, until...." Nema reached up and tapped the edge of his very sharp canines. "Until I caught a glimpse of these last night."

"I'm dead."

Not exactly. "Our hearts beat. We breathe. No, you're not going to be eating hamburgers anymore or drinking beers, but you're not going to be in a grave, either."

His hands clenched. "I didn't choose this."

"Neither did I, Ace. Neither did I." But she knew how he felt. Nema licked her lips and blurted, "I wanted your first rising to be special." Now why had that slipped out?

His gaze met hers.

She pulled the sheet closer to her body. Okay, this wasn't going so good. Dammit, why did things between them always have to get so—

He touched her cheek. "It was."

"Better than waking in a grave, huh?" Shit, could she not keep quiet now?

His brows drew together. "What?"

No sense stopping at this point. Besides, she didn't want anymore secrets between them. "You asked me about my change once."

Slade said nothing, waiting.

"I was seeing this man, Aidan Thomas. We'd been dating a few months."

"Then you slept with him."

She nodded. "Things were intense that night." Intense. Yeah, nice word there. The first part of the night had been great. Hot sex. Great orgasms. Then.... "I didn't even realize he'd bit me until later. Dawn was coming. He told me it was time. I asked, 'Time for what?' Aidan said it was time for me to die."

"Bastard."

"I don't remember much after that." She'd tried to run, but been too weak from blood loss. "The next night, I woke up in the ground. Aidan had buried me, made a makeshift grave and dumped me there." And she still had horrible flashbacks to that night.

"Nema."

She kept talking, fast, wanting to get it all out now. "I dug myself out, hiked through the woods and back to town, and managed to get to my apartment, covered in mud, grime and blood, just as the sun was rising." She rubbed her arms, where sometimes it seemed as if she could still feel that scorching burn.

Nema exhaled. "I trusted him. Stupid mistake, I know." She held his gaze. "I thought I knew him. I cared about him." Back in the days before he'd bled her dry and buried her in the woods.

"Where is good old Aidan now?"

"I don't know. McDermott got on my trail days later, and I had to run. I've been running since." She hadn't gotten the opportunity to hunt down Aidan and give him the ass-kicking he so seriously deserved. Not that she was actually sure she could kick the guy's ass. He was older as a vampire than she was, so he had to be stronger. But she'd still like to give the ass-kicking a try.

Slade cupped her chin into his hand, drew her close for a quick, hard kiss. With he drew back, he stared down at her, his expression hooded.

"I know this isn't what you wanted," she muttered. Really, who wanted to be a vampire? No food, no sunlight, it was not exactly the best way to exist.

His lips hitched just a bit. "Well, I'd say my plans for sunning on a beach somewhere are pretty much screwed at this point."

She winced.

"Give me time, Nema. I'm pissed as hell right now. At McDermott. At that jerk Aidan. At pretty much the whole damn world."

Yeah, she could understand. Been there, done that.

"So let's just get the hell out of here now, okay? I wanna put more distance between us and McDermott, and then figure out exactly how we're gonna stop the bastard."

Sounded like a good plan to her.

He was a vampire. Shit.

Slade stepped up to the gas station counter, tossing down a twenty to cover his gas and tried, very hard, not to stare at the clerk's throat.

A vampire.

And the damn weird thing was, he didn't feel all that different. Sure, he could smell every odor in the station. Could hear whispers of sound and even racing heartbeats, but he didn't feel like some monster out of a horror movie who would go mad at any moment and start attacking humans.

He just felt a little stronger. A little wilder.

His wounds were healed, completely gone, in fact. Not even a hint of pink skin. Yeah, he felt pretty damn good, all things considered.

Meanwhile, Nema was feeling guilty as hell. He didn't need any new psychic powers to tell him that. The woman's face had guilt stamped all over it. She hated that she'd changed him, but he didn't mind so much.

And how insane was that?

Because now that he was like her, Slade was realizing that things were going to be much, much easier. When you wanted to convince a vampire to stay with you forever, well, it kinda helped if you could be around for that length of time instead of say, oh, only forty or fifty more years.

Now, he had forever. And if he had his way, he'd be spending all of his many nights to come with his sexy vampiress.

"That all for ya?" The clerk raised a brow, looking mildly annoyed as Slade continued to stand at the counter.

In an effort not to zero in on the fellow's throat, Slade's gaze drifted to the nearby rack of magazines and newspapers. A black and white headline instantly caught his gaze and his heart leapt.

Houston business tycoon Clayton McDermott found dead.

He grabbed the paper, scanning the story. McDermott had been found just after dawn. The police had been alerted to the fire at his lab, and they'd discovered the remains of his body. No specifics were mentioned in the article, just a few vague references to severe blood loss, throat wounds, and a possible animal attack.

Animal attack. Not damn likely.

Slade dropped the paper and ran for the door.

Nema looked up when he jumped into the truck. "Is everything okay?"

With a swipe of his hand, he opened the glove box and pulled out his gun. Better to have the weapon handy, just in case. Slade tucked the weapon into the back waistband of his jeans.

"Slade?"

He cranked the engine and nearly flew out of the station. "We've got trouble, baby. The killing kind. McDermott was murdered last night." Severe blood loss. Throat wounds. Yeah, that fit the bill and also made McDermott victim number six.

And all the men were linked to Nema. Unless he was very much mistaken, that set him up to be victim number seven.

"Who's doing this?" Nema demanded.

"Gotta be another vampire." He wasn't even sure a human could commit those crimes.

"Another vampire? Who—Slade!"

A black SUV shot from the shadows on the side of the road and slammed into them. The screech of metal filled his ears and the truck flew into the air, spinning in a sickening blur over and over.

Sonofabitch! No! Nema—

The truck crashed into the ground.

Chapter 9

"How the hell are you still alive?" A snarling male voice demanded as a boot rammed into Slade's ribs.

Jesus. He coughed, choking on blood and tried to roll to the left. Every inch of his body burned and he knew he'd scraped a ton of flesh off on the gravel road.

"I'll rip your throat out, just like I did the others." A strong hand clamped around his neck and jerked Slade to his feet. And he came face to face with a killer.

The man's blue eyes shone with a faint glow. His dark hair was wild around his face, and his parted lips revealed his bared fangs.

"It's gonna take more than you to kill me, asshole," Slade managed to growl, spitting blood onto the bastard who held him.

"I don't think it will."

Slade lifted his claws in a flash of motion and buried them in the guy's chest. "Think again."

The blue eyes widened in surprise, and the hold on Slade's throat loosened for just a moment. It was all the time he needed.

The butt of his gun dug into his back. He had one second to be grateful he hadn't lost the weapon in the crash, then he was reaching for it, wrenching it up and out and aiming it dead center between the vampire's eyes.

He smiled as he pulled the trigger and watched the bastard fall to the ground.

"Slade!" Nema's voice.

His head jerked toward her. She was climbing from the wreckage of the truck, pushing aside shards of broken glass from the windshield and slats of wood from the fence they'd crashed into when the truck had finally stopped spinning. Then she was running toward him, her face lit with relief until—

"Aidan?" Nema stumbled to a stop.

Slade glanced down at the still body of the vampire. This was Aidan? The vampire who'd transformed Nema?

"Hello, love." Aidan's eyes flashed open and a twisted smile curved his lips. Then the guy sprang to his feet, his head bleeding where the bullet had ripped into his brain.

Oh, shit.

"Nema—Nema, get out of here." Slade knew they were in serious trouble. He wasn't too sure he understood the whole how to kill a vampire thing, but he would've thought that a shot in the head would have done the trick.

Apparently not.

So what the hell was he supposed to do now?

Aidan's head tilted to the side as his gaze drifted over Nema. A Nema who'd yet to move and follow his instructions to get out of there.

"I've been searching for you, sweet Nema." The guy had an accent. A faint, Scottish brogue that twisted around his words. And damn if the wound between his eyes wasn't already starting to heal.

The bastard was strong.

"Searching for me? You left me in the ground!" The woman was still showing no signs of running, but she definitely appeared to be pissed.

"Um, just a temporary situation only, love. I would have come back for you."

Ah, screw this. Slade lifted the gun and tightened his finger around the trigger. He'd put the bastard down again and—

In a blur of motion, Aidan sprang forward, ripped the gun out of his hands, and tossed the weapon a good hundred feet away. "You had your chance, Brion. Unimpressive though it was. Now, I think it's my turn again."

Brion. So Nema's ex-lover knew his name. No big surprise there. The guy had been waiting to attack them, and, unless he missed his guess, the fellow had a habit of attacking men who had shared Nema's company.

"Don't touch him!" Nema jumped in front of him, her claws lifted.

Slade saw the fury burning in the other vampire's eyes. "Oh, I'll do more than touch him. I'll rip him apart." He shoved Nema to the side, and she flew several feet into the air. She slammed into the truck's hood, groaning.

Aidan's claws were out, his body shaking with rage. "You changed him, you whore! Took him into your body and gave him the gift of our power! I'll fucking rip his head off!"

The fangs in Slade's mouth were burning as they stretched to their full, deadly length. The bloodlust roared through him. Stronger than any force he'd ever known before.

Take.

Kill.

He attacked, fangs snapping, claws cleaving all the way to his victim's bones. The scent of blood filled his nostrils, and the need to destroy Aidan consumed him.

He'd hurt Nema.

Slade was aware of his own vicious wounds. Aidan's fangs slashed against his throat. His flesh split open as the vampire's claws ripped down his side. But the pain only added to Slade's fury and to his strength.

"You'll never touch her again," he growled, his face inches from Aidan's. "Never."

The other vampire laughed. *Laughed.* "Oh, I'll do more than touch her." With a powerful slash, his claws cut across Slade's throat. "She's mine, new breed. Mine. I found her, I chose her, I made her. And I've killed for her."

Six victims. All men who'd known Nema.

"I killed the unworthy. Those who'd dared to touch what belongs to me." His fangs dripped blood as he snarled, "Mine forever."

"Uh, you know what, Aidan?" Nema's soft voice sounded from directly behind him. "I think it's long past time we broke up."

Aidan snarled and spun toward her, releasing his hold on Slade as he lunged for Nema.

"No!" Slade's claws sank fingertips deep into Aidan's side. And he watched as Nema smiled grimly and lifted a broken fence post high into the air.

Then she shoved it straight into Aidan's chest.

The vampire screamed, a high, agonizing sound before he dropped to the ground. His mouth froze in a horrified cry and his eyes stared sightlessly ahead.

"Is he dead?" Slade demanded. Aidan had looked dead before and Slade really didn't want to make that mistake again.

"He'd better be." Nema glared down at the vampire. "And this time the bastard had better stay dead."

Chapter 10

Aidan did, in fact, stay dead. Apparently, Hollywood had gotten one of the vampire legends right. A wooden stake to the heart could stop a vampire permanently.

Nema mentally added stakes to her growing avoidance list as she picked up her shot glass and turned to stare at the dance floor. She wasn't going to drink the whiskey, of course, but it helped her to blend in.

Made her look a little more human.

The door behind her opened and a swirl of cold night air swept into Miguel's.

She sensed him then. Felt the shift in the air. Smelled his scent.

Slade.

He'd been gone for three days. Back to Houston, to "settle up his life" as he'd called it.

Slade had asked her to go with him, but her own memories of Houston were too painful to face. As far as she was concerned, the past was dead. The very long future that stretched in front of her was all that mattered.

Turning slightly in her chair, she watched him stalk toward her. Strong, muscled body. Thick, midnight black hair and gleaming blue eyes alight with hunger. His lips were curved in the faintest of devil-may-care grins and the edge of his tattoo stretched over the collar of his jacket.

The perfect bad boy.

Vaguely, Nema wondered when she'd stopped thinking of Slade as prey and instead began thinking of him as hers.

He stopped at the edge of her table. Leaned over and said, "Dance with me."

She never thought of refusing.

In seconds, she was in his arms, held tight against his body. The band was playing some slow, somebody-left-me song, and Slade's eyes were locked on hers.

His hands dropped to her hips, curved over her ass, and pulled her into the hard cradle of his thighs.

"I've missed you," he muttered, and she had to swallow to clear the sudden lump in her throat.

"Missed me?" She managed. "I would've thought you'd be glad to get away from me."

"No."

"Slade." She'd been thinking about this, about him, nearly every waking moment. And she'd come to the conclusion that she'd really screwed the guy's life up. "Since you've met me, you've been shot in the back, transformed into a vampire, and forced into some kind of alpha-vampire death match with my ex. Not a good way to start a relationship."

He didn't reply, and Nema started to get very nervous. Hell, until he'd walked into the bar moments before, she hadn't even been sure that he would come back to her.

And if he hadn't, well, she wouldn't have blamed the guy. She'd taken away his life. Sex with her had literally been killer.

"You don't understand, do you?" He growled and Nema was surprised to see anger flaring in his gaze.

She could only shake her head.

He cursed, stopped dancing. "There's no going back for me now."

Of course there wasn't. Not for either of them.

"But even if I hadn't changed, I'll still be here, with you."

Oh, she wanted to believe that.

The band shifted tunes, beginning a fast, spinning beat.

His fingers wrapped around her wrist. "Come on." Then he was leading her out of the bar, just as he'd done that first night. Shoving open the entrance door and pulling her along the building's edge until they were covered in shadows.

Her back pressed against the cold building wall. She stared up at him, a desperate hope beginning to stir within her.

There was hunger in his eyes, a dark, swirling lust that made her sex cream and had her rubbing her hips against him, feeling the growing bulge of his arousal press against the front of her skirt.

"God, I thought I could wait," he muttered, and then his mouth was on hers, his lips open and hungry, his tongue thrusting against hers.

Wait. She'd been waiting for three days. Three long days during which she'd begun to worry that she wouldn't see him again, that he wouldn't come back. That she'd never feel his touch again.

His hands were stroking her. Cupping her breasts, fondling the nipples then sliding down her body and caressing her sex through the skirt.

"Damn, I missed you," he growled the words against her lips.

She'd sure as hell missed him. Nema tilted her hips forward, trying to press her sex harder against his hands. She didn't want to play. She wanted him inside her.

Now.

"Slade." There was a warning edge to her voice.

He laughed, but the sound was slightly ragged. Then his hands were on the hem of her shirt. He shoved the soft material up to her hips. She didn't care that they were in the alley. Didn't care that the bricks were chafing her skin or that the night air had a chill or that someone could stumble onto them.

She just wanted him.

Her hands reached for the buckle of his belt. Fumbled, managed to unhook the clasp then unsnap the button on his jeans. The zipper eased down then his thick, bulging erection was filling her hands.

His head jerked back and the veins in his neck tensed. "God, Nema, you're pushing me."

Good. She wanted to keep pushing him right past the edge of control. Her hands closed around him. Her fingers weren't long enough to circle him fully, his cock was too wide for that, but she moved her hands, pumping up and down on his shaft, moving faster, squeezing.

He groaned and pushed his fingers between her thighs, shoving aside her underwear and finding her sex, wet and ready.

Nema parted her legs for him, licking her lips as she watched her hand moving on his body, then his fingers, driving in and out of her. Her stomach tightened. She could come just like this. She could—

His hands were gone.

"No!"

"Shh, relax, baby. I'll take care of you."

He'd better.

He lifted her, holding her against the wall and spreading her legs. Damn but that vampire strength could sure come in handy.

His cock pushed against her and she squirmed, rubbing her clit against him and coating the tip of his erection with her cream.

"Nema." His fangs were out.

So were hers.

She thrust down, taking him all the way into her body in one hard move. Then it was fast. Deep and fast as they both struggled to reach orgasm. His hands were tight around her. Her fingers clenched on his shoulders.

He drove his shaft into her, again and again and she met him thrust for thrust, her gaze locked on his, a heady burst of sensual power filling her as she read the stark desire on his face. Her climax slammed through her, tightening her entire body and sending surges of pleasure to her every nerve.

Slade stiffened against her, growling his pleasure as he pumped into her body, stiffening with his own release.

For a time, one moment, two, they didn't move. Just held each other in the night.

Slade was the first to pull back. He gently set Nema on her feet and straightened her skirt before he arranged his own clothing. His expression was strangely tense as he stared down at her. "I didn't mean for that to happen yet. I wanted to talk first." A hard sigh. "But I can't stay in control when I'm with you." He didn't seem happy about that. No, not happy at all.

She swallowed, not sure what to say. Her sex was still trembling, her thighs were wet, and she felt more vulnerable than she'd ever been in all of her thirty years.

His hands caged her against the wall. "Do you know that I would have killed for you? McDermott? Aidan? I'd have killed them both for hurting you."

She knew that. She'd seen the truth in his eyes first when he'd rescued her from that lab and then later when he'd faced off against Aidan and ordered her to leave. As if she would have left him.

"I wanted you from the first moment I saw you. I thought you might be a killer, but damn if I didn't still want you."

And she'd sure as hell wanted him. She'd just climaxed with him, and, even now, she wanted him again.

His head lifted. "When I realized you were innocent, *when I really saw you*, things changed for me. Everything changed. And we've got to get something straight between us, right now."

Nema wasn't sure she liked the sound of that. "Oh?"

"Yeah, baby. We do." His right hand lifted, stroked down the skin of her neck and she couldn't control the shiver that worked over her. "I don't want you just for a night, or hell, even a few nights." His fingers stilled over the pulse that beat so frantically. "I want forever."

She licked her lips, tasted him. "Forever, that's a long time for us."

"Damn straight it is." Another kiss. This time, his teeth caught her lower lip, nibbling lightly and wrenching a moan from her. When he spoke again, his breath blew lightly over her lips. "When you slept that first day and I watched you, I knew you were mine. *Mine*."

She felt that way about him. In her heart, she believed that he belonged with her.

"I want to spend the rest of my life with you—and I know that's probably gonna be one hell of a long time—but if you'll have me, I swear, I'll be good to you. I'll make you happy, keep the sun off you, and make certain that you're always safe."

Nema blinked quickly, aware that her eyes were starting to sting. "Will you?"

His lips brushed over hers. "Yeah, baby, I will. Nema, my sweet vampiress, you're the only woman that I want to spend my life or death with."

And he was the only man she wanted, period.

Her lips began to curl, and a happiness she couldn't ever remember feeling began to blossom in her chest. "I think I like the sound of that." Yeah, she liked it, a lot.

"I know I'm not perfect, I know I've made some mistakes." He was talking fast now.

"Um." Yeah, he'd screwed up, but so had she. What mattered was that she'd learned the true measure of the man when the chips were down.

"But I swear, you can trust me."

Her fingers wrapped around his shoulders. "I know I can," she told him, her voice absolutely certain.

He blinked.

She laughed. "Slade, you might look like a badass, but I know the truth about you." She knew the truth about her vampire lover.

"And what's that?"

She stood on her toes and licked his lower lip. "That you're a hero inside."

"Ah, Nema, don't be too sure about that."

But she was. The man might be trouble for the rest of the world, but to her, he was just right.

Ex-cop.

Bounty hunter.

Vampire.

With a heart of gold.

How could she not have fallen for him?

"Will you stay with me?" he asked her suddenly. "Forever?"

"You just try to stop me," she whispered and her lips closed over his.

Yeah, forever was a long time for their kind. But she figured that for her and Slade, well, forever was just what they'd need.

Now, if she could just find out if he had an extra set of handcuffs and a Mustang....

Forever with her very own bad boy vampire.

Oh, the wonderful possibilities.

About the Author:

Cynthia Eden is a writer who has a longstanding obsession with the paranormal world. She loves vampires and werewolves, and is thrilled that Red Sage has given her the opportunity to share her creations with others.

Cynthia loves to hear from her readers. Please visit her website at cynthiaeden.com or you may send an email to info@cynthiaeden.com.

Scandalous Behavior

by Anne Rainey

To My Reader:

From the moment I picked up the first **Secrets Volume**, I've been hooked. There's no doubt the passionate storylines and intriguing characters titillate the senses and keep you glued to the pages. So when the idea for *Scandalous Behavior* popped into my head it seemed tailor-made for one of their smokin' hot volumes.

Tess Marley struggles with self-confidence, which is something we can all relate to. She doesn't believe she could hold a man's attention. Especially not a man as virile and intense as Kevin Haines. Lucky for her, Kevin is man enough to prove her wrong and pull her out of her shell.

Oh wow, we should all have a Kevin Haines in our life, right ladies?

Chapter 1

"You have such a gorgeous ass," Kevin whispered into Tess's ear. "So sweetly rounded, just full enough to fill my palms."

Tess quivered as Kevin's hands smoothed over her sensitized skin, his seductive words feeding her desire. His body was pressed all along the back of hers so that she could feel every muscular inch. Slowly, teasingly, she moved her hips back and forth, rubbing her bottom against the head of his jutting erection, before finally allowing him to slide between the globes of her buttocks. When she heard him emit a low growl, she felt triumphant. He clutched her hips between his hard, callused hands and began gliding his rigid length up and down in that smooth seam, sending them both into a frenzy of scorching need.

The cool water of South America's Iguaçu Falls poured down, drenching their overheated skin. The water, so crystal-clear and pure, pooled around their knees. Oversized water lilies tickled her skin. Every sensation intensified the burning inside her aching sex. The wild plants and jungle trees grew high all around them, enveloping them, giving them the impression that they were the only two people left on earth.

Tess wriggled and pleaded with Kevin to enter her. She was now beyond caring how wanton she might sound. She was a sultry temptress, and she reveled in that sinful persona. He rewarded her with a lick against the leaping pulse in her neck, then shifted a hand around the front of her body to palm her right breast. He licked and squeezed, but never once allowed his cock to move lower, to slip inside her swollen folds, where she needed him most. When he pinched her nipple, she lost control. Reaching back, Tess grasped his pulsing heat in her hand and squeezed hard.

"Christ, Tess. That feels so damn good."

She exulted at his guttural words, but she wanted more from him. She wanted him buried deep, thrusting and filling her as he took her to heaven. "I want you. Inside of me. Kevin. Now."

He chuckled. "Not just yet, baby."

She moaned in misery, hating him at that moment for denying her what she craved. But then his other hand released her hip to drift around and cup her mound. She pushed against his hand, eager for something just out of her reach. She pumped him with fingers clenched with desire. Kevin retaliated—his thumb teased her clitoris. Sparks of sharp arousal zipped through Tess's nerve endings, and she gloried when she wrung a bead of moisture from the tip of his penis.

Tess's body began the wild climb towards rapture, when she was jarred by a hand on her shoulder, shaking her. She blinked.

Suddenly her waterfall, her jungle, and her jungle lover were gone, and Tess was left staring at her boss and the platinum blonde plastered against his side.

"Tess, are you feeling okay?"

That question came from the boss, not the blonde. Kevin Haines, concerned employer and the foundation for every fantasy and desire she'd had for the past five years, stood next to her desk.

"Fine, why do you ask?" Tess croaked out and then bit back a groan. She'd failed miserably in her effort to sound cool and collected as she normally did with her boss. But, dang it, how could she keep her cool when lingerie model number whatever was all over Kevin? She'd lost count of how many women this current blonde beauty made. Since she'd been working for the infernal man, there had been quite a few, and every blessed one looked as if she'd just stepped out of a pin-up calendar.

This one, however, also had the cunning appearance of a woman who saw a man with a healthy bank account. The thorns of this particular climbing rose had clearly been sharpened to prickly little points, so she could clutch Kevin as if he were her own personal trellis.

Tess wanted to scream and puke all at the same time. Of course, the timid Tess Marley would do neither.

"You don't look fine," Kevin said, still frowning and staring down and her. "You look overheated."

Under that stare, Tess felt like an odd piece of something at the back of the fridge. "I just felt a little warm there for a minute, must have been something I ate. I'll be fine." Because he continued to stand at her desk and stare, she felt compelled to ask, "Was there something you wanted, Mr. Haines?"

She watched her boss's lips thin as his eyes traveled the length of her. Her face heated and she pushed her glasses higher up on her nose. Even though she knew he couldn't possible see any telltale signs of unrequited lust beneath her heavy brown wool suit, she still felt that quick scan clear to her bones. He seemed satisfied with what he saw, however, and said, "I just wanted to let you know that I was going to knock off early."

She stared pointedly at Blondie and then back at him, saying crisply, "Is there anything you need from me before you leave?"

His arm went around his date and Tess wanted to groan. It didn't help her disposition any either that Kevin looked positively scrumptious in his three-button, black Armani suit with the single pleat trousers. She sat up straighter and kept it professional. Always professional.

"No, you can leave anytime you wish, Tess, thank you," Kevin said.

She nodded, not trusting herself to speak over the lump that had formed in her throat. She watched him lock his office door, and as he left the lobby, blonde in tow, Tess slumped at last. A woman like her could never attract a man like Kevin Haines. She was mousy and drab and he was sexy and wild.

She sighed and began to gather up her things from the desk. He was out of her league.

But a kernel of an idea began to wedge itself into her consciousness as she remembered the passionate temptress under the waterfall. In her fantasy she wasn't mousy, and goodness knows she wasn't drab. That Tess demanded what she wanted, and took it, and took him. In her fantasy.

If only Tess had the courage to do it in real life.

What would Mr. Love and Leave 'Em think if he encountered that Fantasy Tess? If just once he encountered a Tess who allowed herself to break out of her comfortable shell? To change?

Maybe she wouldn't have to change that much—just enough to grab his notice. What would it be like to be on the receiving end of that sensual smile? And to return it with her own sensual smile?

Tess sighed. Whom was she kidding? She wasn't going to change. She was a coward, pure and simple.

She went back to work on the contract she'd been drawing up before she slipped into her fantasy world, but when she hit the backspace for the third time, she gave up and called it a day. It was no use trying to get work done when she couldn't concentrate on anything other than the way Kevin looked in his Armani suit.

He did have the sweetest backside ever. The fine wool trousers had molded to his buttocks perfectly. Enough! She mentally smacked herself. She had to stop daydreaming. Nothing good would come from it.

Tess clicked the save button and shut down her computer. She might as well go home. Tomorrow was Friday, and she'd be right back at her desk, wishing she were anyone but Timid Tess.

For most working folks, Friday was a day to kick back, take the afternoon off, and maybe meet friends for a drink or two. Some would get together with a significant other and enjoy a romantic evening alone. But none of those things were for Tess. Every day was a Monday. She worked eight hours a day, seven days a week, went home to her empty apartment and had an equally empty dinner, where she would then take herself off to an empty bed.

The same routine—twenty-four seven. The highlight of her day happened after her eyes closed. She would dream of Kevin then. His beautiful, hard body taking her with wild abandon. It was the one thing that saved her sanity.

And the next morning she would awake thinking this could be the day, this would be the day she changed. She would break out of her mousy, humdrum mold and live. Really live!

So now it was Friday morning. A brand-new day. The same old Tess.

She got up from her bed, made it up quickly, then went into the bathroom to get started on dressing. But a couple of minutes into her routine, Tess stopped with her hand on her hairbrush and stared at herself in the bathroom mirror. Was today the day she'd become someone new? Nope. She was still just mousy little Tess Marley. Boring, unmemorable, and plain as all get-out.

She heaved a sigh and, as always, pulled her hair back into her sensible brown barrette, securing it in her very smart and dull way. Then she slipped into her nice levelheaded gray suit, matching shoes and added the final touch, tortoise-shell reading glasses. She didn't even need the glasses. They were armor like everything else she wore.

God, she hated herself.

No matter how much she tried to take the modern viewpoint, that she ought to love herself for herself, and she ought to be loved for herself, her thoughts kept coming back to the same certainty. Kevin Haines would never notice her so long as she acted and dressed like an old maid. She could have all the brains, all the money, and all the personality, but he'd still never give her a second glance. As far as a guy like Kevin was concerned, she was just what she looked like—and she didn't look like she deserved his attention.

She needed to do something with her appearance. She needed a makeover—hell more than a makeover, a major overhaul—before he would ever pay attention to her.

A switch inside Tess suddenly snapped, turning off her logical brain for the first time ever. As if in a trance, she watched her own hand slam against the bathroom mirror. She just stood there, awed at her own outburst, her fist aching, the reflection untouched. She'd never so much as raised her voice before, for heaven's sake! She was one of those people who carefully scooped up a spider and set it outside, not wanting to harm even the smallest of creatures. She didn't get angry!

But maybe now the time had come for her to revolutionize herself, to become something new.

She stared at her unchanged image in the mirror. Becoming something new—well, she could start with her appearance. And that appearance needed a makeover—hell, more than a makeover, a major overhaul—before a man like Kevin would ever pay attention to her.

Slowly, as if in a trance, Tess moved away from the mirror and went back to her bedroom. She flung open her closet doors and saw what she had known would be there. All her problems hanging by neat color-coded hangers. It was like suddenly walking into a black and white film. Everything was either black, white, gray, taupe or brown. For her more rowdy days, she had cream. She was completely pitiful.

It was as if the very devil had hold of her. She ripped and grabbed, flinging clothes onto the floor. She heard a wrenching, guttural moan and realized with much surprise that it was her own voice making the feral sound. She sounded like a wildcat gone mad. By the time she was through with her tirade, there wasn't a stitch left hanging. Everything was in tatters and ruined.

She sat among the catastrophe and cried. But this time it wasn't her usual delicate sniffle, but a full-blown flood.

She had no idea how much time had passed when she heard a ringing sound. A familiar one. It seemed to be coming from a distance. She shook herself and tried to focus more fully. Then it struck her, it was her phone! She got up and swung around. Spotting the device on her bedside table, Tess walked over to it.

"Hello." She hoped she sounded civil, but she was sure her voice creaked unsteadily.

"Tess?"

She recognized her boss right away. She'd know Kevin's velvety voice anywhere. "Yes, I, um, it's me."

"Are you okay? You were supposed to be at work half an hour ago. I don't think you've ever missed a single day of work before."

She looked at her alarm clock and grimaced. In her mad frenzy, she hadn't given a thought to the time. Still, that note of surprise and wonder in Kevin's voice had her feeling angry all over again. Good, old, dependable Tess. Always doing the expected. Well, not anymore. That was stopping. Today. She was not going to be the invisible string that kept everything and everyone afloat.

"Yes, well, I'm not feeling quite up to par today. I'll be in this afternoon. I'm sure you can handle one morning without me, can't you?" She knew she sounded waspish, but she'd reached her breaking point.

There was just the slightest hesitation. "Of course, Tess. You take your time and we'll see you this afternoon." As an afterthought, he added, "If there's anything I can do, just call, okay?"

She couldn't believe her ears. It worked! Kevin was backing off and giving her the morning off. Cool! She could get used to this take-charge stuff.

"Thank you. I'll see you this afternoon then." She straightened her spine and grinned.

"Sure, honey, you just relax and take your time."

Honey? Well that was definitely a first. "I'll do that." As if on its own accord, her voice dropped to a seductive whisper, "Goodbye, Kevin."

"Um, yeah, goodbye."

Tess hung up the phone and grinned even more. She would be seeing Kevin this afternoon all right, but this time, she wouldn't be wearing her brown barrette, or her sensible brown or gray suit. He was about to be knocked off his feet, and while she had him down there, she'd see to it that he enjoyed the fall. A lot.

She walked with renewed purpose out of her room. She approached the door to her apartment and glanced at her reflection in the hall mirror. Lord, she was a mess! Her hair was everywhere, her suit was all twisted, and her pantyhose were torn. Tess kicked off her shoes, and stripped out of the ruined hose. It was the first morning she'd gone without pantyhose. She dug her toes into the carpet and wriggled her hips.

It felt good. Bare thighs caressing the material of her skirt. Immediately, she knew she'd never wear hose again.

Absently, she wondered what it'd feel like to go without panties as well. Smiling again, she decided that no one would know if she left them off, so what harm could it possibly do. Unless, of course, she wanted someone to know. Someone like her boss.

Tess stepped out of her plain white cotton panties. It felt sinfully delicious. Liberating. Shyly, she reached under her skirt and cupped herself. She closed her eyes and rubbed slightly. God she needed—hell, she just needed!

She removed her hand and unbuttoned the suit jacket, tossing it over her shoulder, heedless of where it landed. Then she unfastened the top two buttons of her shirt. Last but not least, she yanked out the barrette. She made a silent vow to burn the damn thing later. For now, she was too anxious to go shopping. She shook her hair out and let the long strands fall where they may. Looking at her appearance now shocked her. She couldn't believe the difference just that little bit of change made.

Her slightly closed eyes made it seem as if she was trying to conceal a naughty secret. Her long hair swept over her shoulders and nearly touched the top of her buttocks. Flushed cheeks. Swollen lips. Heck, if she didn't know better, she'd think she had just been truly and thoroughly debauched. She had that sexy, mussed look. Tess Marley sexy? Whoa.

Suddenly, she thought of her ex-boyfriend, Josh. He'd dated her for all of seven months before dumping her. He'd decided she was too boring and wanted a woman who would be willing to toss caution to the wind. She'd wanted to toss the jerk on his ear.

"If he could see me now, he'd be wishing like hell he hadn't thrown me away like so much garbage!"

Grabbing her purse, she headed out the door. She couldn't wait to show her boss just how much fun taking notations and making appointments could be. His desk would do nicely for what she had in mind. It was big, sturdy and hard, just the way he would be when he got a good long look at the new Tess Marley. Now for some new clothes, definitely some new shoes, and a trip to the hairdresser. She was way past due for some pampering.

Chapter 2

Kevin paced his office. He never paced. He was the most in-control, level-headed man he knew. So why was he pacing? Simple. *She* wasn't here. Worse, he wasn't sure why she wasn't here. On the phone she'd sounded distracted, almost flustered. But from what? Or from whom? That last thought kept creeping into his mind, driving him slowly nuts. He just wished he knew why it was driving him nuts. Strike that. He already had a pretty good idea.

He paced some more, back and forth, making a traffic mark on his expensive, dark green carpeting. Tess was his assistant, for crying out loud! He had no business wondering about her personal life. Hell, even if she was romping around in bed right now, it was of no concern to him. Right? Except the very idea set his teeth on edge and made his fists clench.

Tess Marley was dependable, intelligent, and easygoing. All qualities he admired. Though she wasn't exactly drop-dead gorgeous, she wasn't ugly by a long shot. She was a natural woman. The kind that didn't need a lot of camouflage to look good. In fact, if she wasn't always hiding behind a brown or gray suit that always seemed a size too big she would probably be a friggin' knockout. He'd thought of trying to find out what she looked like beneath her ugly clothes, but she always had a hands-off look in her eyes. Anyway, he was her boss, and that meant he couldn't take advantage of her. So, he never gave into his curiosity. But he had a pretty damn good idea that she would be a passionate little thing if she ever let herself go.

Except Tess never let herself go. She never had a hair out of place, her smile rarely slipped and she always dressed totally professionally. She'd been working for him for five years now, keeping him on track and organized, keeping things at his small but thriving company, Invision Computing and Consulting, running—and running smoothly too. He never would have survived this long without her behind him. She had great managerial skills but that didn't explain why his imagination always ran wild around her.

His thoughts would be even wilder if she weren't attired so bulkily, if her hair wasn't pulled back so severely, if her top wasn't always buttoned clear to her chin. Still the way her buttons always strained over her breasts told him that she had more than a handful.

Yeah, he had often wondered what else she had, plenty of times, but wondering was usually all he did.

Guys were that way. It was normal for a man to see a woman between the ages of twenty and forty, and—if she had all the right curves—picture her naked. Nothing wrong with that, a perfectly healthy male thing to do. Add a close working relationship, their single status, and no wonder a stray thought of lust occasionally wriggled its way into his head.

He never let on, of course, never let her notice him watching her a little too closely. Never made her feel uncomfortable by making nasty passes at her. She was what his mother would term a nice girl, and you left the nice girls alone. It was just the way things were.

Secretly though, Kevin knew Tess would be a livewire in bed. He just knew it. That quiet, easy demeanor was bound to rip wide open someday. Who would be the lucky bastard that got to reap the sensual promise of Tess? He supposed it was asking too much to hope it would be him. Although on one occasion, two years ago, he'd come real close to asking her out. A little too close.

It had been a typical workday, filled with client meetings and contract negotiations, nothing to make the day stand out all that much. Except one little incident he liked to think of as the break room episode.

He had just been backing up his computer and getting ready to call it a day, when he'd remembered that he still needed to have Tess reschedule one of his meetings. As he'd peeked out his office door to tell her about it, she hadn't been at her desk. Kevin had gone searching. Looking back now, he realized it would have been smarter if he'd simply left her a note.

He'd found her in the break room, digging into a cabinet for coffee filters, and Kevin had stopped dead in his tracks at the enticing sight that greeted him. His heart had slammed hard against the wall of chest and his body had gone into overdrive in zero to sixty seconds flat.

There she was, bent over, her ass high in the air, her ugly, brown skirt riding high. Kevin had gotten his first glimpse of Tess's smooth, creamy thighs. Her body practically begging for his hand to reach out and grab a handful— wool and all. Like a deer in rut, his body had become instantly aroused, leaping to hot, wicked life. As Kevin stood there, devouring her with his eyes, he had ached to push that skirt up, to bare her clear to the waist, and ease himself between her long, sexy legs.

Tess had been completely oblivious to his presence in the small room, completely unaware of the turmoil she had caused her boss. For a single moment in time, Kevin had nearly shucked his own set of rules of not mixing business with pleasure by asking her out. Thankfully—or regretfully, he still wasn't sure which—he'd come to his senses. He'd quietly exited the room, Tess none the wiser as to what he'd come within a heartbeat of doing.

Not once, before or since, had he gotten another peek at Tess Marley's softer side. Still, that one single vision had fueled more than one erotic dream.

Suddenly, his office door opened, interrupting his thoughts. Kevin roared in an uncharacteristic show of temper, "I said I do not want to be disturbed, Rachael!"

"Well, isn't that just too bad."

It wasn't Rachael. The sultry tone had him whipping around. What stood in his doorway caused his mouth to go slack and his eyes to practically bulge. It took at least three seconds for him to recognize that bedroom voice. Tess Marley. And damn if she didn't look like anything but a nice girl now. In fact, she looked like temptation.

Her blouse sure as hell wasn't buttoned all the way to her chin anymore. Actually, from what he could see she wasn't even wearing a blouse, just a red suit jacket. The matching skirt sat just above her knees, high enough to be alluring but not so high to give a free show. Her legs were just as long and curvy as he had remembered.

He made a slow route up her body with his eyes, looking at his sexy administrative assistant in a whole new light. He smiled when he saw her hair. Now it lay in pleasing disorder, catching the light with little flecks of highlights. He hoped like hell that she had taken the time to burn that ugly barrette.

Gorgeous strands of hair slipped way past her shoulders to her mid-back. Suddenly a carnal image inspired by that time in the break room flashed into his mind. He pictured her from behind as he fucked her that way. Her head would be thrown back and all that hair would be just barely stroking the top of her ass. His expensive, conservative slacks became extremely tight. His hands suddenly itched to grab a fistful of hair, pull her to her knees directly in front of him. Make her suck him—watch her suck him. Her pretty red suit all spread open, baring her tits to him, like a bountiful offering. Imagining those ruby lips of hers sliding over the bulbous head of his cock had him squirming.

Too late he realized he just stood there like some fool, staring at her. "Tess?"

"Yep."

That was all she said, just that one word. Then she moved further into his office. He watched, waited, not sure what she was up to, but suddenly he was willing to bet his new golf club it was not something a nice girl would ever dream of doing.

He didn't have to wait long. Her mouth curved and she turned back toward the door. She was going to leave? Just as he was about to lunge at her in an attempt to keep her in his office and within his grasp, he saw her slowly close the door. The lock tripped into place with a snick of finality. She spun slowly around on one tall-heeled red shoe, then charmed him with that gorgeous smile again. He had no idea what she wanted from him, but he was certainly pleased as punch that she'd chosen him, and not some other son-of-a-bitch.

If it was a wild ride she craved, he'd give it to her tenfold. About damn time too. Five years was long enough. And with any luck she'd stick around when the fires burned low, so he could show her just how sweet it could be when you stoked them back up again.

She was probably feeling pretty damn good about herself, but still he noticed the telltale sign that she was nervous. Her hands were shaking, though she tried to hide it. For her sake, he pretended not to notice. In all honesty, the determined look in her eyes let him know that whatever had brought on such a transformation was important enough to keep her from backing down.

Tess moved forward, away from the safety of the office door and into the middle of the room. She came within inches of him and asked, "Do you like my new suit, Kevin?" She spoke in a barely-there whisper. The tone alone had his blood heating.

Kevin looked at her from head to toe. His gaze stuck once more on her beautiful chest. She had the most amazing amount of flesh showing, and yet he still couldn't see all that he wanted. He wondered how soft her skin would feel against his lips, if she was that same creamy, shade all over. Tess cleared her throat and he looked back to her face. A question. Oh right, she'd asked him something.

"Uh, what did you say?" He sounded like an idiot.

Tess quirked her head to the side. "I wondered if you liked my new suit."

"Right, the suit." Now he remembered what had made his eyes roam freely over hills and valleys. This time he kept them on her face where they were safe. But then there was that mouth, all pretty and painted red and so damn hot. *Geez, get a hold of yourself, Kevin!* This is Tess you're making love to with your eyes.

Dependable, sturdy, hard-working Tess.

"The suit looks real nice." What a friggin' understatement that was! "Did you buy it this morning?"

Her smile was so radiant she practically glowed. Kevin found himself smiling right back at her.

"Yes, I did. In fact I bought quite a few things today."

Kevin had to swallow the knot that formed in his throat so he could ask,

"More suits like this one?" He'd die if she came to work looking this edible everyday.

Her answer was a slow nod and a wink, which had his dick swelling even more. "Well, you look—" but he never got to finish his compliment, because there was another knock on the door. Tess turned and briskly walked over and unlatched it, then opened it wide. Kevin could have strangled her.

On the other side stood one of his sales executives, John Fields. He was a good man, a hard worker who logged a lot of hours at the office. John was also a good friend. Unfortunately, he was also single. And the way he was looking at Tess made Kevin want to serve John his walking papers—good friend or not.

"Tess? Is that you?"

"Hi, John. Yes, it's me." Her voice sounded enticing. Kevin ground his teeth.

"Damn, sweetheart, you look hot!" John's words pissed him off more.

No doubt that had Tess melting all over. Kevin suddenly wanted to kick his own ass for saying she looked nice. What woman wanted to hear that? He should have gone for broke and told her the truth, that she looked like a fucking wet dream. But he was trying to play it safe and keep things professional. And where had that gotten him? Watching from across the room while Tess bestowed John with a thank you hug. If the slimy bastard put his hands on her ass, he'd have to kill him.

To hell with friendship.

Luckily, for John, he kept the hug loose and friendly, but Kevin could tell that the compliment was exactly what Tess had wanted to hear. He realized now that she must have been damn nervous over such a drastic change in appearance.

"Thank you so much, John. I wasn't sure if it was appropriate or not for the office, but I'm just tired of all the tans and browns."

"Well, rest easy, pretty lady, it's entirely appropriate." John crossed his arms over his chest and frowned, as if in great contemplation.

"What?" Tess asked attentively.

"I know this isn't the time or the place, Tess, but would you by chance be free tonight?"

Kevin heard John asking Tess out on a date. In his mind, he saw the tall, muscular man unbuttoning the red suit jacket and seeing Tess Marley's tits splendidly bare.

"No."

John and Tess both turned and stared at Kevin, as if they'd forgotten he was even in the room. Hell, it was his office, for Christ's sake! No way in hell was he going to allow John to come within a mile of Tess's nude breasts.

"I need her tonight," Kevin said. Well, that was true. "She just got here, so we have some catching up to do. It'll probably take us into dinnertime." A lie, but a necessary lie.

Tess pouted prettily and turned back to John. "Can I have a rain check?"

John, the lecher, was only too happy to oblige. "Definitely. Anytime, anywhere. Just say the word." Kevin wondered why he had ever called the dickhead a friend. Just then, John looked over Tess's head and straight at him. The ornery gleam that lit John's eyes just before he sauntered out of his office said it all.

The bastard had been baiting him from the start. He should have known. John always took great pleasure in getting him riled. But with the other women Kevin had dated, John's attempts to make him jealous had never worked. He could have cared less if John wanted to date any one of them. Deep down, Kevin knew that he would never feel the same, cavalier way about Tess. And he wasn't going to delve too deeply into why right now either. Nope, right now he was just glad to have her alone again, without John leering at her bountiful curves.

Tess walked to the door and locked them securely inside once again. When she turned back to him, an impish grin curving her succulent lips, Kevin knew that John was right on the money about one thing. Tess was hot. Now... what to do about it.

"John is a very nice man, isn't he?"

It wasn't so much what Tess said, as the way she said it that put Kevin on edge. He didn't much care for the softness in her voice when she said John's name.

"In what way is he nice?" He knew he sounded testy, but there was no reason for her to be thinking of John at all. He was a coworker, nothing more.

She shrugged. "I just mean that he's very sweet to ask me out, and he was so complimentary, too."

She sounded surprised that a man could possibly want to compliment her. How ridiculous. Any man with half a brain could see she was a knockout.

Kevin quickly waved away those thoughts. "You come to work looking like that and you're bound to get asked out." Probably by every man at his company, but he didn't think she needed to know that.

Tess grinned and Kevin's knees nearly buckled under him. "Dressed like what, Kevin? You think the suit looks nice. John says I look hot." She wagged her eyebrows at him and stepped forward, just a few steps this time, leaving a gaping space of carpet between them. Kevin didn't much like that. "And, you know, I think I like hot way better than nice."

Getting more frustrated by the second, Kevin wondered again what Tess

Marley was up to. He couldn't stifle his curiosity over such a huge change in her. What had finally broken the shell she'd kept herself in for the past five years? More importantly, why had she had a shell at all?

His assistant was a constantly changing puzzle to him, and every time he thought he had her pieced together, she showed him another side that was fascinating.

And she was way too far away.

This time he was the one to close the gap between them. He wanted to give her pretty compliments so she would give him one of those big, chest-to-chest, thank-you hugs.

But being within a few inches of her made his frustration worse. Instead of his breathing slowing down with the knowledge she was all alone with him, it only sped up. To cover his feelings, he gazed down at her and said, "I guess I was a little shocked. That's my only excuse for using such a mundane word as nice to describe how you look today, Tess."

She had to tilt her head back to look into his eyes. He liked that. She wasn't as tall as he was, but she wasn't tiny either. There was a difference of only a few inches. The way he figured it, they'd fit together just right.

Kevin waited patiently to see what Tess would say or do next. He wasn't disappointed.

She reached out and touched his bare forearm. Her delicate fingers felt cool to his inflamed skin. He glanced down when he felt them moving in little circles and was damned glad that he'd decided to wear a casual short-sleeved shirt instead of a long-sleeved dress shirt. It was mid-August and the heat was unbearable this time of year in Ohio, and getting hotter by the second.

"If not nice, then what word would you use to describe my new look, Kevin?"

She kept touching him with those barely-there strokes. It was making him wish her fingers were on his cock instead of his damned arm. He looked into her eyes, staring hard so she wouldn't misunderstand anything he said.

"Just one isn't enough, Tess. One word doesn't even come close to describing what that outfit says to me."

His tone had dropped low as he let her know what she did to him wearing lick-me red lipstick. He flicked a gaze over her once again and growled, "And that suit is sexy as hell for starters."

He moved his head down an inch closer to hers, he needed to taste her lips or die. "Alluring." He smiled, liking the way her cheeks blushed a pretty shade of pink.

"Passion, passion, passion, Tess. So damn much passion." He was real close now. Kevin could feel her quick breaths against his mouth. "And that red is so hot and wild it makes me ache for a taste."

Then he was there, touching her slightly parted mouth with his own, knowing that one kiss would only make him as needy as a kid in a candy store. But to hell with it, he couldn't have stopped now if the office was on fire.

Chapter 3

Tess was in heaven. She couldn't believe she'd gotten her boss to kiss her. So many times, she had secretly wondered what it would be like to be the recipient of his ardor. He was such a masculine man, so dominating and powerfully built that all the women in his company had secret designs on him. He had acquired a polished look over the years, but a woman sensed the restless and primitive creature that lay underneath his business attire. No wonder her fantasy had turned to a hot South American jungle. He truly was a wild creature. She felt that in his kiss.

Small steps Tess, remember? She needed to do this the way she did everything else, in sufficient little stages. First, get herself to his office and get him alone. Done. Second, get him to see her as something other than Tess Marley: efficient assistant extraordinaire. Preferably, Tess Marley: enchanting temptress, like the woman from her jungle dream.

This morning, she'd decided the only way to accomplish that was to get up close and personal with Mr. Kevin Haines and let him have a good long look at what he's been overlooking for the past five years.

Tess had always kept her feelings well hidden, but now, wrapped in Kevin's embrace, smelling his clean male scent, she could revel in the feel of having him where she'd always wanted him—all around her. His dark good looks and dominant nature had been a magnet for women over the five years she'd worked for him. Still, he never seemed to get too cozy with any woman. He put a new spin on casual dating. She'd never seen him with the same woman more than twice.

Lord, he was a good kisser.

Not that she knew good from bad, but even her inexperienced brain knew that what he was doing, the way he was making her feel, took skill. On the tail end of that thought was another.

Maybe she wasn't such a good kisser.

Truth be told, she was so inexperienced that he might actually end up turned off by her lack of finesse. Maybe even stop before they could get much farther. That would be a disaster. Because now that she knew what his lips felt like she wanted to know what all of him felt like. What all of him tasted like. She needed to come up with a way to keep him interested.

His tongue delved into her mouth and suddenly she could care less about strategies and planning.

She closed her eyes and wrapped her arms around his neck, ready to enjoy every inch of Kevin Haines. Her reward was his rumbling groan as he pulled her in closer. Tess's entire body was cuddled up against his, and when he arched against her, she knew for sure that her kiss wasn't making him grow cold. If the hardness pressing into her lower belly was any indication, he was as far gone as she was. This stimulating bit of insight made Tess bold. She let her hands do what they'd been aching to do, what they'd only done in her dreams. She let them loose to roam.

She drifted them down his massive shoulders and over his sexy forearms then on around to his backside. He had the most deliciously squeezable ass she'd ever felt. She couldn't stop the moan of pleasure from escaping as she took her time touching what she had so longed to touch. She allowed her hands to grip, squeeze and massage his chiseled buttocks. Hey if she were going to play ball, she might as well play tackle.

Tess's fingers continued to delve in, kneading and fondling. Oh, god, he felt good. He'd feel so much better with nothing in the way of her questing fingers, but she'd make do with what she had.

Pulling him forward, Tess pressed her pelvis against his, desperate to feel more—every inch of him. She felt, rather than heard, his low chuckle. Then he was thrusting, his moves rubbing that part of her sex weeping for him. He expertly took over the sparring of their lower bodies. His tongue slipped into her mouth and danced with hers even while his hands clutched at her hips, anchoring her to him. She felt drugged by him, impatient to have him naked and inside her overheated body.

Softly, slowly, Kevin left her mouth and moved downward, leaving little kisses in his wake. His lips brushed along her chin, her cheek, and then to her neck where he lingered. His mouth opened and Tess felt his tongue stroke the throbbing pulse he found there. Her heart pounded so hard she thought it would shatter, and her legs felt like rubber. He sucked and nibbled at the skin of her throat. Her breasts swelled, her nipples puckered, aching for his touch.

She wanted to beg him to put her out of her misery, to throw open her suit jacket and suckle her needy breasts, to shove up her skirt and drive himself so deep inside her body that he'd never be able to let her go.

But she didn't.

She simply held onto him, loving the way he took his time, as if they were alone in a cabin in the woods, instead of in his office in the middle of the afternoon. All her thoughts scattered as one of his hands left her hips and smoothed its way down over her skirt to the hemline. At last, she felt skin-on-skin when his warm strong fingers slid underneath.

It was so damned good to have his hand there, so close to where she needed him. He must have liked the feel of her inner thigh as much as she liked the feel of his hand there, because he growled. His lips tracked to the flesh at the V of her suit suckling the top of her cleavage. His fingers slid higher, then higher still. Suddenly, every muscle in his body seemed to go rigid at once. Oh Lord, she'd forgotten she'd decided to go commando today. She opened her eyes just a bit and found him staring down at her.

She braced her shoulders. Timidity was for the old Tess.

The intense look on his face almost had the old, shy Tess returning. But she needed to figure out how to handle the way Kevin was looking at her. As if he wasn't sure whether to throttle her or make wild and crazy love to her. Then again, the fact that his hand was now cupping her mound in a posses-sive, yet lovingly protective, sort of way gave her a pretty darn big clue as to what was on his mind. A warm glow flowed through her. She'd always loved the way this man's mind worked.

She could read his mood in his expression. Kevin was equal parts turned on and pissed off. On one hand he had Tess, beautifully, sexily mussed and minus panties. On the other hand, he would also be remembering that when John had asked her out, she was pantyless. So Kevin had to be wondering if she would have gone without underwear on a date with John?

Tess had to wonder that herself. What had she been thinking coming to the office without underwear?

"Don't get me wrong, I like that my fingers don't have to wrangle a bikini to get to their destination, but would you like to explain what you were think-ing coming to work without any panties?"

Tess shrugged and tried to hide her embarrassment from him, but a beguil-ing blush tinged her cheeks. Apparently, she hadn't figured on him talking about it. No more than she'd probably figured he'd be too far gone by lust to care about her lack of underwear. And Tess would have been right on that one.

"I just felt like it. Does it matter?"

Kevin nearly snarled. "Of course it matters, what if you had to bend over and someone saw up your skirt?" Someone like John he thought, seething.

Tess rolled her eyes. "Are you kidding? No one can tell that I'm not wearing anything underneath this skirt. Besides, it's not so short that I'd be showing anything if I had to bend down. You know that, Kevin."

She was right, but it still rubbed him wrong that John had hugged her while she had no panties on. There was just something about it that was a little too intimate. But he couldn't say that without sounding like a jealous lover, so instead he muttered, "That's not the point, the point is I know."

"Yes, you do." Tess licked her lips suggestively. "And your big, strong hand is still cupping my pussy, isn't it, Kevin?"

He arched a brow at her. He knew Tess never used that kind of language. That she was now, for him, was the best kind of aphrodisiac.

"You're soft, Tess. Soft and wet. Are these juices for me, baby?" He lightly stroked her even while he wondered how far she would go with her sex-talk before balking.

"Yes, god, yes," Tess whimpered.

To Kevin's lust-fogged brain, Tess sounded grateful that he wasn't going to stop their mid-afternoon rendezvous. He liked her candid response.

He moved his fingers even more, rewarding her, and allowing himself to feel her swollen clit nestled in the soft down of her hair. But it occurred to him that, while he had her willing and agreeable, he wanted to get a few things straight before they continued.

"Are you okay with what we're about to do here, Tess? Because I don't want you to regret anything later." Ruthlessly he added, "And I sure as hell don't want any misunderstandings."

Kevin wanted to be fair. He didn't want her feeling as if he had put her in a position where she'd felt obligated to be seduced by her boss.

"Yes, of course I'm okay with it, Kevin. In case you haven't been paying attention, I was the one coming on to you, remember?" Her voice was shaking. "I want to feel desirable, and I want to feel sexy. More than that though, I want you, Kevin." She placed her hand on his forearm, keeping his hand snug against her mound, pleasing the hell out of him. "I want you on top of me, under me, behind me. I want you so bad my legs are trembling." She paused, her words going straight to his crotch, before she gave him a sultry look. "Are we clear?"

One side of his mouth kicked up into a flirtatious grin, but her words nearly did him in. If he came in his pants now he'd never forgive himself. "Yeah, all clear."

He touched his thumb to her clitoris and felt it harden and swell for him even more. He circled it. Tess's warm brown eyes heated and turned drowsy. Her hand dropped away, giving him free rein.

He probed her opening with one finger and was rewarded by her gasp of pleasure. Gently, Kevin eased inside, slowly, moving in and out, savoring the tight squeeze of her inner flesh.

"Please, Kevin, quit teasing me."

She sounded so sincere, so needy. It made his chest ache. Didn't she know he was slowly going insane with wanting her as well? Didn't she realize the effect she had on him?

"I'm dying here, too, Tess, believe me. You aren't the only one being teased." Kevin picked up her hand and flattened it against the fly of his trousers. That was all it took to get her attention. Her eyes shot to his dick and her kiss-swollen lips formed an O. Her expression of combined excitement and awe made him wonder how many men she'd been with. Fuck that, he was not going there.

He withdrew his hand from underneath her skirt and stepped back. Almost at once, he felt the loss, and her little pout told him she did as well.

"Don't move. Not an inch, Tess. Understand?" He knew he sounded autocratic but something about her brought out the pre-historic male in him, made him want to conquer and run away with the spoils—in this case, Tess Marley.

She nodded and stayed still. A man could get used to such a giving woman in bed. In fact, it made Kevin want to please her all the more.

He went straight to his desk and buzzed Rachael. She was Tess's assistant and had been filling in for her throughout the morning.

"Yes, Mr. Haines?"

The mild-mannered voice over the intercom drew him out of his lust-filled haze. "Rachael, Tess and I will be tied up all afternoon and I do not want any interruptions." Hearing Tess's startled intake of breath, Kevin smiled inwardly. She might have her siren's act all worked out, but he had a feeling that down deep, where it counted, she was still a shy, little butterfly.

"Did you want me to reschedule your meeting with Drake and Sons then?"

Damn, he'd forgotten all about that. Drake was a large construction company in need of a major software upgrade and they wanted Invision for the job. But some things were just more important than gaining contracts. "Yes, Rachael, and send my apologies please. Tess and I have enough to catch up on that it will probably run us into the evening."

"Does Ms. Marley need me this evening then, sir?" she asked. "I don't have any other plans."

If Rachael didn't mind working overtime on a Friday night, that was proof Tess was not only good at her job, but an asset to his company. "Uh no, you head on home. We'll handle things fine, Rachael. Thanks, and you have a great weekend."

"You're welcome, Mr. Haines."

He severed the connection and sighed in relief. That he intended to make his evening a damned memorable one was certainly true. Now he could concentrate on finding out exactly what Tess Marley looked like, and felt like, underneath her hot new outfit. Kevin had the sneaking suspicion that her body, whether wrapped in heavy brown wool or a sexy red suit, was as luscious and desirable as he'd always imagined it to be.

He looked up and caught Tess staring at him with an apparent mix of anticipation and uncertainty. "You're mine now, Tess, all mine. You okay with that?"

"Yes."

Christ, her voice turned him on. All soft and husky. She had the bedroom voice down pat and she wasn't even trying. "That's good, because the way I see it, we have the rest of the day and all night to do nothing but enjoy each other." His mouth curved intimately. "That ought to take the edge off some."

"You mean you want to spend the entire evening with me?"

Tess's eyes grew wide as if in alarm, but this time, Kevin was the one confused. "Of course. What did you think?" he asked purposefully. "That a quick fuck in the office would be enough to satisfy me?"

"But, I—the entire night?"

Kevin winked. "All night, Tess," he confirmed.

When she still looked so full of wonder, he added, "Trust me, sweetheart."

With a jerky nod, Tess surrendered, filling Kevin with supreme male satisfaction.

He moved away from the desk and looked around his large office. It was the first time Kevin had ever thought to thank his mom for the couch she insisted he buy. At the time, it seemed a waste of money. Now, well, he would definitely be buying her a big bouquet of roses.

It was a roomy, comfy thing and would do nicely for their first time together. At least he wouldn't have to bend her over the desk—how cliché was that? Still, the thought of Tess in that position did have its upside.

"Uh, Kevin, are you having second thoughts?"

Kevin looked at Tess and knew he must have looked odd standing in the middle of the room looking from his desk, to his couch and back to his desk. Truth, always the best route. "Nope, no second thoughts. Just wondering which way would be better, the couch or the desk."

She looked at the couch, then at the desk. Her face flamed red. "Oh."

Kevin had to hide a smile. He didn't want to embarrass her, but damn she was such a contrary lady. One minute she was begging him to get on with it, and the next she was blushing crimson. Go figure.

He moved closer, circling her until he stood directly behind her. He now had a perfect view of her luscious behind. He could easily see her naked and bent over the desk, her legs spread wide for his view and her full, heavy tits pressed against the cherry wood surface. Maybe he'd ask her which she preferred. His voice came out guttural and rough with desire. "What do you want Tess, the desk or the couch?"

"I-I-it's up to you." Her shoulders slumped as she muttered the words. "To be honest, Kevin, I'm not quite as experienced as you. I've never made love in anything but a bed. Maybe this wasn't a good idea."

Was she backing out on him? Not just no, but hell no! Kevin stayed where he was, because he sensed she was more at ease when she wasn't looking directly at him. He wrapped his arm around her body and fingered the buttons on her suit jacket. "You want me, Tess. I know you do," he insisted. "Tell me. Just say the words."

Tess only nodded.

"Okay, I'll let you get away with a nod this time." A slip of his index finger and thumb, and the top button was free. "A few minutes ago you were wet in my palm. Your sweet scent fills me up even now, Tess." Pop, another button free. "And if you think telling a man that you aren't experienced, that you've not slept with many men, is a downer, think again, babe." Pop, and the third was free.

So close, but not quite.

He wanted the jacket off already. He wanted to see the creamy swell of her tits without any hindrance. Only then would he allow himself to touch. "Knowing that we'll be doing things you've never done before," he said in a thick voice, "that I'll be the first man to have you on a couch, on top of a desk, and every other place we can dream up, is like throwing gas on an open flame."

"Oh, God."

The last button popped and the jacket hung open. Kevin nibbled her ear while drifting the jacket off her shoulders and down her arms. "I want to see you sitting on top of me with your breasts in my face. I want to suckle and play while I fuck you. So, first the couch. Okay with you, Tess?"

The jacket fell to the floor as she nodded eagerly. Ah, so she liked it when he talked dirty to her. He'd remember that.

Without the jacket in his way, he could finally see that he was right. There was not even a camisole next to her skin, only a bra. It pushed her tits together to create cleavage, though from his vantage point she didn't need any help in that area. Silly woman. She had perfect, round, heavy breasts that didn't need wires and cleverly angled pads. And, although the bra was red and lacy and extremely sexy, it'd be even sexier on the floor, with the jacket.

"Have you ever thought of us together, Tess? Fantasized?" When her breathing increased, he knew he had his answer. Still he wanted to hear it for himself. "And I won't accept a nod this time, so answer me, babe."

Chapter 4

"Yes, I've thought about us," she whispered, "dreamed about... this."

"Mmm, that's what I thought." Kevin lifted one strap away from her shoulder and kissed the spot where it rested before sliding it down her arm. "A woman doesn't just suddenly decide she wants to sleep with a man she's known for five years. You had to work yourself up to it, I think." His voice gentled. "Still, I'll bet you didn't know that I thought of you as well, did you?" She shuddered under his fingers. "My sweet, shy, little Tess."

"I had no idea you thought of me in a sexual way."

Unable to help himself, Kevin kissed the crook of her neck, her shoulder, and rubbed his nose in her hair. It very nearly caused him lose the thread of the conversation.

"You never said a word, Kevin. Never once. Why?"

"You work for me. I don't date women that work for me." He was always clear about keeping his personal life personal—until she had walked into the room today. "I never would have compromised our working relationship that way."

He loved the way her body was put together, all curvy and voluptuous, not like most of the women he dated who thought they had to be supermodel thin. Now he realized that he didn't want to make love to a skeleton. He wanted something to stroke and squeeze, hills and valleys and other places to roam and play. Why on earth Tess had been wearing oversized ugly suits to cover the playground she had, he had no idea. He made a promise to himself to get to the bottom of that with her. For now, it was recess.

He slipped her other strap off, then frowned when Tess reached up to hold the bra in place as she cleared her throat. "Then why now, Kevin?" she asked. "Why break your own rules?"

"Simple," he groused. "If I don't have you, I'll go insane. Do you want to see me in a padded cell?" Kevin's heart thundered as Tess quickly shook her head. He unhooked the back closure and reached around to cover her hands with his own. Slowly, he slid her hands down her body and the bra with them. He felt her tremble. Probably a combination of nerves and exhilaration. He felt it, too.

"Don't be shy with me, Tess. I like the way nature put you together. I just can't believe you've been hiding these all this time." His hands left hers to once again cup her breasts in his warm calloused palms. "God, you are a handful aren't you?"

He massaged and kneaded her breasts. He was anxious to taste her erect nipples, but he didn't think she was quite ready for him to move in front of her yet. Not that being behind was so bad. He pushed closer, so close he felt the indention of her ass with his hard-on. He pressed himself against her bottom, letting her feel how hard she was making him.

"Do you like the way I'm touching you?" She moaned and dropped her head back against him, giving herself to him. He couldn't stand much more.

"I want you naked. I can't wait any longer." Then he released her breasts. Her unhappy whimper pleased him.

He turned her to face him and made fast work of unbuttoning and unzipping her skirt. It quickly joined the rest of her newly acquired clothing at their feet. Now he could look his fill.

"You are so fucking hot," he murmured. "How is it that you've been right under my nose all this time?"

She didn't answer him, but the look in her eyes was enough. Tess probably felt vulnerable standing in only her stilettos. Kevin wanted to remove his own constricting clothing, but he would wait a few moments longer.

Tess had a body like the starlets of old. A perfect hourglass figure. It was as if she were shaped specifically with his hands in mind. From her C-cup breasts to her tight tapered waist and sweetly rounded hips, Tess's body was designed for a man to worship. For him to worship.

Kevin reached out and touched one mauve nipple with his index finger. It puckered right before his eyes. "You have very sensitive nipples, don't you, baby?"

She closed her eyes and nodded.

"I'll bet you felt that all over." He lightly pinched her, rolling the distended bud between his fingers. "Do you feel it between your legs, Tess? Is your pussy dripping for me?" Reaching out with his other hand, he touched her there and was rewarded by the dewy softness of her. Her knees buckled. She had to grab onto him for support and Kevin took full advantage, separating her soft folds and sliding his middle finger all the way in, while still playing with her nipple.

"Oh, Kevin, that feels...."

"Mmm, yeah, I know." He groaned and stepped closer, not willing to wait any longer to taste the creamy swell of her breasts. He bent his head, sucking as much of the round globe into his mouth as he could, then laved her with his tongue. He felt Tess's delicate fingers dig into his hair, pulling him to her. He wiggled his finger inside her, enjoying her slippery heat. Her legs spread even further apart for him, allowing him deeper access. She was snug, and Kevin wondered how long it'd been for her. He wanted to give her as much pleasure as possible, make her forget any other lover she'd ever had. Just then she pushed him away, and he was forced to pull his finger free. His heart dropped. Had Tess changed her mind?

"It's not fair that you're still dressed," she told him with a little pout.

Kevin bit back a triumphant roar. He loved the way she was issuing more demands–demands that he could easily obey.

He began by yanking his shirt up and off. He tossed it carelessly aside and nearly grinned at the hot look in Tess's eyes. He had never been as glad of his daily workouts as he was at that moment. He was tugging at his belt when an intriguing idea came to mind.

Looking directly at Tess, Kevin issued a command of his own. "You want me undressed, you're going to have to do it yourself."

Tess was pretty darned sure that drooling was not a very sophisticated thing to do. And yet, that's exactly what she was doing. Staring and drooling over the perfection of her boss's chest. He had a yummy amount of chest hair, muscles that were well-defined but not overdone, and a lean waist that told her he took care of his body.

And she was very glad he did too, she thought with a shiver.

Kevin wanted her to do the rest of the undressing for him? Oh god, she had never undressed a man before. She didn't know how to be sensual and alluring about it. Tess had never done anything so bold in her entire adult life. Kevin's electrifying touches and words caused her pulse to pound frantically. Now, it was her turn and she didn't want to disappoint him.

"Tess? You chickening out on me?"

This stiffened her spine. "Chickening out? Not a chance."

No way, no how, Tess thought smugly. She was just taking a minute to figure out the best way to start. A sophisticated woman didn't just start yanking and ripping, for crying out loud. There needed to be a sort of seduction about it.

So, with her mind set on her role as the seductive temptress, Tess stepped forward, looked directly at Kevin and smiled. His pale blue eyes caught at hers, daring her, urging her on, until she refused to look away. She breathed in his scent, enjoying again the clean smell of soap and man. She liked that he didn't use cologne. For her, that would only mask this man's appeal.

She touched his bare chest with both her hands, flattening her palms against him first, needing the contact. She was intent on savoring every moment she had with Kevin. Tess watched transfixed as her own fingers eagerly sifted through the soft, dark curls that covered his pectorals. Her fingers followed the tempting trail downward, only to be stymied by the barrier of his slacks. Just that quickly though, her shyness disappeared, replaced by a curious fever that heated her insides.

She wanted to gloat when her fingers deftly dispensed with his belt buckle, and her body tingled when the button slipped through the hole on his trousers. She licked her lips in anticipation as she inched the zipper down. Kevin's simple white cotton briefs were stretched taut to accommodate his impressive erection. Her fingers moved again. Slipping inside the opening of his slacks, she began stroking his sex. When she felt his entire body shudder and vibrate, she sighed and closed her eyes, relishing the hard, masculine feel of him in her palm. That's when Kevin's patience seemed to snap.

"Stop taking so long, dammit," Kevin growled. Then he tried to push his pants and underwear down his legs and nearly toppled because he hadn't yet taken off his shoes.

To see such a powerful man so hungry for her empowered Tess. She watched as Kevin pulled, tugged, and tossed, and when he straightened again he was standing barefoot and as naked as the day he was born. The only thing preventing her from yanking him to her and shoving his heavy cock inside her body was her lack of experience. She might be as hot as he was right now, but she was still out of her league.

Still, she was experienced enough to recognize what she wanted. "I want to touch you, Kevin. May I?"

As if unable to speak, Kevin bobbed his head.

Tess's gaze left his face and strayed to his throbbing erection. She could swear he swelled yet another inch. She moved around to the back of him, impatient to feel his perfectly sculpted buttocks in the palms of her hands. Light as a feather, she touched his shoulder blades, reveling at the sharp intake of breath from Kevin. Slowly, she drifted her hands downward, closing her eyes as she felt the smooth, bronzed skin of her boss. As she reached his ass, however, Tess opened her eyes and watched as her fingers gripped and squeezed the taut flesh.

"Jesus, Tess," he ground out between clenched teeth.

A knot rose in her throat as she let her hands skim over his hips to his jutting penis. She licked her lips, imagining the taste of him, and then wrapped her small hand around his long length, gripping him in a tight fist. She heard Kevin groan low in his throat and the first slow stroke of her palm evoked a muttered curse from him. A sticky drop of fluid appeared at his bulbous tip. She took that as a thumbs-up.

Tess moved out from behind Kevin, anxious to see the magnificence of his aroused flesh in her palm. The thick weight of him had her body on fire.

She used her index finger to spread the liquid heat over the head of Kevin's manhood, lightly, teasingly, all the while watching him watch her. It was the single most erotic thing she'd ever done. She felt a surge of feminine power at the naked longing she saw in Kevin's eyes.

"I like touching you, Kevin," Tess whispered huskily, "I like it a lot."

"I like you touching me, too, baby, but if you don't stop, the fun'll be over before it even starts."

Tess stilled the soft caressing motion of her hand, and looked into a pair of blazing blue eyes. Kevin's jaw was locked and his neck veins were pumping furiously, as if he were having a hard time holding back. She liked that. Never before had she gotten that kind of reaction from a man, and it felt good. It felt powerful.

Chapter 5

Kevin knew that nothing stood between him and paradise. He had Tess restless, turned-on, and best of all, all to himself. Her quick breaths and slumberous eyes were speaking volumes, telling him that she wanted him to hurry with his perusal of her body so they could get on to the big show. He, on the other hand, intended to take advantage of the moment and look his fill.

Tess Marley was everything he ever imagined her to be and more. She had smooth, ivory skin, soft, supple curves, and her dense patch of pubic hair made it obvious that she must have never shaved her bikini line a day in her life. He liked that. It was so unlike the other women he'd been with, who seemed to feel less was more. But Kevin liked Tess's natural beauty. All that hair just dared him to find the jeweled treasure underneath.

The easy contour of her hips tapered upward to a trim waist, only to bloom outward again to full, heavy, womanly breasts. It was like ripping open an ugly brown paper bag and finding a flawless diamond inside. He would make it his life's mission to see to it that she never wore another brown, tan, or cream-colored article of clothing again. He was so adamant about it that he voiced his feelings aloud.

"If you haven't burned every last piece of your old wardrobe yet, then I damned sure will," he insisted. Then he reached out and touched a fingertip to her shoulder. He slid it over and down her breast, barely touching her ribcage, until he was at her hip. He clutched her there and urged her to walk forward while he walked backwards.

"I've changed my mind, first the desk," he commanded. He watched Tess follow him as if an invisible thread pulled her along.

When they reached the massive expanse of his desk, Kevin moved her to the left side, facing it and away from him, opposite the flat screen monitor. With no more thought than it took to swat at a fly, Kevin shoved everything but the monitor out of his way. Papers, pens and backup disks crashed to the floor. Tess looked at him over her shoulder as if surprised and he only winked.

"Bend forward." Then he gave her a little push in the center of her back, forcing her to obey.

She bent until she was flat against the cherry wood, then gasped. The cold was a shock to her hot skin no doubt.

"Does the cold make your nipples pucker, Tess?"

She muttered, "Yes."

"Want me to warm you, baby?" She nodded, clearly too far gone to speak. "Spread your legs for me, honey."

She did, but it wasn't enough. Kevin prodded her legs wider with his knee. She wiggled around as he wedged himself between her spread thighs, covering her with his body.

"Do you trust me?"

Another nod, and Kevin kissed her neck in approval.

"Stretch your arms out then, and grab hold of the desk on the other side."

Tess complied.

"Are you okay?"

All she managed was a murmured yes. And seeing her body sprawled out as if she were a banquet nearly had Kevin climaxing like a teenager. Thank God she wasn't short. As it was, her body was stretched seductively taut. Still, he wanted her to enjoy herself, not feel as if she was being pulled like a rubber band. "You aren't too uncomfortable?"

"No." It wasn't so much what she said but the pleading way she said it. Tess was on fire. It fueled his own lust all the more.

Smoothing her mahogany brown hair to one side, he kissed his way down her spine, inhaling the unique scent that seemed to belong to her alone. He stopped and looked at her from behind. Her breasts were flattened against his desk, her legs spread so far apart that her feet barely touched the ground. He wanted to thank the man—and it was damned sure a man—who had invented high heels.

Her barely visible cleft was wet and slick with her juices. Kevin felt a surge of possessiveness arise at the sight of her. "You're so fucking beautiful like this."

Then his mouth was on her again, kissing and nipping at her rounded, upraised buttocks.

Kevin's hands roamed over her body, constantly stroking and touching, warming and urging her on at the same time. Then he touched her between her bottom cheeks. He wet his index finger with her juices and rubbed her tight pucker. She wriggled and squirmed for him, as if wanting more, but unsure how to go about getting it. Kevin spread her open and eased a different finger between her glistening feminine folds, delving in just once, teasing a moan from her, all the while delicately probing her anus.

"Taste your pussy for me, baby." He touched her mouth with his wet finger. Her tongue darted out and licked his finger greedily, before sucking it into her mouth completely. This time he was the one moaning.

"Damn," was all he managed before he was on his knees behind her. He parted her, finding her hard clit and licked hungrily.

Tess arched up off the desk at the first contact of his tongue. He moaned his appreciation and licked again and again, before he sucked her tiny nub into his mouth. Tasting and eating at her, taking his time to find the right rhythm and pressure that would give her the most satisfaction. He delved between her folds to find what he sought and slid two fingers in. Tess came undone. She screamed and bucked, moaning his name and undulating against his face and hand as her orgasm went on and on. But Kevin didn't stop his pleasurable assault until he had wrung every last gasp and moan from her.

Once her body settled and quieted, Kevin sat back on his haunches and surveyed his handy work. Her vulva was sopping wet and puffy from his loving, and the sight drove Kevin insane with lust. Tess had come magnificently for him, and so quickly that he knew it'd been awhile for her. She was sexily sprawled out, totally abandoned, wonderfully sated, and blissful unaware of his perusal.

He could feast from her pussy for hours and never get tired, never get enough. He felt a kind of crazy obsession for Tess's body that he'd never known with other women. She had stirred something inside of him and he could feel a new kind of pleasure building as he stared at her pulsing heat. The thought that he could pound himself into her right now until she milked him of every last drop of fluid had him feeling greedy and impatient as hell.

And though he wanted to make her come a thousand times over, to bring her a kind of desire that she'd never felt before, he also felt curiously tender towards Tess. He wanted to make this memorable for her.

Kevin stood up and pressed his cock into the cleft of Tess's ass, smiling as she arched and practically vibrated for him, never once releasing her hold on the desk. His nature was to dominate, to take the lead sexually. And he'd wondered what Tess would be like, because she was always so in control. She was never one to hesitate or wait around to be told what to do. But apparently when it came to sex, she was content to let him be the one in the lead. Damn, he liked that.

Kevin heard her whimper and knew that she was way past ready for him and he was close to exploding himself. He pressed up against her opening and almost shook at how good it felt. Too good. Oops, and he knew why too.

"Christ, I can't believe I almost forgot," he grumbled.

"What is it?"

"No condom." And that hadn't happened since he was a teenager. He never forgot to protect the woman. His father had ingrained that in him from the time he'd caught Kevin with his first nudie magazine. Thankfully, he had one in his wallet.

He released his grip on Tess's hips and frantically looked around the room for his pants. When he located them, he started to step over to get them, but he felt Tess attempting to get up off the desk. He pressed her back down by covering her hands that still held onto the side and said, "Just where do you think you're going?"

She tried to rise up again, but he kept her still.

"Uh, I thought you said you don't have a condom."

He smoothed his hand down her arm, her side, to her sweetly raised bottom. Kevin was becoming a complete glutton over her ass. "I have one in my wallet. Stay put."

"Oh, okay," she said, as she relaxed for him.

He hurried over to his pants and nearly ripped the back pocket off as he yanked out his wallet. When he turned back around, Tess was grinning and staring at his cock. The smile lit up her face, and he found himself smiling right back. "What are you grinning at?"

Tess quirked her eyebrows. "Those pants are ruined, you know."

A laugh bubbled out of her, and Kevin didn't think he'd ever heard such a lovely sound in his life. "Fuck it, I've got other pants."

Once settled back between her thighs, Kevin tore open the packet and rolled the condom on. He looked down at Tess. Her breathing came in fast pants, and the teasing laugh was gone. He spread her open and nudged his way into her wetness.

"Damn, you're tight." He didn't want to hurt her so he took it slow, easing in an inch at a time, and then back out again until he thought he was going to die from the sweet pleasure of it. When Tess's muscles tightened, he whispered, "Don't tense up on me, baby."

"You're too big, Kevin. I-I don't think...."

The statement hung in the air between them as if she were unsure what to say. Kevin heard her fear and knew whatever experience she'd had with men was either pretty damn lousy or too meager to count.

"We'll fit." He said softly, "You trust me, remember?"

A few seconds went by before he saw her tentative nod.

Kevin reached between their bodies with his right hand, found her clit, and began rubbing her with his thumb. When she finally relaxed and began to slowly move against him, he took the advantage and slid all the way in.

This time she arched all the way off the desk, her hands pushing her body to a standing position, and moaning. He held himself inside of her, unmoving, just feeling. Kevin wrapped his left arm around her waist, and Tess wrapped her arm around his neck. They held each other that way as Kevin made slow sweet love to her from behind.

His fingers petted and stroked her clit, and when he pulled out and thrust back in again Tess shouted out her climax. He moved faster then, frantic to bury himself inside of her. Going in as deep as he could and then back out again, fucking her fast and hard. Her inner body squeezed him as her climax went on and on, and then Kevin was blissfully sailing over that edge with her.

As their breathing slowed and their hearts quieted, he felt Tess start to squirm, attempting to move away. She wanted distance, physically and emotionally, but he would have none of it.

"Remember what I said, Tess." His deep voice whispered in her ear. "I want all night. I want at least that long with you," he reminded her, and then he released his hold. She wobbled a little before catching herself against the desk. She stood there like that, looking around the room at the mess they'd created.

Their clothes were strewn everywhere, the contents of his desk were scattered all over the floor and his only coherent thought was that he wanted to take her in a hundred different ways before their night was up. He hoped she was up to it, because he sure as hell was. He felt intoxicated by Tess's body. And, like a junkie, he was already craving his next fix. He couldn't wait to get her home.

Kevin's thoughts scattered when he saw Tess bury her face in her hands and her shoulders begin to quiver. Oh god, she was crying, already regretting what they had done. At once, he was there, holding her in his arms, rubbing her back, totally lost as to how to handle a woman in tears.

"What is it, baby?" Kevin coaxed. She was too quiet and it scared him more than he cared admit. "Please tell me, Tess, we can deal with it together."

Then he heard what sounded suspiciously like a chuckle. *What the hell?* Kevin pushed Tess away from his chest and pulled her hands away from her face. To Kevin's immense relief Tess was actually laughing.

"You want to share the joke with the rest of the class, Marley?" Kevin insisted. He felt just a tad bit defensive, but also relieved that he wasn't going to have to make Tess stop crying. However, there were two things that were never a good sign from a woman after sex: crying, or hysterical laughter. Both emotions spoke volumes as to the man's sexual prowess.

He watched as Tess seemed to get a grip on herself. "I can't believe we just did that!" She squeaked with all the excitement of a woman who badly needed to let her hair down. Once more she looked around the room. But

Kevin's gaze was riveted.

She was still naked, except for her come-and-get-it shoes. Her hair was disheveled and her cheeks rosy. It made for the most appealing sight Kevin had ever seen. When she started laughing all over again, he grew hard, despite the fact he'd just had the most awesome sex of his life. And he couldn't help but laugh right along with her, because Tess's excitement was contagious.

He reached out and turned her so she faced him, then he yanked her back into his arms. He kissed her soundly on the lips. She sobered instantly and relaxed against him, whimpering. He released her mouth.

"I want to get you home. I want you in my bed, Tess." Kevin breathed the words against her lips anxious to have her all over again.

Tess was still in shock, but she did have the presence of mind to wonder if what they had just shared meant anything at all to Kevin. Before she went any further, she wanted to know at least that much.

"Kevin, I need to know how you feel about me. I need to know what this meant to you." There, it was out and she couldn't take it back. Kevin's lips thinned and Tess's heart sank. She wasn't going to like what he was about to say.

"I liked what we just did, Tess. Christ, I liked it a helluva lot. That's why I want you to come home with me."

Tess could see that he was hedging. She knew him well enough to know when he was trying to speak with caution. She tried not to let it tear her up. After all, she had come to him knowing full well what would happen. She had no illusions when it came to Kevin and relationships. He was a one-night stand kind of man and it was that simple.

Kevin reached for her, but she stepped backwards. He sighed heavily and shoved a hand through his hair.

"What's the problem, Tess? You said you wanted this with me. You knew what you were doing when you came in here. You damn well knew where this would lead. So why the sudden change of heart now?"

Tess struggled with her emotions, unwilling to cry in front of him. She didn't want his guilt. What they had shared was more than she could have ever dreamed of, and she didn't want that marred by Kevin's pity.

"I did want this, Kevin. And it was beautiful. It was more than I could have ever imagined. You gave me a taste of paradise. You were incredibly affectionate and so generous."

His gaze softened a fraction, and he started towards her again, this time not stopping when she moved away from him. She suddenly felt like she'd just become her jungle lover's next meal. She hadn't thought it possible, but his predatory gaze had her breasts and clit tingling even more than before.

Tess held up a hand to hold him at bay. "I need some time, Kevin. I'm sorry, but I just can't go home with you. I just can't. Please try and understand."

She watched a muscle in his jaw jump, but he stopped pursuing her and nodded briskly. She should have been relieved, but she couldn't feel anything past the thick cloud of misery threatening to engulf her.

Silently, they both got dressed. More than once, she felt Kevin's eyes on her, but he never said another word. He went to his desk and sat down behind it. She left, quietly shutting the door behind her. What was she supposed to do now? She felt sick and she began to wonder if she'd been better off keeping Kevin a fantasy in her head. It hurt less that way. But no, what they had shared was more than she'd every hoped. She'd wanted every second of their loving and she'd cherish it until the day she died.

Well, now what the fuck was he supposed to do?

Kevin watched in angry silence as Tess glided out of his office in the same erotic and elusive way that she had come. One minute she was there, coming apart in his arms. The next, he was left staring at the back of a door. An unfamiliar ache welled up and threatened to consume him, as if he'd somehow just let something very precious slip between his fingers. He didn't like feeling so helpless and out of control. It wasn't in his nature to sit and do nothing. If he wanted something, he went for it, to hell with the risks.

Still, that little squeeze to his heart kept him from leaping out of his chair and racing after Tess. He needed time, as did Tess. But damn, he had been envisioning taking Tess home with him. It had been in his mind to take her sixty different ways before dawn broke. Having sex with her in his office had been phenomenal, no doubt about it, but he wanted her in his bed as well. If Kevin was being completely honest, he'd admit that he wouldn't mind having her on his kitchen counter, in his shower, on the floor, and every other place he could dream up.

As it stood, however, he wouldn't be christening his apartment with Tess's delectable body. It appeared that he was sentenced to going home alone to an empty bed. The prospect sent him into a nasty, brooding stupor. He had half a mind to stop and pick up a twelve-pack of beer on his way home. Maybe if he got rip-roaring drunk he'd be able to forget how juicy Tess's pussy was. But Kevin had never been one to drown his sorrows in alcohol, and he damn well wouldn't start now.

He'd give them both time to think things through. Maybe, just maybe, he'd even forget how melodic her husky voice had sounded as she had climaxed all around his dick, shouting his name—but he wouldn't place any bets on that. He was still hearing the echoes.

Kevin pushed his fingers through his hair and let loose a few expletives, then he went back to work on his office. If he wasn't going to be burying himself between Tess Marley's silky thighs, then he may as well clean up the mess they'd made of his desk.

As Tess took the elevator down, leaving the building and Kevin behind, slowly making her way to her car, a loud wolf whistle stopped her in her tracks. She turned towards the sound and saw John Fields striding towards her. She shook her head and smirked. He was such an outrageous flirt, but a harmless one.

"I figured you were gone for the day, John. Why aren't you off partying with some lucky lady right now?"

John came up beside her and slowed his pace to match hers. "I was gone, but I remembered a file I wanted to look at this weekend, so I came back to get it."

She nodded. John was a hard worker, putting in as many hours as Kevin, and that was saying something. "All work and no play, John," she said, enjoying the easy friendship she had with him. He was one of the few men that she didn't feel quite so timid with. But John was a very likeable man. He made people feel comfortable. No doubt that quality aided him as their sales executive.

He cocked his head to the side and leaned towards her when they reached their car. "Speaking of all work and no play, I don't have a date for the Employee Recognition Dinner tomorrow night. Want to go with me, Tess?"

Oh, no! She'd completely forgotten all about that dinner. It was quite possible that Kevin had forgotten too, considering what they'd just been doing. Her face heated when she imagined Kevin sitting behind his large, sturdy desk, his office in disarray. Her body was frantic for him all over again. What was she going to do? She couldn't possibly face him, not now when she was feeling so fragile. She'd barely escaped as it was. If she went back up to his office to remind him, in the state she was in, he'd have her agreeing to just about anything, including that one-night stand.

"It wasn't that hard a question, Tess."

She looked at John and realized she'd been staring off into space. Then she thought of his words. He wanted to be her escort. The sexy John Fields was asking her to the dinner as his date. She wondered—should she?

She gazed up at him and gave him his answer. "I'd love to be your date, John."

He grinned and opened her car door for her. Once she was settled inside, he leaned down into the open space and murmured, "We'll knock him on his ass, pretty lady." Then he winked and closed the car door, causing her to stare, dumbfounded, wondering what he could have possibly meant by such an odd statement.

Then she thought of Kevin and the dinner. Perhaps Rachael would remind him, Tess thought with a flicker of hope. Ever the efficient assistant, however, Tess knew that she should be the one to remind him of the event. She groaned, heart plummeting as the truth crashed in on her. It was her job to keep her boss apprised of these things, not Rachael's. Still, she didn't want to speak to him directly—coward that she was. So she called his home number, leaving a brief message with the details. She clicked her cell phone off and pulled out of the parking lot, still reflecting on John's odd statement.

Chapter 6

Originally, Tess had thought to wear one of her cream-colored suits to the Recognition Dinner this evening. But that was before she'd gone berserk and trashed her old, ugly clothes. Now, as she stared at her reflection, she was surprised by the joy that began to spread through her. She liked what she saw staring back at her.

She'd gone shopping earlier in the day and found the perfect dress in a consignment shop. It was a sleeveless, silky little number in red, high at the neck with a hemline that fluttered like butterfly wings around her calves. She loved the feel of the material against her skin. She felt decadent but modest all at the same time. The dress wasn't revealing, but its thin material molded to her curves like a soft glove. The red heels from yesterday complemented the outfit perfectly. She stared, enjoying the way her hair hung in long, loose curls. It was still such a strange sensation to have it down instead of pulled tight into a bun. For once in her life, she felt confident and secure in her appearance.

Unfortunately, she would need all the confidence she could muster for the night and Kevin. This time, as she looked across the ballroom at him, she'd know just exactly how his mouth tasted. She'd know how his touches caused her body to go up in flames. The images flitting through her head were wild and untamed and she wanted badly to be with him again.

The doorbell rang, and suddenly she remembered her date. John. She looked at the clock. He was right on time, of course. She took a deep breath and let it out, determined to enjoy the novelty of being out with a man, even if that man was just a friend. It was better than going to the dinner alone, as she'd previously assumed she would, just like every other year.

Tess grabbed her matching shawl and purse and swung open the door to greet her escort. "Hi, John," she said, determined to enjoy her evening, even though it wasn't Kevin standing at her door, smiling.

John looked her over, slowly making a heated journey from the top of her head to the tips of her shoes. When his gaze came back to hers, he was grinning lecherously. "I'll be the envy of every man there, pretty lady."

John had called her that before, but she never took much stock in the term. Now it gave her a zing of pleasure to hear it. "And I'll be the envy of every female I'm sure." And she meant it. John was wearing a pair of charcoal-grey slacks and an ivory shirt open at the collar. With his wild dark hair and tall, muscular frame, he could pose for GQ.

He held out his arm and said, "Let's go make an entrance." She laughed, feeling lighthearted and carefree for the first time since leaving Kevin sitting at his desk.

The Employee Recognition Dinner was always a lively event for Invision Computing. It was a small company yet, so the agenda wasn't long. Still, as the ceremony got underway, Tess still hadn't spotted Kevin, and she was beginning to wonder if he got her message.

The preliminaries were already over, and when the music started several people had begun swaying and moving to the slow rhythm. She'd never danced at the Recognition Dinner, just watched from the side, sipping her water and counting the minutes until she could make a quiet exit. So when John leaned towards her, whispering, "May I have this dance, pretty lady?" she felt a quick spurt of excitement laced with a heavy amount of fear.

"I've never danced before, John," she answered him honestly.

He stood and held his hand out to her. "There's nothing to it, sweetheart. Let me do all the work. You just hold on tight."

As he entered the ballroom, Kevin was feeling like a thundercloud ready to burst wide open. He'd gotten very little sleep, and now he had to smile and be polite, when what he really wanted to do was hit something. Then he saw Tess. That little weasel John was leading her out to the miniscule dance floor. When he took her waist in his hands, Kevin no longer wanted to hit something, but someone. An employee. No, he couldn't do that, not at the Employee Recognition Dinner.

So Kevin rubbed a hand over his face and found a seat off to the corner, intent on being left alone so that he could watch Tess's body sway back and forth to the music.

Christ, she was stunning. So perfect in every way. The red dress she wore was really nothing more than pretty paint. He could see her breasts bobbing beneath the flimsy material. Had she forgone bra and underwear both this time? As he memorized every soft, fleshy curve of her, his hands fisted on the table in front of him in a pathetic attempt to keep himself calm.

He hadn't stopped wanting her since she'd walked out of his office. For over an hour, he'd sat there, staring at the closed door, willing her to come back to him, dying to take her home to his bed where he could have her all over again. She'd become an obsession, one that had monopolized his thoughts all last night and all day today.

But she hadn't come back, and now she was here with another man. He wanted to shout to the moon that she was his and his alone. No other man had a right to touch her! Then, as the song ended and another started, he watched John pull Tess closer until she was flush against him. Her luscious tits, that same bountiful swell of skin that Kevin had worshiped with his lips and tongue, were now pressed against the hard planes of John's chest. Kevin stood. Enough was enough.

As he made his way over to them, he saw something else that set his blood to boiling. Tess was wearing the shoes. Those fuck-me pumps that pushed her ass up in the most sexy way imaginable. The shoes she'd worn when he'd taken her from behind.

"Bullshit." In two long strides, Kevin reached Tess. He yanked her out of John's arms, whipping her around to face him. "What the hell do you think you're doing?" he growled, pinning her with an angry glare. He was ready to explode and completely oblivious to any onlookers.

Tess's eyes went wide with surprise. "Kevin, what on earth?"

He cut her off with a look of warning, then his gaze quickly shot toward John. "She's mine, Fields," he ground out. "So back the hell off."

John, the idiot, merely smiled. "I don't see a brand on her, Kevin." Then he looked at Tess and wagged his eyebrows. With a leer, he added, "Unless your mark is somewhere beneath that pretty red dress."

Kevin stepped towards John, putting himself between Tess and his rival. Then he issued a single, deadly warning. "She's not to be played with, John. This isn't an effing game."

John rubbed his jaw and stared back at Kevin, who suddenly felt slightly uncomfortable under his employee and friend's intelligent scrutiny. "Fine. But, Kevin, she's a dear friend, so I hope you mean what you say."

"Doesn't anyone care what I have to say?" Tess shouted.

Kevin could hear her anger. Was she mad that she wasn't able to dance with John anymore? Was John more than a friend to her, then? That ugly thought caused him to squeeze Tess's wrist harder than he'd intended as he pulled her out of the room full of shocked employees. It would be the talk around the water-cooler come Monday morning, but he didn't give a shit. He wanted Tess far away from John. Now.

"Kevin, please stop. You're hurting my wrist."

He stopped and immediately lessened the pressure on her wrist, but he didn't let her go. He could never let her go. They were alone in the parking lot, hidden from view by parked cars, when he turned to her and asked, "Do you want him, Tess?"

Tess blinked and her mouth fell open. She was dressed like a temptress, but she still acted like an innocent. He liked that volatile combination in her.

When no answer came, Kevin stepped closer, just barely allowing his body to touch all along the length of hers. He whispered, "Do you have panties on, Tess?" He stroked a hand down her side to her hip where he pulled her towards him. "Answer me, or I'll find out for myself. Right here, right now."

She seemed to shake herself out of her daze. "Of course I'm wearing panties, Kevin," she said hurriedly.

He looked down the front of her and saw the indentations of her areolas and the hard nubs of her nipples pressing against the red silk. "Well, if you have a bra, it must be pretty damned flimsy, because I can see every line of your tits. You look ready to fuck, baby." He looked back into her eyes and demanded, "Is that what you had planned for John tonight? Were you going to let him fuck you, Tess?"

Tess flushed. She pushed against him, but he didn't budge. He had been an idiot when he let her walk out on him yesterday and he'd regretted it ever since. She wasn't escaping him this time. He chose another tactic when she stayed rigid and mute in his arms.

He drifted his fingers over her body, touching the turgid peaks of her breasts and then sliding down over her ribs, her stomach on his path to her hot center. "Does he turn you on?" he asked in a rough snarl. "Does he make you wet the way I do, Tess? Because I know you're wet for me, aren't you? Tell me the truth now, no lies."

Tess closed her eyes and sighed heavily as if admitting defeat. "No, he doesn't make me feel the way you do, Kevin. John's a friend, nothing more."

He smiled, though he felt like exploding with repressed sexual desire. "Answer the other part of my question, Tess. Are you wet for me right now?" As if to accentuate his point, he slid one finger along the soft seam of her swollen vulva, which the flimsy silk of her dress barely hid. He was rewarded when he felt her body bow and vibrate. "Yes! Damn you. I am wet, Kevin. You know I am. Please don't torture me this way."

She was shaking and her voice broke with emotion. Kevin gentled his tone. "I'm not torturing you, baby. I'm torturing me. I want you so bad I can't see straight."

She opened her eyes and looked down at his fly, her warm eyes zeroing in on him. He felt his dick pulsate and swell with need. She looked back up at him and he saw something more than desire in her eyes.

She loved him.

The emotion was there, mingling with the desire. Of course she did, he realized with a surge of triumph. A woman like Tess would never give herself to a man if her heart wasn't involved. He didn't know what he felt for Tess, but he knew that he had never felt the kind of jealous rage that had torn him apart when he saw John holding Tess. He'd wanted to tear the man apart with his bare hands. To rip Tess away and spirit her off to his cave. It was primal and uncivilized and completely undeniable. And while he didn't have a cave, he did have an apartment. He intended to get them out of the parking lot and into his cozy bed right away.

"Come on," he said, ushering her toward his car. This time she didn't pull back, and he felt victorious.

Kevin drove to his apartment like a man on fire. Considering the way he ignored the speed limit, Tess was thankful they'd gotten there in one piece.

As soon as he got her inside the door, he started touching and kissing her. Already, there in his hallway, she was lost to his passion. He seemed intent on having her again. He was insatiable! And now so was she. Reason flew out the window as need rushed in. She was on fire. Her insides melted to liquid lava. If she couldn't have his love, then she'd damn well take what she could get. This night might be her last time with Kevin and she meant to make the most of every second.

Tess wrapped her arms around Kevin's neck and in one swift move, he pinned her against the front door with the hard length of his body. She wriggled against him, eager and ready for him to fill her.

"Do. Not. Move. Tess," he ground out, his voice a hot demand. Then, his mouth found her breast, sucking her through the red silky material of her dress.

She arched against him and shouted, ""Kevin, please, I need you!"

She felt the absence of Kevin's mouth as he raised his head. His eyes were fierce with need and anger?

"Why did you let John touch you, dammit?"

She started to protest, but he clamped a hand over her mouth instead. "No more talking. I want to fuck you now. If you don't want me, then shake your head no. I'll stop."

Tess closed her eyes and willed her heart to slow down. He was giving her a chance to call a halt. Even as wild and angry as he was, he would never hurt her, Kevin simply wasn't like that. So she lifted her hand to his cheek and tried to communicate the way she felt with her eyes, hoping he understood that her need was as great as his.

Kevin let out a breath and growled low, "Then you're mine now, Tess, and right now the only thing I want is to feel your sweet pussy holding me tight. So no words."

Tess nodded, and Kevin went back to her breasts, using his mouth to drive her into fits of pleasure. His fingers slowly drifted lower over her ribs and lower still to her hipbone. Grabbing her dress in his fist, he tugged it upwards, baring her clear to her waist. He lifted his head, and eased away from her slowly, as if afraid she would run if he gave her too much space. Tess didn't bother to tell him that she was right where she wanted to be.

He looked down at the flimsy red panties and snarled, "It's a damn good thing you weren't lying about wearing panties." She wanted to smack him for thinking she would have lied, but he slipped his fingers under the slim lace edge and yanked, tearing them apart. She yelped. He jerked them away from her body and tucked them into his back pocket, then went down on his knees in front of her. Tess watched in wonder as his nostrils flared, and then he rubbed his lips back and forth over her swollen heat. She moaned.

Kevin looked up at her and whispered, "You left me yesterday, baby." His voice sounded raw and she saw something akin to pain in his eyes. Could it be that he cared? But all thought fled as Kevin's tongue darted out and licked the sensitive fleshy folds as if she were his own personal ice cream cone. She pushed her lower body into his hungry mouth and he forced her legs wide while he lapped at her hot center, wiggling a finger into her while sucking at her clitoris. Tess fisted her hands in his hair and felt him groan his approval. She pressed forward, frantic for release. Then, without even a hint of warning, her body seized and clenched.

"Kevin, oh God, it's too much!"

"No!" came Kevin's deep rumble. "All of it, Tess. I want every last drop." Then his tongue swirled around her clit and he took the tiny distended bit of flesh between his teeth and sucked greedily.

Tess shouted as she flew into a million tiny pieces, her body obeying Kevin's every wish and command. She would have collapsed if not for Kevin's strong hold on her, anchoring her to the door. He released her, stood to his feet and took a condom out of his wallet. He then unzipped the fly of his expensively tailored navy-blue slacks, freeing his throbbing cock from its tight confines.

He handed her the foil packet and ordered, "Put it on me, Tess."

She'd never done that before. Anxiety filled her and threatened to swallow her whole at the thought of messing this up, of disappointing Kevin. But when she saw the feral look on his face, she knew she wanted to do this for him. On some elemental level, Tess knew that Kevin was intent on pushing her to the very edge of her comfort zone, in part because she'd danced with John. She urgently wanted to prove to him that she saw him and only him.

Dropping to her knees, Tess tore the foil apart. With shaking, inexperienced fingers, she began to roll the rubber down Kevin's thick penis. It got twisted a couple of times, but eventually she had it all the way on. She felt proud of herself. When she stood again, the warm, gentle expression on Kevin's face had her blood coursing through her veins. He dipped his head, and his lips feathered soft against hers. She wrapped her arms around his neck and leaned into him. Giving him everything.

He lifted just a breath away and softly ordered, "Put your left leg around my waist, baby."

She did, offering him her absolute trust. He anchored his hands by her head, caging her in. Kevin bent his knees and plunged into her in one smooth stroke. Tess cried out and clutched onto his shoulders for support. He took her mouth with the same fervor, sliding his tongue inside, filling every part of her that he could.

Tess felt his powerful thrusts clear through to her womb. Pleasure spiked anew within her. All at once, she felt Kevin stiffen. He shoved against her pelvis with such force that he lifted her off the floor completely, pushing her body into a spiral of sensation. Kevin shouted out her name as he spent himself inside her honeyed heat. Tess wrapped her other leg around him, straddling him where he stood, and hugged him tight as she claimed her own fulfillment. His breathing was labored, and after several long seconds, he lifted up and pulled himself out of her. At once, she ached to have him back, right where he belonged, inside the very heart of her.

He stared down at her and said tenderly, "Christ, I'm sorry."

Tess frowned. "What on earth for?"

Kevin gave her a disbelieving look. "I just took you against the front door like a wild animal!"

She cuddled into his neck and whispered, "Yes, you did, but I wasn't complaining."

He groaned and wrapped his arms around her bottom, holding her snugly against his groin. "Well, I'm glad you liked it, baby, but I could have used a little finesse."

She pushed away from his chest so she could see his face. "You were angry with me, Kevin."

He scowled. "I didn't like you dancing with John."

She gave him a half-smile and looked down at his still-heaving chest. "So I gathered. But he really is just a friend, Kevin."

He tipped her chin up so she was forced to look into his eyes. "I know, baby. I suppose I'm a possessive bastard. Truth is, I can't seem to help it around you." She was about to tell him she understood, that she'd feel the same way if she saw him dancing with another woman, but her stomach rumbled just then. He looked at her suspiciously.

"Didn't you eat anything at the dinner, Tess?"

"Huh?" The statement had come so far out of left field that she couldn't be sure she'd heard him correctly.

Kevin cocked his head to the side. "Did you eat, or did you just dance?"

She saw that same wild look coming into his eyes again at the mention of dancing. Quickly she answered him. "No, but we can eat later, don't you think?" She wanted to get him to bed. She wasn't nearly done with him yet.

Unexpectedly, he set her back on her feet and straightened her dress, then pulled her away from the door and brought her into the kitchen. Once there, he lifted her into a stool at the counter.

"I'll be right back. Stay put."

He wasn't gone long, but when he reappeared, his clothes were restored to order. He walked straight to the massive, stainless steel refrigerator. Tess didn't even know they made refrigerators that large.

"I'm going to make you some dinner."

She started to object, because never in her life had a man cooked for her. It seemed so intimate. Absurd, considering all they'd done so far.

"Don't try and talk me out of it either, Tess." He turned and gave her a wide grin. "Now that I have you all to myself, I intend to do this right. First, I'm going to feed you, and then we'll play some more."

Was it the devilish grin or the promise of sustenance that had her accepting his offer? But she couldn't sit and do nothing while he did all the work. That just wasn't her thing. She got up off the stool and insisted, "Okay, food sounds wonderful, but I'm helping."

He had been in the process of getting out various greens and condiments but her words stopped him. He crossed his arms over his chest and glared at her. "Why can't you ever accept anything nice from me?"

She hadn't seen that one coming. "I don't understand." Then she thought about it a minute and said softly, "I guess I'm just not used to being waited on."

He pulled her into his arms. "Over the five years you've worked for me, you've never once accepted presents or cards or anything from me. I know you've accepted presents from other employees. Why not me, Tess?"

He began stroking her back, soothing her frazzled nerves. It was odd that he knew she needed that. "You're my boss and I suppose I just wanted to keep things professional between us." In a quieter voice she said, "I didn't want anyone saying bad things about you."

He pulled back and looked into her eyes. "You are such a puzzle at times, and other times you're an open book. I swear you don't seem to know how to conceal your emotions. When you get this vulnerable look in your eyes, like now, I have this need to protect you from the swindlers and shysters of the world." He paused and then, "I want one thing made clear right now, I don't give a damn what people say about me," he said harshly, "but if you're worried that your coworkers will talk about you now that we've had sex, think again."

She started to object, but he hushed her with a light, teasing kiss to her lips.

"I have zero tolerance for office gossip and everyone at Invision knows it, Tess." Then he smiled, but it was a cold, merciless look that had her shivering. "Besides, no one would be stupid enough to say anything about you. I'd fire them immediately if they did. I'm betting they know that too."

She didn't know what to say to such an outlandish claim. He couldn't very well go around firing anyone who spoke badly of her. She would deserve the nasty comments, anyway. She did have sex with her boss, on his desk no less! And then he'd gone all Neanderthal on her at the Recognition Dinner in front of everyone. That kind of thing always garnered catty comments. Still, she remembered sadly, it was a moot point. She wouldn't be working there any longer than it would take to type up a formal resignation.

Tess could never work for Kevin and watch him with other women. And she was sure there would be more women. She didn't have a monopoly on him. But, to see Kevin with someone besides her, it would be akin to a slow death. It had been different before—hard but manageable. Now that she knew his passion first hand, she could never go to work every day and maintain a discreet distance. So the future didn't matter. Only this moment mattered.

With that in mind, she gave him a flirty wink and murmured, "I love that you're willing to slay my dragons, but I'm sure it won't be necessary."

He puffed out his chest and said, "Anytime you have a dragon you need slain, just call Sir Kevin."

Tess laughed, pushed out of his arms, and moved towards the sink. "Now show me what you want me to do. I'm starving."

Kevin rolled his eyes and said, "Why do I get the feeling I just lost that round?"

Tess began to wash her hands, but she could feel Kevin's eyes traveling over her body. She turned to see if she was right. She was. He just stood there, staring at her, his gaze a hot lick down the length of her.

"What?"

He shook his head. "I can't seem to get enough of your delectable ass. Those heels and that dress are a lethal combination, baby. And you have the longest, sexiest legs I've ever seen." Then he stopped at her feet and frowned. "But I want you to change out of those clothes and get something more comfortable on. Those shoes have got to be killing you, because I know damn well you aren't used to wearing heels. And if you put up a fight this time, I'll undress you myself and skip the damned meal. Not exactly a big sacrifice on my part."

She looked down at her dress, noticing for the first time how rumpled she looked. Well, that was his fault for carting her around like she was a sack of potatoes.

Chapter 7

Kevin entwined his fingers in hers and tugged her down the hall. "You can wear something of mine since you don't have anything with you."

She stayed silent beside him, but when they reached the bedroom she started forward.

"Where do you think you're going?"

She turned her big brown eyes on him and said, "I'm going to go change."

Amused, Kevin crossed his arms over his chest and leaned against the doorframe. "Would you like to know which drawer the clothes are in first?"

"Oh, right." Tess turned three shades of red.

What was going on inside that fascinating mind of hers now? Kevin mused. Had he done something wrong again? He'd been working with Tess long enough to know when something wasn't right. Her brows would pull together and her cheeks would turn rosy. Same as they were now.

He walked over to her, knowing only that he needed to touch her and try to reassure her. She was clasping her hands together in front of her, as if to protect herself. He gently separated them and twined their fingers together once more. It seemed such a natural thing to do. Amazing how well she fit with him. How could he have been so blind to that before? She belonged with him. If she didn't know that already, she soon would.

He bent down to look her in the eyes. "Why are you blushing, babe?" he asked softly. "Did I say something wrong?"

"No, of course not." Tess was quick to reassure him, but then she ruined it by blushing further.

Kevin brought her hand to his lips and brushed her knuckles with a feathery kiss. Then, without looking up, he whispered, "Don't lie to me, Tess. Don't ever lie to me."

He watched her take a deep breath before saying, "When you asked me to go change, I looked down at myself and figured you were having second thoughts about tonight, and maybe even about what we've already done."

Kevin could not believe what he was hearing. He tugged her across the room without saying a word, loving that she trusted him enough to follow without question. When they reached the freestanding mirror, her tiny hand still in his much larger one, Tess faltered.

"What are you doing, Kevin? I already have a fair idea of what I look like right now. I don't need it thrown in my face."

He rolled his eyes at her irritated tone. "Do you?" He pushed her in front of him even as she stiffened her shoulders. "Look at your reflection, Tess."

She did, albeit reluctantly.

He bent and feathered her ear with his lips. "Let me tell you what I see, that way there won't be any more ridiculous guesses." He continued kissing her, just barely touching. He allowed her scent to fill his lungs. Christ, she smelled good. She had an elusive barely-there smell that tempted a man to get closer.

He'd already discovered that she had a particularly sensitive spot behind her ear, and the elegant line of her neck got his special attention too. He raised his head and held her gaze in the mirror.

"I'm not a poetic guy, Tess. You've worked with me long enough to know that sweet romantic words don't come easily to me."

She nodded at him in the mirror in agreement.

"So I'll keep it simple for both our sakes. Yesterday, when you left me, you had the look of a woman who'd been very thoroughly loved, babe." His eyes heated with a possessive fury that he'd never felt before. "Right now, standing here with that sexy painted-on dress, you look good enough to eat. I wanted John in a casket for touching you, for holding you. It made me crazy seeing that."

Tess's eyes grew big and her pretty mouth formed an O. Kevin clenched his jaw, attempting to tame the need to take her all over again. He stared at her wrinkled silk dress and tousled hair and half moaned in predatory delight.

"All this long hair, and this wrinkled dress," he said and stroked his hands down her sides until he was gripping her hips. "And your pretty cheeks are showing signs of a slight whisker burn, I think." He winced. "Damn, I'm truly sorry about that part." Her skin was too delicate for him to be so careless.

He gave her a crooked half-smile. "If I'd known I was going to drag you back to my apartment and ravish you, I would have taken more care in shaving this morning."

He took one hand from her hip and stroked the reddened cheek with his thumb, watching as she went all soft and drowsy with arousal. Uh-oh, he'd better bring this to a close before they both got sidetracked and forgot about dinner. He'd already skipped lunch, because he'd been too agitated with thoughts of Tess. He wasn't about to neglect Tess's health too. They needed to eat, then he would take his time enjoying her supple body, he thought with lusty intent. But there was something even more important to settle first.

"Tess?" he said, then waited until he had her full attention before continuing. "Why don't you know how pretty you are?"

She blinked rapidly at him and he knew he'd hit a nerve when her face practically closed down. He wasn't going to let her do that, not anymore. "I look at you and instantly I'm hard as hell."

"The clothes. It's just the red dress, and the shoes," she said.

He shook his head. "I don't think so. The clothes only help to show off what you've had hidden from me for the past five years."

She started to protest, but he wasn't having it.

"Let's not forget I've seen you without the clothes, Tess. And believe me when I say that men don't care about the pretty trappings. What a man wants, what I want, is to see you in nothing at all." He stroked her hip, moving his hand around until it was spread wide over her bottom. "As much as humanly possible, in fact." He winked at her furious blush in the mirror and said, "As far as I can see, you in the buff ought to be how I start my day as well as finish it."

"You're kidding."

He thought about it for a moment, warming to the idea, even as he massaged her bottom. "No. I mean it. Every morning when I wake up, I'll turn over and find you next to me... naked, warm, soft. Then when I crawl into bed at night, I get to wrap my arms around your luscious tits and cuddle up to your curvy bottom. Mmm, yeah, that'd be real nice."

Tess's mouth was hanging open in shock. Her innocence was such a refreshing change for Kevin. None of the women he'd been with had blushed in the way Tess was doing now. She was such a rare treasure and yet she had no clue.

"Yep, hell of an idea." He ran a finger down her cheek to her neck and then over her breast. He felt her nipple harden instantly for him. Such sensitivity was another sweet quality about her. He'd barely touched her. It had him asking a question he hadn't really intended to ask. Yet. "When was the last time a man made love to you, baby?"

"It's been a while," she hedged.

His eyes turned hard as he stared at her in the reflection. "Not good enough, Tess. How long?"

Wrangling an answer out of her was proving to be a challenge. But Kevin never backed down from something he wanted.

"Um, over a year?" Tess squeaked out.

It was clear she hadn't wanted to admit exactly how long. But she could never tell a lie worth a damn. Still, her answer was too vague. He wanted more.

"You mean you aren't sure?" Kevin said, trying hard to imagine going that long without sex. He couldn't. It was impossible to even conceive. Why would anyone want to?

Kevin saw her eyes close, and she took a deep breath before answering. "It's been five years for me, Kevin, and I wasn't really all that into it even then. The last time wasn't worth repeating." She shrugged. "So I didn't."

Kevin very nearly choked. Five years? Damn. If he'd known that before hand, it would have made him too nervous. Talk about performance anxiety. Then again, if he had known, he would have made it better for her, like in a bed for starters. God, he was a cad.

That's when it hit him.

Five years. That was how long she'd been working for him. Could the length of time be more than a coincidence? The last guy must have been a bungling idiot for Tess to decide abstinence was better. Again, he was thankful she'd come to him, instead of some other lucky yokel.

"Tess, if I'd known that I never would have taken you like I did yesterday. I would have brought you back here first, been more gentle with you, baby."

"I can't believe what you're saying!" She whipped around and grabbed hold of his shoulders. "For the record, so there's no ridiculous guessing, it couldn't possibly have been any better, and I didn't want gentle."

Kevin felt her words all the way to his groin. He knew she had enjoyed herself, but it never hurt to have confirmation. Men needed that as much as women did; they just weren't always willing to ask. Male pride and all that bullshit.

Suddenly, a thought occurred to him. "We still need food. If we don't eat we won't have any energy, and we're going to damn well need energy." He could feel more than see Tess protesting, but he wouldn't let her distract him from his chosen course. He wanted her tummy as satisfied as the rest of her body.

Kevin kissed her, keeping it short and sweet, lest he get waylaid. "You freshen up, or whatever you women do, and I'll go make us something to eat." He went to a tall dresser and opened a couple of drawers. Grabbing a t-shirt and boxers, he tossed them onto the bed. "Wear those."

Tess picked up the shorts. "I can help you cook. Just give me a minute."

Kevin shook his head. He wanted to treat her, which was another new sensation for him. Usually when he was with a woman he was ready to either crawl into bed and have sex or send them on their merry way so he could get some sleep. Now he was starting to see the beauty of spending time with a woman who was still wearing her clothes.

"No, you cater to me all day long, Tess. Let me do this for you. I'm not saying it'll be anything extravagant. I'm not a great cook." Now he wished he had let his sister Bella show him a few things in the kitchen the way she'd wanted to a couple of months back. At the time, he had insisted that he knew enough to keep from starving, and all the rest was just nonsense. He'd have to give Bella a call next week and ask her—or beg rather—for a few pointers, so he could impress Tess and prove to her that he was more than a good lay.

In the meantime, Kevin worked to hide his smile as he saw Tess's eyebrows scrunch up. She was confused by him. Good, now she knew how he felt.

"Okay…" she finally said.

"Just grilled cheese sandwiches and a salad. Work for you?" She nodded and he gave her one last peck on her forehead before striding from the room.

Tess was lost in this new foreplay. She'd figured Kevin for a let's-get-busy kind of guy, but now he wanted to feed her. And it seemed that no matter what she said, he was determined to have his own way. Oh, well, she supposed there were worse things in life than a hunky, dark-haired, blue-eyed man cooking dinner for you.

When they had stood in front of the mirror, Tess couldn't take her gaze away from Kevin's. She'd felt spellbound. He was so intense, so male, yet so gentle and sweet.

He'd asked when the last time she'd made love was and she had wanted to say never. That would've been closer to the truth, because she'd never been in love before now. But he wasn't really asking that, so instead she'd kept that to herself.

Tess hated the feelings of inadequacy that had trapped her for her entire life. The whole reason for going through her transformation was to shed that awful skin and show the true, daring self that lay beneath.

Maybe this red dress was just another skin.

Quickly she went to the bed and unzipped her dress.

As she did this, she looked around now, assessing his bedroom against what she now knew of him. Her gaze settled on the room's focal point, a king-sized four-poster bed. It was so big and inviting, with its plushy, cream-colored down comforter. Then she transferred her appraisal back to the freestanding mirror, cherry wood like the bed, and its matching dresser. There was also an overstuffed cream-colored chair sitting by a window, obviously big enough for two people. Suddenly, Tess had a vision of her sitting astride Kevin's lap as he made slow, sweet love to her.

Yep, she was definitely getting in too deep.

She sighed, then sat on the edge of the big bed and slipped out of her shoes, grimacing. She wasn't entirely sure she'd be wearing those torturous things ever again, regardless of how sexy they made her look and feel.

She stood up and took off the dress. Snagging the black boxers that Kevin had gotten out for her, she slid into them, feeling a thrill go up her spine at the notion that she was wearing Kevin's clothes. It was a heady thought. She put the huge grey t-shirt on next. It nearly swallowed her up, but it was comfortable and it smelled of Kevin.

She felt silly, but she did what the hair stylist had suggested and flipped her head forward, finger combing it before flipping it back again. Hmm, not bad. It did look sort of sexy and tousled. She went to the mirror and looked again. Now, in his t-shirt and boxers, she looked more like a woman who had just spent the night with a man, making love into the wee hours of the morning. The thought appealed to her greatly. It was politically incorrect, but it was true nonetheless— clothes could make a person feel and act more self-assured.

Tess suspected this new sense of self was a combination of finally shucking years of self-pity and of having Kevin treat her with such loving care. She no longer felt like she was trying to be someone else, just that she was trying to be more like the real Tess Marley.

Well, she thought nervously, Kevin might see her like this and still want to give her the let's be friends spiel. But she at least felt like she'd accomplished a middle ground between the temptress and the timid. It was time to go show the handsome cook her new found confidence.

Chapter 8

Who would have thought that a thirty-two year old confirmed bachelor would actually enjoy cooking dinner for a woman, all the while plotting how he was going to convince her to marry him? Because that was exactly what he wanted. To marry Tess and make her Mrs. Kevin Haines. He'd come to the realization that he loved her when he was staring at her in the mirror. It had hit him like a ton of bricks.

He'd been so blind.

She was the one constant in his life, his reason for coming to work everyday. When she hadn't shown up on Friday morning, he'd been thrown for a loop. Even after she'd arrived and taken over his office with her allure, he'd convinced himself that his desire was only for sex. It had taken seeing her dancing with John to make him see reason. She wasn't going to sit around and wait on his dumb ass forever. A woman like Tess wouldn't spend her life alone and unloved.

He wanted to be the one to love her. But she knew him too well. She'd spent five years watching him seduce and discard women, after all. Who could blame her if she decided he wasn't good for the long haul?

So first he had to convince her that he wasn't such a bad catch.

And it started tonight. First, he would fill her belly with food and fill her needs sexually. Then maybe he had at least a small chance of making her see he could be better than he'd been before, that he could make her happy.

He had been so sure that he knew what women needed—just a night of loving with a man to see to their pleasures and ease their sexual cravings and then to send them on their way, satisfied. Now he was starting to see that sexual desire was only a small fraction of it. With an intelligent woman like Tess, he needed all the ammo he could get to make her see that there was more to their relationship than satisfying cravings.

He had just taken the second grilled cheese out of the pan when he saw Tess enter the room from the corner of his eye. He put the sandwich on the plate and looked up in greeting.

"Christ," he mumbled, and then his mouth went dry at the vision in front of him.

Tess dressed up was an exquisite feast, exciting to be sure. But Tess dressed down, now that was something else entirely. She looked adorable in his clothes, and Kevin wanted to see a lot more of that in the future. Then she fidgeted, and he saw the way she twitched her ankles uncomfortably. He went to her, taking her hand and anchoring her to him.

"You okay, babe?"

She waved him away. "My feet are a little sore. You were right, I'm not used to those shoes yet."

And she would never get used to them, Kevin thought, because he wasn't letting her wear them again. At least not in public. Just the thought had him grinding his teeth. The fuck-me shoes were for his viewing alone.

He led her to the breakfast bar. "Sit down and be prepared to eat your fill." When she was settled in, he went back to the counter and got their plates.

As he placed them on the bar and sat, he frowned down at the blandness of it. He wasn't really kidding when he had said it wouldn't be anything to write home about. Grilled cheese sandwiches, salads and colas were not the way to charm your woman. Sheepishly, he said, "I didn't know if you liked regular or diet pop, but all I had was regular."

"I like regular just fine."

He leaned over and pressed his lips to hers. Kevin hoped his possessive kiss communicated to her how powerfully he felt about her. He couldn't stand to be sitting next to her and not kiss her.

His voice was a rough thread of sound when he finally released her mouth. "You're very sexy, Tess."

"Oh, uh, thank you," Tess said feebly. Then, as if remembering her manners, she said, "The meal looks wonderful, thank you." Kevin was mesmerized when after taking a quick bite her face lit with pleasure and she licked her lips. "Mmm. That's good."

"Well, it's nothing great, but it'll give us what we need, energy." He grinned lecherously at her eagerness. Damn, she was cute. "Later, I'll give you a foot massage that's out of this world." At least he hoped it would be out of this world, massaging women's feet was new territory, like everything else tonight.

Instantly, she was refusing him. "Oh no, Kevin, really. My feet will be fine by tomorrow I'm sure."

Hadn't anyone ever pampered this woman? No, he decided, probably not. He didn't know much about her upbringing, but he knew enough to know she didn't have any brothers or sisters. From what little she'd said, her parents barely even knew she existed.

He touched her cheek and spoke in a soft, coaxing voice. "I've never given a woman a massage before, Tess." Her mouth dropped open. "I know that's hard to believe. Lord knows, I've been with plenty of women."

"So I've noticed," she said dryly.

A spark of something that looked a little like jealousy lit her eyes, giving him hope. "It's true, though, baby. You wouldn't deny me this opportunity, would you?"

"How can I say no? Besides, I wouldn't want to disappoint you. After all, you're the boss."

Her voice was wickedly teasing and Kevin had a sudden image of sweeping her off her feet, plopping her onto the breakfast bar and making love right there in the kitchen.

Eat, he reminded himself once more.

They ate the rest of their meal in silence. It seemed that neither one of them wanted to delay their night for even one more second. Once finished, Tess had to laugh when Kevin haphazardly tossed plates and silverware into the sink, insisting that they could wait. He led her back to his bedroom and she felt almost more nervous now than she had at the office. It was more personal being in his home. In his bed.

When she lay down in the center of the bed, Tess was finally able to find out that the huge thing was every bit as comfortable as it looked. Kevin slipped out of the room and into an adjoining bathroom, where he retrieved what appeared to be a tube of cream.

"Close your eyes, Tess," he said, and she did. It was scary how much she trusted this man. "I can't guarantee that this massage cream will smell as pretty as you do, but it should do the job."

Then he quit talking and slid his hands over her toes. Oh, God, his touch was magical on her. How was it possible that he'd never done this before? She thought she moaned a few times, but soon she was completely lost in how good it felt and had no idea what she did.

"Kevin, that feels heavenly." He mumbled something and she whispered, "I could seriously get used to this."

"I'm counting on it."

Her eyes flew open, and she raised her head to look back at him. He was seated at the side of the bed, staring at her with such feral heat darkening his blue eyes. "Why are you counting on it?"

His hands stopped on her foot, and he stared at her for so long it made her squirm. Then, slowly, he recapped the tube of cream and tossed it aside, never taking his eyes off her. He climbed further onto the bed and straddled her thighs, careful to keep most of his weight off her. She had been lying with her arms down at her sides, but now Kevin was raising them up and over her head. Twining his fingers through hers, he held her immobile with his hands and eyes. He looked serious, too serious. She had the awful feeling that her heart was about to be crushed.

"What is it, Kevin?" she asked nervously.

"Both times we've had sex, I was the one in control," he said.

She could feel her body flush all over as she remembered every wonderful second.

"But this time I want you to take the lead," he added.

"Oh," Tess murmured reluctantly. Be in charge of their sexual satisfaction? She didn't know if she was uninhibited enough for that yet. But for Kevin, she would do just about anything.

"I can hear how nervous you are, but don't worry, we won't do anything that makes you uncomfortable. Okay, baby?"

She hesitated only a second before whispering, "Okay."

Kevin moved off her and stood beside the bed. He made quick work of his clothes and was soon naked, his erection level with her body. If she moved a scant inch to her left and turned on her side, she'd have him between her soft lips.

"I was hard throughout dinner, now I feel like I'm going to explode." As if unsure if he trusted himself not to close the gap for her, he said roughly, "What would you like me to do, Tess?"

She knew leaving it all up to her wasn't easy for him. It wasn't in Kevin's nature to relinquish command. She was glad he was giving her a chance, because Tess needed this from him. In order for her to see herself as the desirable woman that she was, she needed to not only take off the shell, but destroy the damned thing completely.

Tess sat up and whipped her shirt up and over her head. She tossed it to the floor and watched Kevin's nostrils flare. His fists clenched and unclenched at his sides. She couldn't believe he was willing to let her run the show when he'd always been such a take-charge guy. Well, if Kevin could sail into unfamiliar territory, then she certainly could as well.

Tess left the bed. Now she stood on the opposite side from Kevin. "Lie down on your back," she instructed him a little nervously. She shimmied the soft fabric of the boxers down her legs, thrilling at the way his incredible blue eyes watched her every movement, even as he did as she instructed.

She was left in her red bra, which she decided not to remove just yet. She needed the scrap of lace for armor.

"I can't believe you danced with John," Kevin said, his eyes blazing. "You are so fucking hot. Any man who sees you is going to want you under them, Tess. And I'd have to kill them."

She almost lost her composure right then at another revealing confession of jealousy. But, seeing him laid out for her, he really was her jungle lover come to life. The sight was enough for her to stay in the game. "And you are magnificent, Kevin. So big, so hard, and so mine."

He smiled arrogantly at her, but her gaze was glued to his engorged cock. It made her mouth water. She badly wanted to taste him, and it was her show, so....

Tess heard him emit a low growl when she boldly straddled his thighs. Her voice came out husky and raw as she whispered, "I want you in my mouth, Kevin. I want to feel your dick on my tongue. I would love to play with you for awhile, but I don't think I can wait. Okay with you?" His jaw clenched as he nodded. With obvious effort, he folded his arms beneath his head and watched and waited, letting her call the shots. It turned her on, knowing his hot gaze never left her face.

Tess swept her hair to one side and bent down until her breasts touched his thick, strong thighs and his hardness rested against her closed mouth. She kept her lips pressed together as she used her hand to rub her lace-covered breasts against his erection. When she was rewarded with a drop of moisture, she opened her mouth and licked the sticky fluid, careful to use only her tongue, teasing a groan from him.

Tess grinned at Kevin's intense expression. She felt brazen and wanton. "I want to watch you climax, Kevin. I want to taste your hot come on my tongue, swallow it down my throat."

She grasped him and squeezed his length. Kevin cursed, and she closed her eyes, concentrating on the task of pleasuring her lover, sucking and licking, taking as much of him into the warm, wet cavern of her mouth as she could. Her left hand squeezed and fondled his balls while her right held him steady for her eager mouth.

His fingers dug into her scalp, forcing her to take more of him. A moan coursed from within her only to stay trapped in her throat. She had no idea that giving him head would have her clit throbbing and her nipples fairly begging to be rubbed and teased. It was such sweet torture. There was a wild pleasure in knowing that she had the ability to make Kevin lose control.

It was making her wet. Turning her on. Holding him inside her mouth, being the one in control of his satisfaction, it was all a powerful sort of fore-play for her.

Within seconds, Tess felt the pressure building inside Kevin. His thighs flexed underneath her and his balls tightened under her touch. Swiftly, she opened her eyes, unwilling to miss a thing. He was looking at her with such a raw expression, so possessive and male. Tess let her tongue coast over the swollen head of his penis one last time, pushing him over the jagged edge of reason.

Tess nearly winced when Kevin's fingers tightened in her hair, pulling almost painfully, shouting as he filled her mouth with his seed. It was so electrifying and passionate to have him watching her as she swallowed every last bit of his salty fluid.

She straightened and then sat on the edge of the bed, swiped the back of her hand across her mouth, and grinned. "Did you like that, Kevin?"

"Hell, yes." Kevin's voice was just a husky thread of sound in the room. Then he reached his hand to her and pulled her forward onto his rock hard body before locking his arms around her and twisting in a blur of motion. Now, Tess lay beneath him. He cupped her mound protectively and said, "My turn." Tess shivered with deep, hot anticipation.

Kevin began by dragging her bra straps downward, baring the tops of her breasts, and letting her nipples spring free. To Tess's disappointment, however, Kevin never touched her breasts. He simply moved to her mound. For a long moment, he stared at her, as if committing her body to memory, before parting her dewy lips with his thumbs and sucking on her. She moaned incoherent sounds of need and her hips lifted off the bed with the first contact of his tongue to her distended clit. His gaze flew to hers, watching as he played with her, never once allowing his tongue or fingers to enter her.

Oh, God, it wasn't enough. She wanted his fingers inside her sheath. She wanted to feel him stretching her with the heavy weight of his shaft. She squirmed around on top of the bed and begged, "Please, Kevin."

His expression was rife with intent. "I know the feeling, Tess, believe me." He took her clit between his thumb and forefinger and squeezed lightly, making her moan louder. "You want more, but you feel torn between what you should do, and what you want to do. Is that it, baby?"

She nodded, unsure if her voice would work. He slipped his finger into her then, as if rewarding her good behavior. He stroked her channel with a single talented finger, bringing her to the very edge of sanity. Tess was so close to coming, yet paradise sat just out of reach. She didn't know what to do or how to tell him that she needed more.

"That's what I've been going through for the past five years. Frustrating as hell, let me tell you. I knew what I wanted to do, but I knew I shouldn't. And all your signals were telling me to stay away. Keep it professional. You've been making me nuts, Tess." Kevin's deep timbre paused as he wiggled a second finger in. He pushed deep inside of her tight opening, stretching and filling her. She wanted to say something, deny his claim, but she was lost to the feelings of her body. "But you've had it your way, baby," Kevin warned. "It's my turn now."

She wanted to tell him something, but then his mouth opened around her breast, sucking hard, biting gently, eliciting another series of moans from her. Her thoughts scattered.

Kevin spent long moments on one breast, before moving to the other saying, "Christ, you have incredible tits." Then he gave her a crazed expression and rasped, "No more dancing with other men. Not ever again, baby." He pulled his fingers free of her aching sex and put them both into his mouth, sucking on her juices. She watched him watching her and when he was through, he hooked her legs in the crooks of his elbows, spreading her wide. "I like seeing you this way, Tess. So sweetly open and ready for me."

"I'm ready for you, Kevin. Now. I need you now!" Her voice was husky and raw, her entire body shaking with desire. Kevin reached over and opened his bedside drawer. Putting on the condom seemed to take an eternity, but eventually she felt the head of his erection pushing against her opening. He stroked a hand down the valley between her breasts and then rested a palm against her belly.

"Relax and let me in, baby."

She closed her eyes and willed her body to do whatever Kevin wanted. Then she heard the velvety sound of Kevin's voice murmuring his approval.

"You're beautiful, Tess. I love having you this way. Everything I want is right here at my fingertips." He stroked a finger over her pink folds, eliciting another moan from somewhere deep within. "All creamy heat and anxiousness."

She trembled at his words, and then he pressed forward, burying himself completely. She squirmed against him, glorying in the feel of his big, solid body on top of hers. Using her hands, she gripped his hips and tried to pull him more fully into her. Tess needed him to move, she ached to feel his body hammering into hers.

He chuckled at her untamed behavior. "Take it easy, baby, we've got all night." He leaned down to kiss her then, forcing her legs further apart.

The kiss went on forever. It was demanding and hot as he pushed his tongue into the dark recesses of her mouth to toy with her tongue. Only as Tess sighed in surrender did he begin to move his lower body.

His actions were gentle and deliberate, but Tess wanted so much more. She wanted it all. She pushed her mound into him and Kevin's eyes shown with carnal intent. He released her legs, so that he could interlace her fingers with his and raise her arms high above her head. It left her completely vulnerable to him. His mouth clamped down onto her shoulder and sucked hard, creating a purplish bruise.

He raised his head then, staring at the spot he'd left on her body and snarled, "There. Now you do have my mark."

Tess was shocked speechless and so blissfully close to coming. He licked the darkened skin with a gentle swipe of his tongue and then began moving inside of her again. His thrusts starting slow, then moving faster until he was fairly driving her body into the mattress with the force.

Tess flew apart, screaming his name as she climaxed. Kevin went wild, fucking her as if he couldn't get enough. He was a glorious sight to see. His heavily muscled hips pumped against hers. His body glistened with his sweat, teeth gritted as if barely holding himself in check.

Her breasts bounced as she squirmed and bucked up and into his groin. Just when she thought her body couldn't possibly take any more, another orgasm took her. The pleasures he pulled out of her seemed never-ending.

Kevin shouted and ground her into the mattress as he rocketed out of control. His eyes and body pinned her in place while he filled her with his hot come.

Drifting back down to earth, Tess's first thought was of how quickly and easily she had become his willing sex slave. And she didn't even care. She'd do anything for Kevin. In fact, it seemed like a great way to start each morning- with him filling her up and taking her to heaven.

He released her hands, cupped the back of her head and kissed her deep. She let out a soft sigh when he broke the connection. Kevin left her to dispose of the condom, then came back to the bed and lay down next to her. She allowed him to drag her limp body on top of him, using her as a human blanket.

"Poor little thing. Wore yourself out, didn't you?"

She didn't have the strength to answer his remark. All she managed was a sigh.

Kevin pulled the sheet over their bodies and smoothed her hair off her cheek. "Sleep for now, baby. When you wake, we're going to talk."

Seconds before sleep engulfed her, she felt Kevin press a light kiss to her forehead.

Chapter 9

Two hours later, Tess woke in the warm cocoon of Kevin's embrace. She was careful not to wake him when she freed herself and got up to use the bathroom. But when she slipped back into bed beside him wearing his shirt, he was awake and frowning.

"What?" she said.

"I love your modesty, baby, but eventually you'll get used to me and you won't need the shirt."

He rolled over until he was on top of her, gaining her full attention instantly. A soft smile curved her lips and her body melted against his. He was going to take her again, and her body eagerly responded. But he didn't pull her closer.

"I've been patient long enough, Tess. It's time we had a talk."

His words sent a shiver of fear through her. She didn't think she wanted to hear what he had to say.

"I was going to make love to you once more before I said this, but I don't think it can wait. I don't think it would be wise to wait."

Tess's passion dried up and she felt her smile disappear. Oh God, it was worse than she thought. He was growing bored with her already. Why had she thought she could keep his interest? Tears burned, threatening to spill over, but Tess wouldn't let him see her acting like a sniveling baby. She didn't want him feeling pity for her, and she definitely didn't want him thinking he'd made a mistake by giving in to her seduction. So, she cut him off at the pass.

"I know what you're going to say, Kevin."

He blinked, as if surprised. "You do?"

Tess willed her stomach to settle and her heart to calm. "Yes," she said, her voice quivering, "and it's okay. I knew that this would only be sex. I'm a big girl, Kevin. You don't have to worry about me getting too attached." He looked about to say something so she hastily added, "Besides, I like this new vamp persona of mine." She tried for a flirtatious smile but was pretty sure it fell flat. "And I'm thinking there may be other unsuspecting males that I can try it out on." There, that ought to set his mind at ease that she wasn't going to get clingy.

Up until that moment, Tess's hands had been resting idly beside her. But very swiftly, Kevin twined their hands together and raised them above her head, stretching and forcing her body into a submissive position. His voice went hard as steel and his eyes were cold when he said, "Like hell you will," and then he was kissing her.

It was a hard, punishing kiss. Tess thought that she really should be pushing Kevin away, but it just felt too good, and he was all at once greedy and territorial. Tess's blood heated and the juncture between her thighs grew moist. His musky scent filled her nostrils, and she was a goner.

Just as abruptly as the kiss had started, it stopped. Kevin lifted his head away from hers, his eyes piercing as he demanded, "You want this to be nothing more than a good fuck, Tess?" His eyes snared her gaze, daring her to look away. "Damn it, is this about John again?"

He appeared ready to combust and Tess knew she had to set him straight on at least one issue. "This is not about John. I told you he's just a friend and I meant it. Besides, don't you want this to be about sex? That's what you said at the office." She was more lost than ever. She knew how she felt. She was in love with Kevin, but she had no clue how Kevin felt.

He frowned at her. Unexpectedly his anger evaporated and his face softened. "You think I want you just for sex," he stated, as if just grasping her meaning. "A weekend of sweaty bodies and tangled sheets. Is that it, Tess?"

Tess's voice came out softer, more cautious. "Kevin, you never get serious." Rushing to reassure him, she said, "And I understand that, believe me, I do."

"I never did before, that much is true, but it's different now." His mouth went crooked. "You're different, baby."

She blinked in surprise. "I am?" she said suspiciously.

"Damn right. I've never cooked for any woman but you, Tess. And you can bet that I've never wanted to massage a woman's feet—not when there were other, more interesting body parts demanding my attention." He raked her body with his darkened gaze, grinning. "I've never, ever wanted to spend an entire weekend with a woman." He released one of her hands and smoothed her hair away from her face. "What does that tell you, honey?"

"I'm not sure. I haven't had enough experience with men to know where this is all leading, Kevin," she said, getting frustrated by the minute.

Yeah, he liked that part, her lack of experience, Kevin thought with possessive satisfaction. "That's something I'm truly happy about, by the way." He touched the side of her face, her lips, until he reached her breasts. He let his thumb coast over her nipple and felt it harden through the cotton of his shirt. He groaned, ready for her all over again. He seemed to have a permanent hard-on where Tess was concerned.

"I'm in love with you, Tess."

Her eyes grew round and her mouth dropped open. "Am I dreaming?"

Well, Kevin thought, he had her attention now. Time to lay it all out on the line and hope he didn't get his heart drop-kicked in the process.

"No, you aren't dreaming. I realized my feelings when I saw you with John. I knew if I didn't get off my ass and do something, you'd be swept right away from me." His voice came out rough as he told her how he truly felt. "You've been in my life for five years and I'm just now realizing that I'm in love with you." And he wanted to kick his own ass for not seeing it before now.

"The clothes," she squeaked out.

He shook his head, knowing what she meant. "No, babe. It's way more than that. It just took you breaking out of your cozy, little shell to make me see you for who you really are."

He played with her other nipple, enjoying the way her breathing grew more rapid and her chocolate brown eyes turned warm. "You've kept yourself wrapped so tightly that you practically had a neon sign that said: Back Off." He moved his hand down her body and spread it out over her concave belly. "I want to spend the rest of my life with you, Tess. I saw the woman beneath the dowdy appearance and I desperately wanted to know what made her tick."

"Oh, Kevin." Tess started to cry and Kevin trembled. He could handle anything, but not Tess in tears.

"Why are you crying, baby?" Kevin asked worriedly, wiping a tear off her cheek. "Tell me."

"Because I very nearly left Invision. I was going to quit. And because I love you, too," Tess said, her voice full of hope.

Kevin let out a breath that he hadn't even known he was holding. She loved him! Whew, talk about sweating bullets. "Thank God I told you tonight instead of waiting. But either way, I never would have let you get away from me. I was all prepared to kidnap you, just in case. But that still doesn't explain the tears."

"I've been in love with you since the day I started working for you. But you were strict about not getting involved with coworkers, and I was too shy to do anything about my feelings." She stared at him questioningly. "And since you never seemed to see me in that way...." She let the statement hang.

"You still want to know why now? How I could have fallen in love so fast?"

"Yeah. Tell me."

Kevin cupped her chin in his palm. "You think it's impossible, don't you? For me to love you?"

Tess only shrugged, causing Kevin to frown.

"Who told you you weren't lovable?" he exclaimed. "Tell me! Is that why you've been hiding behind bulky clothes and heavy glasses, Tess? Why don't you see how pretty you are?"

"My mother," Tess responded after a few minutes of quiet contemplation.

Tess's tiny voice spoke volumes to Kevin. Clearly, the issue of her mother was a very touchy subject, but he wasn't about to let her hide from it. Not anymore.

"What about her?" He prompted.

Tess licked her lips, and the innocently seductive action very nearly had Kevin losing the thread of the conversation. However, her next words had the effect of a dash of cold water to Kevin's libido.

"She used to say that I'd do good to accept the fact that I was no raving beauty," Tess stuttered out. "She would tell me that I should try hard in academics, because a woman with less than average looks couldn't hope for a man to come along and sweep her off her feet." Kevin noticed her voice quivered a little as she attempted to defend her mother's insensitive remarks. "I suppose, in her own way, she didn't mean to say that I was ugly, but when I started dating and all the guys would grow bored so quick, it seemed to back up everything she said."

Kevin had his own thoughts about Tess's mother and her nasty barbs. None of them were kind. Those comments had been a devastating blow to Tess's self-esteem, and that alone was enough to arouse his temper. Hell, it was no wonder she had played down her natural beauty for so many years. And the men she'd dated were clearly blind fools.

He leaned down and kissed her forehead, determined to erase the pain that Tess's thoughtless mother had caused. "For the record, you are definitely a raving beauty, Tess. You can believe I damn well did think about you in that way, too. More than I should have probably." Tenderly, he murmured against her cheek, "And I think I've been in love with you for a long time, but we were both too busy being professional and proper."

He kissed her lips, unable to help himself. "You hid away in your heavy brown suits, Tess, and I hid behind my title. It took John hugging you, dancing with you, to make me see that I would lose you if I didn't do something, and quick." He nibbled at her fuller lower lip, loving the way she tasted, smelled, responded so restlessly.

"What's all this about John anyway?"

"His arms were around you, Tess." Kevin cringed, seeing the pleasure on John's face all over again. "He was holding you, dammit, and all I could think about was that it should be me holding you, moving to the rhythm of the music, feeling your pretty tits against my chest. That it should be me paying you compliments that would make your eyes light up with such delight." He paused, then admitted, "Well, that and how good it would feel to grind John's face into the floor."

"Oh."

Kevin laughed at her reply. "Now, there's just one last thing to settle before I move on with my diabolical plans for your luscious bod."

Kevin loved the giggle that Tess couldn't suppress, but it was the husky, "Okay," that had all his muscles pumping hard.

Christ, he reveled in her willingness. More nervous than he'd ever been in his life, Kevin sucked in a breath and went for broke. "Will you marry me, Tess?" Do it or die trying, that had always been his motto. And if she refused him, he would surely die.

"This has to be a dream, because there's no way this is truly happening."

"It's not a dream. I'm achingly hard and proposing marriage."

Tess started crying again, even as she was busily nodding her head. Happiness swamped Kevin and his voice turned harsh with emotion. He kissed away her tears one at a time. "Tears of joy, I hope?"

She nodded again, the tears mixing with laughter. "Accepting you as my husband will forever be the most wonderful thing I've ever done."

"Okay, tears of joy I can handle." Then he got off her and left the bed altogether. Kevin stood beside her, staring down at his future bride. He wanted to shout to the world that she was his, now and forever.

Soon the fact that he and Tess were an item would be all over the office. Kevin grinned like an idiot. Knowing that Tess was now off-limits was sure to have the hopeful men at Invision crying into their beer. And instead of trying so hard to keep his personal and professional life separate, he had just happily mixed the two. To his surprise, the thought didn't make him uncomfortable as it once would have.

"You know what?" Tess murmured.

What, baby?"

"I feel like I just won a battle. A battle for my heart and my future."

Kevin dipped his head and kissed her. He liked it that she thought she'd won, but Tess was getting far too serious for his liking. He wanted to see that sultry glow lighting up her eyes again. So he let his gaze roam over her body, looking at her from head to toe, then Kevin smiled sinfully and whispered, "So, how are you with bondage, baby?"

It was Tess's shy yet naughty smile that got him. Oh, yeah, life with Tess was sure to be one hell of a ride.

About the Author:

Anne lives in a small town way out in the middle of no-where-ville. She is a gorgeous blonde with wonderful curves and a money tree in the backyard. She never wants for anything and she always loves everyone. Of course, Anne is a mere figment. A ghostly figure that pops in and out like a drive-by author. Her wicked imagination will bring you fantasies and erotic delights that will leave you panting and grabbing the ice water.

Enter the Hero

❧◦✽(ೞ)✽◦❧

by Sedonia Guillone

To My Reader:

I hope you enjoy Kass and Lian's escape to Paradise. The wonderful man of my life gave me this title, *Enter the Hero*, because he knows how much I love martial arts films and watching Jet Li in action. Here's the sexy and romantic twist I envision for my own Jet Li film. *wink* Hugs, Sedonia

Chapter 1

Year: 2071 Location: Area B, Zone 5 (Formerly Known As Nevada)

"Prisoner 342, next."

The guard shoved Kassie through the doorway into a white room, empty but for the speaker box mounted on the wall and a window of one-way glass. He followed close behind her with his phazer brandished and set, no doubt, on kill. A second guard slammed and locked the door behind them. As if she could possibly escape these tremendous black-uniformed, phazered guards. All five feet six inches of her, wearing nothing but a prison-issue gray cotton shift.

No, she could not fight her way out of Central under these conditions. Not even with her soldier's training. Not even with the martial arts skills Lian had taught her.

"Strip her," the disembodied male voice said through the loudspeaker.

The words sent chills through her veins.

The guard stepped in close and insinuated his body against hers. The scent of his sweat invaded her nostrils, churned her stomach.

"Lift your arms," he said close to her ear. His breath blew across her skin in a malevolent, tobacco-soaked wind.

She tensed with the instinct to turn and kick him in the balls the way Lian had taught her. But she remembered Lian's hurried warning the moment of their arrest. Police hover vehicles had encircled them with roof-mounted phazers pointed right at their chests.

"Don't fight them, Kass," he'd said. "Whatever they do, don't give them a reason to kill you."

A pang shot through her chest at the memory. What if she never saw Lian again? No. That was unacceptable. She would obey him. If she did as she was told and didn't make trouble, they would eventually release her and she'd see Lian again.

She lifted her arms. The guard grabbed hold of the hem of her shift and pulled it upward.

She was left standing naked.

She folded her arms protectively over her breasts to lessen the horrible feeling of exposure in the cold, white-tiled room.

"Uncover yourself," the voice said.

She lowered her arms before the guard could do it for her. The floor tiles were like blocks of ice under her bare feet and the cold air in the small room penetrated her skin. Slowly she became more aware of the one-way glass. Whoever was behind there was staring at her and evaluating her naked body. Gooseflesh rose on her skin and her nipples puckered into erect nubs.

She heard a soft grunt of approval and saw with revulsion the way the guard ogled her. She itched to slice a hand chop to his throat.

Don't fight, Kass, Lian's voice warned inside her. She took a deep breath.

Before she could turn away, the guard smoothed a meaty hand over her backside.

"That's enough," the voice reprimanded. "Turn around, 342."

Obedient to her invisible captor, she turned her back to the one-way glass. Unfortunately, that exposed her front to the guard. The bastard's gaze moved hungrily over her breasts, down her stomach, and lower, over her pubic mound.

She fought the tears that sprang to her eyes. Lian should have been the first man to see and touch her body. The only thing that kept her in control, that allowed her to withstand this humiliation, was her determination to see Lian again. She didn't know if he was in love with her the way she was with him, but she didn't care. He was everything to her.

"Turn back around, 342. And raise your arms."

She did as she was told and sensed the guard's lustful gaze rake over her the entire time. Her cold nipples jutted out mercilessly and she longed to put her shift back on. Not even her long blond hair covered her because it had been pulled back into a severe bun by one of the female guards.

The only thing that warmed her and made her feel safe was thinking of Lian. Knowing that her childhood friend was somewhere inside this building helped her feel less frightened. Less alone.

"Arms down."

She crossed her arms over her breasts.

"Get dressed."

She glanced at the guard.

With a tiny sideways grin, he gestured toward her shift, a puddle of gray cotton on the tile floor.

She knelt down to retrieve it, taking care not to give the hulking cretin another clear view of her ass. He'd seen more than enough. She slipped on her shift while still crouched, then stood up.

Several moments of silence passed as she stared through the dark glass and tried to picture the person who held her fate in his hands. She waited for further interrogation about Lian's and her escape plans, but they had already grilled her for several hours earlier. All they'd gotten was her refusal to incriminate Lian or herself. It didn't matter what the Confederation mole who'd squealed on them had said. She kept to her story, and she knew Lian would too. But she knew that in the eyes hidden behind the glass, she and Lian were guilty.

"342, turn to receive sentence."

Her hands curled into fists at her sides and she struggled not to appear as breathlessly frightened as she was. Lian's voice came to her mind again, repeating years of secret lessons. *Deep breath. Center yourself, Kassie. Don't fight what you feel. Let it flow.* Before the New Order, Lian's father had helped him master the combined arts of meditation and combat. Lian, in turn, had taught her these disciplines.

As always, his teaching worked to reassure her. She uncurled her fists. Her breathing evened and she waited.

"Prisoner 342, for the crime of conspiracy to abandon the Border Guards, for political insubordination and psychological treason—"

Her heart lurched. The crimes he was enumerating were punishable by death.

"—you are sentenced to fifteen years service in the S Sector. The balance of your sentence will be declared when that period is served. Dismissed."

Her breath hitched sharply. Relief flooded her entire body with such force she nearly lost her balance. She had escaped death.

But she had not escaped Sector S.

Sexual servitude.

The history books taught that Sector S had once been called Las Vegas in the former state of Nevada. People had vacationed there, drinking and gambling their money away in funny colorful machines. Now, Sector S was the pleasure city reserved solely for the Upper Party members of the Confederation.

"Guard, get her on the next transport."

The guard yanked out a pair of handcuffs. "Come on, sugar buns," he drawled. He clapped the restraints on her wrists and pushed her back out the door.

Her stomach yawed like a boat pitching in a storm as the guard led her down a long institutional corridor of closed doors. In her mind she pictured Lian's face, his ebony hair and soft full lips, his large, almond-shaped brown eyes that always blazed with intensity. He would be accused of the same crimes she was. But would he receive an equally lenient sentence? And if he did, would they send him to the same place? She could only hope that his handsome face and muscular physique would make him eligible for the same sentence. That hope helped her win the struggle not to escape the guard and run down the hall, screaming for Lian, desperate with the need to know where he was.

At the end of the hallway, the guard slid a pass card through the sensor on the wall, and the glass door opened. A small hover bus stood at the curb with the engine running. The guard prodded her up the steps into the bus.

She searched every seat for Lian.

But he wasn't there.

Two guards took up the front seats. In the row behind the guards, one other young and pretty woman sat dressed in the same gray prison shift as Kass. Kass glanced at the girl's handcuffed wrists and knew she had just been sentenced to the same place. The young woman glanced at her, then away out the window. The door to the bus closed and the driver shifted gears.

Kass plunked down in a seat and stared out the dirty window, her gaze trained on the door to the building as if Lian might emerge any second. Had their escape plan worked, they would have been on the other side of the border in Paradise by now. For twelve years, Lian had made certain that they stayed together. He'd trained her in wu shu so she'd be strong enough and skilled enough to be chosen for the Border Guards, as was he. This ensured she'd be able to escape with him.

But someone had found them out, a Confederation mole who'd been placed in the Border Guard Unit to ferret out anyone who might be using their post as a mode of escape. She and Lian had been just about to lower the force field when the police surrounded them, phazers set on kill and pointed at their chests.

Kass would never forget that moment of sheer, bone-chilling terror when they separated her from Lian. Now, sitting in the seat of the bus about to take her to Sector S, she knew that her only reason to survive was to see him again.

If he was alive.

If Kass hadn't been handcuffed and guarded, she would have thought she was simply staying in a fancy hotel.

Starting in the parking lot, she'd observed her surroundings, searched for any possible way of escape. But there were phazered guards at every entrance to the building, and the all doors had force fields that required valid identity cards.

"Here you go, hon." Her new guard, a large red-headed woman in the usual dark green uniform of the Confed, was surprisingly kind, a welcome release from the drooling beast back in Central. She lifted the force field of the third door down a long, carpeted corridor.

Kass stepped into her cell, and then the guard was behind her to unlock her cuffs. At one time a room for hotel guests, this prison cell at least had its own bathroom, complete with shower, sink, toilet and a view to the outside.

"I think you'll be comfy enough here." The guard went over to a chest of drawers and pulled out something black and lacy. "This is what you'll be wearing tonight."

Wordlessly, Kass took the article from her and examined it. The completely see-through scrap made Kass's prison shift look like heavy winter clothing. "This?"

The guard grinned. "That's right. Gotta show off the goods."

Kass's heart clenched. People would be seeing her body in those skimpy clothes? Like the women who sold their bodies in the Combat Zones.

"And these." The guard held up a pair of black shoes with very thin high heels. "Now, you'll shower and brush your hair. Leave it loose. I'll come to get you and make sure you've followed your instructions. Any questions?"

Kass swallowed hard. Her heart pounded and a sweat broke out on her body. She shivered even though the room was a comfortable temperature. Her tongue felt so horribly thick and dry that she could barely get the question out.

"Yes. What exactly will I be doing?"

The guard raised her eyebrows and laughed as if Kass had asked the most ridiculous question. "Honey, are you kidding?"

Kass clenched her fists and fought for control. She imagined that was what Lian would do in this situation. "I mean, I know what they do here, I just wanted to know what to expect."

"Well, I can't say for certain what they'll have you do, but I can guarantee it will involve a naked man with gorgeous muscles and a hard cock."

Kass's breath caught. She fought back sudden tears as the ramifications of her prison sentence sunk in. "You mean, a man and me?"

The large woman waggled her eyebrows then winked in a suggestive way. "Uh huh. Almost makes me wish I'd get arrested and put here, if you know what I mean. Does that answer your question?"

Kass forced herself to nod. Her heart and hope were both sinking fast as her dream of giving Lian her virginity died yet a bit more.

"If you're worried about them inflicting physical pain or something like that honey, don't you worry. I haven't been told your actual assignment yet, but I can guarantee you one thing. Nothing but pleasure in this place, even for you prisoners." She paused, as if waiting for Kass to question her some more.

Kass breathed deeply to stay centered and hide her distress from the guard see. "All right."

"I'll be back for you after they give you your supper." The guard pointed her phazer at Kass as she raised the force field, stepped through and lowered it again. Then she locked the door in one smooth, seamless move. She might be sympathetic, even kind, but she was also obviously highly trained and competent. Getting past her would be difficult, if not impossible.

Kass sank onto her bed. Tears slipped freely down her cheeks and she covered her face with both hands. Lian was supposed to have been her first man. Her only man. At least in every dream and fantasy that had ever kept her company through lonely nights in the women's barracks.

She sobbed quietly until no more tears could come. The only thought that brought her any comfort was remembering the first moment she'd ever met Lian on Children's Farm 16. She was eleven and he was twelve, and they were both loners.

One day on the playground, two boys taunted Lian about his Asian features. A head shorter than both of them, Lian must have appeared an easy target until he whirled around so fast he was nearly invisible and delivered a sharp sideways kick to one boy.

That tormentor went straight down into the dust on his butt and sat there in shock. Lian stood over him, fists in an attack pose. His dark eyes flashed and his face was a mask of ferocity.

The boy scrambled to his feet and ran away with the other bully close behind him. The ferocity drained from Lian's face and he sank onto a nearby bench, staring down at his hands.

Like a magnet, she was drawn to sit beside him. He looked up at her with large brown eyes full of sadness. To her surprise, he took her hand and held it. They sat there quietly on the bench as if they were long lost friends who'd just found each other.

From then on, they were inseparable. They even developed a secret language by scratching their fingertips in the palm of each other's hand. But she'd never told him she loved him.

And maybe now she never would.

Kass turned onto her back and stared up at the ceiling. She forced herself not to think of the night ahead, when some man would do the things to her body that only Lian should do. She closed her eyes as new tears slipped out.

Chapter 2

Kass showered and brushed out her long hair as instructed, then went back into the room to get dressed.

She slipped on the thong and frowned. The strap between her butt cheeks felt weird. Before putting on the negligee, she held it up to her front and stared at her reflection in the mirror above the chest of drawers. She'd never worn anything except for her uniform, plain white underclothes and the Confed-issue ankle-length cotton nightgown that all the girls wore. The silky material of the negligee against her skin felt kind of nice. She tilted her head and turned this way and that, marveling at the unfamiliar mature woman she saw in the glass.

A pang squeezed her chest. How she wished Lian could have seen her in something like this. Even if he hadn't been in love with her before, seeing her like this, like a woman instead of a soldier, might have made him fall in love. But now some other man, some stranger, would see her instead.

With a deep sigh, she slipped the thing on and tied it in front, just above her bare breasts. She frowned. Whatever she could see of her body, anyone else there would also see. Her nipples not only poked through the lacy material, but were completely visible, as was her pubic area through her thong. Nothing left to the imagination. Nothing kept back. She felt the need to cry again but fought it down. She refused to let the guard, or anyone else, see her distress.

It was almost time. Kass slipped into the spike-heeled shoes and took a few steps. She teetered and grabbed onto the edge of the bureau. Damn. What if they expected her to walk around or something? She couldn't look sexy while stumbling around in these things. She'd fall for sure. She'd never worn anything on her feet but socks and heavy boots.

She let go of the bureau and practiced walking in front of the mirror. Standing back a few paces, she got a glimpse of her legs in her reflection. The heels showed off her legs in a way she'd never seen before. Her thighs and calves were more shapely and more feminine than she would have guessed.

The women who sold their bodies in the pleasure zones probably wore stuff like this to tempt the men who came around. Kass's heart skipped in her chest. Had Lian been to those women? He'd never mentioned it to her. Of course, he wouldn't. It wasn't something you discussed with someone under your command, even a friend like her. Some things a man didn't discuss with a woman.

Of course, she'd never asked him. And would never have asked.

Waiting for the guard, Kass watched the sun set through her window. There was a clear view to the outside, but Kass heard the hum of the force field over the glass. One touch and she'd be stunned, the alarm tripped.

She wished that Lian were in the room with her. Even though their circumstances had never enabled them to openly show affection, she would have wanted to crawl into his arms and stay there forever if she could. Safe. Even in a place like this.

Shortly after dark, the door's force field lifted and the door slid open. The guard stepped through, her phazer pointed at Kass to prevent her from trying to escape. The instant the guard was in the room, the force field buzzed shut again.

"Come on, 342. It's show time." She regarded Kass from her towering, big-bosomed height. "Let me check you first. Got to make sure you're ready."

Kass surreptitiously clenched her fists and went over to her for inspection. She squeezed her eyes shut as the guard smoothed her hands over her hair. Thankfully, the woman's touch was impersonal and gentler than the male guard's had been back in Central.

"Turn in a circle, please."

Kass obeyed and felt the woman's gaze, an assessing look that reminded Kass of the way buyers at the market used to inspect her father's horses when she was a little girl before the days of the Confederation.

"Very good, hon. You're going to be a crowd pleaser, that's for sure." She cuffed Kass's wrists and raised the force field. "Let's go."

Kass's heart lurched. The moment she'd been dreading was getting closer with each passing second. She bit back tears as the guard led her from the room and down the hall. They went up some stairs into another hall. With each step they took, Kass's heart pounded harder. Every nerve ending in her body felt tight, prepared to fight, although she was powerless to do anything but let the guard lead her to her fate. Only imagining Lian's face—his almond-shaped eyes and high cheekbones, the sexy curve of his full lips when he smiled— brought her any peace at all.

Halfway down the hall, the guard slid her pass card through the sensor and led Kass into a huge room.

Kass pulled in a tight breath. Half the room was blocked off by a panel of that one-way glass the Confed officials seemed to favor. The half of the room visible to Kass contained a large platform bed covered with silken pillows and sheets, but no blanket. A pair of leather wrist cuffs hung from short chains from the brass headboard.

She blinked hard. Her heart thrashed in her chest like two wrestlers locked in combat. A strange pulsing sprang up in her sex as the guard led her forward. Each tap of her spiky heels on the parquet reminded her of what was about to happen. She clenched her jaw and tried to disconnect her mind from her body. Impossible. She'd never been able to shut down her emotions all her life, no matter how frightened or upset she was. Now was no different and her body and heart warred viciously inside her.

A second guard followed them to the platform. "This way, sweetheart. Up you go."

Slowly, she climbed up the platform steps and onto the bed.

"Lie down."

As soon as Kass lay back against the pillows, the guards un-cuffed her hands, raised her arms and locked the new leather cuffs around her wrists. The leather pressed into her wrists but she remained still. There was no way she could escape, not without getting killed. She watched the guards repeat the process with her legs. They cuffed her ankles, leaving her knees slightly bent. Shivers of terror slipped through her as she watched them retreat, leaving her spread out, completely prone.

As soon as she was alone, the lights brightened and a spotlight shone on Kass. She glanced at the one-way glass and realized the people behind it could see her now as clearly as if she were on a movie screen or a stage.

After another moment, the door opened again. Kass turned her head at the sound and caught her breath.

A man, naked except for a loincloth, stood there, watching her. He must have been six feet two. His muscular frame filled the doorway. Even from a distance, Kass could see the serial number tattooed in bluish-green ink on his left upper arm. A transporter. He'd probably gotten arrested selling black market luxury goods from over the border.

Her gaze locked with his. A tiny grin curved his lips. He wasn't familiar, and she would remember him if she'd ever turned him back from a checkpoint. He must have been arrested out of her jurisdiction.

Broad-shouldered, rippling yet lean, his body a sculpture of chiseled muscle, he stood quietly, obviously waiting for the guard to unlock his handcuffs. He continued to watch her from across the room, and she saw an appreciative gleam come into his eyes.

A strange ripple of heat cascaded through Kass's body. This man was going to touch her. And more. And there was nothing she could do to prevent it. Her heartbeat sped up as the man's cuffs came off.

As soon as he was free, he started for the platform. He moved smoothly, a strange contrast to his brawny body.

A drumbeat, primal and rhythmic, echoed through the room. Kass glanced up to see a speaker by the ceiling in the corner. The drumbeat echoed the muscular man's footsteps as he drew closer.

Kass tried to shrink back. She pulled against her bonds. To no avail. She was forced to watch the man approach.

One by one, he took the few steps to the side of the bed until he stood only inches away. The light glinted off his closely shorn head and the golden hairs sprinkled over his chest.

Kass swallowed hard. Her gaze locked with his. She could practically feel the sexual hunger that radiated from him as he stared down at her. His blue eyes never left hers, and his chest rose and fell heavily. He gave her a tight nod, so brief that it would have been invisible to anyone else. Slowly, he climbed onto the bed and slunk over to her on all fours, his movements sleek and graceful as a panther's.

She could hear his breathing like a crashing sound in her ears. Energy sizzled off his body, and the air crackled with his testosterone. She wanted to close her eyes as if to hide, but stared at him with her body tensed in fight mode.

He hovered for a moment then bent over. His arm muscles flexed with the movement. Kass yanked backward, away from him, but she could barely move an inch. She clenched her teeth and stared at him. His eyes roved over her body as he bent in closer, his obvious erection straining the front of his loincloth. His warm breath caressed her skin.

For a moment, he didn't move but just stared into her eyes as if searching for something there. She picked up his scent, a blend of soap and an aroma she recognized from the moments Lian had stood close to her while training her. Her heartbeat thrummed harder. She recognized that scent.

Man.

Without breaking eye contact, he reached out and pressed his fingers to her bare shoulder. His caress was surprisingly gentle, but Kass yanked back until she was halted by the bonds. She couldn't get away from him, from his touch, from his penetrating stare. Her breath came in short hard gasps as her second dream was crushed. Strange men had already seen her naked and one had pawed her. And now another one was about to take her virginity. None of them, Lian.

The man slid his fingertips down her bare arm. His touch was like a trail of fire along her skin.

Against her will, her body responded. A warm tingling sensation erupted wherever their skin made contact. She fought back hard, thrashing to avoid his fingertips. It didn't work. He kept his hand on her arm, squeezing it gently in his hold.

That aching pulse in the juncture between her thighs intensified with the continuous drumbeat. She'd never known a man's sensual caress, and with each passing second, her body awakened more. A near lifetime of unrequited desires and needs simmered in her core.

Horrified at her body's response, she pulled against her cuffs. But it was to no avail. He trailed his fingertips back up her arm. The sensitive skin at the inner juncture of her elbow tingled from the warm touch.

As if sensing the budding of desire in her, he knelt between her thighs and bent close. His face was within inches of hers.

She gasped and pulled back, but his only response was to lower his body, invading her with his masculine heat and scent. His broad chest grazed her nipples through the negligee. The bulge in his loincloth pressed lightly against the thin panel of lace that covered her mound.

Her sex pulsed now, deeper with each brush of his chest on her nipples and of his hips against her inner thighs.

He was grinning down at her as he rocked his pelvis against hers. He seemed to be enjoying this slow taunting, this preview of the male invasion about to happen. The more she pulled back or turned her head away from him, the more he teased her.

With no means to fight back and no other alternative, she glared at him.

He shook his head slowly, almost sadly, and brushed his lips over the side of her throat. He nuzzled the sensitive skin there and flicked the tip of his tongue just under her ear.

She moaned softly and clenched her jaw.

He pulled back with a triumphant gleam in his blue eyes and skimmed the palm of his hand over the lacy negligee covering her breasts. Heat zinged through her nipples.

Damn Lian. Damn their failure. If only they hadn't been caught, or even tried to escape. They'd still be together. She wouldn't be here, forced to submit to another man.

Not that Lian had ever promised her anything.

The man leaned closer. She closed her eyes to avoid his simmering blue gaze, but that only intensified the physical sensations, so she opened them again. His fingertips slid over her nipples and grazed that intimate flesh through the thin panel of lace. His touch was warm and soft even though she hadn't invited it. Oh, nothing had ever felt like that before.

She hadn't expected pleasure.

She fought the haze that threatened to saturate her. He was seducing her. He wasn't forcing her, damn him. He was making her want him, coaxing her body to relax and her sex to become slippery. Preparing her body for his possession.

When she dared to glance at his face, his hungry gaze was riveted on hers. A question seemed to fill his eyes. No, she mouthed, not daring to speak.

The drumbeat mingled with their heavy breathing. She pulled and thrashed and resisted, but he continued to touch her, caressed her over the negligee, first one breast, then the other.

She didn't want it to feel good.

Lian had never told her he loved her, never promised her anything. So did she owe him something now? It should have been his touch warming her skin.

But it wasn't.

Her mind understood the difference. So did her heart.

But her body was a traitor.

The man reached under the black negligee and slid his fingertips across her stomach. Kass's body tingled under his sensual caress. Her flesh acted on its own will with its overwhelming need for touch. For comfort. For a means to forget her desolation over Lian, even if only for a moment.

But she didn't want to forget Lian, now or ever.

"You want me now, don't you?" the man whispered so softly that she thought she might have imagined it. And maybe she had. She stared at his carved lips but they didn't move.

She shook her head no just the same.

His eyes glittered as he gingerly pulled open the lace tie on the negligee. His fingertips brushed her skin. She caught her breath. The filmy material fell open, completely revealing her body, naked except for the tiny covering of lace thong.

He groaned softly and knelt over her. His playful teasing of earlier seemed to fade, replaced by deeper lust. His erection tented the white cloth of his loincloth, and Kass couldn't resist staring at it. She felt a wild desire to see his cock, the instrument of her undoing. That male part had always been a mystery to her and she wanted to end the mystery.

With Lian.

Who wasn't here.

The man's fingers hovered an inch above her stomach, then he touched her again. The pads of his fingertips sent warm shudders through her flesh. His touch remained gentle, seductive, and her disloyal body ached for more.

He slid his fingers upward and slowly traced the undersides of her breasts. Her breath hitched as he closed one hand over her left breast and squeezed it softly then gently pinched the nipple.

Tingling fire pulsated through her nipple with each tiny squeeze. The sensation traveled down between her legs, weakened her, made her sex ache with want. Her eyes closed. Instinctively, before she could stop herself, she arched her back up into his hand.

No, her mind screamed, and she flattened her spine against the mattress.

She moaned softly, strained against her bonds. Her control was slipping and she didn't know how she would withstand the seductive onslaught much longer.

Suddenly, a loud bang echoed through the room.

Kass gasped and her eyelids shot up. The man jerked away from her and sat up. They both looked toward the door, which hung wide open.

Kass caught her breath.

At first she thought it was a ghost, a trick of her mind. The heated blood swirling through her body concentrated in her heart, which gave a sudden leap in her chest.

He wasn't dead.

He was here.

He stood in the doorway, his dark eyes blazing over a bare chest and scanty loincloth.

Lian.

Chapter 3

The drumbeat halted.

Lian's gaze flicked to the man on the bed and then to Kass. The possessive gleam in Lian's eyes intensified. His nostrils flared and his face darkened with the determined ferocity he always showed before a fight. His hands were cuffed behind his back and the muscles of his broad chest heaved like a wild animal trapped in a cage.

The drum resumed, beating out a fevered rhythm.

The man on the bed rose on his knees with his back to Kass. His physical tension radiated through the mattress, and Kass sensed the fight to come.

Slowly, he climbed off the bed and down the platform. His gaze locked on Lian, who obviously chafed at his shackles as he waited impatiently for the guard to free him. A fierce sizzle of combat simmered in the air between the two men.

Kass's heart thrummed, her limbs rigid, her breath tight. She pulled at her cuffs. Had she been free, she would have bounded off the bed and leapt to Lian's side. Now, she was forced into the role of spectator as Lian and the man who'd been forcibly seducing her sized each other up.

The drum tempo increased to match the pounding of her heart. The staccato beats thundered in her ears and blended with the whoosh of blood through her body.

The click of keys in Lian's handcuffs echoed through the room. Kass watched the glinting steel being slipped off his wrists.

Cautiously, Lian watched his opponent. The blond man was tall, a veritable giant. But Lian's fierce strength emanated from a place deep inside him. Kass sensed him assessing his opponent, planning his strategy. Lian had seen that man touching her, so he'd be furious. Whether Lian was in love with her, she didn't know, but he'd always been fiercely protective of her. More than once in the past twelve years he'd come to her defense, on the playground and then later in the Border Guards. No man who ever hassled her got away with it when Lian was around.

And this man had done more than hassle her.

Slowly, the two men circled around each other, their chests heaving, their hands tensed into fists.

Kass stared at Lian, unable to pull her gaze away from his dark eyes, his flawless golden skin, and the glint of the soft lighting on his cropped ebony hair. His body tensed and rippled with finely etched muscles. His broad chest and back emanated the physical power and prowess she had often seen in action. Lian was a defensive fighter. He wouldn't strike his opponent until the man went at him. And then he would force his opponent to bend to his style of fighting, a strategy that made him nearly invincible in hand to hand combat. But his rage might unbalance him, and his opponent was strong.

Her heart continued to thunder, pounding blood through her entire body until even her fingertips tingled. If Lian lost this fight, the man would return to the bed, to her, to finish what he started.

But if Lian won, maybe he would be the one to join her on the bed and claim her as his prize.

Her body hummed madly, and she hungered for a quick and harmless end to the fight so that Lian could be with her. The mere thought of his touch and his kiss, of his strong hard body over hers, penetrating her, filling her, made her dizzy with longing.

The two men circled each other like prowling beasts. Suddenly, the blond man lunged at Lian and threw a ham-fisted punch.

Lian blocked it, grabbed his opponent's arm and pushed it down, then punched the man's stomach.

The other man grunted and staggered backward under the force of Lian's belly-caving punch. Before he had a chance to recover his footing, Lian charged him and delivered a sharp kick with the sole of his foot to the same spot he'd punched. While the man stumbled, Lian whirled around and landed a second kick to his chest with equal force.

The fight was over.

The blond man fell back against a guard who almost toppled under his weight. A second guard reached in to help. Together, the two guards dragged the stunned, defeated man from the room, leaving Lian alone in the center of the floor. His broad chest heaved, and his strong hands clenched and unclenched. A sheen of sweat gleamed on his smooth skin.

Kass watched him, captivated. Her own breath rose and fell in unison with his. Her blood swirled icy-hot through her veins and every nerve in her body tingled.

Suddenly, Lian spun around. His gaze locked with hers. He bounded over to the platform then leaped onto the bed. He leaned over her, his warm strong hands on her shoulders.

A sense of safety and protection flooded her, mingled with the arousal that coursed through her entire body. She stared up at him, lost in his liquid brown eyes with their intoxicating mixture of concern, relief and desire.

Desire.

Never before had she seen that in his eyes. Whether the need burning there was a result of the fight or of the adrenalin-heated moment, she didn't know. Neither of them dared speak. To reveal their friendship to the guards or audience would only provide a weapon to be used against them.

But she didn't care about their forced silence. Lian was here, alive and whole and touching her. In moments, their bodies would fuse together and the deepest desires she'd ever carried in her woman's heart would be fulfilled. She would give herself to the man she loved.

Lian gazed at her a moment longer. He leaned in and closed his mouth over hers.

All thought melted instantly away. Kass's eyes fluttered closed. Lust simmered from his mouth to hers and she parted her lips to silently beg for the wet heat of his tongue. A murmur of delight escaped her throat when their tongues met and swirled intensely around each other's as if they could drink in each other's souls through the kiss.

Kass licked up his salty musky flavor, the most delicious thing she'd ever tasted. She sighed deeply and her body sank underneath him, under the warm press of his muscular body. She felt high. Elated. All sense and feeling concentrated in the passionate exchange of their mouths. Years of longing for him poured from a well deep within her and channeled through her hungry kiss.

He slid his hands from her shoulders and up the length of her arms, his path to her hands interrupted by her shackles. She longed to pull out of them so she could embrace him and feel the warm flexing of his broad back as he took her. That wasn't to be, so she delighted instead in her complete surrender to the erotic promise of their heated kisses.

Lian maneuvered his body between her parted legs, his lips never leaving hers.

He sank down on top of her. The warm press of his bare chest on her breasts was the most delicious sensation she'd ever experienced. His hard erection nested in the heated juncture of her thighs. Even through his loincloth and her scrap of black lace, she could feel his passion against her swollen core.

The drumbeat pounded a sinuous sensual rhythm that melted into her blood and beat in syncopation with Lian's pelvic grinding. Blending with the drumbeat, a soft groan vibrated from his throat into her mouth.

She bucked her hips against him. Even over her thong, the friction of his cock against her clit made her wild. Her mind melted in a glorious oblivion in which only Lian existed. His muscular chest rubbed her nipples to hard peaks, and his erection rubbed her inner sex. His tongue massaged hers in hungry strokes, and his clean musky scent filled her senses.

He slipped his hands around her back, encircling her completely with his strong arms so tenderly yet with such desire. A warm shiver passed through her at the sensation.

Lian lifted his mouth from her swollen and tingling lips, leaving her breathless. He lowered his face to one of her breasts. His breath pulsed warmly on her skin and his ebony lashes fluttered against his cheeks as he closed his lips over her nipple.

She moaned softly. Nothing had ever felt like that in her life. He swirled the tip of his tongue around the sensitive tip. Kass arched her back, tried to push her breast deeper into Lian's mouth.

He seemed to understand her silent plea and tightened his lips on her nipple. Jolts of white-hot pleasure radiated through her, into her entire body, especially into her sex. She felt slippery and open, and her arousal soaked the crotch panel of the thong. She moaned softly and ground her hips against his. Her instinct was to wrap her legs around his hips, but the bonds on her ankles held her legs in place. She was forced to rely solely on Lian to pleasure her body.

Lian lifted his lips from her breast and kissed a fervent trail on her skin to the other nipple, which he suckled wildly for a long time. Each tug of his lips sent a dart of heat into her sex and several times, a tingling wave surged deep in her core. She liked that feeling.

His cock ground harder against her and the rasp of his loincloth back and forth over her clitoris sent a delicious wave of pressure through her sex.

Lian lightly dappled the pads of his fingertips on her back, and in the haze of her fevered mind, she realized he was speaking to her in the silent childhood language they'd invented so long ago.

Want you now, his fingertips spelled in heated patterns on her flesh while his tongue swirled over her nipple.

Want you.

Now.

A jolt of wild arousal surged through her. Oh God, he wanted to be inside her. He wanted her!

She didn't care that it was the heat of the moment or that under different circumstances, he might not have felt this way. She only wanted him inside her. Buried deep inside.

"Yes," she whispered. She arched her back to push her breast deeper into his hungry mouth. "Yes."

Lian lifted his face from her breast. His gaze seared her with a bone-melting blend of passion and tenderness. His brown eyes simmered under heavy lids. His golden complexion was darkly flushed.

Her entire body tingled madly and her breath rose and fell heavily. *I love you* she thought silently but didn't dare tell him, instead praying that somehow he would understand.

He leaned down and captured her mouth in a brief but hot kiss, then levered himself up and knelt between her spread legs. His heated gaze fell on the thong. He slipped several fingers under the waistband and gave a soft yank. The flimsy snap closures gave way and he slipped the thong off her and threw it aside.

Then his hands went to the tie of his loincloth. The white cotton fell away.

Kass's breath hitched. She'd spent years imagining him naked like this. And now, it was real. Better than she'd ever dreamed.

Lian was glorious. Beautiful. Breathtaking. The parts of him that she'd never seen before were as incredible as she'd imagined them to be.

His waist melted seamlessly into narrow hips and round hard buttocks. His fully erect penis, reddish gold with small veins, jutted thick and hard from a nest of dark hair.

Her heart slammed hard and she trembled. She licked her lips. Her hands ached to touch him, to brush his dark brown nipples and to skim her palms over his hard muscles and smooth skin. Had she not been restrained, she would have leaned forward and stroked his shaft with one hand and caressed the heavy sac underneath them with her other.

He reached between her thighs and brushed his fingertips over her swollen aching folds. With his gaze never leaving hers, he rubbed the pads of his fingertips up and down her slit.

Kass pulled in a shuddering breath. His touch was so delicious, so intoxicating. She whimpered and stopped herself from whispering his name out loud.

He continued to explore her, tracing all the sensitive contours of her inner sex, gathering her moisture of arousal on his fingertips. He slid two fingers inside her, slowly, gently stretching her.

The sensation of fullness weakened her further. She moaned and ground her hips against his hand.

After several more moments of caressing her intimately, he slid his fingers out. He held his fingertips to his nose. His eyes closed as he breathed in her musk.

Kass felt her cheeks burn, but she stared, riveted. She watched him lick her moisture off his fingertips. His eyes appeared dazed, as if her were drunk from her scent and taste.

He then lowered his body back down between her legs, settled gently on top of her. The head of his cock nudged her slick opening.

Kass caught her breath softly. A near lifetime of yearning was about to be fulfilled. Her mind spun and her body tingled from the contact of his male warmth and hardness against her.

With a tiny thrust, he pushed the swollen head of his erection in and stopped.

She caught her breath. Lian was inside her, not all the way, but there, his body joined with hers in the way she had dreamed of for so long.

He lowered his face to hers and kissed her softly. She sighed and surrendered willingly to the tender brush of his lips back and forth over hers. He pushed his hips forward, just a bit more, and filled her a little deeper.

She caught her breath and moaned softly into his mouth. The head of his cock pushed up against the barrier of her virginity.

She could feel how cautious he was being with her, how careful, knowing she was a virgin. His care only made her love him more, only made her heart burn more fiercely for him.

He caressed her cheek with the fingertips of one hand and reached down with the other to where they were joined. He shifted his body slightly to the side and rubbed her clit in gentle circles.

The erotic massage felt so hot and sweet. Her arousal coated his fingertips, made her passage more slippery. He pushed again. A quick thrust and he tore through.

She gasped. A small sting of pain and then a flood of pleasure. His touch on her clit washed away the sudden sharp pain, and he didn't stop rubbing it as he moved inside her, thrust slowly in and out.

Lian was inside her. The thought swirled in her mind as he stretched her open and filled her with his maleness. She didn't care about anything else, not even the audience watching her make love for the first time. She only wished she could put her arms around him and hold him as he made her his own.

He pulled out his hand from between them and once again licked her musk from his fingertips. Kass felt her cheeks burn again but also found his savoring of her femininity incredibly arousing.

Lian made a show of devouring her juices from his hand and then put it back down between them to rub her clit in quick little circles, matching his faster, more heated rhythm of thrusts.

The pleasure filled her womb and burned in her belly until she came. The waves gripped her body and made her arms and legs strain helplessly against her bonds.

When her orgasm had wrung itself away, Lian removed his hand and braced himself on either side of her with his hands pressed into the mattress. He moved his hips a bit faster and sank the length of his erection deep inside her. The friction rubbed her already sensitive core and she moaned with her head tilted back, completely, gladly under his power.

He pulled back and then pushed, a gentle but firm thrust into her again. The mixture of pleasure and pain was intoxicating. She opened her eyes and watched the muscles of Lian's body flex and tense with each motion he made. Instinctively, she squeezed her lower muscles around his shaft.

He groaned and moved faster.

She bucked her hips against him as much as she could in her restrained state. She squeezed his cock again and again. He groaned each time and moved in a more fevered rhythm.

Suddenly he tensed, groaned again and closed his lips over hers. He let out a heavy rasping breath and she felt his cock pulse inside her, felt him fill her. The tension ran out of his body and he lowered himself, covering her body with his, breathing heavily against her shoulder.

She buried her face in the crook of his neck and breathed in his warm male scent. His damp skin fused against hers and she wished they could stay here like this. She was his now.

He slipped his arms around her back and she felt his fingertips move against her skin.

Your room?

She took a deep breath to cover her rising panic. How would she answer him with her hands tied?

With a kiss.

She put her lips to his neck and feathered the tip of her tongue on his smooth skin. She managed to sign the number, tasting the delicious saltines of his skin as he did. 231. She had seen the number on the door when she was first brought to the room.

321. Me, he answered.

She fought to appear normal through her joy. Just knowing where he was made her feel less frightened.

The dramatic light faded and the normal lights went back on. From the corner of her eye, Kass saw the guards approaching. Her heart sank at her coming separation from Lian. It wasn't supposed to be that way. They should be able to lie together all night.

Lian's tongue flickered softly on the side of her neck, just as one guard unlocked her right handcuff. Kass realized Lian was telling her something else. The message came through and made her breath catch.

We will escape.

"Come on, get up." The guard's voice was like a death sentence.

Chapter 4

Lian paced his prison room. He felt more than ever like a caged beast, especially after making love to Kassie. For hours after leaving her, her scent had lingered on his skin as had the tangy flavor of her sex on his tongue.

He halted and clenched his fists. They would escape. They had to. There were too many risks in staying. They could be separated. He could be forced to watch another man have her. They could be put into violent, possibly deadly scenarios. Even if he could make love to her every night of their prison sentence, there was no guarantee of what would happen to them at the end.

Even if they finished their sentence alive and together, no doubt Kass would be transferred to the Breeding Division and impregnated repeatedly until she was too old to provide the Confederation with future generations. He couldn't bear that. He wanted her for himself. Always.

He'd fallen in love with Kassie the day she sat down next to him on the bench after he'd defended himself against some playground bullies. In her he saw a fellow human being, a pretty girl, as hungry for hope and friendship as he was.

Everything he'd done since that day was intended to keep them together somehow. But the threat of separation grew every day, until Kassie was sixteen and he was seventeen, near the age when the sexes were divided from each other.

Every word they'd said, and every feeling he'd had that night were etched in his memory.

The night had begun as usual. He and Kassie climbed the fence after lights out and ran across the overgrown field that had probably once belonged to a farmer. The farmers too had been rounded up and put to work on collective farms.

Kassie seemed particularly troubled about something. He saw it in her blue eyes as he guided her in a stance before a kick. The moonlight splashed into the barn and cast a soft glow on Kassie's face and upper body. Her breasts pushed against her t-shirt, making small indentations as the material stretched between the soft mounds. His hands were on her shoulders, and he was particularly aware of her warm skin, just a thin layer of t-shirt away from his fingertips.

"Kassie, what's wrong?"

She raised sad eyes to him, and he remembered he was touching her. He kept his hands where they were.

She lifted one arm and he released his hold. She pulled back the short sleeve. "This."

At first he couldn't see anything, but when he looked closer, the moonlight revealed a small line on the inside of her upper arm, no deeper than a scratch. Without thinking he reached up and smoothed one fingertip along the line. Another jolt of energy shivered through him at the softness of her skin.

"What is that?"

She furrowed her brow. "Don't you know?"

His heart lurched. It couldn't be good. "No."

"It's an infertility implant. All the girls get one when they turn sixteen. It's so we can't get pregnant."

Pregnant. The word shot through him and reminded him of the way his body responded to hers every time they were together. But it also reminded him of something else. Something bad. The thing in her arm meant that they'd take her away from here pretty soon.

"They'll remove it later." She sniffled. "When they send me off to breed."

Lian's blood ran cold. This wasn't something the men were told about.

"They call it the creation of our future," Kassie went on. Her voice shook and Lian could feel her fear and horror as if it were his own. "Breeding the future champions of the Confederation, but what if I don't want to? They'll make me—you know."

Lian's shock turned to anger. No one was going to touch Kassie against her will. He grasped her arm again and squeezed both arms gently. "Kassie, look at me."

Her troubled blue gaze turned up at him.

"I promise you, you'll never have to go there."

Her bottom lips trembled. "But—how—how can you?"

"Listen. Work really hard. Build up your strength. Show them you have what it takes to be a Border Guard. That's where I plan to go, and they take women too. Pass their tests. We have a chance at staying together if you do. And then I'll find a way to get us over the border to Paradise. Please. Promise me you'll try."

Kassie nodded. "I promise, Lian," she whispered.

A tear pushed from her eye and rolled down her cheek. He reached out and brushed it away with a fingertip. She was so close he could practically feel her breath on his face. He wanted to show her what she meant to him. Just one kiss. But not here. Not while they were prisoners of the Confederation.

And now they were Confederation prisoners of another kind. Despite all their careful planning and training.

His mind was full of images, memories of how they'd snuck out for wu shu training at night when they were supposed to be in bed. He'd loved to see the determination in her blue eyes as she tried to imitate the forms he showed her, the kicks and punches. It was a way for them to be together, a way for him to steal touches, his hands on her shoulders or legs as he corrected a stance.

So many times he'd wanted to kiss her. It would have been easy, standing there in front of her, Kassie's eyes closed in concentration. So many times he could have just leaned forward and pressed his lips to hers.

Lian continued to pace his cell. Now he wished she knew how he felt about her. He'd never told her he loved her, not even in their secret way of communicating. He refused to let his feelings show until they reached Paradise.

He sighed, frustrated at his own stubbornness. But he couldn't help it. His father taught him to hold fast always to deep truths. For Lian, telling Kass the truth was only something he could do once they were safe in Paradise. Once he claimed her, Lian knew that her loyal heart would cling to him. If he didn't survive their attempt to escape, he couldn't bear the thought she would live out her life alone, refusing to find someone else.

After a day pacing his cell, he showered reluctantly and tied on the cursed loincloth so he'd be ready when the guard arrived. He didn't want to wash Kassie's sweet female scent off his skin, and he dreaded the prospect of having to perform with a different woman. In this Godforsaken place, anything could happen.

Shortly after the evening meal, the guard lowered the force field and stepped through the door with a phazer pointed at Lian's chest.

Lian studied the beefy man as he'd done each time the guard had come to his cell with meals or to fetch him for the previous night's performance. He crossed the room with his wrists out to be cuffed but never stopped evaluating the guard. Like all the guards, male and female, this one was large and burly with a meaty face. By scanning his facial structure and posture, Lian was able to estimate his weaknesses. In Lian's escape plan, this guard would be the first obstacle to overcome.

The guard wore a smirk.

"Kung fu guy," he said as he slapped the cuffs on Lian, "It seems you and the blonde were a hit last night. Your audience has asked for an encore."

Kassie! They were putting them together again. Thank the gods.

Lian kept his expression blank and hard, not betraying the surge of adrenaline that the guard's words caused.

The guard clicked the cuffs shut. "Apparently the party bigwigs not only liked the way you kicked that guy's ass in three shots, but you and the chick really got them all hot and bothered, like you weren't putting on a show. I heard one of them say it was like they were actually peeking into someone's bedroom. Good for you they like that shit." He yanked Lian in the direction of the door. "I'd have to say I agree. I was there, myself. Man, if I didn't know better, I'd say she's pretty hot for you."

Lian didn't respond, though his face and chest burned with anger. He remained silent.

The guard cocked his head and studied Lian with that crooked smirk still pasted on his meaty face.

"I thought you'd be excited about that. I sure as hell would be. She's a sweet piece of ass. Well, not all guys like girls." He yanked on the lead attached to Lian's handcuffs and deactivated the force field.

Lian gritted his teeth and followed the guard through the doorway. It took every ounce of discipline he possessed not to beat the bastard into the ground. Lian had never liked that kind of speech about women, not even toward the women who sold their favors to men. They were sharing their bodies with men, after all, and deserved to be honored. At times, he himself had gone to those women with his Pleasure Pass so that if he ever got a chance with Kass, he'd know how to satisfy her.

But still, he'd always respected those women. To hear them belittled bothered him enough. To hear that kind of talk about Kassie made him want to kill.

The guard led Lian to the same large room from the night before. The guard stopped at the doorway and passed his card through.

The door slid open.

Lian's blood ran cold.

At the far end of the room, Kassie was leaning back against the wall and staring at a large man who'd been put into the room with her. Her hands were bound in front of her, and she wore the same sheer cloth and the same high heels as the night before. Her blue eyes radiated fear and anger.

Shorter than the man from the night before, this man bulged with corded, tensed muscle. Long brown hair hung past his shoulders, and he practically drooled as his gaze raked up and down her body.

Lian growled and lunged, but the guards yanked him back into the doorway. They both brandished their phazers, very likely set on kill rather than stun.

So to spare his own life and Kassie's, Lian remained still as he was forced to watch the scene with murderous rage burning through every muscle and sinew of his body.

Kassie looked up. Her gaze locked with Lian's and there was no mistaking the relief in her expression. Even from across the room, Lian saw a tiny muscle in her jaw twitch and recognized a spark of determination in that almost imperceptible movement. He'd seen that transition slide across her features many times during their training, and he knew the strength and power that poured from her in such moments.

She turned her attention back to her assailant. The man had stepped closer to her. His broad back heaved and his huge hands were poised to grab her.

Lian clenched his fists. His heart pounded. This man obviously intended to rape Kassie, and there was nothing Lian could do to help her.

She sagged against the wall with her bound hands hanging uselessly in front of her. She appeared ready to submit. As she licked her lips, her pink tongue darted out and slid enticingly across her full, soft lips.

The man stepped closer and pressed his body against hers. His large, meaty hands grasped her shoulders and pushed her back against the wall.

Lian's breath hitched in his throat.

Kassie's knee flashed into the man's groin. He released a strangled wail and staggered back, clutching the front of his loincloth.

Before he could recover, Kassie stepped away from the wall with her eyes blazing. She lifted her bound hands and pounded one sharp, determined punch into his throat.

Without a sound, his bulky frame toppled to the floor, his arms flailing to clutch his injured groin and throat all at once.

Relief prickled like icy heat through Lian's chest and veins. The guard unlocked his cuffs while a third guard dragged the injured man from the room. Kassie watched and sagged back against the wall.

Lian charged across the room. He stood in front of her, resisting the urge to call out her name. With his hands pressed into the wall, he bridged her body and stared into her eyes.

Her breasts were heaving under the sheer black negligee and her dusky pink lips were slightly parted. She lifted her bound hands and pressed them to his chest. Her fingertips moved rapidly against his skin.

Only you, Lian, she spelled in tiny movements that to the untrained eye would appear to be fervent caresses. *Only you.*

Lian's blood surged hotly and pounded in his groin, which tightened possessively. He understood exactly what she meant and her secret message only made him burn for her more than he ever could have imagined.

He stepped closer. The heat shimmering off her body warmed his chest, and her light musk invaded his senses. His eye caught the little pulse in her neck. He leaned in and kissed it, pressing his lips to her damp and salty skin.

A tiny sigh escaped her. She seemed to love his kiss. He moved closer, slid his hands to her shoulders, and feathered the tip of his tongue over her soft flesh. Mmm, she was so delicious. He almost put his arms around her and told her secretly how much he loved her, but he resisted that nearly overwhelming need. To do that here in front of their audience would not only violate the promise he'd made to himself, but would also be too dangerous. All he could do was try to communicate his love for her through the way he touched her, licked her, and made love to her.

He dappled tiny kisses on her neck and throat. She tilted her head back, and he tasted the soft underside of her jaw, then inched upward to her lips. His cock was hard and strained with want. He pressed his body to hers and nestled his erection into the soft, warm crevice of her sex. He wanted nothing more than to pull off the panties she wore and slide into her, but he held back, wanting first to give her as much pleasure as he could.

Kassie moaned softly and answered the press of his groin by opening her legs and moving her hips against his.

He sucked in his breath. The friction against his cock sent licks of heat up the shaft. He took her mouth, tugged her soft lips against his tongue.

She answered his kiss with her own fervent gulping, as if she could inhale him and take him inside her. Her desire radiated through her kiss, unleashed from inside her the wild woman who wanted to devour him.

Kassie lowered her bound hands between their bodies. Her fingertips blazed down his skin and left tingling fire on his stomach as she reached for the loincloth tie. In one quick movement, she pulled it open and the white material slid off his hips to the floor. Her mouth sought his for the deepest kisses she could take and then pulled away to hungrily suckle his skin in a fiery trail down his neck and over his chest.

He grasped her shoulders as her hot tongue on his skin robbed him of his ability to think. Grasping her shoulders, he turned them both so he could support his sagging weight on the wall. She kissed his chest again, teased a hot trail with her tongue over to one nipple.

He sucked in a breath. Even the women in the combat zones hadn't done that to him. Kassie flickered her tongue teasingly over the hard tip, the way he'd done to her the night before. He panted, slid his fingers into her silky hair, and followed her movements. She sucked and teased until Lian thought his cock would explode, then she dragged her mouth across his chest again and lingered the same way on his other nipple.

After several intoxicating moments, she continued down his torso. Her warm moist lips made his skin feel like it was on fire. His cock twitched as the heat of her mouth drew closer. She paused at his navel and swiveled the tip of her tongue in the indentation while lowering herself to her knees. Lian nearly lost his mind.

Kassie's slid her bound hands up his inner thighs, brushed her fingertips over his balls.

He sucked in a breath. She teased the underside of his balls, back and forth, while her hot breath caressed his cock. He worried he'd spill himself too soon, before he could pleasure her, and fought for control when she leaned in and swiped her tongue up the length of his rigid shaft.

He groaned. She did it again. He squeezed his eyes shut and tilted his head back against the hard wall. Damn! Like an angel of pleasure she took his cock into her mouth. Greedily, her sweet pink lips engulfed the swollen head. She pulled her lips tight and sucked.

Lian groaned again. He couldn't think, could only sag against the wall and struggle to hold up his weight.

Kassie took him in halfway. She moaned softly, the sound vibrating against his cock. The moist heat of her mouth massaged his shaft, made his body feel like mush. She pulled back and swallowed him in again, one slide after the other, fondling his balls at the same time with her fingertips.

He moaned, panted, tried to gather his strength to stop her and lay her back. All he wanted was her body underneath his, his cock sheathed in her hot cavern. She pulled several more groans of pleasure from him and his fingers tightened in her soft golden hair. He followed her bobbing movements as she sucked his cock, until he couldn't bear not being inside her a moment longer.

In one hard effort, he stilled her head, pulled out of her mouth, and crouched down in front of her. He scooped her up and carried her up the platform steps to the bed they'd shared the night before. Gently, but with firm determination, he laid her onto her back. She stared up at him, her lips gleaming from sucking him, her blue eyes wild with heat.

He climbed onto the bed and slid the lace panties down her legs over her high-heeled shoes. He threw the flimsy little things aside and pushed her legs apart. Her legs fell wide open and freed him to kiss his way back up her leg. The smooth skin practically melted under his tongue. He flicked his tongue along her inner thigh, that baby soft skin he wanted to devour. She moaned and sighed, then moved her hips back and forth in silent invitation.

Just as he reached the core of her womanhood, her musky feminine scent filled his nostrils and drove him wild. He kissed the last few inches of her thigh and spread her lower lips with gentle thumbs.

She let out a soft cry and inched closer as if to push her sex onto his mouth. He swiped his tongue gently over her clit, then paused and breathed in her musk. She moved again and whimpered, and he understood her silent plea. He took her inner sex between his lips and tongue. Her tangy juices coated his lips and her hips bucked against his mouth. He laved the tiny hard bud of her clit with his tongue, gauging her pleasure by the moans that slid from her throat one after the other. She tasted so incredible and she seemed to love his mouth on her.

Urged on, he pushed one finger, then two, inside her. Her open, silky passage swallowed his fingers over and over as he pulsed them gently in and out.

She cried out and arched her hips. Her tiny inner muscles tightened around his fingers. He continued teasing and licking her until she went limp. Her breasts heaved as her heavy-lidded eyes watched him with wonder and desire.

His erection throbbed and tensed painfully. He couldn't wait a second longer.

Moving up on her body, he lifted her arms above her head and opened her completely to him. With one hand he spread her already wet sex and slid in, carefully but hungrily.

Her sheath closed around him with a mind-blowing mixture of moist tightness. He nearly came there and then.

He paused to give her a few moments to get used to him being inside her. He imagined she was still tender from the night before and didn't want to hurt her, even though her body, a sweet mixture of soft curves and firm lithe muscle, was driving him to madness.

Her inner muscles squeezed him. He groaned, no longer able to hold back. He thrust harder, pushing deeply into her and grinding his pelvis against hers.

Pleasure shuddered through his body. He sank onto her welcoming softness and kissed her, giving her a taste of her own female juices. His lips were slick and he kissed her wildly, spreading her musk over her lips and chin. Her scent filled the air, wild and primal and he couldn't hold back. He drove into her tight sheath again and again, completely, utterly intoxicated with her.

She gasped softly and writhed underneath him.

They fit perfectly together in every way.

She bucked her hips against him, demanding more. Her legs were unbound and she pulled them back. Her thighs squeezed his hips and she panted into his mouth.

Lian slid his hands around her back and pulled her close against him, driven by the reality that their moments together were precious and by the fear that each encounter could be their last.

He held on as long as he could and alternated deep hot kisses with thrusts inside her until her tight moistness pulled his climax from him. In driving waves, the pleasure crashed through his body and left him breathless. He collapsed lightly on top of her.

He closed his eyes and pressed his face into her hair, breathing in her scent. He stayed inside her, wishing that his seed could take root. Of course, it couldn't because of the sterilization implant.

Lian rested inside of her, feeling his erection begin to stir once again. He wanted nothing more than to make love to Kassie forever, but one of the guards called out to them and he pulled out and lifted away from her before the guards could do it for him.

He reached for his loincloth and tied it on in a casual way that belied his heartache. He hated having to pretend that leaving her was nothing more than the fulfillment of his duty as a performer in Sector S, when inside, the separation tore at his heart.

Now, after having made love to Kassie and feeling the way she opened her body to him, Lian knew the separation tore at her heart, too.

"In case you haven't guessed, you and the Chinaman are the main attraction of this hotel." The guard's green eyes shone from her ruddy face. She put up the force field and lowered her phazer.

Kass looked at her. She held her wrists out to be cuffed as she'd done every night for the past few weeks. "What do you mean?"

The guard chuckled as she did her nightly inspection of Kass's most recent next-to-nothing outfit and loose hair. "The Party bigwigs rave about the way you and the Chinaman get down. Haven't you noticed that the muckamucks put you two together every night?"

"No, I guess I haven't." Kass felt her face burn at the lie. Of course, she'd noticed. She'd given a performance with Lian every day for several weeks now, and it was always the same pattern. First one of them had to fight off an opponent, then they made love. Kass wouldn't be happy about so much fighting except it kept her in form for the day when they made their escape.

The guard ran one hand down the length of Kass's hair. "The buzz I've managed to catch is that your audiences feel like they're spying on private moments. It really does it for them. And the fighting! The way you defend each other and beat your opponents before you do it." Her voice fell to a whisper on the last phrase, as if sex embarrassed her.

But Kass wasn't embarrassed. The only thing she minded was that they could never have their arms around each other at the same time. One or the other was always bound at the wrists. She longed for the day when they could embrace for as long as they wanted. That was, if Lian wanted it, too.

The guard took out the cuffs. "When I watch, I always get the feeling that you're in love."

Kass's heart nearly jumped up her throat. She'd been trying not to let her feelings for Lian show. God forbid their true relationship be found out and thwart their upcoming escape.

Each night during their performances, Lian used their secret language to tell her as much as he could of the escape plan he'd made. It took several sessions before she knew the whole thing. He was going to use the nerve press on his guard's neck to render him unconscious, steal his uniform and scan card, and then come to her room and get her. From there, they'd find a way to sneak out of the building and make their way to the border.

It seemed an impossible task, but Lian was absolutely determined to escape and Kass took heart from his confidence that they would somehow succeed. Or die together trying. There was no in between.

"I'm not in love. I don't even know his name," she managed to say.

The guard lowered the force field and led Kass through. "Well, just keep up the good work. The more they want to watch you, the better it is for both of you."

Kass shivered at the words, which haunted her through the whole evening and almost daunted her pleasure with Lian.

But after they'd finished making love for their audience and Lian lay holding her, she felt his fingers brush her back just as the guards started the end-of-show procedure.

The same anxiety caused her heart to lurch each time she and Lian were separated, but this time, her breath hitched extra hard.

Lian just barely finished his message before the guards pulled them apart.

Escape.

Tomorrow night.

Chapter 5

Something was terribly wrong.

Kass paced her room, dressed and ready as if she were going to their regular performance. But the evening meal had come and gone, and still she waited. Lian had planned to overpower the guard when he delivered the evening meal to Lian's cell. That meant that Lian would have fetched her within minutes.

So where was he?

Maybe he hadn't tried to escape. Or maybe he had tried, and failed. He could even be dead.

Her heart raced painfully and she clenched her fists until her nails dug into her palms. She shivered even though the room was rather warm.

The force field rose and her door slid open.

Her breath hitched and she turned, desperate to see Lian.

Instead, her world nearly collapsed when she saw her guard's uniformed large frame filling the doorway. Two male guards flanked her.

A wide grin spread across the woman guard's pale face. "You and the Chinaman have hit the big time," she said in a singsong. With the handcuffs ready, she stepped into Kass's room.

Kass almost sagged with utter relief. The guard wouldn't be talking like that if something obviously bad had happened to Lian. But then, why hadn't he escaped? A chill of dread touched her heart. Something must have gone wrong.

"What do you mean?" Suspended between conflicting emotions, Kass teetered on her spiky heels, her vision blurred. She held out her wrists.

The guard came toward her. "Well, one of the High Commissioners of the Party is vacationing here with his wife. They saw you two last night and requested a personal session."

The woman was practically giggling with glee. She wasn't an unkind person and actually treated Kass rather humanely, despite being a prison guard. However, Kass would have liked to see how gleeful she'd be if their positions were reversed.

"A personal session with me?"

"With both of you. The Chinaman has already been brought upstairs. I'm supposed to check your hair and make sure you're presentable."

So that was it. A change in routine made escape too risky. If she had two additional male guards, then certainly there had been several guards waiting for Lian as well. Three large, fully armed guards who would have made his plan impossible to execute without dying in the process.

A chill snaked up her spine.

The guard circled Kass and clucked her approval. "I think you'll do very nicely. Although I don't understand why the muckamucks around here care so much about what you're wearing, especially a girl as pretty as you." She clapped on the handcuffs, steered Kass to the doorway, then used her scan card to lower the force field.

Even though her words were probably meant as a compliment, Kass couldn't bring herself to thank her, especially when she started down the hallway surrounded by guards with phazers.

The guard chuckled. "Yeah, I can't understand why they care so much about what you wear in this place. You never stay dressed for long."

The High Commissioner's suite was on the top floor of the hotel. One guard opened the door and Kass found herself in a large, luxurious hotel room. She scanned the room in desperate search for Lian.

He wasn't there.

Kass's gut clenched as she was led to the center of the room. Recessed lighting cast a sensual glow on the decor heavy on animal print pillows, and the plate glass windows showed the twinkling night cityscape.

"Stay right there," her guard said. "There is a lot of security stationed here." The woman gave her a pointed look and Kass understood the warning underneath it. Don't try anything. You won't make it out alive.

Kass's heartbeat increased and she could feel the heat begin in the recesses of her body. What had happened to Lian? What if the guard had lied to her about performing here with him? What if he'd actually tried to put their plan into action and had gotten caught? She fought back tears and struggled to breathe normally.

She heard the door to the suite click and then open. She stared ahead and stifled a cry of relief.

There he was, being led toward her. As usual, he wore only his loincloth and handcuffs.

Her gaze locked with his, but she forced herself not to smile in her joy. Lian nodded his head, a movement so small, she could only know what it meant from their years together of communicating in secret.

"Well, hello there."

Kass turned at the sound of the silky female voice and saw a woman of her height with a mane of frizzy blond hair. Her silk robe whispered around her slim body as she moved.

Immediately Kass recognized the High Commissioner's wife from many telescreen broadcasts over the last few years. Her husband, formerly the vice president of the United States, had led the coup which began the establishment of the New Order.

Kass gritted her teeth. Tension made her body clench all over. In her entire life, she'd never felt hatred for anyone except this woman and her husband, the people who'd destroyed so many lives and enslaved even more. It figured they wanted slaves for sex too.

The woman came to a stop in front of Lian and Kass. Large brown eyes under a fringe of heavy lashes raked over her face and nearly naked body with sensual heavy-lidded hunger. The woman moved over a step and did the same with Lian. The way she checked Lian out, as if he were a piece of meat instead of a man, sent chills through Kass's whole body.

"Do you want them bound or unbound, Ma'am?" One of the guards stood over them as if they were going to try to escape right then and there. "Don't worry. Our phazers are set on kill should they try anything."

The woman tapped one manicured fingernail reflectively against her cheek while her gaze slipped over Kass and then Lian. She licked her lips.

"Hmm, isn't that a decision everyone would like to make?" Her dusky lips curled into a grin. "Unbound, please. I want them to be able to touch us back."

Kass stared at her as the guards uncuffed her and Lian. Apparently, these people didn't intend to observe a performance. They intended to participate.

The guards saluted the High Commissioner's wife. "We will be right outside the door if there are any problems."

When he was gone, she turned back around. Kass's heart thumped. Her throat went dry and she felt again that horrid sense of violation she'd had in Central when the guard had made her strip for the voice behind the glass. Thank God for Lian standing close beside her.

"So beautiful," she breathed, "Both of you are so beautiful."

She ran her fingertips across Lian's cheek.

Gripped by a horrible fear, Kass glanced at him and tried to measure his response. Had he liked this woman's touch? If he did, his expression didn't show it. She clenched her fists and fought back the wave of possessiveness that gripped her. Of course, she had no claim on Lian but that didn't make it any easier to watch another woman ogle him, especially one who was probably going to have sex with him. Damn. She wanted to be Lian's only lover.

The woman slid her hand across Lian's chest and down his stomach. Kass wanted to tear her gaze away but stared at the woman's hand, watching its trail on Lian's skin as her fingertips headed downward.

Kass caught her breath. The woman's hand stopped at the border of Lian's loincloth. Kass exhaled, unable to suppress her relief. Maybe, just maybe, the High Comissioner's wife would only want to touch him a little and leave it at that. Maybe Kass wouldn't have to share him completely.

The woman switched her attention to Kass and smoothed her touch over Kass's shoulder. "Mmm, so soft." She turned her doe-like eyes toward another doorway and smiled at the tall man standing there. "Aren't they just scrumptious, darling?"

Kass recognized him immediately. The High Commissioner. The man who was the cause of their suffering all these years. He was tall and handsome with chiseled features and dark hair streaked with silver at the temples. Bare-chested, he wore only silk undershorts—the kind only Upper Party members could afford—tented in front by his erection. Had the circumstances been radically different, Kass could have seen him as an attractive man, but the reality was, he'd destroyed their lives and now had her and Lian as his sex slaves.

He puffed out his muscular chest with its coating of dark hair. Kass swore she could see the cold heart beating bloodlessly in that broad chest.

He strode across the room to them, a wineglass tilted casually in one large hand. His blue eyes roved over Kass but lingered on her breasts, just visible through her lacy get-up. Kass's skin shivered as if the man's eyes were hands. He perused the rest of her and then trained his eyes on her sex.

Kass felt her cheeks heat up and she dug her nails into her palms. One of the worst feelings in the world was being leered at by someone she absolutely hated. A sideways glance showed her the subtle tightening in Lian's jaw and in the fist at his side. His possessive anger practically simmered in the air.

"Yes," the High Commissioner said. "You have exquisite taste, my dear."

His wife ran her fingertips down Kass's arm. The light graze of her nail made Kass shiver. She pressed her lips together and wished this were already over.

The woman turned back to Lian. She put her hand palm down on one side of his chest. Kass caught her breath. Again Lian's expression remained neutral and Kass couldn't even hear a change in his breathing. She wished desperately she knew what he was thinking.

"This one is so exotic, honey. I knew when we saw him last night he was perfect for you."

The High Commissioner reached out his free hand and brushed his thumb across Lian's bottom lip. "Yes, darling, you thought correctly."

Kass's heartbeat raced and sweat beaded on her upper lip. How much longer were she and Lian going to have to stand there and take this? His wife slid her hand over Lian's torso. She toyed with the tie of his loincloth. Kass held her breath and from the corner of her eye watched the woman run her hands over Lian's groin. Damn her! For one second Kass seriously considered attacking her. Death had to be better than this torment.

When Lian didn't get an erection, Kass breathed a small sigh of relief. At this point she didn't care if it was because of Lian's self-discipline, she was just glad he wasn't responding to the other woman's touch.

"Don't be nervous, sweetheart. We don't bite." She giggled. "Not unless you want us to."

Kass dug her fingertips into her palm. Her heart thrashed as if it were trying to escape her chest. How were Lian and she going to have sex with these people? They didn't care about anything but their own selfish pleasures. They certainly didn't care about her and Lian, yet they expected their sex slaves to behave as if their passions were mutual. In that moment, Kass would have preferred a sentence of hard labor.

Beside her, she felt Lian tense. She moved closer to him until their arms lightly touched. Even the mere whisper of contact comforted her and infused her with greater strength.

The woman untied Lian's loincloth and let it fall to the floor. A large smile spread across her face and her brown eyes widened. "Ooh, just as nice close up!"

Kass caught her breath softly, terrified that the woman was going to touch his penis. Lian didn't have an erection and the High Commissioner's wife undoubtedly would want to correct that.

Lian's hand closed softly around Kass's, his fingertips worked surreptitiously in her palm.

No fear. We leave soon. Follow me.

The woman slid her hand around Lian's hip. Her red-manicured nails grazed Lian's buttock.

Kass's heart crashed in her chest.

From the corner of her eye, Kass saw the High Commissioner rub a large hand over Lian's shoulder. He and his wife were both closing in on Lian. They seemed to find him of more erotic interest. Kass had to help him.

Emboldened, she released Lian's hand, stepped forward and whispered her hands over the woman's arms.

The woman looked wide-eyed at Kass.

Kass gave her as silky a smile as she could muster and passed her tongue across her lips. For a split-second, Kass thought she'd been too bold and was now in trouble.

In the next second, however, the woman turned her full attention on Kass and slid her fingertips over Kass's arms. Her touch eased over Kass's shoulders to her breasts, passing lightly across her nipples. The contact sent a zing of energy through her body.

The woman's hands played over Kass's torso and loosened the negligee's strings until the black sheer material fell away. She purred and squeezed Kass's bare breasts. "This is going to be fun."

She looked at her husband and Kass followed her gaze. The High Commissioner was running one large hand over Lian's chest and arms the way his wife was doing to Kass. Kass searched Lian's unreadable expression, but his features were stony and his body was in a rigid stance.

A wave of fear shivered over her. She didn't want Lian to enjoy these people, but if they weren't pleased, they could have him punished. However, neither the High Commissioner nor his wife seemed to notice Lian's lack of response.

The woman grasped Kass's arms, gave her another suggestive smile and tugged her in the direction of the bedroom.

Kass glanced at Lian. He nodded as they passed through the doorway into the bedroom.

The huge bed, a plateau of animal-print pillows and shiny silk, jutted into the center of the room. Its size could easily accommodate all four of them.

At the end of the room was a sitting area of plump pillows and a low table with a vase of flowers. The Commissioner's and his wife's uniforms lay slung over the arms of the beige love seat, and their boots sat on the floor close by.

The Commissioner set his wineglass on the nightstand and threw back the covers on the giant bed. A large grin curved his lips and rugged cheeks. His wine-drunk eyes were still leering at Lian as if Lian were the most incredible thing he'd ever seen.

"I can't wait to feel those beautiful lips of yours on my cock," he said. He put his hands on Lian's shoulders and pushed at him to get into the bed.

"I'd love to see that, darling," his wife said.

Kass felt her mouth drop open, but Lian glanced at her and jerked his chin toward the woman. Sensing Lian had a plan, Kass obediently turned to the wife.

The woman had already shed her robe and climbed in. She smiled at Kass and patted the space next to her. Kass clenched her teeth even though she tried to act like she was really glad to be there.

The High Commissioner's wife had a lithe, athletic body and turned to jut her ample breasts toward Lian's face as soon as he was in the bed beside her. She crooned something again about Lian's beautiful physique as she ran her hand over Lian's back muscles. Jealousy stabbed at Kass.

The High Commissioner climbed in beside him and turned onto his side.

"And I want to watch the girl eat your pussy at the same time."

"Ooh, I can't wait." The woman smiled and purred. She smoothed a manicured hand down Kass's backside. Kass suppressed a shiver and looked at Lian.

"All your wishes will be granted, Sir," Lian said quietly.

To the untrained ear, Lian sounded agreeable and accommodating, but Kass had known him for far too long not to hear the string of tension coiled in his voice. She knew then that he had a plan and that she had only to go along with what was happening in the moment to find out what that plan was.

The High Commissioner's wife turned once again to Kass and maneuvered her body into Kass's arms. She rolled onto her back, pulling Kass over her, and slipped her hands into Kass's hair.

"Kiss me," she whispered.

Kass obeyed. She brushed her lips over the other woman's.

A murmur sounded in the woman's throat and her fingers tightened in Kass's hair. She pushed her tongue between Kass's lips and danced it hungrily against Kass's tongue.

Kass pretended to surrender. She sank her upper body onto the woman's and pressed their breasts together. But as she continued her submissive ruse, she watched Lian for his signal.

Lian had turned over. The curves and bulges of his back muscles were shadowed and accentuated by the soft lighting in the room. He leaned over the High Commissioner and Kass saw one of his hands on the man's chest.

The Commissioner lay on his back with one hand caressing Lian's spine. In the next second, his hand fell limp. Lian had done a nerve press on his neck which had caused him to black out.

She turned her attention back to his wife and dipped her tongue sensuously between the woman's lips. The woman seemed oblivious to anything except Kass's erotic advances, including Lian turning over in the bed next to her.

Lian brushed his fingertips over the woman's neck. She moaned softly into Kass's mouth. Kass opened her eyes and her gaze met Lian's. Again he nodded and caressed the woman's neck. This time, she pulled her mouth from Kass's, turned to Lian and smiled.

"Oh," she purred, "Don't stop."

Lian smiled at her as he danced his fingertips over the delicate pulse in her throat. With a barely perceptible movement he pressed down. Without a sound, her eyes closed and she blacked out.

"They won't be unconscious for long," he whispered. "Let's go."

Her blood ran cold. Their chance to be free was now, this second. They wouldn't have another.

She climbed out of the bed and helped Lian pull the covers over the Commissioner and his wife to tuck them in. When they'd finished, the unconscious couple appeared to be sleeping peacefully. But when they woke up, they'd want to execute Lian and her.

Kass followed Lian to the loveseat where they hurriedly dressed in the Commissioner's and his wife's uniforms. Kass was buckling the belt of the baggy trousers when Lian slipped one foot into the Commissioner's boot and then lifted it out again. His fingers curled around the handle of the phazer that had been hidden within.

Kass froze.

He looked at her. "Check yours," he said softly.

She found a second phazer tucked in the woman's right boot.

"Set it on stun," he said.

Kass did as he told her and they finished getting dressed. She put on the boots and uttered a silent prayer of thanks that the clothing fit them well enough. No casual observer would realize the uniforms were not their own.

When they were dressed, Lian stood close in front of her. He put one hand on her shoulder. "We're going to the door now and ring the service button. When the guards walk in, we'll stun them."

She nodded. Her heart clawed and hammered in her chest. She wondered if Lian was as frightened as she was. He'd learned long ago to hide his fear under a cool mask, and she took heart from the certainty that darkened his handsome features.

Lian cupped her cheek gently. His touch infused her with warmth and strength.

"We're going to make it," he whispered. "I've given us no choice."

She nodded and put her hand over his. She loved touching him so much and prayed that she'd have more chances to do so soon.

He bowed his head and kissed her lips softly. When he lifted his mouth from hers, his eyes burned with determination.

"It's time, Kassie. Come."

He lifted his hand from her cheek and led her to the door of the suite.

Chapter 6

Lian stood on one side of the door and Kass stood on the other, their phazers poised and ready. He held up his fingers.

One. Two. Three.

On the third finger count, he lifted his hand to the service button by the door.

She caught her breath. A cold sweat erupted on her body.

He pressed the button.

The door opened. First one guard entered, followed by a second. They took several steps into the room.

"Commissioner? You called?"

Lian nodded at Kass. In unison they turned and fired.

Both guards passed out in a heap of black uniforms to the soft carpet.

Two more guards poured through the doorway with their phazers pointed. Lian and Kass stunned them before they could turn and see them.

Lian holstered his phazer. "Hurry."

He grabbed one of the guards by the boots and dragged him into the room. Kass helped him do the same with the second guard.

"Take a scan card," he told her.

They each unclipped a card from a sleeping guard's gun belt and shoved it in their pockets.

No more guards came in. Lian peered through the doorway and checked the hall.

"All clear."

Kass followed him out into the hall. Her heavy boots sank into the plush red carpet with each hurried step.

Lian shut the door behind them and hung a Do Not Disturb sign on the knob. With a ranking member of the Party staying here, that sign would surely be honored, giving them some extra time to get out of the hotel before anyone discovered they were missing.

They made their way down the hall to the service elevator that had brought them upstairs. Lian pressed the down button and they waited.

Kass stared at the steel doors. She fought to keep her breathing normal. Next to her, Lian stood comfortingly close, and she could hear by the deep rhythm of his breathing that he was working hard on the same thing.

Finally the bell on the elevator dinged and the steel doors parted. Kass caught her breath.

A waiter in a red jacket emerged, pushing a room service cart. He nodded politely to them. His expression did not betray any surprise he might feel at seeing people in Party uniforms using the service elevator.

Thankfully, he moved on and they stepped inside. Kass held her breath until the doors closed, then heaved a sigh of relief. Her blood pounded through her body. She saw Lian's chest heave with a deep breath, too, and he sagged against the wall.

Reaching for her hand, he pulled her so close that she could see the light sheen of sweat on his golden skin. His brown eyes simmered and made her heart jump. In spite of their dire circumstances, he could melt her heart and body with a simple look.

"Wo ai ni," he said softly.

She blinked. In all the time she'd known Lian, the only times he'd ever spoken Chinese was while teaching her the terminology of kung fu. The words he'd just said were unfamiliar. "What did you say?"

He reached up and smoothed her hair back. "I'll tell you when we get to Paradise."

She stared at him while her heart raced. She noticed he'd said when and not if. She prayed he was right.

Kass glanced at the floor counter on the control panel. They'd nearly reached the third floor. She took a deep breath. Another few seconds and they'd be on their way out of the building. Out of their prison.

Suddenly, the bell dinged.

She gasped.

They were stopping too soon.

Lian stepped in front of her and pressed her to the wall with his back to the elevator doors. He bowed his head and kissed her mouth in wild, passionate gulps.

Kass understood what he was doing and added to the scene. She locked one leg around his hip and moaned loudly into his mouth. She pulled him into her arms and rubbed his strong back through the scratchy Party shirt. Their first embrace. Ever. Except that he didn't embrace her back, but set his palms flat against the wall on either side of her head.

In the back of her consciousness she heard the doors slide open. Lost in their role playing, she surged against Lian and squeezed his body tightly to hers.

Whoever had been waiting for the elevator was now getting an eyeful of two people passionately making out.

Lian raised one hand, waving the person away, as if it were completely within his rights to usurp the elevator for his carnal needs. Because of the uniform he wore, Kass knew he'd be obeyed.

"Yes, Sir," Kass heard a female voice say.

The doors closed, leaving them alone again.

Lian's body relaxed. He lifted his mouth from their kiss to sigh deeply and rested his forehead against hers.

His warm breath pulsed on her face and passed across her lips, swollen and throbbing from those wild kisses.

His erection pressed into her belly through the heavy canvas trousers. Apparently, their act was not completely an act for him, either.

Kass let her leg slip back down, but kept her arms around him, palms resting on the chiseled planes of muscle in his back. She loved holding him like this, even though it was not yet a complete embrace. His hands remained pressed into the wall on either side of her.

"I'm scared, Lian," she whispered as the elevator continued its rapid descent to the ground floor.

He raised his head and looked at her, his dark eyes smoldering.

"So am I, Kassie. But we'll do this. Together."

She nodded just as the elevator landed.

The doors slid open to reveal the large hotel kitchens. Uniformed waiters bearing trays and carts bustled in and out of the swinging doors. Chefs worked behind sizzling grills and chopped and mixed at long stainless steel counters. Random workers raised their heads to stare blankly at Kass and Lian as if they couldn't possibly comprehend the presence of visitors in the work area.

Lian slung his arm nonchalantly across her shoulders and planted a large, loud kiss on her cheek. He laughed and sauntered casually out of the elevator with Kass under his arm.

She kissed him back and giggled, doing her part to add to the illusion of a honeymoon couple oblivious to the world.

He leaned down and pretended to whisper something in her ear. She giggled loudly as if he'd told her the funniest joke she'd ever heard.

They passed a waiter pushing a cart and Lian tapped him on the shoulder.

"Hey, buddy." Lian slurred his voice to sound a bit drunk. "Where's the door in this place? My wife and I took a wrong turn somewhere."

The uniforms they wore spoke loudly, and the waiter left his cart to escort Kass and Lian to a service door. A guard stood at the door with a phazer rifle slung over his shoulder.

Kass caught her breath. She had to work hard to maintain her giggly demeanor. One slip and they were dead.

The guard stood at attention and saluted them as they came near. Then he stood aside and passed his scan card over the control panel.

The door clicked open and the guard held it for them.

Lian took his arm off Kass's shoulder and gallantly gestured for her to pass through first.

She simpered at him as she passed by.

Lian followed her through the door then bestowed a glance at the guard.

"Thanks, man," he said, playing the role of a cocky young officer in the Party to his utmost.

The door closed behind them and Lian took her hand.

"Keep up the act a bit longer," he said softly. He tugged her gently to follow him. "We have to get out to the street and find a cab."

The night was arid and cool and the hotel's service parking lot was pleasantly quiet and devoid of other people.

Kass walked at Lian's side and they emerged onto the sidewalk of a street that ran behind the hotel.

The glow of colorful neon signs and honking car horns directed them toward the main part of the city. They walked at a more brisk pace the closer they got.

❧❀❦

A phazer set on stun worked on its victim for about twelve minutes. Kass didn't know exactly how many minutes had passed since they'd used their phazers on the guards, but she guessed that the men would be waking up pretty soon.

They would find the Commissioner and his wife in the bed, unconscious.

They would find the prisoners had disappeared.

The search for the escaped prisoners would begin.

Lian led her over to the first taxi they saw. He slid his arm over her shoulders again, affecting that same casual air as before in the hotel kitchen.

The driver was a beat-up scrag whose age was hard to tell because of his patchy beard and stringy hair. He sat in the driver's seat next to an open window with tobacco smoke billowing through it.

"'Scuse me, man," Lian said. He made himself sound like he'd just come from reveling. "Can I buy your car?"

The driver gaped at them as if they had green skin and three heads each. In the background, his tele-radio was flashing the latest newsbreaks across the tiny screen.

Kass's heart kicked up its pounding another notch. All they would need is for the news flash of their disappearance to come through before they could get safely away.

"Are you kidding?" the cabbie answered. "I mean no disrespect, sir, but this is a junk heap. They won't give us the newer models. This is a '65. Not even turbo channels in the damn thing. Forget about hovering."

Lian chuckled. "I don't care. It's for my girl here. We just tied the knot a few minutes ago and I promised her a night drive in the desert. You know how it is."

The driver eyed Kass for a second and took a puff of his tobacco. "I don't know, Sir. I'm still on payments. Cheap ass bastards in dispatch. I'll be paying off this shit box for the next five years."

Lian reached into his pocket and pulled out a wad of currency. Kass stifled a soft gasp as Lian thrust the High Commissioner's money in the cabbie's face.

The older man's eyes widened and he tossed his tobacco stick out onto the pavement. "You're shittin' me! There's gotta be 10 g's there!"

"I'd guess," Lian answered as if he were wildly rich. "How 'bout it, man? You'd be able to pay off this thing and buy yourself three more."

The tele-radio blared on. "Two prisoners have escaped—"

Kass squeezed Lian's other hand. He returned her squeeze, letting her know he'd heard it too.

The man's eyes never left the wad of bills in Lian's extended fist.

"—A man with Asian features and a Caucasian woman—"

Oblivious to the news report, the cabbie opened the door and stepped aside. Wordlessly, he took the payment from Lian's hand.

"Starter laser's in the ignition," he said and stuffed the money in his pants pocket as if he feared Lian would change his mind and snatch it back.

"Thanks, man. Have a good one." Lian slipped into the driver's seat and waited for Kass to get in.

The second she shut the passenger door, he revved the engine, shifted gears, and peeled away from the curb.

Lian wove through the traffic as fast as he could without attracting attention. It would have been difficult to go any faster because of the taxis and Committee vehicles leisurely cruising for prostitutes down the streets or checking out the sexual displays of live nude bodies in the storefront windows.

Every so often on the tele-radio, the report of their escape crossed the screen with a news update and a flash of their mug shots from the prison. Each time Kass saw them, her blood ran cold and her pulse skittered.

At last, they left the city's congestion and headed into the desert night.

She drew a few deep breaths to calm herself. "We're probably in range now. I'm going to try to radio Paradise station so they'll know to be on the lookout for us."

"Good idea."

Suddenly her blood chilled. In their concentration to escape, Kass realized, they'd forgotten a crucial thing.

"Lian, I know this is a horrible time to ask, but how are we going to lower the force field?" She didn't need to remind him that the police had confiscated their mobilizers during their arrest.

"Shit. I hadn't even thought about it. Maybe we can drive to a lag point and fight our way through. We have the phazers." He glanced at her and Kass saw him grin. "All that training in wu shu will have to be useful sometime, huh?"

In spite of the situation, she smiled. His confidence always bolstered her. Protecting lag points was one of the main duties of the Border Guards. The Confederation had not yet figured out a way to keep the force field uniform along the entire border of Paradise. It was just too damn long. So guards were stationed at the gaps. Lag points were fiercely guarded with barbed wire and automatic phazers coordinated by higher-ranked guards. Any movement through the lag point and the phazers would shoot wide radius beams. Lian had never had the coordinates to disarm them and so he had never been able to plan their escape by this means.

"I'm not sure we should do that. I don't see how we could duck the auto-phazers even if we did get past the guards."

He frowned. "You're right."

Kass reached across the front seat to stroke his arm. Lian had always been humble, quick to admit his errors, and with a good sense of humor about his faults. Those qualities only made her admire him more.

Their vehicle's headlights shone on the junction signs.

"We'll take 234," Lian said. "A bit longer to the border but hopefully they'll expect us to take the shortest route to the lag point. We might catch them by surprise."

"Good idea." Her heart pumped like mad as he jerked the wheel and ground the accelerator to the floor. The engine ground and hummed loudly over the empty desert highway.

Lian grunted. "That cabbie was right. This thing is a shit box. We're lucky to have gotten this far."

Kass stared through the window into the darkness. She'd always liked the desert, still and cool at night. When on watch, she used to pretend that there was no Confederation, only the sand and desert creatures and the clear stars above.

And Lian.

Her heartbeat sped up. Even in the dark Kass recognized where they were, roughly ten miles from one of the lag points.

They were so close now.

She caught her breath. Headlights shone from the oncoming direction. Kass's heart lurched. "Lian!"

"I see it." His hands tightened visibly on the steering wheel. "Let's hope they're joyriders."

The lights drew closer, rising above the ground as the gap closed between the two vehicles. Between tight breaths, Kass fiddled with the tele-screen control to find a coordinate for the other car. She hit on it and the sound of two guys laughing like crazy crackled through the speaker.

They drew closer and she could see that their vehicle was a late model police hover, junked and then salvaged, common among joyriders. The laughter grew louder, hit a high point then softened just as the headlights washed over the cab's interior.

She blew out a breath of relief and sank against the seat.

"You were right." She closed her eyes briefly as relief prickled along her arms.

"This time. But that doesn't mean they haven't heard the reports." He glanced through the side window.

Kass leaned forward again and switched through the various channels on the radio until she heard a male voice say, "Paradise Border Station." What a glorious sound that was!

She locked onto the channel and picked up the receiver. "Two defectors coming from the Confederation. Do you copy?"

"I copy. You understand we can't retrieve you, but we can open the gate."

"I understand."

"Names?"

Kass glanced at Lian. He returned her look and the energy zinged between them. She pressed the button again. "Lian and Kassandra. White female and Asian male dressed in Confederation uniforms. We'll be running like hell."

"I copy," the voice said. "Get here safely."

At that, Lian floored the accelerator and the dark ribbon of highway stretched out before them, lit only by the moon.

About a half mile from the border, the end of the road came into view. The pavement there had been booby trapped with spikes and sensors to destroy the tires or hover capability of any vehicle that tried to get over the border. The road spikes gleamed in their headlights.

Lian screeched to a halt and threw the car into park. He froze with his hand on the door handle. Kass scanned the night landscape until she saw what he saw.

Under a spotlight, two Border Guards stood with their phazer rifles pointed straight at the taxi. Immediately Kass recognized Charlie and Dan, two of the people who had served in her unit. They had once respected Lian as a fair and strong leader of their division. She prayed their respect endured.

Charlie held a transmitter to his mouth. "Drop any weapons you're carrying and come out with your hands up." His voice blared over speakers mounted on a nearby pole.

Lian turned to her. "This is it, Kass. Come on. Leave your phazer in the car."

She nodded, slipped the weapon from its holster at her waist, and left it on the seat behind her. Slowly, she got out of the car.

Dan aimed a flashlight at them and for a moment Kass was blinded. The light was lowered quickly.

"Captain, it really is you. Hey, Kass!" Charlie lowered his phazer and walked toward them.

"Charlie, what are you doing? They're traitors." Dan remained in place, his phazer rifle still poised.

"Come on, Dan, are you crazy? This is our captain. You don't believe that trumped-up charge, do you? He was framed for sure."

Charlie's loyalty stirred Kass's heart, and she dared to hope that they might succeed.

"It's not true, is it, sir?" Charlie asked. "You weren't involved in a conspiracy to assassinate the Prime Commissioner and then escape over the border?"

Lian sighed, his hands still raised. "To escape, yes. But not to kill. Murder is never my way."

Charlie nodded. "I knew it. But wait, you wanted to escape? I thought you were happy here. We have it good, you know."

"Captain, sir." Dan obviously referred not to Lian but to Charlie. "Call them in."

Kass looked at Dan, not surprised at his attitude. He'd always been a strong Party supporter.

"Dan, lower your weapon." Charlie ordered.

"But, sir, we have them now."

"Now."

"Sir, I don't think you understand."

"Now, or I'll be forced to report your earlier disciplinary infractions to Central."

With excruciating slowness, Dan obeyed.

Charlie turned back to Lian. "Why did you want to leave, sir?" His voice held genuine confusion. "I don't understand. You're a captain. You would have worked your way up. Maybe even to a high official. They'd have given you a house, a wife, whatever you want."

Kass's stomach clenched at the mention of a wife for Lian.

"Those things mean nothing if they are given to keep you imprisoned, Charlie," Lian answered. "I've always wanted to return home to San Francisco. My parents raised me there until the roundups. Kassie and I just want to live in freedom. You're the only one who can help us now, friend. Please, let us through. We're at your mercy."

Charlie didn't move.

"Will you let us through?" Lian's voice remained calm, patient.

Charlie eyed him uncertainly. Then his gaze flickered to Kass.

She nodded. "Please, Charlie. They'll kill us now if we don't leave. We're already held like beasts in a cage, forced to...." She trailed off, unable to admit what they'd done.

Charlie stood for another excruciating few seconds, obviously deliberating. Finally he stood straighter, his shoulders back, and saluted Lian.

"Dan!"

"Sir."

Lights and sirens sounded in the distance. The battering whir of a helicopter cut through the air in the distance.

Kass's blood ran cold.

They were coming.

"Torch the car. You'll get merit points for having performed an immediate and crucial execution of two prisoners, armed and dangerous."

Execution. Kass's eyes widened and she nearly forgot to breathe. It sounded as if Charlie might have changed his mind about their innocence. Maybe he wanted to hold them until the police came. The lights and sirens drew closer. The helicopter was almost overhead and the air churned from the whir of the rotor-blades.

But he'd saluted Lian, a sign of respect and obedience, and his phazer remained lowered.

"I don't understand your decision, Captain," Charlie said, "but I respect it. Go on. Hurry."

He stood aside and gestured toward the neutral zone beyond the force field. He pressed the button on his mobilizer and the force field dropped.

"Thank you, Charlie." Lian held out his hand.

Charlie stepped forward and accepted his offer of a handshake. "You're welcome. Now go." He pushed Lian toward the opening.

"Yes, Charlie, thank you," she breathed as the sweet rush of relief flooded her veins.

Charlie waved at the open space. "Quickly."

"Come on, Kassie." Lian grasped her hand and pulled her toward the border. Side by side, hand in hand, they ran with perfectly matched strides. Though she was a bit shorter, Lian didn't have to hold back for her sake. His heart raced and his blood surged in his veins. They were almost there. They were alive. Together. He was moments away from realizing his dream. There was no time to look back. The lights of the Paradise border station were still a quarter mile away, across the neutral zone, beyond the force field's reach.

Behind him thundered the explosion of their car being torched, blending with the battering of the helicopter's rotor-blades. The night glowed with the inferno of the burning vehicle that was supposed to have their dead bodies inside it.

The force field came back up with its strange electric buzz. But the sound was behind him. Not before him.

They were over the border. In the no-man's land. If the helicopter spotted them now, they'd be mowed down without hesitation. But the Paradise border station loomed closer with each step.

His breath pounded in his ears and cold sweat erupted all over his body. It wasn't a long run, but it was a hard one. He tightened his hold on Kassie's hand and glanced at her. Her hair whipped out behind her and her boots thudded on the sand in a rhythm with his. Even though the helicopter blades sounded a bit too much like machine gun fire, even though he might die any second, seeing her like this made it worth it.

How would he know when they were safe on Paradise land? How would the gunners in the chopper know? If he couldn't see the exact border, then neither could anyone else. Besides, bullets knew no boundaries. They had to make it inside the border station in order to be safe.

And they were close enough now that he could see the panes in each window.

Suddenly, Kass's hand slipped from his and she sprawled in the dirt.

Lian skidded to a halt. No!

He dropped to her side but was afraid to touch her. Where was the blood? He didn't see any bullet wounds.

She lifted her head, panting. "I tripped."

He could barely hear her over the helicopter.

"You're okay? I thought you'd been shot."

She nodded and her heavy breathing stirred the wisps of grass between them. What he wouldn't give to be able to hold her now, check her for injuries, wallow in his own relief. But the helicopter hovered over the Confederation border with its high beam trained on their burning car. The distraction was working, but that didn't mean they could linger at the crossing.

"Let's go."

But she waved him off. "Go ahead. I'll catch up."

His heart surged. This woman had been with him through hell, and even though he'd never said a word to her, she'd shown him nothing but devotion and loyalty. Fate had brought them together under nightmarish circumstances and had given them the rarest of chances. This was the moment he'd spent half his life working for and praying for.

Lian slid an arm under her shoulders and lifted her gently to her feet.

"Like hell I'll leave you, Kassie. We're going in together. Or not at all."

Before she could answer, he tugged her hand. "Can you run?"

She nodded, breathless, and by the lights that shone from the nearby border station, he could see unshed tears glistening above a tender smile. "Let's go."

He resisted the urge to kiss her then and there. The next kiss they'd have would be in Paradise.

Chapter 7

Kass's heart pounded even though they ran a bit slower now. Was she imagining it, or did her body instinctively know when they reached official Paradise soil? Her feet felt suddenly lighter in the clunky Party-issue boots. The coarse shirt collar no longer chafed her throat. Even Lian's hand in hers felt more tender and less tense.

They'd made it.

A guard opened the big metal door and ushered them into the border station. From the corner of her eyes, she saw the gate close behind them and the sign over it that said in bold letters, PARADISE.

The tears she'd almost shed when Lian refused to go on without her now slipped from her eyes. He pulled her close.

Without thinking, she wrapped her arms around him and squeezed him. A soft cry escaped her when his arms closed around her and the heat of his hard chest was pressed against her breasts. One hand slipped into her hair, and she felt his face nuzzled into the curve of her neck. No chains. No secrecy. Just them.

Their first real embrace.

For what felt like a long time, she held him and let her tears slide into his shirt. He seemed just as reluctant to let her go. Finally Lian lifted his face and smiled at her. He pressed his forehead to hers.

"We're here," he whispered.

She laughed and sniffled. The reality had not quite settled in and she felt stunned.

"We're here," she echoed. After all Lian's planning and determination. She felt another surge of love for him. For his courage and refusal to give up. For bringing her with him. For always believing that freedom was worth risking everything for.

One of the guards coughed discreetly. "We've been hoping you'd make it."

"As soon as you're able," the guard said, "we need to search you for arms."

"That's fine," Lian said between breaths, "as long as we can stay."

"Of course you can stay." The guard motioned to them to stand apart.

Kass hated being even a few feet away from Lian while the guard patted him down and the second guard checked her.

"They're clean," the first guard said. "Greg, bring them in to Dr. Brighton."

"Yes, sir. This way." The guard named Greg radioed that they were on their way.

"I'm not quite ready yet," Lian said. "May I have a minute?"

"Take your time."

Kass looked at Lian, puzzled.

He came up to her and stood very close.

"I wanted to do this before," he said softly. "But not until we were free."

He reached up and cupped her cheek, then pressed his lips to hers.

Kass's heartbeat leaped to sprinting speed again. Her eyelids fluttered and she sighed. She never wanted it to end.

She felt the dampness of tears wetting her skin. When he finally lifted his mouth from hers, his dark eyes glistened.

"We made it, Kassie."

She nodded, her eyes filling too. They had made it, yes. But now what? Just because they were here didn't mean that he was in love with her. Or that he wanted to stay with her. When the kiss might be nothing more than a celebration of crossing the border.

≈⋙(℧⅋)⋘≈

Lian and Kass were processed, then were fed a meal of soup, bread and fruit. They sat together on a sofa by a large picture window framing a view of the mountains, dark hulking forms against the night sky.

Dr. Brighton sat in a chair opposite them. She had put on a pair of glasses and held a clipboard and pen. Although she looked official, she wore a warm smile that made them feel welcome and safe.

"Now, Kass and Lian, we need you to stay here for two weeks under quarantine. We'll have to do a few tests on you to make certain you aren't carrying any illnesses into the region. I'm sorry to have to tell you that."

"It's all right," Lian assured her. "Anything is fine as long as we never have to go back."

Dr. Brighton laughed softly, but then her smile faded and she fixed them with a serious gaze. "I assure you, you'll never have to go back. It is our fervent hope, of course, that the whole so-called New Order will topple before long and everyone can live freely again without having to risk their lives like you did."

"Thank you very much," Kass said. "I would like to try to find my parents."

"So would I," Lian said. "There was no way to do so back there."

Dr. Brighton nodded. "Yes. I understand. We'll help you contact any family you might have living on this side. And before you leave, we'll provide you with some currency and clothing to help you get started."

Kass's whole being tingled with the anticipation of living in Paradise. The only thing that tamped down her joy was the fear that her new life would not include Lian. What if he wanted to make a whole new beginning? Would he want to find a new woman to share his new free life with? Perhaps Kass would only remind him of his painful past.

She shifted uncomfortably, trying to hide her rising panic.

"Dr. Brighton," Lian said, a strange quaver in his voice, "Do you, um, are you able to reverse sterilization implants? Kassie was forced to have one, like all the girls there."

Kass's heart lurched and her gaze whipped to Lian's face. Why would he ask such a question?

"Yes, we can do that. Of course, once the implant is removed, it may take as many as several months for you to conceive. Your body will need time to get back to normal." Dr. Brighton smiled, her brown eyes sympathetic. "After that, however, you shouldn't have any problems. If you want, Kass, I can do the procedure now. It takes about ten minutes."

Kass's vision blurred and her heart raced. So much had happened that she couldn't process it all. Why had Lian brought up the issue of her sterilization? "Lian?" But how could she ask him?

Dr. Brighton stood up. "I think you two need a bit of privacy. I have a few things to attend to right now. I'll check back in here soon. All right?"

Lian nodded. "Yes, thank you."

She gave Kass's shoulder a friendly squeeze as she passed on her way out.

After the doctor left, Lian turned to her. His dark eyes simmered with a turbulent emotion she couldn't identify.

He picked up her hand and slowly turned it over, palm upward. His breathing rose and fell heavily, giving her the sense he was anxious as he skated his fingertips on her skin.

The pad of his index finger brushed her skin pleasantly and she watched, barely breathing as he traced his message.

I love you.

Her breath caught sharply. Hot tears crowded her eyes. She stared at him, blinking away the salty moisture that blurred her vision.

"Lian," she breathed as understanding flooded her with tingling warmth. "Is that what you said to me in the elevator?"

He nodded. His gaze never left hers. "Forgive me, Kassie, for never telling you. I couldn't—not until—not when we were enslaved. I wanted to tell you when we were here, in Paradise. Now, when I can begin to realize my dreams." He fell silent and watched her with a hopeful expression burning in his brown eyes.

She stared at him, momentarily dumbstruck. Could it possibly be true that life had taken such a glorious turn?

"There's nothing to forgive, Lian. I just can't believe you love me, too."

His eyes lit up. "Of course I do. I loved you from that first moment you came to me on the bench. The way you did that, so sweetly. You wanted to comfort me."

She nodded. Tears welled in her eyes. "I did want to comfort you," she whispered. The lump in her throat made speech difficult. "I always want to."

Lian watched her for another moment. His eyes darkened, and their brown depths took on a velvety sheen. "My father's surname was Hsu," he said softly. "Hsu Wan Li." He took a deep breath. "I'm taking his name back. I want to give it to you, Kassie."

She caught her breath. "You don't mean like a—like a—"

"Wife." He touched her cheek. "Will you be my wife, Kass?"

"Yes, Lian, yes!" She squeezed him, buried her face in the warm, strong curve of his neck.

His arms came up around her and squeezed in return.

Tears of joy pooled in her eyes and ran down her cheeks. She could just hear him continuing to speak, saying things about redwood trees and building a cabin for her and watching her belly swell with his child.

They remained in their tight embrace for what seemed a long time before Kass pulled away and looked at him, sniffling. She wiped her cheeks with the heel of one hand, her other hand rested in Lian's.

"Kassandra Hsu." She tried the name, loving the sound of it. Then it hit her. Never again would Lian and she be forced apart. They were free now. Free to love each other openly.

"Lian, we can say it out loud now. We don't have to hide it."

Lian's eyes burned with light. He cupped her cheeks and kissed her mouth tenderly.

"I love you, Kassie," he said softly. "I love you."

"I love you, too," she answered.

He smiled. "No, I'm saying it too softly." He threw his head back. "I love you!"

His voice reverberated through the room. She began laughing and crying all at once as joy elated her heart.

"I love you!" she shouted. "I love you!"

They fell into each other's arms again, laughing and sobbing and rocking each other.

Dr. Brighton came in.

By habit, Kass pulled away and sat up quickly, trying to act innocent. Lian did the same and they traded sheepish glances.

The doctor smiled. "I'm sorry to interrupt. I just wanted to make sure you were all right."

Kass breathed a sigh of relief. They weren't going to be punished or pulled apart. Lian slipped his hand into Kass's and laced their fingers together "Kassie just agreed to be my wife," he said.

Her smile widened. "Well! Congratulations to you both." She sat down in her chair and marked something on her clipboard. "Kass, I guess you'll want that implant out today."

Kass nodded happily. This day would be etched forever in her heart as one of the best in her life. Next to the day she met Lian.

Less than an hour later, Lian and Kass were shown to their "honeymoon suite" as Dr. Brighton cheerfully referred to it. Dr. Brighton bid them farewell and closed the door behind her.

Lian went to the door. He opened and closed it a couple of times as he grinned at Kass.

She knew exactly what he was doing and returned his grin.

He turned the deadbolt to the locked position. As he'd done with the door, he unlocked and locked it repeatedly. They could come and go as they pleased, or stay here and keep the rest of the world out. What luxury.

Kass stood in the middle of the small room and looked at him. Sudden shyness overcame her.

If she wasn't mistaken, he also appeared hesitant, and Kass sensed their mutual thoughts. They would be husband and wife. After all this time of uncertainty and fighting for survival, they were together. Free. And in love.

A terrible wave of doubt assailed her. What if she didn't please him? What if the passion he showered on her before an audience during their imprisonment had been from the heat of battle, or because of loneliness and duress? Kass didn't think she could bear finding out it hadn't been real.

On the other hand, she couldn't bear not being with him, either.

She could only hope that his searing heat and magnetism was real in their new circumstances and not an illusion from Sector S.

She smiled hesitantly and glanced at the small but comfortable bed in the corner.

Their bed.

Nothing could have seemed more wonderful to Kass in that moment. Except the fact that the room was theirs to share. Their medical tests didn't begin until the following afternoon, so they had the rest of the night and morning to do whatever they wanted. Together. No one could send them back to separate prison cells or to punish them for being intimate.

He eased closer to her.

Kass's heart fluttered. She stood face to face with Lian. She gazed into his eyes. Her whole body trembled, caught in the terrible clutch between her desire to throw herself into his arms and her terror of what might lay behind the illusions.

He reached out and closed his large hands around her upper arms. His touch radiated warmth through the black shirt.

"I'm nervous, Kassie," he said. Tension tightened the skin around his eyes. "When we were together before, those times, we had to—I mean, I wanted to so much, but you didn't have a choice. I'm so afraid you won't want me after—" He fell silent and looked down.

His confession drained all her doubt away. Emboldened, she stepped close enough to press her body to his. She couldn't get enough of embracing him now that they'd had their first real hug after crossing into Paradise.

"Lian, all I've ever wanted is you. All these years."

Lian closed his arms around her and held her so snugly to his chest that she swore she could feel his heartbeat.

She squeezed him, her hands splaying on the hard planes of his back. His body heat warmed her and released his clean male scent. She closed her eyes and rested.

Lian nuzzled her hair, pressing his lips into it. "You're so soft, Kassie," he said softly. "So pretty."

Kass felt her cheeks heat up. "Thank you. So are you. Beautiful, I mean."

He nuzzled her hair again. "I'm glad you feel that way."

Kass felt the heat of arousal between them. He squeezed her again and his back muscles flexed. Instinctively, she began a leisurely exploration of his back. Her fingertips traced the slopes and valleys of chiseled muscle underneath his shirt.

The more she touched him, the more her body tingled.

Lian slipped his hands under her shirt. His trembling fingertips skated over her skin in widening circles. "You're so soft," he said again.

His touch warmed her skin and sent pleasant shivers through her. The heat traveled to her sex and she pushed her body more firmly against his.

He continued to caress her back, then dipped his touch downward. His fingertips slid pleasantly along her spine and ventured under the waistband of her baggy pants. Heated moisture pooled in her sex and left her tingling, wanting. He ground his hips slowly against hers, and the hard evidence of his desire pressed into her pelvic bone.

The contact touched off erotic memories of his naked body over hers, possessing her wildly.

Gently, Lian pulled away and gazed down at her, his eyelids sensuously heavy. His eyes darkened and smoldered, and his breath grew huskier.

Struck by how devastatingly handsome he was, she reached up and brushed a fingertip across his bottom lip and down over his chin. The light roughness of his beard rasped the pad of her finger.

Lian unfastened the top button of her shirt. He unhooked the second one, then the third, and pulled the material apart. His gaze slid over her face and down her throat, and his fingertips slid along the same path, trailing his heated touch down across her collarbone.

"I could touch you forever," he murmured.

Kass's heart pounded. His touch sent whispers of desire through her and her nipples hardened. The erect tips pushed against the rough material of her shirt.

Lian trailed his fingertips across her chest. His full lips parted slightly with his ragged breaths. He unbuttoned the next few buttons in a painfully slow way, finally reaching the bottom. The shirt fell open and he slid it over her shoulders. The shirt slipped off and puddled on the floor.

Lian's breath caught softly and his face darkened with a hungry expression. Gently, he grasped her upper arms and slanted his lips over hers.

Eagerly Kass parted her lips to accept the delicious intrusion of Lian's tongue. Their kiss was deep and sweet, as if they were drinking from each other and tasting each other's souls. Her eyelids fluttered closed and she groped for his shirt and worked open the buttons with mounting fervor.

When she'd gotten his shirt unbuttoned to the bottom, she pushed it back to reveal his broad chest and beautifully sculpted torso. She put her hands palms down on his chest and lightly squeezed each rounded hard pectoral muscle. Each small brown nipple hardened under her touch, and he groaned softly.

"You're so beautiful, Lian," she breathed.

He traced the fingertips of one hand across her chest. "You're the beautiful one."

His touch circled around the swell of her breast, brushing several times back and forth over her nipple, which puckered into an erect bud. His other hand slipped down to the waistband of her trousers. He unsnapped the button and pulled down the zipper.

The trousers slipped past her hips and fell around her ankles. She heard Lian's soft intake of breath just before he stepped closer and pulled her against him. He claimed her mouth in a deep kiss.

For several moments they tasted each other, swirling their tongues around each other's in a sensual dance. Lian caressed her bare back with growing ardor.

He lifted his lips from hers and knelt down. With quick hands, he unbuckled the heavy boots and lifted her feet out of them, freeing her of both boots and trousers. He stood up and took her hand.

"Come." He led her toward the bathroom, where he turned on the shower and held his hand under the spray until it ran sufficiently hot. He unbuckled his trousers and divested himself of them and his boots.

A warm rush passed through Kass's sex, which pulsed at the sight of his naked body.

He drew aside the shower curtain and guided her in with him. Under the pleasantly hot water, he pulled her into his arms and bowed his head to hers, kissing her as the water soaked their hair and skin.

The kiss lasted for what seemed a long time before he pulled away, gazing down at her as if he couldn't believe she was really there.

She stared back at him and drank in the sight of the water gleaming in his short hair and beading off his smooth skin and hard muscles. Each time she looked at him was like the first time. His masculine strength never failed to overwhelm her in the most wonderful way.

He picked up a cloth and soap and started to lather her skin. He was so soft with the cloth, smoothing it over her skin with tender care. He rubbed her back and around to her breasts. The material rubbed her nipples pleasantly and caused them to tingle and harden.

Her eyelids fluttered closed under Lian's cushioned touch. She tilted her head back and lost herself in the pleasure.

Lian dipped the cloth over her stomach and pushed it between her legs.

She moaned softly and moved her feet farther apart to give him access to her sex. Tingling heat whirled through her and she had to anchor her hands on his shoulders to keep from falling.

He rubbed the cloth back and forth gently along her slit, weakening her further. Her lips parted and he claimed them in a kiss. Resting the cloth on her hot core, he kissed her deeply and swirled his warm tongue greedily against hers.

Lian's kiss heated more with each passing second. The cloth dropped onto the tiles of the shower floor with a soft thud. Lian gently backed her up against the wall. The cool tiles felt good against her heated skin, and the hot spray battered them with delicious warmth, washing them clean of the past.

Lian rained soft kisses all over her, devouring her neck and throat, her shoulders and chest, down to her breasts.

Slowing down, he tasted each nipple in languorous circles with his tongue until the bud peaked and tightened and Kass felt nearly breathless.

She clasped her arms lightly around his head. Her fingertips brushed the softness of his hair and followed the movements of his head as he pleasured her.

The shower had a built-in tiled seat at one end. Lian picked up one of her feet and set it on the bench. He continued a trail of kisses from her breasts down her stomach. The soft suction of his lips on her wet skin made her melt and sag against the tile wall.

He knelt down in front of her and spread open her lower lips. His breath passed deliciously hot over her wet, aching clit and she pushed her hips forward, needing his mouth on her flesh.

Lian groaned softly. The sound conveyed the wild effect that her most intimate part had on him. He pressed his mouth to her inner sex, swollen with need. The first swipe of his tongue on her clit drew a cry of pleasure from her. Her fingers tightened in his hair. Her thumbs brushed his cheeks and felt the tensing of his jaw as he tasted her.

Lian splayed his hands on her hips, drew her sex tighter against his mouth. He swirled his tongue in tiny circles over the engorged nub. It drove her wild. But as incredible as it felt, she needed him inside her, filling her, his cock sheathed in her core.

She drew his face away from her sex.

He looked up at her, his lips parted, his chest panting.

"Please, Lian," she breathed. She grasped his shoulders and tugged on him.

He rose to his feet. His cock, hard and jutting, pressed against her curls and slid along her pubic bone.

"You want me inside you, Kassie?" He nipped gently at her lower lip. "Is that what you want? Tell me."

"Yes," she said over the loud spray of the shower. She sagged back against the wall, her body weak with need. "I want you inside me."

Without hesitation, Lian reached down, spread her open and nudged at her opening. He captured her mouth in a kiss.

She embraced him, pulled him close and thrust her hips forward. The movement made him slide in deeper.

Lian groaned. He bent his knees and pushed up, sheathing himself deep inside her.

"Kassie," he whispered as their bodies met.

Kass pressed her lips into his neck, damp and warm. She loved the taste of his smooth skin, and she sipped the droplets of water off him as if she could imbibe his essence through them. She closed her eyes and squeezed him in her arms. All there was in the world was them, together, their bodies intimately connected.

"Kassie," he whispered again into her ear.

There was no mistaking the passion and tenderness in his voice and the heated way he drove into her, over and over, as if he were trying to climb inside her and make them one person. His lovemaking washed away her doubts about his love just as the shower washed away the dirt of their painful past.

Suddenly, he pulled out and stepped back. His chest heaved and he grasped her shoulders. His simmering gaze bore into hers.

"Not like this, Kassie." He reached past her and turned off the water.

She stared at him as her heart pounded. Her body pulsed and tingled, unfulfilled. "What is it?"

"Come on." He grabbed their towels and led her, soaking wet, by the hand into the bedroom where he spread the towels swiftly across the bed. "We finally can do whatever we want."

He bent and kissed her mouth with a sweet passionate touch of his lips to hers. Then he grasped her upper arms and bid her to lie down.

Her heart pounded as the warmth of his hard body closed over hers. She spread her legs so he could settle between them. His body, warm and wet, fused to hers and gently flattened her breasts against his strong chest. His hard cock nudged her slippery opening.

He looked down at her, his lids heavy over his huge beautiful eyes. Kass's heart melted and she put her arms around him and held him tight. And he slipped his arms around her to hold her completely in his embrace.

This was the moment she'd wanted her whole life.

Tears surged to her eyes and slipped onto her cheeks.

Lian lowered his face to hers and kissed her tears. "Kassie," he whispered between soft kisses.

His kisses heated up, and he covered her lips, his tongue hungry against hers.

Kass whimpered and moved her hips against his, demanding him inside her again. She was already so wet and open that with one small push, he sheathed his cock deep inside her. He stroked her insides with deft thrusts.

Kass slid her hands down his back and grasped his hard buttocks. The round muscles flexed with each thrust of his cock inside her. He felt so delicious, warm and strong in her arms, and she savored each second. She followed his movements in and out. The thickness of his shaft rubbed against her clit, drove her closer and closer to the edge. What he'd begun with his mouth and hands in the shower, he finished in the bed with his cock.

Her lower muscles clenched around his shaft as her orgasm gripped her. She dug her fingertips hard into his butt until every last drop of pleasure had passed.

When she sagged limply into the mattress, Lian slowed down and kissed her again.

"I wanted to make it last for you, Kassie." Disappointment laced his voice.

She gazed at him and cupped one cheek. Her body felt completely languid and satisfied, and her heart and soul were bursting with joy because he loved her and because they were beginning a new life together. He would make her his wife. He'd give her his name. And someday, his child would grow inside her. Everything she'd ever hoped for.

"Don't you know how good this is?" she teased softly. She squeezed her muscles around his cock again and bucked her hips.

His breath hitched in his throat and he started moving again.

"Yes," she breathed, "Don't stop. Don't ever stop."

She rocked again and felt his control slip. His mouth, insistent and deliciously slick from the water, crashed down on hers. He gulped greedily at her lips and tongue while he rode her faster and harder.

She moaned from the pleasure of the friction and gripped his backside to pull him deeper into her, She moved her hips against his until she felt his cock twitch and pulse inside her and fill her with his warm seed.

Lian sagged against her, his lips pressed into the side of her neck. His breath pulsed hot on her skin.

She smiled and hugged him close as his chest heaved against hers.

Slowly, as he recovered his breath, he slipped his arms around her and held her tight. One hand slipped into her wet hair and cradled the back of her head.

She closed her eyes and rested, happy for the first time she could remember since she was a girl. She felt ready for whatever challenges they faced, whatever happiness and sorrow the future might hold.

Because as long as she was in Lian's arms, she was truly in Paradise.

About the Author:

Sedonia Guillone is a multi-published, award nominated author of both m/f and m/m erotic romance. The man in her life is her inspiration and provides all the hands-on research she needs. When she's not writing, she's cuddling, watching samurai flicks and thinking about the next naughty, delicious tale she wants to write.

Up to No Good

by Natasha Moore

To My Reader:

I'm thrilled to be able to share Mac and Allie's story with you. I love sexy banter and these two really get into it. Don't you just love to see two stubborn people clash? Enjoy!

Chapter 1

Mac could tell she was up to no good the minute she walked through the door. She sauntered up to the bar with that heady self-confidence reserved for those too young to know life was just waiting for the chance to cut them down to size.

He wondered what she wanted besides a drink.

He watched her out of the corner of his eye as he poured a Bud for Wally. A mane of wavy red hair spilled down her back, nearly tickling her shapely ass. Her long, firm legs traveled miles before they reached the floor.

Bouncing impatiently on her stiletto heels, the front of her white, tight shirt rose and fell in interesting bounces as well. The deep, plunging neckline gave him a breathtaking view of her generous cleavage.

Man, he loved summer, loved skimpy shirts and short skirts. The warm weather season was too short in western New York not to enjoy every second while it lasted. Mac took his time finishing the next drink order, taking advantage of the fact that the young woman seemed to have a problem with patience.

"Hey, Mac, you getting that tequila sunrise ready or are you going to be sight-seeing 'til the sun rises tomorrow?"

The sarcastic snap of Denise's voice made him pull his eyes away from the far end of the bar and back on his work where it belonged. There had been plenty of pretty young women in his bar over the years. This one was nothing to get excited about.

He poured tequila in the glass and added the ice and grenadine. While he reached for the orange juice, he managed to sneak a peek again. She'd stopped bouncing—damn—and was now beating out some kind of rhythm on the bar with her hands.

Denise grabbed the glass out of his hand while he was still stirring it and headed over to the table in the corner, shaking her head as she did. He barely realized his gaze had drifted down to the young woman again until he caught her looking back at him.

In the darkness of the Jolly Roger, he couldn't make out the color of her eyes. Her mouth was way too wide for her face, her lips full and lush. He got an instant image of what a mouth like that could do to a man. Oh, yeah, his cock got the picture too, rising to attention, straining against his trousers.

He wiped his hands on a towel and moved down the bar toward the young woman. The closer he got, the prettier she was. The better she smelled. The younger she looked.

He resisted the impulse to suck in his stomach. He didn't even have a gut yet, not like a lot of guys at thirty-five. He looked into those wide eyes and sucked in anyway. "How can I help you?"

In the brightness of her smile he thought her eyes were blue. "I'm looking for a man."

The heads of all the regulars popped up along the bar like a row of ducks. Rather than satisfy his curiosity, she'd managed to arouse it even more.

"A particular man?" Mac asked, crossing his arms in front of him. "Or will just any man do?"

"A very particular man."

Her voice was sweet and rich, like a good Irish whiskey. He'd bet she'd taste just as sweet, just as intoxicating.

"The trouble is I don't know which bar he's at," she went on. "I can't remember."

"Now what man in his right mind would let a pretty little thing like you run around alone?" Seth called out. The balding orthodontist had sat on that same stool for as long as Mac had owned the place, coming on to all the women in his less-than-subtle style. Seth waved his pudgy hand around the room. "He should be looking for you."

Mac noticed her smile didn't quite reach those lovely eyes. "Well, thank you, but he doesn't know I'm here."

"Oh, you're going to be a surprise, huh?" Seth replied. He raised his eyebrows in what ended up looking like a bad imitation of Groucho Marx.

"Something like that." She looked up at Mac with a plea for help written in her eyes.

"Would you like something to quench your thirst while you wait?" Mac asked.

"You don't need to wait for him, honey," Seth said, standing up and swaggering toward her stool. "You've got all the man you need right here."

"Seth, give the girl a break," Denise said, wedging her tiny body in between them. "She doesn't know you're bluffing, but the rest of us do." Laughter rose up around the room; warm laughter born of long-standing friendships. Seth blushed and returned to his seat next to Wally.

The young woman looked relieved and turned back to Mac. She ran her tongue across her lips, leaving that wide mouth wet and shiny. "I could go for a sloe comfortable screw."

"Couldn't we all?"

She laughed, a short, surprised burst of music. Amusement shone in her eyes.

Oh, hell, had he said that out loud? He cleared his throat and took a step back. At least he could satisfy a little of his curiosity about her. "May I see some ID, please?"

"Sure."

She reached into the back pocket of her tight, short skirt. Mac swallowed hard as he watched her slowly draw the wallet along that shapely bottom. He imagined his hand following the same path, caressing that firm cheek, squeezing her soft ass. He drew in a shaky breath when she fished out her license and handed it to him.

The year of birth on the Pennsylvania license made her twenty-two. Barely old enough to drink. Way too young for him.

"Alison Chandler?" The name sounded familiar.

"Call me Allie."

Mac handed her back the license and turned away before he could watch her replace the wallet. "Okay, Allie. One sloe comfortable screw coming right up."

He shook the sloe gin, Southern Comfort, orange juice and ice a little harder than he normally did. Suddenly he had all this extra energy he didn't know what to do with.

That was a lie. He knew exactly how to spend that energy. His cock was hard and throbbing. A screw, slow or otherwise, was exactly what he needed. It had been too long since he'd buried himself in a soft, feminine body. But he shouldn't be imagining it with a young thing who just walked into his bar looking for a man who wasn't him.

She sat on a stool and took a sip from the glass he gave her. Mac couldn't help but watch her. Her lips were wet again and suddenly he wanted to know how she tasted.

"It has a man's name," she said, looking up from the glass.

He dragged his thoughts away from lips and tongues and wide, wet mouths. "What?"

"The bar. It has a man's name in it. Do you know how many bars have a man's name in them?"

"I have no idea."

"I have a list," she said. "This is the third place I've been to tonight."

Mac was drawn again to those lips as she pulled them into a little pout.

They were painted some color that wasn't really red and wasn't really pink. Whatever it was, it made her lips slick and shiny and the thought of them going down on his hard, throbbing cock nearly made him groan.

Denise walked back to the bar. "I need another fuzzy navel."

Mac dragged his eyes away from Allie's mouth and reached for a glass. "Why do drinks have names even stranger than the bars they're served in?"

He picked up the bottle of peach schnapps and didn't risk looking up. "I don't name them, I just make them."

"But where did these names come from? Fuzzy navels and tequila sunrises?"

He looked up at her anyway. "And sloe comfortable screws?"

"Exactly. I think it's laughable."

Just the sound of her voice tempted him to forget what he was doing. It was a perfectly simple drink and he couldn't remember what to do next. His annoyance made him speak a little sharper than he normally would, at least to a paying customer. "Do you have an opinion on everything?"

"Of course, doesn't everyone?"

"Everyone doesn't announce them like they're hoping to start an argument."

"'I have the right to foist my opinion on anyone with an ear.'"

"What?" Mac stared at her, not believing those words had come out of that incredible mouth. It had to be a coincidence. "That's the most idiotic thing I've ever heard."

"Mac!" Denise said in a loud whisper. The look of astonishment on her face was justified, but he couldn't help himself. "Mac doesn't like arguments," Denise said to Allie, as if she thought she needed to apologize for his behavior.

Of course, Denise was thinking about business. Mac could only think about wide slick lips, long slender legs, and a mocking voice quoting words he'd written over a decade ago.

"In fact, for a bartender," Denise went on, "our Mac isn't much of a conversationalist."

Mac frowned. "Bartenders make drinks. Not chit-chat." He handed Denise the drink and left to check on the rest of his customers sitting at the bar. But he didn't move so far away he couldn't eavesdrop if necessary.

"So this guy you're meeting," Denise said when she returned to the bar, "is he cute?"

"Well, I've never actually met him."

"Oh, a blind date, huh?"

"Not exactly." She cleared her throat and looked around the bar. The determined look that suddenly appeared on her face made Mac nervous. What she was up to? She grabbed her glass and took a long drink.

When she spoke again, she raised her voice loud enough to be heard half a block away.

"I'm looking for a man named Simon MacKenzie. He used to write a column in the papers called 'Simon Says' and I was told he owns a bar around here. Does anyone know him?"

The noisy chatter cut off instantly. In the uneasy silence, Mac's head pounded. Alison Chandler. Of course. How could he have forgotten the bold signature on all those annoying letters?

"I've heard the name, of course, but not for years," Denise said, filling in the silence as she always could do best. "You must have been just a kid when he was writing those columns."

"I took a college course from a friend of his. He used 'Simon Says' columns as a teaching tool all semester. I couldn't get enough of it. That wonderful writing. All those daring opinions. I've been hooked on Simon MacKenzie ever since."

"So why's a pretty little thing like you looking for an old, washed-up writer?" Seth asked loudly. Mac was close enough to see the glint of amusement in Seth's eyes.

"I'm a writer," Allie replied with a sense of pride Mac could have related to once. "I want to interview him for an upcoming issue of *Writer's World* magazine."

"Who cares what happened to a man who hasn't written anything in years?" Wally asked.

"Everyone loves a mystery," Allie said. "Five years ago, Simon MacKenzie was the most widely syndicated columnist in the entire country. Then one day he disappears. Boom. No reason why. No hint of where he ran away to. Just gone from the face of the earth."

"What makes you think he ran away?" Mac asked, struggling to keep his voice neutral.

"He disappeared at the height of his career. Some people say he couldn't handle the pressure. Most people think he lost his ability to write." She looked up at Mac. "A few people say he's dead."

"But you don't believe that?" Mac asked.

When she shook her head, hair the color of an Irish Setter swirled around her face. "I want to find out why he turned his back on that tremendous talent. I'll print the truth and set the record straight once and for all."

Images flashed through his mind. Scrawled handwriting. Police reports.

Photographs of blood and terror.

Mac closed his eyes and fought the images, pushing them back into that part of his mind he tried to keep locked up. What right did she have to come into his bar and try to uncork all the emotions he'd worked so hard to bottle up?

"Why don't you just call him?" Denise asked. Mac's eyes flew open. Denise avoided looking his way, but she did have the nerve to plop down onto the stool next to Allie.

"His number's unlisted. He doesn't have a website or e-mail. I tried snail mail, but he hasn't answered my letters."

"You must have his address, then," Wally said.

"Only a post office box here in Buffalo. Professor Kelsey told me the name of the bar he owns, but I lost the piece of paper I wrote it on."

"You just remember it had a man's name," Denise said.

"Right, so can anyone help me?"

A few of the guys shook their heads and the rest stared in silence. Mac released the breath he didn't know he'd been holding. These people were the closest thing to friends he had and he'd do anything to make sure they never found out the shame that haunted him every day of his life.

Now to get the troublemaker out of here before the liquor loosened someone's lips. He picked up her nearly full glass and wiped the bar in front of her. "So I guess you'll be off to the next place then."

She shook her head and appeared to settle onto her stool. "I'll have a club soda with lemon now. The other bars will have to wait 'til tomorrow."

✳꧁☙☸☙꧂✳

Allie yawned. She'd never been a night person. She resisted the urge to check her watch. She knew she'd feel more tired than she already did if she knew how late it really was.

Her hands had finally stopped shaking and her stomach was no longer churning. She'd given her pitch to a bar full of strange men three times and was no closer to finding Simon MacKenzie than when she started. For the first time, the word "fail" snuck into her brain.

She pushed it back out. She wouldn't allow herself to think like that. Giving up was not allowed.

"Yeah," Seth called out when the rollicking strains of "Hound Dog" filled the bar. "Elvis was the king." He curled his lip in a bad Elvis impression.

Allie smiled, glad for the distraction. "He was in a class by himself," she agreed. She went over and made a couple of selections of her own on the jukebox.

She'd been so nervous when she'd come in tonight. She always talked too loud and too much when she got nervous. Like saying she needed a slow comfortable screw. Her face grew hot, just thinking about it. When she sat back down, she shook out a piece of ice from the bottom of her glass and ran it lightly over her face.

"Um, are you alright?" Mac said, his voice a little rough around the edges.

Allie looked up. She was going to smile at him but, when his gaze caught hers, somehow she couldn't move. Her heart started pounding in an uneven rhythm she didn't recognize. She almost forgot to breathe, but then she finally took in a ragged breath, breaking the spell. She dropped the ice cube and it went skittering across the bar.

Wow, he was hot. Not real tall, not real young, but Allie could picture a well-sculpted body beneath the loose white shirt and tight black pants. His dark hair looked black in the shadows of the bar, and while his face looked as though it had never been smooth, all the features came together in a pretty appealing package.

"This is the stuff I usually hear booming out of some kid's car, even with the windows up," Seth said.

Allie dragged her attention away from Mac. One of the songs she'd picked was playing. "Don't tell me you never turned up the volume on 'Jailhouse Rock'."

"Well, yeah," he admitted. "It's okay, I guess."

"I knew you'd like it," Allie said. "You have to try all kinds or you can miss out on some really great stuff." She smiled. "Give it to me any way. Fast or slow, quiet or wild."

"Sounds good to me."

At the sound of the deep, lazy voice, Allie looked up to see Mac standing in front of her again. The innuendo wrapped in those few words caused all sorts of erotic pictures to move through her mind.

Dancing with Mac, slow and close in the late night shadows. Bodies rubbing against each other, swaying in time to the music. Her nipples beading as they brushed across his muscular chest. Her hands caressing his strong back, coaxing him closer to her. Close enough to feel his hard arousal pressed against her.

And then they were having sex, fast and wild, on top of this bar. Arms and legs tangled. Mouths dropped kisses onto sweat-soaked skin. Their bodies slammed onto the top of the bar as they –

She snatched her hands off the smooth surface of the bar. Where did those thoughts come from? She picked up a napkin to fan herself. When did this place get so hot?

She had to swallow before she could get the words out. "I was talking about the music."

"So was I." He smiled and his face was transformed from merely good-looking to sexy as hell. What did that expression mean? Was he imagining sex on the bar too?

Allie wasn't sure how to react. She'd had guys flirt with her before. But it wasn't often that her nipples tingled just from having a guy look at her. She didn't usually find her panties damp from having erotic daydreams about a man she'd barely met.

But she was here to do a job. Having a fling with a sexy bartender didn't fit into her plans, no matter how much she was attracted to him.

Besides, there was another man who held her heart at the moment. Another man she dreamed of sharing her love—and her body—with. She couldn't get involved with any one else until she settled things with him.

If she could only find him.

With more than a small twinge of regret, Allie turned away from Mac and the hint of what might have been. Sometimes it was better to stop before you ever got started.

"So, Denise," Allie said to the pretty blonde waitress, partly to get her mind off Mac, partly because she already liked the woman who knew how to put all the men here in their place. "Are you usually the only woman in this place?"

"Sometimes," she replied, leaning over to rub the calf of her leg. "We get a lot of couples on the weekend. But during the week it's usually the regulars."

Allie took a handful of peanuts from the basket in front of her. "I don't know if I'd like working at night."

"My husband's a cop and he works nights," Denise told her. "I used to waitress during the day and we never saw each other. This works out much better."

"Well, this is a great place," Allie said, then yawned before she could stop herself. "I'll have to stop in again after I hook up with Simon MacKenzie."

"What if you can't find him?" Denise asked.

The possibility twisted like a fist in Allie's stomach. "I'll find him."

"What if he won't give you the interview?"

"Can't and won't aren't in my vocabulary," Allie told her. "I'm going to find Simon MacKenzie and I'm going to get that interview." It was the only way she could see it.

"How can you be so sure?" This time it was Mac who questioned her and his voice seemed laced with ice.

"I can do anything I put my mind to," Allie said, repeating the words her father, a lifelong military man, had drilled into her head. "Simon MacKenzie has never granted an interview before, but I'm going to be the first writer he gives one to."

"You can't control what somebody else is going to do," Mac said.

"I'm not worried," Allie said, smiling up at him. "I can be very persuasive."

"You can't make somebody do something they don't want to do," Mac told her. His eyes flashed in the darkness and he seemed to loom above her like some dark angel of vengeance.

Wrong word. There was nothing angelic about him.

"I thought you didn't like to argue," she shot back, her heart beating furiously.

He ignored her comment. His face got darker. "Just how persuasive are you planning to be?"

Suddenly the lighthearted banter wasn't light anymore. "I don't know what you mean," Allie said with a frown. "I'll talk to him. I'm very good with words."

"And if words aren't enough?" he asked, his voice low and dangerous.

Allie glanced around her. The others at the bar were staring silently at them. "Mac, you're scaring me a little here. What is your problem?"

"There are some women who are not above using their bodies to get what they want."

"You're asking if I would fuck Simon MacKenzie to get an interview?" She jumped off the stool and balled her hands into fists.

"Oh, Mac." Denise said.

"I am a professional writer," Allie told him, fighting to keep her voice level. "I have written dozens of articles and interviews for a variety of magazines. I certainly don't need to resort to screwing someone to get a story."

Mac stepped back and wiped his hand over his face. He didn't look so dangerous anymore. Only tired.

Well, maybe a little dangerous.

"I'm sorry," Mac said. "I had no right to suggest something like that. I knew a woman. Well, she still makes me angry when I think about her."

"So don't think about her."

He laughed but Allie thought she caught a hint of underlying bitterness there. Someone had messed with this guy's mind. "Why didn't I think of that?"

Relieved laughter rang around them. Whew. She wouldn't want to get Mac really mad at her. But she could sure picture that passion released in another direction.

She got hot again just thinking about it.

Allie was so tired, her steps were unsteady when she finally left the bar. She shouldn't have stayed so late, not after driving all day and barhopping all night, but she'd had a hard time making herself leave. She'd never had trouble talking with strangers, but she had rarely felt such camaraderie with people she'd just met as she did at the Jolly Roger.

She couldn't wait to get back to the hotel and hit the mattress. Her brain was fuzzy. Her eyes were gritty. Her body itched from being so tired.

She stopped in front of a dark alley that ran between the Jolly Roger and a beauty shop called Maxine's to fish for the key that was in the front pocket of her slim skirt.

Maybe she'd come back here again before she left town. She'd let them all know how well her exclusive interview with Simon MacKenzie went. She'd deserve a celebration.

Of course, if things went the way she hoped with Simon MacKenzie, she might not be interested in taking another look at the sexy man who tended bar at the Jolly Roger. She felt a strange sense of loss that she'd probably never see him again.

Allie found the car key and began to pull it out of the pocket with two fingers. At the thought of Mac, Allie whirled around on her stiletto heels to look at the building, as if she would be able to see him through the block walls. The world spun around her and the single key went flying from her hand. She heard a faint clink as the key landed somewhere in the darkness of the alley.

Damn. Allie took a couple steps into the dark alley. She was never going to see where the key landed without some sort of light. She could go into the bar and ask for a flashlight, but pride stopped her from letting Mac know she was too clumsy and too tired to get where she was going on her own.

Then she remembered the flashlight in the glove compartment of her car. She could grab it and be back here in a couple seconds to find the key. She turned and took two steps before coming to a halt.

A deep groan escaped her lips. Shit. She needed the key to unlock the car in the first place.

There was no way around it, she was going to have to venture into that dark alley and find her key. She wasn't afraid of snakes and mice and other creepy crawlies. Growing up with two older brothers cured her of that. But she wasn't relishing the idea of what other disgusting things she might find while on hands and knees in there. She peered into the darkness, trying to make out shapes and shadows. She took a deep breath of sour air and pushed back a wave of nausea. She wished she could crawl back to her hotel and collapse. Dropping to her knees, Allie reminded herself if she couldn't find the car key, that might be the only way she'd get back to that mattress.

The pavement was hard and gritty against her knees. She reached out her hands, sweeping the open palms before her, encountering nothing but damp dirt, stones, and bits of paper. The foul odor of garbage hung in the muggy air. Grimacing, she crawled forward, determined to find the stupid key. Even if she had stones imbedded in her knees and broken fingernails, she wasn't going to give up. Giving up wasn't in her vocabulary either.

Suddenly she crashed into something large and metal. And hard. Stars exploded in her head. She grabbed her head and propped herself up against the side of what must have been the dumpster. Maybe she'd rest a minute before she continued her search, just long enough to let her stomach settle and her head stop pounding.

How darkness could whirl around was a mystery to her. But one mystery a night was her limit.

She closed her eyes and settled into the corner between the dumpster and the wall. It wasn't a bad resting place. She'd stay here a couple of minutes, just until the world stopped spinning every time she opened her eyes.

Just a couple of minutes more.

Chapter 2

The hour after closing was the time Mac liked best. He always drew a sigh of relief when everyone was gone. He did all the cleaning himself, taking satisfaction in the shining glasses, the gleaming bar, and the spotless floor. He liked the quiet, appreciated the time alone with himself and his thoughts.

As long as the thoughts didn't get too deep.

Right now, his thoughts were on a certain troublesome redhead. On her beautiful breasts and smart mouth and go-on-forever legs. How could he hope he never saw her again, yet pray she came back tomorrow night?

He had to be crazy. He could never trust her in a million years. Didn't his time with Robyn teach him anything?

Mac tied up the bag of trash and started toward the door, shutting off the lights and making a final security check as he went. Night after night he went through the same routine. Night after night he went home by himself.

Another day gone. Another day alone.

Grabbing a flashlight, he reminded himself this was what he wanted. He wasn't lonely. Not like Wally, who lost his wife of thirty years to cancer two years ago. Or Seth, who broke down tonight and admitted he hadn't had a date in over a year. Mac wasn't like any of the regulars who used the Jolly Roger as a substitute for home and family. He was content with his life, just the way it was. Really.

Mac locked the door behind him and carried the trash bag into the alley. In the dim flashlight beam, he saw the shadow of a figure propped up limply against the dumpster. At first he thought it was a drunk passed out in the alley, until the beam caught a shock of red hair.

He dropped the bag and ran over to Allie. Had she been attacked as she left the bar? He pictured her bloodied and beaten. It was too damn dark out here.

His hands shook as he pressed his fingers to her throat and found a steady pulse. He ran the flashlight beam over her. He found no obvious wounds, no signs that she had been attacked or robbed or raped. Just as he leaned forward to make sure she was breathing, a soft snore escaped her parted lips.

"Allie?" He shook her gently by the shoulder. "Allie? You have to get up now." When she didn't respond, he shook her harder. "Allie!"

She groaned, but didn't move.

What the hell was he going to do with her now? He had no idea where she was staying but he couldn't leave her here.

No way was he taking her back to his place. He never brought anyone there. He didn't want anyone invading his privacy.

Especially a nosy writer with an incredible mouth.

Mac stared at her and his head started to pound. He sighed, then knelt down to pick her up, sliding one arm under her knees and the other around her shoulders. He struggled to his feet. He had fantasized tonight about having Allie in his arms, but this sure wasn't what he had in mind.

Her hair tickled his face, soft and silky. Her scent was clean and fresh, a sharp contrast to the sour smells around him. Mac cursed as he nearly tripped over the garbage bag he'd left lying at the mouth of the alley. He kicked it back toward the dumpster and hoped it made it somewhere close.

Getting her up into his Jeep Wrangler was the next struggle, but he finally lifted her into the passenger seat and slammed the door before she could fall out.

He didn't need this. First she'd pestered him with her annoying letters, wanting to dredge up the past and invade his privacy. Then she barged into his bar, intending to do the same thing. He should have thrown her out when he found out who she was.

Now he was going to have to take her into his house.

She awoke with a hideous pounding in her head. Or was it the sloppy kiss across her face that woke her up? She couldn't bring herself to open her eyes yet, but when she reached up to wipe off her face, she felt fur. Allie found her arms wrapped around what felt like a shaggy dog.

Where was she?

She didn't own a dog. She didn't get headaches. She didn't have a lumpy mattress that wasn't long enough for her legs. Allie faced the awful truth with a groan. She was going to have to open her eyes.

Only a slit at first, she promised herself, just to test the light. Allie peeked through grainy eyelids to discover the sun was a faint glow through the huge multi-paned window. Did that mean it was morning or evening?

This wasn't her hotel room. She would have remembered the vaulted ceiling and warm oak trim. But the room was as bare and uncluttered as one. Where was she and whose gigantic sheep dog was this sitting beside her, wagging its fluffy tail and doing what could only be described as smiling an honest-to-goodness smile at her?

Allie tried to remember what had happened the evening before and frighteningly, drew a complete blank. She clutched the soft cotton blanket that someone had spread over her and tried not to panic. She lifted her hand to her head and winced when she touched a large goose egg. What had happened to her?

When she peeked beneath the blanket, she was relieved to find herself completely clothed. But with a cry she saw that her knees were skinned and her skirt was never going to be the same. This didn't make any sense. If someone had hit her on the head and dragged her here, why would they tuck her in on the sofa with a friendly dog to look over her?

She wasn't going to discover a damn thing by lying and whining on a too-short sofa. She sat up, but the pounding in her head went into double time. Groaning, she dropped her head into her hands, wishing she could curl up into a ball and hide from the pain. The jolly dog nosed through her fingers, rubbing his face against hers, as if to offer comfort.

Jolly?

Memories of the Jolly Roger came flooding back. And of how late she'd stayed there last night. She always paid the price the next morning if she didn't get enough sleep. No wonder her head felt as if it were being hammered and her tongue resembled sandpaper.

"I have to find some aspirin," she said to the dog. He simply wagged his tail. Allie rose unsteadily to her feet. "Where am I?"

She padded through the living room, the soft brown carpet tickling her bare feet. With the dog at her heels, she found the bathroom right off the kitchen. Aspirin was the only thing in the medicine cabinet besides a tooth brush and toothpaste.

She popped three tablets in her mouth. A healthy person lived here. Not even one prescription bottle to give her a name. Not one special touch to make this any more personal than a motel bathroom. She splashed some cold water on her face and dabbed some on her tender knees, then stepped out into the hall.

She needed a strong cup of coffee. Someone who didn't take medicine probably wouldn't need to rely on something like caffeine. She discovered a coffee maker behind the appliance doors in the corner, however, so she took that as an encouraging sign. She finally found Columbian coffee in the refrigerator and had a pot brewing.

Soon she poured a steaming cup. Inhaling its rich aroma, she sighed and reached down to pat the dog on the head. "So who is your master and how long does he or she sleep?"

The dog refused to talk.

"I'll have to find out myself." She tiptoed down the long hall and slowly opened the first door. The knob slipped in her sweaty hand. A home gym. Weight training equipment. A treadmill. Someone liked to keep in shape, but still no hint of who.

She closed the door and walked on to the next one. She slowly turned the handle and pushed open the door. The room was very dark. Heavy shades covered the windows.

A man was sprawled across the bed, his face buried in the pillow. The light from the doorway reflected off his bare back, bringing the well-defined muscles into sharp relief against the navy blue sheets. His torso tapered from wide shoulders to narrow hips barely covered by the sheet. Allie knew she should back out of the room, but she couldn't drag her gaze away from him. Her fingers curled into her palms in an attempt to resist the urge reach out and—

He stirred and Allie dashed out of the room and gently closed the door. Her pulse raced and wild thoughts flew through her head. Who was that? What happened last night? How did she end up in this man's house?

The dog bounded to the front door and wagged its tail in obvious desperation. "I'm trusting you to come back," she said sternly as she opened the door. "I don't want to have to explain to your master that I let you run away." The dog ran down the front steps and disappeared around the corner of the house.

The sky was lightening. The aspirin and caffeine were helping to relieve her headache, so she was able to enjoy the gold and pink streaking across the sky. Allie noted the house had a fenced-in yard before she closed the door against the cool early morning air.

There was only one picture on the living room wall, and that was of the dog. The tables were bare except for a lamp beside the leather sofa. No books, no magazines or newspapers to read with her morning coffee. No television or radio to check the morning news.

She had to get out of here. She'd leave a note to thank whoever it was for their hospitality, whatever the reason. There had to be something she could write on. She had papers and pens lying all over her apartment. She often worked on several stories at once and she had to be prepared to jot down ideas whenever they came to her. How did anyone get through the day without pen and paper?

Allie started her search by opening the drawer in the lamp table. The mail that she would have left covering the kitchen counter was piled neatly in the drawer. Allie grabbed a few envelopes and stared at them as if she didn't trust her own eyes. Suddenly her legs buckled and she sank down onto the sofa.

They were addressed to Simon MacKenzie.

She looked around in awe. This was Simon MacKenzie's house? How did she get here? If she met him last night, why didn't she remember? Did it have something to do with the large bump on her head? Did she have amnesia?

The idea was so absurd, she laughed out loud. It had been her dream for the past three years to meet Simon MacKenzie and now she couldn't even remember it!

A thousand thoughts flew through her head. Through all that chaos a dog barked. She stared at the envelopes in her hand and watched them shake. She dropped them onto her lap and clasped her hands together to stop the trembling.

She'd started falling in love with Simon MacKenzie the first day she read his wonderful words. And now she was in his house. A nervous thrill danced through her stomach. That meant Simon MacKenzie was in that bed in there.

Why couldn't she remember? What happened last night? How did they meet? And if she went home with Simon MacKenzie, why did she spend the night on the sofa?

Her head was pounding again. A dog barked insistently somewhere in the distance. She went back over the whole evening in her mind. She remembered stopping at three bars last night. She went to the Jolly Roger last. She hadn't been drunk, she'd only had a few sips of her drink at each of the places. She remembered arguing with that sexy bartender, Mac. She left the bar by herself.

Why couldn't she remember meeting Simon MacKenzie?

"Damn it, Roger!" a familiar voice boomed. "What are you barking at?"

She looked up to see Mac stumble into the room, hair tousled, muscles flexing, wearing nothing but navy blue boxer shorts. He slid to a halt in the middle of the room, staring back at her. He looked down at the mail in her lap and his expression changed instantly from sleepy to suspicious.

"What the hell are you doing?"

"I... I was just looking for some paper to leave you a note." She stood up, letting the envelopes fall to the floor. She couldn't take her eyes off him. Who cared about excuses at a time like this? "You're Simon MacKenzie?"

He ignored her question and walked over to the front door. "Were you planning on leaving my dog outside all morning?"

"Oh, the dog. I'm sorry. I forgot about him."

He opened the door, and the dog named Roger bounded in and jumped up on Allie, bestowing her with another sloppy kiss.

Mac walked over to her in slow, determined steps. A nervous thrill ran through her. He leaned over, picked the envelopes up off the floor and shoved them back into the drawer. "You helped yourself to my coffee and my mail, but you forgot about my dog?"

She patted the dog's shaggy head, but her mind was racing as she looked at the nearly naked man in front of her. She ran her tongue over her lips as she tried to figure out how this was possible. Mac?

Of course, Mac. MacKenzie. Simon MacKenzie. She nearly laughed. So the man she had the hots for last night was the same man she'd been dreaming about for years? She slowly looked him up from bare toes, to lean thighs, silk boxers, muscled chest, thick dark hair. Shivers of awareness ran through her body.

"Well, you're certainly not dead."

Not even the hint of a smile. He stood in the middle of the living room, somehow looking quite dignified in nothing but boxer shorts. Dignified and angry. She hadn't made the best impression, but there was nothing she could do about it now. Now was the time to repair the damage and move forward.

Allie had no doubt they could reach an amicable agreement.

She never imagined making her pitch with skinned knees to a man in boxer shorts, but couldn't be helped. She tried to ignore the clenching in her stomach and grasped her hands together so they wouldn't shake. She took a deep breath and prepared to make her appeal. But somehow the words in her mind didn't come out of her mouth. The words in her heart did.

"Why didn't you answer my letters?"

He turned his back on her and walked into the kitchen. She followed without hesitation.

"That should have been obvious," he replied finally, reaching into a cupboard and taking down a mug with a skull and crossbones on it. "I don't want to be interviewed."

"But don't you want to set the record straight?"

He poured the steaming coffee into the mug and then turned to face her. "No."

"But people are spreading all sorts of rumors about you."

He sat down at a small table in the corner. "I have absolutely no interest in what is said about Simon MacKenzie. Just as you obviously have no interest in my privacy."

She had started refilling her mug, but stopped with the coffee pot in mid-air. "Mr. MacKenzie, I don't want to invade your privacy."

The anger flashing in his eyes made her back up until the counter pressed into her back. "What do you call going through my mail? Questioning my friends? You probably faked passing out in the alley just to trick me into taking you home."

The alley! It all came back to her in a flash. She slammed the pot back onto the heating plate. "That's ridiculous, I didn't fake anything. I just…."

His dark brown eyes snapped. "What?"

"Well, I hate to admit it after all the things you've been saying about me, but I had a real good time last night at your place and I didn't want to leave. That's why I was so tired. And once I fall asleep, I'm dead to the world."

She thought he almost smiled this time. "You sure are. I thought you were dead until you snored."

Allie winced. She snored?

He stared at her, his gaze burning her with its intensity. "How can you look so great with only a few hours sleep?"

She didn't respond to the compliment, but her heart did a little skip. "I'm always up at the crack of dawn, no matter what time I go to sleep. Something in my metabolism, I guess."

She turned away before she did something foolish like kiss away the frown lines on his forehead. She walked over to his refrigerator and took a quick survey of the interior. She pulled out a carton of eggs.

"How do you like them? Scrambled? Sunny side up? Over easy?" She glanced at him over her shoulder. Sitting behind that table, he looked completely naked. His striking face and sculpted chest showed above the table top. His long legs and bare feet stuck out below. Her stomach did a flip.

"What are you doing?" he growled. "Get out of my stuff."

"I'm fixing you breakfast. It's the least I can do after you rescued me and gave me a place to stay for the night."

"I don't eat breakfast for hours yet," he said, rising to his feet.

"That's okay, I don't mind." She rattled around in the utensil drawer, trying to steady her nerves. "If you'd feel a little more comfortable with some clothes on, you could get dressed while I'm cooking. But don't do it on my account." She grabbed a spatula and turned to look at him. The grin popped out before she could stop it. Tousled hair and bare skin, what a combination. "I've been enjoying the scenery."

He grabbed his coffee cup and practically snarled. "Over easy," he said, stalking from the room. Over his shoulder he called, "And don't break the yolks."

"Don't you have anything chocolate in this place?"

Mac looked up from the plate of delicious eggs, to the shapely ass of the whirlwind who had taken over his kitchen. How the hell had that happened? Bent over as she was, her skirt barely covered those firm cheeks. He scooped up another forkful of eggs before he could reach out to cup them with his hands. "Chocolate?"

"Yeah. How about Cocoa Puffs cereal? Or a chocolate covered doughnut? Ah-hah!" She pulled her head out from the cupboard she'd been searching, a bag in her hand. He'd forgotten all about those cookies. If her interviewing techniques were anything like her chocolate hunting prowess, she'd be very thorough. He had to get her out of his house.

"Ah, chocolate chip cookies," she said.

"For breakfast?"

She walked over to him, her bare legs tempting him, her polished toes teasing him. He looked up as she sat down across from him at the table.

"I eat chocolate any time."

He didn't want her here, but he couldn't help but love watching her. She was so animated. Her eyes sparkled. Her hands flew when she talked, whether it was to illustrate a point or to talk about chocolate. He usually liked to savor the silence with his coffee, but Allie turned talking into a spectator sport. He almost couldn't wait to hear what she was going to say next.

"Don't you get a morning paper?"

"I don't read the newspaper."

She stared at him as if he'd said he didn't breathe air. "I don't see a radio or television, either. How do you know the world didn't blow up overnight?"

"Someone at the bar would let me know."

She fidgeted in her chair and tapped out a tune on her coffee mug. "What do you read with your coffee?"

She started bouncing in her seat, just enough to make the shadows of her cleavage shift as her breasts moved. "I don't," he replied.

"Magazines?" she asked, her voice a tiny bit desperate. "Books?"

"No."

"Are you sure you're Simon MacKenzie? The man who lived by his words and shared them with the world?"

"No, I'm not. Not anymore."

She frowned and studied him, searching his face as if something there would give her the answers she wanted. He should have kept his mouth shut. Making a woman like Allie curious was a big mistake.

She was quiet then, almost too quiet. He'd already gotten used to her nonstop chatter. She just sipped her coffee and munched on Chips Ahoy. The early morning sun lit up the highlights in her hair, lit up her dark blue eyes, too. He didn't usually experience the sun shining through the windows in the breakfast nook. Normally, he'd be in bed for hours yet. Looking at Allie, at the rays of soft light bathing her smooth skin in a rosy glow, Mac wondered what else he'd been missing.

"Can we talk about the interview now?"

He was missing nothing but his privacy. Distracted by the early morning ambience and the tantalizing cleavage before him, it had been too easy to forget why she was here. "No."

She set down a half-eaten cookie beside the coffee mug. "Mr. MacKenzie, please listen to what I have to say."

He picked up the rest of the cookie and popped it in his mouth. He made her wait until he chewed and swallowed before he replied. He chewed nice and slow.

"Miss Chandler," he finally replied, "there is nothing you can say that I want to hear. I used to write. I don't anymore. My reasons are no one's business but my own. End of story."

She finished her coffee in one final gulp and set the mug gently down on the table. "All right." Her voice was quiet, resigned.

If she was trying to make him feel guilty, it didn't work. He lived with enough guilt already. The last thing he needed was his whole sordid past dragged out for the world to see. After five years, he was still trying to forget. Why couldn't the rest of the world? Why couldn't she?

"Is it far to the Jolly Roger from here?" she asked, standing up and smoothing the impossibly wrinkled skirt with her long fingers. Roger got up from his place beneath the table and circled around her legs, as if he wanted to keep her here. "If it's too far to walk, I'll call a taxi."

He stood up too, oddly reluctant to see her go. "That's right, you left your car at the Jolly Roger."

"I left my key there," she told him as she turned and walked away from him.

He followed her into the living room, right behind Roger. "What?"

She whirled around and bumped into him as Roger jumped out of the way. His arms found their way around her slender waist. Her hands splayed across his chest as she tried to keep her balance. The heat from her fingertips seared him. His hand found a bare patch of skin above the waistband of her skirt, and he stroked the warm skin he found there.

His heart hammered as it tried to pump blood thickened by desire. He had no doubt she could feel his heart pounding beneath her fingers. And feel his hard cock pushing against her hips.

Nose to nose. Eye to eye. Heart to hand. They didn't move, as if bound by a spell. What did he see in those bright blue eyes? Desire, certainly. Passion as well. A love of life he almost envied.

Without a conscious thought, he raised his hand and brushed his fingers against her soft cheek. If only she wasn't so young. If only she wasn't here to ruin in his life.

But at the moment his body didn't give a damn about those things. Her scent wove through his brain wiping out all thoughts of the past he needed to hide and the future he had no reason to look forward to. All that mattered was here. Now. Allie.

He knew kissing her was the worst thing he could do. He wanted her out of his life, not bound more closely to it. But he stared at her lips, the way her tongue darted out and moistened them and he knew he was going to do it anyway. Desire buzzed through his body and he combed his fingers through her silky hair as he bent to touch his lips to hers.

Suddenly, Allie gasped and pulled her head away. At least one of them had some sense. Mac's hands shook as he let go of her and stepped away.

Allie cleared her throat. "I, uh, I dropped my car key last night and it rolled into the alley. That's why I was down on the alley floor in the dark. Then I bumped my head on the dumpster." She took his hand and placed it on a large, obviously painful bump on her head.

He snatched his hand away and realized why she'd pulled back. It wasn't the kiss. He'd hurt her. "I'm sorry. Are you okay?"

"I appear to be." She avoided his gaze and walked away from him. She slipped her feet into the shoes he'd placed by the sofa last night.

He should have been relieved that the kiss never happened, but he would always wonder now how she would have tasted. "I'll give you a ride."

She leaned over to pet the dog, giving her attention to Roger instead. Giving Mac a bird's eye view of those tempting breasts. "That's all right. A taxi will be fine."

"But what if you can't find the key?"

She smiled and glanced up at him, her hand still buried in Roger's fur. "Can't isn't in my vocabulary, remember?" From the sparkle in her eye, he knew without a doubt she wasn't talking only about the key.

Chapter 3

Mac never overslept. But when he fell out of bed five minutes before he should have been unlocking the doors of the Jolly Roger, he knew whose fault it was. Whose carelessness woke him up when he had been barely asleep. Whose veiled threats kept him from falling back to sleep after he left her in the alley where he found her.

Whose generous mouth and silky voice filled his dreams, tempting him to stay and listen a little bit longer.

When Mac got to the Jolly Roger, Denise was behind the bar leafing through the bartender's guide he stashed there. Luckily, there were only a couple of customers in the place.

"Sorry, I'm late," he said, coming up beside her. "How are you doing?"

"Wally's Bud was no problem," she said in a low voice, "but the guy over in the corner wants a mixed drink." She started flipping pages again. "I never said I could tend bar."

"I know. Thanks for opening for me. I'll get it." Denise threw down the book and sighed with obvious relief. "What does he want?"

"A Harvey Wallbanger."

Mac rolled his eyes. He tried not to, but he pictured Allie's laughing eyes as he floated the Galliano on top of the vodka and orange juice. It was a stupid name for a drink.

"What happened to you?" Denise asked as she skirted the bar with the glass in her hand.

"I ran into a hurricane this morning."

She stopped and turned to look at him as if he'd had one too many. "Mac, we don't have hurricanes around here."

"Oh, yes, we do. This one blew in from Pennsylvania last night and swept me along in her wake."

Denise laughed and turned to deliver the drink, leaving Mac to wonder what was so funny.

"So what happened with Allie?" Denise asked when she returned to the bar.

"She knows who I am."

"How did she find out?" Denise asked, her eyes wide. "None of us told her, Mac, honest."

"I know. She found some of my mail when she was snooping around my house."

"She broke into your house?" Denise cried.

"No, she didn't break into my house," he said. "It was my own fault. I should have known better than to bring her there last night."

Denise grinned and her eyes gleamed. Mac had always been amazed at the range of emotions Denise could cover in the blink of an eye. "Whoa, Mac. I knew it. I saw those sparks flying between you two last night."

Why did she keep jumping to the wrong conclusions? Mac grabbed a rag and started washing the already clean glasses. "No, that's not what happened."

She ignored his denial. "I knew it the minute you starting arguing. You never disagree with any one, Mac, and you were actually fighting with her. I thought, wow, she's the one to finally turn Mac upside down."

"Denise."

He tried to sound angry and forbidding, but Denise grinned again and climbed up on a stool. "So are you going to do the interview?"

"Absolutely not. She wants to dig into all my dirty little secrets and blab them to the world."

Denise laughed and stood up as two couples walked in. "Mac, anyone who knows you knows you don't have any secrets, dirty or otherwise."

He didn't say anything. Denise didn't know him as well as she thought she did. No one did. No one knew.

"Chuck and I are taking the boat out tomorrow," she said. "Why don't you come along? Brush up on your water skiing. Forget about your problems."

Forget about Allie? Not likely.

"Come on, Mac. Water skiing? You know you want to."

Maybe it would get his mind off Allie. "Okay. Thanks."

He watched Denise walk away to wait on the newcomers. If he couldn't admit the truth about his past to Denise, how the hell could Allie think she deserved to know just because she asked?

He is still a man of strong convictions, even if he doesn't put them into print any longer. Surrounded by loyal friends, he lives by night, dispensing drinks and lending an ear. His strong jaw is accented by a small, sexy cleft and his eyes are clear and bright, touched with a trace of sadness. Why is

he sad? Does he miss the life he used to know; the notoriety, the success, the writing itself? Or is it something else?

Allie stopped typing and stared at the words on the screen of her notebook computer. Somehow she'd lost the impersonal slant she needed for the story. Sexy cleft in his chin? Touch of sadness in his eyes? Where had that come from? She had to get back on track if she was going to get the lead finished. Of course, it had never been impersonal. Not with Simon MacKenzie. But she had to think of this like any of the other interviews she'd done in the past. Scanning the words she'd written so far, she stopped with her finger still poised over the delete key. Mac was sad?

Her cell phone rang before she could think about it any further. She leaned across the king-sized bed and picked it up off the end table.

"So, Allie, how's it going?"

At the sound of her friend's raspy voice, Allie smiled. "Great, Marcia. Couldn't be better." Well, maybe a little better, but she'd never admit it out loud.

"So did you get the interview?"

"I'll be talking with him today," Allie told her. She wasn't really lying, just not explaining everything to the woman who also happened to be her editor at *Writer's World* magazine.

"That's fantastic. I think an exclusive with Simon MacKenzie deserves the cover. How soon can you get the article to me?"

Allie flopped back on the bed, her heart beating wildly. Cover? The cover?

"Allie? How soon?"

First things first. She couldn't get too excited yet. "Well, I'm still feeling him out," Allie told her carefully. "I'm not sure he'll be totally candid in the first interview. I may have to meet with him more than once."

"Two weeks at the latest. Can you do that?"

She swallowed and crossed her fingers. "Sure."

"I'm depending on you to come through again for me."

"You can always count on me."

"Great. Gotta go now. Talk to you soon."

Marcia hung up. Allie stared at the telephone as if it could tell her why on earth she promised an interview she hadn't even been granted yet. The cursor on her computer blinked at her. It seemed to be laughing, mocking her. If she couldn't get the interview, she would be known as unreliable. She'd never get another assignment on spec. She'd probably never get another assignment for the rest of her life if she couldn't deliver what she promised.

Wow. A cover article.

Allie jumped to her feet and tossed the cell phone onto the bed. She could do anything she put in mind to, including convince Simon MacKenzie to give her an interview. She glanced at the clock on the nightstand, then pulled the bikini she bought last night out of the drawer. It was time to get to work.

⁂

The sun was hot enough to dry the mist from the wake almost before the boat cut through it. Man, he loved summer. Mac leaned back in the seat that stretched across the back of the motor boat. He closed his eyes and let Chuck take them wherever he wanted.

Denise got up from her seat beside her husband, and sat down beside Mac. "We're making a quick stop to pick up another passenger."

"Lisa?" he asked.

"That airhead?" Chuck called out.

Denise jumped up and swatted her husband playfully. "My sister is not an airhead!"

Chuck put an arm around Denise and hugged her close. "Well, she's a lovable airhead."

Mac sat in silence and watched them exchange their little smiles, looks meant only for each other. A pang of longing struck him deep in his chest, surprising him both with its intensity and with the fact that it happened at all.

Once he'd thought he'd found someone with whom to share those smiles, those looks. But that was before he discovered he couldn't trust anyone, not even the one closest to him. The one he thought he loved. The one who lied through her teeth when she pressed her luscious body up against him and said she loved him too.

Mac had closed that part of himself off forever. He was never going to risk falling in love again.

The boat began a slow turn toward shore and Mac lazily turned his head to look in that direction. He told himself he wasn't surprised by what he saw, even though his body reacted instantly. It wasn't a short blonde standing at the end of the dock, as he expected. One glimpse of the tall redhead had his heart suddenly going into double time.

"Denise?"

Even he was surprised by the low growl that came out of his mouth.

Denise turned and gave him a sheepish grin. "Oh, didn't I mention I ran into Allie downtown yesterday?"

"No."

"Must have slipped my mind."

Mac let his gaze slide back to Allie. She wore a big yellow T-shirt and sandals, with nothing but her long legs in between. Mac groaned to himself.

He had to remember she was the enemy. But that didn't stop his body from buzzing with the need to touch her. Taste her. Take her.

He didn't move as Chuck helped Allie climb on board. He just sat back and watched as if he didn't care that his hormones were raging like a horny teenager's. Allie smiled brightly and sat down beside him. Mac managed to smile politely, pretending that her scent didn't drive him wild, and the sight of all that skin didn't make his palms itch.

And the memory of the kiss they almost shared didn't make him thirsty.

"This is awesome," Allie said, digging into a huge tote bag and pulling out a pair of over-sized sunglasses. She plopped them on her face. "I've never been on a boat before."

"Really?" Denise said. "I grew up with boats. Dad owned a marina until he retired."

Allie tipped her face up to the sun. Mac ran his eyes along her long throat and swallowed hard. He longed to press his lips there, taste her skin, test her pulse-rate. Would it be beating as fast as his? He cleared his throat and banished the image. "I thought you were going back to PA."

Her smile faltered slightly and Mac was sorry he blurted the statement out so abruptly. "I decided to stay on for a few days. A little vacation."

He should have known she wouldn't leave that easily. Why wasn't he furious? Why did his emotions run closer to... what? Relief? Frustration? Desire?

"A vacation?" he repeated.

"I'm allowed." She stood up and looked away from him. "What a beautiful day."

Just then the boat caught the edge of a wake left by a speed boat that cut in front of them. Allie was thrown off balance, and Mac caught her in his arms, saving her from sprawling on the deck or pitching over the side. She was on his lap before Chuck had finished with his string of curses aimed at the people in the boat that was already out of sight.

Mac could feel Allie's heart thudding beneath his hand. For a moment, she seemed too stunned to move. Her fingers curled into his arm, her eyes wide. His hand cupped one of her soft breasts and her tight little ass sat cradled between his thighs. If they were alone, his fingers would have found her taut nipple and played with it through the soft fabric. His mouth watered with the thought of taking the swollen peak and teasing it with his teeth.

She squirmed on his lap, rubbing against his already hard cock. He knew she was trying to get up, but his body didn't read her movements that way. To his straining cock, she was teasing him. Tempting him. Before he got into any more trouble, he lifted her over to the seat beside him.

"The first rule of boating is to stay seated when the boat is in motion," he told her tightly.

"I'll remember that," she replied, clutching the back of the seat with a white-knuckled grip.

"There are always a bunch of fools out on the water, just like on the roads," Chuck muttered. "I can't get away from them no matter where I go."

Denise patted him on the arm. "Settle down, Officer. You're off duty now."

"Well, I'm okay and the weather's terrific," Allie said, "so let's not let them ruin our day."

While his whole day might not have been ruined, Mac's peace of mind certainly was. He couldn't relax with Allie sitting next to him. "I thought we were picking up Lisa," he said, his voice sounding a little more grumpy than he thought it would.

"Who's Lisa?" Allie asked.

"My sister," Denise said. She turned to look at Mac. "I didn't say we were picking up Lisa, you assumed that all on your own."

"I always wished I had a sister, but I got two older brothers," Allie said. "How about you, Mac? Do you have any brothers or sisters?"

He started to answer, then snapped his mouth shut. He narrowed his eyes. "Why do you want to know?"

"What?"

"I'm not answering any questions from you."

"Mac!" Denise cried. He refused to look her way or let her make him feel guilty.

"I was simply making conversation," Allie replied, appearing perfectly innocent. "Can't we have a conversation?"

"No, we can't." This wasn't a conversation, this was an interview.

She lifted that cute little nose of hers into the air and had the audacity to quote him. "'Anyone reluctant to answer a simple question probably has more important things to hide.'"

"I was talking about politicians at the time and stop quoting me."

"If the shoe fits." Allie retorted.

Mac smirked. "You can't be much of a writer if you can only come up with clichés and quotes."

"Oh, don't worry. I can come up with plenty of words to fight my own battles," Allie said. Her blazing eyes were so bright, they rivaled the sun shining above them. Mac had forgotten how enjoyable an argument could be.

Chuck began humming some old 50s song as he liked to do too often, and Allie starting singing along. Soon the two of them were belting out two-part harmony in voices loud enough to be heard across the lake in Canada.

There was no way she was water skiing. Allie was quite content to sit in the boat and watch Denise and Chuck each take their turn. Sure, it looked like fun, but that didn't mean she wanted to get out there in the middle of one of the Great Lakes. They made it look easy, but then, they'd been doing it for years.

She watched Mac put on a life jacket and jump over the side of the boat. She couldn't blame him for not trusting her. After all, she was trying to get information from him. Information he was clearly unwilling to give to her. All she could hope today was to break down the barrier a little and maybe within a day or two she could convince him she didn't mean him any harm. How much time could she take?

Allie couldn't drag her eyes off Mac as he cut through the water behind the boat. His tight, navy blue trunks clung to his wet body, not leaving much to the imagination. With fluid agility, he gracefully wove the skis back and forth across the water. As he grasped the rope and made the skis dance beneath him, his strongly muscled arms and legs easily took the punishment speed and water dished out.

What would it feel like to have those arms and legs wrapped around her? Her skin tingled at the thought. Her body heated with the need to touch him as she ached to. She knew he felt the same attraction. How long would it be before they wound up in bed together?

Who would have thought she'd be so wildly attracted to the body of the man whose mind and ideas first captured her heart? It made the attraction even more exciting. He didn't know it yet, but they were the perfect match. She just had to convince him of that.

And get that interview to boot.

"It's a heavy plastic sled, Allie," Denise explained. "You lay down on it, and the boat pulls you along behind. It's a lot of fun, and much easier than water skis."

Allie didn't look convinced. Mac was surprised to see the always confident Allie unsure. "I thought you could do anything you put your mind to."

Her lips trembled slightly when she smiled. "Yeah, but that's when my mind is telling me to go ahead. Right now it's screaming that I have to be out of my mind."

"How about if Mac rides with you the first time?" Chuck suggested. "You lay on the sled, and then he'll get on behind you. You might feel more secure that way."

Mac glared at Chuck. Didn't he have any say in this?

Denise must have seen the look on his face. "You don't mind, do you, Mac?"

Sure. No problem. He could touch Allie's bare skin and keep his head about him. Wrap himself around her soft body and keep from wanting more.

He was pretty good at lying to himself. He nodded at Denise, then held his breath as, with obvious reluctance, Allie pulled the yellow T-shirt up over her head, revealing a skimpy yellow and white striped bikini.

Mac forgot to breathe.

The tiny bikini did little to cover her firm, rounded breasts, breasts that he knew now would feel heavy in the palm of his hand. The suit stretched across her body in ways that made his mouth dry, revealing her long legs and a flat stomach adorned with a gold ring in her navel.

She accepted a life jacket from Chuck and fumbled with the buckles and straps. Denise helped her fasten it. Allie turned and looked at Mac, smiling a little sheepishly. "I'm not usually this chicken." She shrugged. "It's all this water."

"Hey, if you don't want to go, we'll all understand," Mac said, eagerly grabbing a way out of climbing on that little sled with her. "No one wants to force you into doing this."

"No. No. I want to do it. It sounds like fun, it really does. I'll be fine."

"Okay. Let's go, then." Mac turned and jumped into the water before he could change his mind.

He was able to keep his thoughts impersonal until Allie joined him by the sled. Bobbing in the water beside him, Allie grabbed his arm to steady herself. Her eyes were wide, but although he tried to tell himself it was all from excitement, he was pretty sure it was partly from fear.

"Are you all right?" he asked, treading water so close to her that their feet brushed.

She nodded, but seemed to be shivering. "Sure. It's just… well… I don't know how to swim."

"What?"

She looked at him sheepishly, her eyes looking huge in her pale face. "I know. Stupid, huh? I guess I never got around to learning."

He put his hand on her arm and noticed that she held the edge of the sled in a white-knuckled grip. "Are you sure you want to do this?"

"No, but I'm willing to try." She patted her bright life jacket with her other hand. "This thing will keep me afloat, right?"

He nodded. "Of course, it will."

"Okay then."

Mac helped Allie get into position, face down on the sled, her hands grasping the ropes at the top. Then, steeling himself against the sensations he knew would come, he slid his body between her slick legs, stretched out on top of her, and grabbed onto the ropes at the top of the sled.

Her body was wet and soft beneath him. She wriggled to get a better position on the sled and her round ass rubbed against his stomach. Heat flooded his body. Even the cool water of Lake Erie did nothing to chill the desire rushing through his veins. He could imagine her lying in his bed, stretched out on her stomach like this. He would take her from behind, her legs spread wide for him. He'd grab that fabulous ass and plunge his throbbing cock into her wet and ready body. He'd ride her like they were going to ride this sled.

Suddenly, being pulled behind a boat at thirty miles an hour was the farthest thing from his mind. But Chuck and Denise were waiting in the boat for their signal.

Mac cleared his throat. "Ready?"

"Ready as I'll ever be," she called over her shoulder.

Mac gave Chuck the thumbs-up sign. "Hold on." Chuck pulled out slowly. Mac could hear Allie's laughter ringing around them and he found himself laughing with her.

He remembered when he used to be like that, young and enthusiastic. Looking at life as an adventure and grasping every opportunity that came along. He knew exactly when life's realities hit him with an upper cut to the jaw. He hoped Allie never got hit that hard.

Chuck began to give the boat more throttle, pulling them faster and faster. They rode up and over the swells. The exhilaration of the ride almost took Mac's mind off the way Allie's body bumped into his. The way her slick skin slid against his.

Almost.

The boat rounded a corner, making them slide back and forth on the sled. Allie almost lost her grip on the ropes, but Mac managed to help her steady herself. As they crossed a busy section on the water, the sled bounced wildly. Chuck must not have realized the size of the wakes they were going to have to cross when he decided to go this way.

Cursing loudly, Mac struggled to hang on. Allie shrieked as they rode over a swell of water so high they couldn't even see the boat. Mac let go of the sled with one hand and touched Allie's shoulder, trying to steady her.

Crashing down on the other side of the swell, the sled slammed onto the water. He lost his grip on the wet sled. Water splashed over the sled, slapping him in the face, momentarily blinding him. He scrambled to hold on, instinctively grabbing for anything he could. His fingers clawed and caught something, but it wasn't enough to keep him from being thrown from the sled.

Bobbing in the water, he shook the water from his eyes and looked at what he clutched in his hands. A yellow and white striped bikini bottom.

Chapter 4

Allie had struggled to keep her precarious grip on the sled as it bounced over a hard wave. She felt Mac grab for something to hold onto behind her. Then the sled bucked some more and she wasn't sure what she was feeling, what was happening. Mac's hands were all over her body, which wasn't a bad thing, but with the riotous waves of water and the churning sled, she wasn't able to enjoy it all that much. Suddenly she felt Mac catch on something and then he was gone.

It took her only a split second to figure out what happened and then, even though she would lose her lifeline to the boat, she let go of the sled so her now bare bottom would be beneath the water.

Bobbing in the waves, she frantically looked for Mac. Water streamed off her hair and into her face, so it was almost impossible to see anything. It didn't bother her that the boat that had been pulling them was still heading in the other direction, or that she was floating around in the middle of one of the Great Lakes. She didn't even worry about not being able to swim. She was only concerned with one thing. The bottom half of her brand new bikini.

"Hey!" she shouted when she saw Mac swimming toward her.

"Missing something?"

He was smiling! Like he thought it was funny to undress her in the middle of Lake Erie. Like he thought it was funny that her bottom was unprotected from whatever creatures may be swimming around her right now. He swam closer and held up her bikini bottom. And grinned even wider.

She hardly had time to consider the fact that a smile from Mac was pretty rare.

She thought about the sled hitting the big wave, Mac scrambling to stay on the sled, grabbing anything he could find. Actually, it was pretty funny.

She tried not to laugh. She didn't have time. "Quick. Give me that." She saw the boat turning around to come back to get them.

With Mac's help, she managed to thread her feet through the legs of the bikini bottom, trying to ignore the fact that he had to perfect view of anything he wanted to see. She was just shimmying the fabric over her hips when Chuck brought the boat alongside them.

"Are you guys okay?"

"Fine," Allie called out.

"You want to try it again?"

"No, thanks. I think I've had enough water for today."

"So how long have you known this grumpy guy behind the bar?"

Mac glanced up from the tap he was pulling and saw Allie sit down on the stool next to Wally. Mac grumbled and narrowed his eyes, but neither Allie nor Wally looked his way. He went on filling orders, but made sure he could eavesdrop on their conversation at the same time.

"Been coming here for a couple years," Wally said. "Place gets to be like home and the people like family."

"Don't you have a family at home?"

"Did. Had a beautiful wife. Sandra. She died two years ago Thanksgiving."

"Oh, God, Wally. I'm so sorry." Mac could see the tears spring to her eyes. "Me and my big mouth."

"It's okay. Rest of my family's in Chicago. Guys at work, they kinda avoided me after she died. Didn't know what to say, I suppose. But Mac's a good listener. And I guess that's what I needed. Anyway, Mac and everyone here got me through."

Mac remembered that time. Wally was a mess. Mac served him one drink a night, then switched him to coffee. Looking at Wally now, Mac had forgotten how far he had come.

"Sounds like you have a lot of good things to say about Mac."

Wally shook his finger at her. "Don't you say anything bad about him."

She held up her hands in a gesture of surrender. "I won't. I just asked."

Mac couldn't keep quiet any longer. "I'd appreciate it if you didn't grill my customers."

"We're having a conversation," Allie said, her blue eyes all wide and innocent. "You've heard of conversations, haven't you?"

"You gonna order a drink or are you just here to hassle my customers?"

She smiled widely and his pulse leapt. He noticed the mischievous glint in her eye just before she spoke.

"I'd love a Screaming Orgasm."

Wally laughed, spitting out a mouthful of beer. "Whoa, she's a live one, Mac."

Mac tried not to smile. He didn't want to encourage her. But the thought of giving Allie a screaming orgasm was almost more than he could take. He could picture her lying naked on his bed, crying out with the pleasure his cock had given her. Or maybe he'd drive her wild with his mouth, sucking that little clit until she came over and over again. His whole body throbbed. He was going to have to buy some roomier trousers.

He had to clear his throat before he could speak. "A Screaming Orgasm, huh? Do you even know what's in one of them?"

She raised her eyebrows and smiled slyly. "I'm entirely familiar with what is required for a Screaming Orgasm."

And he didn't think his cock could get any harder. "Okay, tell me."

"You mean you don't know?" Her silky voice slid along his skin, sending shivers of awareness through him.

He could play this game too. He winked at her and stepped as close as he could with the bar between them. "I've given my share of Screaming Orgasms."

The blue of her eyes seemed to deepen. "Oh, then you're an expert."

"Are you kidding? Honey, I'm a professional."

"Then I put myself in your capable hands."

Mac groaned. Right out loud. If only she were in his hands. Any part of her. Those breasts. That gorgeous ass he had the opportunity to see this afternoon. He turned away to make the drink.

Wally had been shamelessly listening in on the exchange and he started to laugh. "Hey, Mac. You might want to stick one of those ice cubes down your pants."

Not a bad idea.

Allie could sit on this stool all night long, just watching Mac and listening to him talk. She even seemed to be getting used to staying up later. While she sometimes got that tired buzzing in her head, she was doing better than she had before.

She never tired of looking at Mac, and not just admiring his strong arms or broad chest or cute buns, though they were all great. She loved to watch his face as he served the customers at the bar. He didn't talk all that much, but his expressions said more than words ever could.

She enjoyed seeing him flirt with two older women who came in to celebrate a birthday. They laughed and blushed in response to something Mac said. He laughed back and Allie's breath caught in her throat at the irresistible sight he made.

Would he ever laugh like that with her? Would he ever let his guard down? Ever let her get to really know him?

She pushed away the twinge of despair that tried to worm itself into her head. She couldn't give up yet. She just had to hang around and let him get used to her, as if he were a wounded animal. Sooner or later she'd wear down his resistance and he'd realize she wasn't here to hurt him. She was here to help him.

Help him clear the air.

Help him find his soul mate.

How could she convince him that they were meant to be together? The air sizzled between them, didn't he realize that? He was fighting her because the attraction was so strong.

Wally nudged her with his elbow. She'd forgotten he was there. "Hey, isn't this the song you played the other night?"

"Yeah. Bruce Springsteen." She started to move her head in time to the music. "Simon says, 'Springsteen is a classic for any generation.'"

"Stop quoting me," Mac growled from down the bar.

Allie just smiled and kept moving on the stool in time to the heavy beat of the music. She started humming along with the Boss. She'd get under Mac's skin one way or another.

She hadn't planned on staying until closing, but she'd started talking with Seth, who added a couple more stories about Mac. Then she'd talked to some of the other regulars and even ended up helping Denise with a few tables when she was rushed. Somehow Allie found herself still at the Jolly Roger when all the customers had gone.

She'd never minded being alone. With two older brothers, she'd relished any time she could spend by herself. And being in a military family meant they'd moved around a lot. Allie had had to become comfortable with her own company until she could make new friends again.

But tonight, she didn't want to think about going back to that impersonal hotel room and tossing and turning by herself in that big bed with the hard mattress. She knew she'd lay there thinking of Mac. Imagining his hands on her, caressing her skin, kneading her breasts, stroking her pussy. His mouth on her, kissing her lips, sucking her nipples, teasing her clit. She'd spend the night yearning instead of sleeping.

"Whew, what a night! Thanks for the help." Denise untied her apron and hung it on a hook inside the storeroom. "Walk you out?" she asked Allie.

"Thanks, but I'll help Mac clean up." The words just popped out of her mouth before she had time to think. She didn't dare look at Mac to see his reaction.

"I like to clean by myself," his deep voice growled behind her.

"Nonsense. With two of us it will go twice as fast." She smiled at Denise, still not looking behind her. "Go on home to that cute husband of yours. I'll help Mac."

Allie watched Denise until she disappeared through the front door. Then she finally turned to face Mac. She didn't let his intimidating glare sway her. In fact, it made her pulse race. His white button-down shirt was open at the throat and rolled up at the sleeves. She swallowed hard and fought the urge to undo the rest of those buttons and rip that shirt off his broad shoulders.

"Give me a rag," she said lightly, "and I'll get the tables." He didn't move for a moment, then tossed her a wet rag.

There was a different atmosphere to the place now that there were no other people here. The shadows weren't softened by cheery laughter or friendly chatter. She wiped sticky spills and peanut crumbs off the table. The place didn't look so jolly now. It was dark and more than a little sad.

Sad, because Allie saw the Jolly Roger as a substitute. Oh, not for the group of students who came in here to party or the couples who stopped in to flirt and talk. But people like Wally and Seth, who were missing a significant relationship with someone in their lives, who came here to try to fill that empty space inside them.

The Jolly Roger had to be a substitute for Mac too. She knew what he was capable of doing, of writing. He'd made such a difference in people's lives. What could have been so traumatic that he turned his back on who he was? Why did he bury himself here, trying to fill that empty space inside him? Why—

"Thanks for the help."

She jumped at the sound of his voice and dropped the rag onto the table. She didn't want to face him with her face flushed and her heart pounding, so she didn't turn around right away. She took a deep, shaky breath and willed her body to relax.

Then she felt his hands on her shoulders. Warm hands. Strong hands. They were the hands that wrote all those wonderful words that attracted her to him in the first place. He began to knead her shoulders, loosening the tension she hadn't realized was there. With a soft moan, she backed up against him.

She dropped her head back against his shoulder. Her cheek brushed against his, setting off shivers of awareness through her body. The smell of beer and liquor in the air only intensified his own unique scent. She closed her eyes and breathed him in.

"Allie," he whispered, his lips touching her ear. His warm breath caressed her face.

She opened her eyes and turned her head to look at him. Their cheeks brushed again. His rough jaw line scraped her face, awakening her senses even further. It was a good thing she was leaning back against him, because her shaky knees threatened to give out on her.

Through a haze of passion, she smiled.

Without breaking eye contact, he began to move his hands down her sides. He gently skimmed her ribs, slowly brushing the outer curve of her breasts with his fingers. She'd have loved him to linger there, but he continued moving his hands down to her waist. Her breasts swelled in anticipation, her nipples puckered and tingled. She needed his hands there, touching, squeezing. She moaned and moved against him, pressing her bottom into his hard arousal.

He moved his hands lower still, caressing her hips. Then at the same time, he brushed her ear with his lips before taking the lobe between his teeth and gently teasing the sensitive flesh.

Her knees weakened. His warm breath blew in her ear as he nipped at her earlobe. His tongue played with the two hoops that swung there. Her hands hung by her side, aching to touch him as he was touching her. But her back was pressed up against him and his hands held her in place, grasping her hips and pulling her even more tightly against him.

She reached up and combed her fingers through his hair, keeping his head down where his tongue still played with her earrings. Her body was one big itchy ache. She brought her other hand up to one of her breasts and massaged it through her thin T-shirt. She plucked at an aching nipple with her fingers. Her pussy tingled and grew damp with need. She moaned and began to pulse her body against him, pressing her ass into his hard cock, over and over again.

He must have sensed her frustration. He brought his hands up and cupped her breasts. He squeezed them roughly and they seemed to swell beneath his touch. When he rolled the sensitive nipples between his fingers, desire shot straight to her core and her knees nearly melted beneath her.

She sighed and rained light kisses along his jaw line. He tasted of salt and sin.

Silently, he turned her around to face him. He caressed her face with his gaze and she swore she could feel his touch. Then, he finally took her face in his hands and lowered his lips to hers.

This was what she had been dreaming of for far too long. But that was only a fleeting thought in a far corner of her mind. Then she was beyond thought. She lost herself in the kiss, throwing herself headlong into it as she did anything she was passionate about.

Mac nibbled at her lips, tentatively at first, as if he was trying to find out who she was, what she wanted. She returned the kiss, offering her tongue to deepen it, to intensify the sparks that ran through her body. To show him she was simply Allie and all she really wanted was him.

She lapped his mouth with her tongue, her moans going down his throat. A mere taste of him wasn't enough. She wanted to devour him, to inhale him. To make him a part of her.

Her body came alive with desire. It thrummed through her like an electrical current, charging her body with excitement, igniting her senses with need.

This was the man she had fallen in love with years ago. This was the man she was falling in love with now. Only now it was more than his words that she was attracted to. More than his words that made her feel alive.

She stepped back and in one swift motion, pulled her shirt over her head. His eyes widened but he didn't say a word. Her wispy bra was barely there and with a flick of Mac's fingers, it wasn't there at all.

He stood there and simply looked at her for a moment. She should have felt self-conscious, should have felt exposed. Instead she felt incredibly attractive. Incredibly aroused. Moisture pooled between her legs and she had to force herself to stand still and not give in to the wriggle her body wanted to indulge in.

"Beautiful," he murmured. "You are so beautiful."

He stepped forward and gathered her breasts into his hands. He pressed them together and buried his face in the cleavage. His breath warmed her skin.

She grasped his head with her hands, savoring the feel of his soft hair against her palms. He placed circles of kisses along her skin, coming closer and ever closer to the sensitized nipples that seemed to grow and beg for his touch. She gasped when he finally captured one with his hot mouth and sucked it deep inside.

She threw her head back, arching her body against him. He sucked her nipple hard, almost to the point of pain. All her senses were heightened, her body was one giant buzz.

She grabbed his shoulders and felt the strength in his muscles, the hard maleness of him. This was the man she wanted. Couldn't he see that she was the woman he needed?

All too soon, he stopped teasing her nipples. He straightened and placed a light kiss on her lips. His face was pretty much in the shadows, but Allie was certain she saw deep emotion on his face.

What emotion, she wasn't sure.

Why did he stop? Her body ached for satisfaction. Her body yearned for him to bury himself deep inside her, to finally make them one. But what did he want?

She took his face in his hands. If she asked him, would he tell her? She looked into his deep brown eyes, trying to see inside the man. But the shadows hid him from her.

"Why did you run away?"

They sure weren't the words she'd planned to say, but maybe they were the ones closest to her heart. It was too late to take them back, anyway.

He brushed her hands away from his face and stepped back from her, breathing heavily. He stood completely in the shadows now. "I didn't run away."

She missed his touch already. She wished she hadn't brought it up, wished they could have finished what they had started. But the question hung in the air between them and she knew that Mac had to face it as much as she needed to know the answer.

"What else would you call it?" she asked. Her mind craved answers as much as her body craved satisfaction. "You had an award-winning career. You were doing something you were obviously born to do. And you ran away from it. I'm trying to understand why."

"I didn't run away," he repeated, his voice low, almost dangerous. He turned from her and walked slowly back to the bar.

"Your words had such power," she said, following him across the room, unable to stop the words from pouring out of her. Maybe if he understood what his writing had meant to her it would make a difference to him as well. "You gave me the courage to say whatever I wanted to say. You let me know I could be whatever I wanted to be. Just with your words. How could you give that up?"

"You're giving me a lot more credit than I deserve," he said, his voice raw and rough. "Old newspaper columns do not give a person courage. You had that yourself, Allie. Give yourself the credit."

"But your words did influence me," she said, putting her hand on his arm. He flinched and pulled away from her. Tears sprung to her eyes. How could she make him understand? "Your words influence everyone who reads them. Why do you think your columns were so popular? Because of the integrity in your writing. Because of the power in those words."

"I never wanted that kind of power!"

The wild look in his eyes might have frightened her if she hadn't seen the anguish in his face. He turned his back to her and he grasped the edge of the bar.

Allie wanted to reach out to him, but she knew he wouldn't want her to. She wished he would confide in her, but she understood why he didn't trust her. She watched his shoulders rise and fall, heard his heavy breathing. He took one last deep breath and turned to face her again. His face was a frozen mask.

Without another word, he walked past her and picked up her shirt and bra. He shoved them into her hands. "Get dressed. I'll walk you to your car."

Her hands shook as she hooked her bra and then drew her shirt back over her head. "Mac, I—."

"I don't want to talk about it anymore." He turned away from her to switch off the lights, then led her to the front door. It was as if what they shared tonight had never happened. He walked her out of the bar and to her car, never touching her. He watched her unlock it, open the door and climb in. As she drove away she realized he'd never said another word.

Mac walked back into the Jolly Roger, but didn't switch the lights back on. He sank into the closest chair. His body ached, his cock throbbed with the need for release. What was he going to do about her? Why couldn't she leave it alone? Leave him alone, instead of teasing him with her body. Why did she have to keep raking up the past? Why did she have to keep reminding him?

All that talk about integrity and power. What a joke.

If she only knew.

But she never would. The untold story of Simon MacKenzie would stay locked up inside him until the day he died.

Tonight was a big mistake. He'd just finished telling himself he was going to keep his hands off her, the next thing he knew, he'd wrapped his arms around her. He was drawn to her like there was some kind of magnetic pull between the two of them.

They should never have gone so far tonight. He would have taken her on the floor if she hadn't opened that big mouth of hers. He would have plunged his cock into her over and over again, sliding his hard shaft into her wet, waiting flesh, driving her ass into the floor until he was satisfied. And she would have been satisfied too, her climax squeezing him dry. He'd have made sure of it.

She wouldn't want him if she ever found out the truth. He wasn't the man she thought he was. That man had never existed. He was nothing but a lie.

Allie couldn't sleep when she got back to her room. The feeling of Mac's lips on hers wouldn't go away. She still tasted him on her tongue. She couldn't pretend it had never happened. She wouldn't pretend. She wrapped her arms around herself, trying to recapture the feeling of Mac's arms around her.

How could she have been so stupid? She'd actually been in Simon MacKenzie's arms. They'd been enjoying blood-pounding foreplay and she had to blow it. Why couldn't she turn off that inquisitive mind of hers once in a while? Why did she always have to say what she was thinking? She'd never known when to keep her mouth shut.

Since she was restless anyway, she turned on her laptop to get down the stories about Mac she heard tonight before she forgot them. As if she'd ever forget anything about Mac. She laughed out loud as she typed in the story Denise told her about Mac giving Chuck a bachelor party at the Jolly Roger, then arranging to have Denise jump out of the cake. Wally and Seth had their own stories and it would all make for a well-rounded interview. She had Mac's words from his columns; she had the stories from his friends. Now she just needed the answers from the man himself.

But right now the answers didn't seem as important as the man.

She still couldn't sleep, so she grabbed the remote and flipped through the channels on the small screen TV, but she didn't want to watch infomercials and she sure didn't want to watch other people having sex. She felt like writing. Felt like using this pent-up energy for something productive, but there wasn't anything more she could add to the article tonight. So what should she write about?

A little voice in the back of her head started whispering, reminding her of the novel she'd always wanted to write. What about that mystery she'd always dreamed about? Allie grasped the laptop in her hands but didn't open the lid.

Could she fit more writing into her day? A novel sounded so daunting. Could she invest months, maybe years, on one project that might or might not sell? How would she even start a big project like that?

In an alley.

The first scene came to her, full-blown in that instant. A young woman had to venture into a dark alley in search of something important. Allie knew exactly how she would feel. What she would hear. What she would smell. And someone was following her. He wanted that important something too.

What would happen when they met up in that dark alley?

So many possibilities. Excitement swelled up in Allie as she imagined what could be. She opened the laptop and started typing.

When the telephone rang the next morning, she realized she'd fallen asleep propped up in the bed, the computer still on her lap. After she reached across the pillow and picked up the phone, Allie stifled a groan. "Hi, Marcia. I didn't expect to hear from you today."

"I didn't expect to find you still in Buffalo," her editor replied. "I thought you'd be back in Pittsburgh by now, putting the finishing touches on the article you promised me."

"I can put the finishing touches on the article in Buffalo, Marcia," she told her, trying not to panic. "I have my laptop right here. I've been hanging out at this cool little bar called the Jolly Roger."

"Allie, I don't care about a damn bar."

"Well, would you care if I told you the bar is owned and operated by one very handsome Simon MacKenzie?"

"It's going well then?" Marcia asked, the eagerness clear in her rough voice. "I can't wait to read it. Maybe you should e-mail me what you have so far."

What she had so far was a disjointed mess of paragraphs with nothing to tie them together. She couldn't send that to Marcia. She cleared her throat. "Give me a few more days, okay? To be honest, Mr. MacKenzie hasn't been as forthcoming with information as I would have liked."

"What does that mean? Are you going to have the article for me or not?"

"I'll have it, Marcia," she said. "Just give me a few more days."

"You're making me nervous here, Allie. I expect a progress report e-mailed to me within two days."

"Okay, Marcia," Allie replied. But the editor had already hung up.

Allie sighed and hung up the phone. She grabbed a pillow and held it against her stomach to try to calm the nerves that were gathering there. How was she going to get Mac to tell her what happened to make him stop writing? Something dramatic had to have happened. One event that changed him forever.

It was no good to speculate. She couldn't use guess work in an article. She couldn't ask Denise or anyone else at the bar. She'd never ask them to betray a confidence, and she was willing to bet they didn't know what happened anyway.

It had to come from Mac. And Mac wasn't talking. She stood up and started pacing around the small room. There had to be a way to work this out. There had to be a way to get the interview and get Mac too.

She didn't have much time. Tonight night was going to have to be the night. She told herself that this was for Mac's sake too. Whatever happened to him was obviously still eating at him and probably always would until he got it out in the open and dealt with it. She was going to have to convince Mac one way or another that he wanted to give her the interview.

And that he wanted her.

All the talking in the world hadn't done any good. She could only think of one other thing to do.

She picked up the telephone and called Denise's number. "Are you busy today before work?"

"No, just housework, but that's always there. What did you have in mind?"

She reminded herself that this was for Mac's own good. "Shopping."

"You called the right person. Shopping's my middle name."

After she arranged to meet Denise later, the day stretched out before her. What could she do besides fantasize about Mac in her bed, his mouth on her breasts and his teeth teasing her nipples, his cock filling her up, pumping into her over and over against until they both exploded in shattering orgasms. She didn't need the frustration.

The knot was still in her stomach from Marcia's phone call, the near panic was fresh in her mind. A picture of the young woman venturing into that dark alley flashed in her head. The scene she'd been working on before she fell asleep. This young woman knew she was being followed. She fought the panic bubbling up inside her and began to run.

Allie sat down at her computer and got to work.

Chapter 5

Wally was fidgeting tonight. It was only a few minutes after opening and he and Mac were the only people in the bar. He had no idea where Denise was.

Mac handed Wally his beer. "Got something on your mind?"

Wally looked into the mug, as if he could find the answers there. "No. I've got to leave early tonight, though."

"You know, there's no time requirement to sit at my bar. You can come and go as you please."

Wally chuckled. "I know." He took a sip of beer and cleared his throat. "There is one thing, Mac."

"Sure. What is it?"

"I loved my wife, you know."

"I know, Wally."

"Loved her with all my heart. I never cheated on her the whole time we were married and we were married a long time."

"I know, Wally."

"Well, I started going to these meetings at that book store down the street. You know where people get together and talk about the books that everyone's reading. It's a mystery book club."

"Yeah, I've heard of those."

Wally stared into his beer as he talked. "Well, there's, um, there's this woman that comes to the meetings too. She's real smart, and funny, and nice looking too. She's divorced." He looked up at Mac. "It, um, it came up in conversation."

Mac nodded and tried not to smile.

"I asked her out to dinner and she said yes." Wally looked up at Mac. "I didn't really think she'd say yes, I mean, I haven't asked anyone out for a date in so long I didn't even think I knew how. But I stumbled through it and she actually said yes."

"That's great, Wally."

"Yeah, that's what I thought too." He pushed the beer mug from one hand to the other, but didn't drink anymore. "But now I keep thinking about Sandra.

I still love her, Mac. I'll never stop. How can I think about going out with another woman when I still love her?"

Oh, man. "Sandra was a good woman, Wally. She'd want you to be happy, wouldn't she? She wouldn't want you to be lonely anymore."

"Yeah, there's nothing worse than being lonely," Wally said. "Man wasn't meant to live alone."

Sure he was. Mac opened his mouth, but closed it again. He'd lived alone for so long, he couldn't imagine it any other way. He didn't want it any other way.

Or did he? Lately, in some weak moments he'd been picturing Allie with him around the house, taking over his kitchen like she did when he first met her. Playing with Roger. Sharing his bed.

Since Allie had come into his life, he could understand what Wally was feeling. The guy deserved every chance at happiness. Mac grabbed the half-empty beer mug off the bar and dumped it out. "Then what are you sitting here for? Go get ready for dinner."

Wally broke into a big grin. "You're a good friend, Mac." He shook Mac's hand and jumped off the stool. "I'll see you later."

Mac watched the big man leave the bar. He had a feeling Wally wouldn't be stopping in so much anymore.

Denise rushed in the door a few minutes later. "Sorry, I'm late." She started bustling around, getting the place ready for customers.

Mac shrugged. "No problem." He waited for Denise to get some supplies out of the storeroom and come back into the bar. "You missed Wally."

"Wally's come and gone already?"

Mac nodded. "Wally met a woman."

Denise stopped in her tracks and stared at Mac, a handful of napkins in her hand. "Wally? Our Wally?"

"Yep. He's taking her out to dinner tonight."

"Good for him." She stacked the napkins in their spot behind the bar. "I hope things work out for him." She grabbed her apron and stared at Mac as she tied it on. "You know, I don't want to be a busybody, but I hope things work out for you too."

"What are you talking about?"

"You and Allie."

"Denise."

"Come on, Mac. I've known you for too long. I can tell the difference in you when she's around."

"She's not much more than a kid. I'm too old for her."

Denise put her hands on her hips. "Age has nothing to do with it, and you know it. It has everything to do with the way she makes you feel."

"Trying to play matchmaker?"

Denise climbed up on the barstool in front of him and looked him in the eye. "I don't want you to be lonely anymore."

"I'm not lonely."

"Yeah, just like Wally hasn't been lonely. You're glad to see him going out on a date. Maybe it's time to follow your own advice."

He was so close to doing just that. "Have you forgotten why Allie is here? What she wants to do?"

Denise hopped off the stool and walked over to straighten up a couple chairs. "I don't understand why it's such a big deal anymore."

"You wouldn't."

"It's just one little article in an obscure writer's magazine. It's not like it's going to be on the front page of the New York Times." Denise whirled around. "And what if it was? What does it matter? You're still going to be you. You're still going to own this bar. You're still going to be a retired writer. What does it matter?"

Mac turned away. He couldn't explain to Denise why it mattered. He couldn't bear to see the look of disappointment in the faces of his friends if they ever found out the truth.

Customers started filtering in and Mac was glad for the familiar busyness of bartending. He might build drinks now the way he used to build sentences, but no one cared what he was thinking about while he was making them.

He heard a couple low whistles before he looked up and saw her. If the wine glass he'd just filled hadn't already been sitting on the bar, he would have dropped it. She strolled over to the bar as if she had no idea every man in the place was tripping over his tongue. Her eyes were locked on his and never left his face.

She'd swept her hair up off her neck tonight, leaving a few tendrils curling around her face. The short white dress she wore hugged her body like a lover before it flared out to swing around her legs.

Her legs. Mac could have written an entire column on those long, firm legs. Those long, firm, bare legs he fantasized about when he was hardly aware of it. Those legs he ached to have wrapped around him.

And the buttons that ran from the deep neckline to the hem. Oh man, a million little buttons teasing him. Testing his self control. His hands shook as he kept himself from reaching out to touch them.

He knew he was staring at her. He knew he was still gripping the wine glass. He knew the bar was filled with other people and they must have been talking. The jukebox must have been playing. But he couldn't hear anything but his own ragged breathing. He was mesmerized by her and he couldn't seem to snap out of it. She smiled lazily and he thought he must have smiled back.

"Hey, Mac. Put your tongue back in your mouth and wipe up the drool before you hand me that glass."

Leave it to Denise to bring him back to earth.

Allie laughed and sat down on the stool in front of him. "Hi, Mac."

He didn't trust himself to speak yet, so he nodded and cleared his throat. "Hi." The word came out like a moan.

Was there laughter in her eyes?

She slowly licked her lips. He couldn't look away from that wide, wicked mouth. "How about a Blow Job tonight?" she asked, her voice low and sensual.

He almost choked. He glanced around to see if anyone heard her. "What?"

There was definitely laughter in her eyes. "Kahlua? Irish Crème? Vodka?"

He didn't let himself smile. "Oh. The drink."

"Well, yeah. What did you think I was talking about?" She slid her finger in her mouth and slowly pulled it back out, shiny and wet. "Oh. That."

He was still staring at her mouth and the image of her going down on his cock made it grow hard and throbbing. "Allie, you're killing me."

If she was trying for an innocent expression on her face, it wasn't working. She was pure temptress tonight. Wide eyes outlined with some kind of smoky makeup. Wet lips covered with dark red slick and shine. White dress shining in the dim shadows, barely held up by impossibly skinny straps.

"Blow job," she repeated, licking her lips. "It sounds yummy."

His pants tightened even more as his cock pulsed in reaction to her smooth, low voice speaking those words. He turned away before he grabbed her and took her behind the bar, the hell with the customers.

He grabbed a small rocks glass and poured in the Kahlua. Then he had to take a deep breath to steady his hands before he floated the Irish Crème liqueur over the Kahlua and then layered the vodka on top.

He steeled himself against the sensations she stirred up in him. Then he handed her the glass. "Bottom's up."

A sly smile slid across her face. She tossed back the drink like a pro.

"Whoo. That's so good," she said. "I can feel that going through my whole body."

Mac swallowed. "Um, we aim to please."

"I went shopping today. Denise and I went down to the Galleria Mall."

So that's why Denise had been late. She must have had something to do with that unbelievable dress Allie was wearing. The one oozing sex. The one with buttons that had his name written on them.

"Shopping, huh? I suppose you picked up that little number you're wearing?"

"This old thing?"

He laughed out loud. Man, he wished they were alone. He wished they were at his place. Everything he said to Denise went out the window. He was going to die before he could get his hands on Allie. How many more hours until closing?

He cleared his throat again. "So, you spent all day shopping?"

"Well, actually...."

The woman who brazenly walked into his bar and ordered a Blow Job was blushing. What had she been up to? His stomach clenched. Had she been snooping and found out something?

"I started a book," she said before he could accuse her of anything else. "A novel. A mystery."

"Really?" He wouldn't bother to mention how tough the fiction market was, she had to know. And he wouldn't mention the suspicions he'd almost thrown her way. "How's it going?"

"Oh, Mac, it's going great." Her face lit up and her hands started moving along with her expression. "I couldn't believe it. Once I got started, the words just poured out of me. I mean, I know it'll need a lot of work. And I still don't have a real handle on the characterization yet, but it's coming great."

"That's great. I'd love to read it."

"Oh, it's not ready for anyone to read yet," Allie replied quickly. "Maybe when I'm done."

But where would she be then? For the first time, Mac admitted to himself that he didn't want her to go. It didn't matter to him anymore why she was here, just that she was.

So what was he going to do about it?

A new couple sat down at the end of the bar. He signaled to them that he'd be right there. "Well, let me know when you're ready."

She grinned up at him. "I'm ready now, but I guess we'll have to wait 'til the bar closes."

Chapter 6

It was the longest night of Mac's life. Business was brisk and conversation lively, but he had to resist the urge to chase everyone out of the bar and lock the door behind them. All he could think about was taking Allie back to his place and opening each and every one of those little buttons.

Allie joked around with Seth and the other guys at the bar, but Mac caught the flirtatious glances she threw his way. One time when he looked her way, she dipped her finger into her glass of wine and then sucked on it, pulling the finger slowly in and out of her mouth. And then had the nerve to laugh when he missed the glass and splashed vodka all over the bar.

Mac had already finished washing the last of the glasses when closing time finally rolled around and the last patron left. Denise hung her apron up and smiled at Allie, still sitting on her barstool.

"I suppose you're going to help Mac clean up again?" Denise asked.

Allie nodded. "Give Chuck a kiss for me."

"My pleasure," Denise said. "'Night, Mac." She gave him a wink and was out the door.

Allie turned to look at him, her eyes bright even in the dim light of the barroom. She still took his breath away. He couldn't imagine not seeing her every night. Talking with her. Laughing with her. Holding her in his arms.

When Robyn left him and he moved from New York City to Buffalo, he'd closed himself off from opinions, from emotions. From life. He thought he'd been protecting himself.

For the first time he wondered if he'd been punishing himself instead.

"Toss me a rag?" she said. Funny, he could have sworn her expression was saying, "Kiss me?"

All logical thought scrambled in his brain. He handed her a damp cloth, his touch lingering on her fingers. She curled her fingers around his for a second, then tossed him a sassy grin and jumped off the stool. She wiggled those hips a little more than usual as she walked away from him.

He watched her lean over to wipe off the table in the corner. Her shapely little ass seemed to beckon him to come and touch. Her legs stretched out below the flirty skirt, teasing him with their shapely curves. Mac had to force himself to stay behind the bar and finish his work so they could head to his house and his big bed.

He grabbed the broom and did a quick sweep behind the bar. He swept up the crumbs beneath the tables and quickly made his way over the last corner Allie was working in. He brushed up against her bare arm as he reached out to sweep beneath the table. She didn't look his way, but leaned into him as she scrubbed the table, rubbing her leg against his.

He swallowed the moan that threatened to escape his lips. He dropped a light kiss on her shoulder and dragged himself away from her, sweeping the rest of the crumbs over to the pile by the trash. After he'd scooped them into the can with the dustpan, he turned around to look at Allie. But she wasn't there.

Then he heard Elvis begin crooning over the speakers. He turned around and saw Allie leaning against the jukebox, smiling at him. The lights from the jukebox pulsed around her, turning her hair to fire and his knees to jelly.

His heart stumbled in his chest, trying to find a new rhythm, one that beat in time with the love he felt for her.

Love?

He almost dropped the broom. Had he fallen in love with Allie? When the hell had that happened? He'd been fighting it for what seemed like ages. He stared at her and knew it had probably been building since the first moment he saw her. But it had taken until this very moment for him to make the tumble.

Love.

Love he couldn't explain or describe in mere words, even though words had come easy to him for most of his life. That big, empty hole inside him seemed to fill with something warm and significant.

How could he have fallen in love with a woman he didn't trust? It wasn't possible. Didn't love and trust go hand in hand?

Or deep down inside did he trust her after all?

He'd been rooted in the same spot since the song started. Allie slowly sashayed over to him, and whatever he'd been thinking about went out the window. She smiled and took the broom and dustpan he'd forgotten he was still holding. She leaned them against the wall and turned back to him.

"Dance with me?"

"I've been waiting all night." He opened his arms and gathered her to him. She rested her head on his shoulder, burrowing her face into his neck. They swayed in time to the music, her soft breasts pressed against his chest. Her lips pressed against his throat.

She stroked his back, making light circles with her fingernails. He shivered in response. He brushed his lips lightly across her temple, then with a single finger he lifted her chin.

Her lips were already parted when they met his. Soft and wet, they slid against his. Then she slipped out her tongue and ran it across his bottom lip. He groaned and pulled her closer against him, pressing his hard cock against her hips as he took her tongue into his mouth.

She tasted of tangy wine, tart yet sweet. He sucked her tongue gently, drinking her in like a man who'd abstained for way too long. She moaned and leaned into him, rubbing her soft body against him. And still they continued to sway to the music floating around them.

She smelled like soft flowers. She felt like she belonged in his arms. He wished he could get closer to her, to climb inside and become one with her. To love her inside and out and beg her not to go.

The song ended before he got around to begging, and they slowly backed out of the embrace.

"Wow," Allie said. Mac was pleased to hear a little shakiness in her voice. "You're some dancer." Her hands lay lightly on his chest and she began to play with the buttons on his white shirt.

Buttons. How could he have forgotten about that row of tiny buttons running up Allie's dress? His fingers itched at the reminder. He began playing with her buttons too and was frustrated to find his fingers fumbling with the little round pieces of plastic. He used to be able to unhook a bra strap one-handed, damn it. Now his fingers felt big and clumsy and he couldn't get a grip on some stupid little buttons.

But, of course, with a little more work, he could. And he did. The top button popped open, revealing the creamy, rounded swells of her breasts. She looked up at him with a mischievous glint in her eye and licked her lips again. She unbuttoned his top button as well.

He thought he had been hard when he was dancing with her, but just the sight of those soft, full mounds left him straining against his zipper. The hell with going to his apartment. No one was out on the street at this time of night to look in the window. This room was too dark anyway. There was only a small light over the bar still burning.

Mac wanted to plunge his hands into her soft hair, but a large clip held that beautiful bounty up on her head. He grasped the clip and squeezed. It released her mass of curls, and he tossed it away. He heard it clatter across the floor and stop when it hit the wall.

Allie laughed and shook her head, tossing the hair around her shoulders. He let the soft strands slip through his fingers and settle around her lovely face.

He lowered his lips to her breasts, sweeping them across her soft skin. She let her head fall back, her hair cascading behind her, her chest coming even closer to him. He swept her breasts into his palms. She wasn't wearing a bra. All right. He wouldn't have to worry about those little hooks.

He took one breast into his mouth, soaking the fabric that was the only barrier between them. He found and teased her swollen nipple with his teeth. She clutched his shoulders and swayed backwards. They were close to the bar, so he led her back to lean against it, never taking the nipple out of this mouth.

"Oh, Mac," she moaned, her fingers grasping his shoulders tighter. "You're driving me crazy."

He reluctantly relinquished his hold on her breast to reply, "It's only fair. You've been driving me crazy all night."

"I have?" She smiled, that wide wet mouth once again causing his head to spin. "That was the idea."

"Oh, it was?" She'd planned to seduce him? Why didn't the thought bother him? Somewhere in the back of his mind, he knew it should. Robyn's name drifted through his mind like a wisp of smoke and was gone. All he could do was grin like an idiot. "So you're saying you bought that dress for me?"

"Of course I did."

He undid one more button without too much trouble. Her breasts strained against the fabric, threatening to spill out. One more button would do it, but Mac didn't touch it yet. His fingers hovered over them, tingling with anticipation. He leaned forward, capturing her sweet lips once again. While he continued with the kiss, his fingers quickly unfastened the rest of the buttons down to her waist.

He stepped back and looked at her. "You are so beautiful." He cupped her breasts in his hands and buried his face between them. Her arms wrapped around his head. Though some parts of his body had other ideas, he could have stayed where he was all night long, nestled in Allie's warm embrace.

There was so much more he wanted to experience with Allie and he didn't want it over too soon. He wanted time to discover all of Allie, every part of her. The way she felt. The way she tasted.

"Hold on to my shoulders," he said suddenly.

"What?"

He put his hands at her waist. "Hold onto my shoulders."

"Okay."

He was glad he lifted weights daily. He might be getting older, but he could lift Allie up onto the bar with no problem at all. She laughed when he set her down on the smooth surface of the bar.

The dim light over the bar shone down on her like a soft spotlight. She glanced over to the picture window. "Can anyone see us?"

It was dark outside, without even a streetlight to illuminate the sidewalk in front of the Jolly Roger. Mac could see their faint reflection in the glass. "Yeah, if someone was out there and really wanted to watch, I guess they could."

"Oh." A small smile turned up her lips.

He rubbed his hand up her leg until it disappeared under her skirt. "Does that bother you?"

She shook her head and grinned. "I thought it might, but it really doesn't." She rocked her pussy against the bar. "In fact, I'm getting even wetter just thinking that someone might catch us."

Mac's laugh came out more like a moan. So Allie had a little bit of the exhibitionist in her. Her legs swung lightly on either side of him. He ran his hands gently along her legs, soft and bare, her feet in strappy heels. The little gold ring decorating her navel caught his eye and he couldn't resist kissing her belly, tangling his tongue in the ring that dangled there.

Then he turned his attention to the bottom button on the skirt but soon he realized that it was going to take way too long to free all those buttons. With impatient hands, he shoved the skirt up her thighs. Long lengths of firm flesh stretched out before him. He slid his hands along her bare thighs, every nerve ending in his skin tingling with awareness. And when he reached her white, lacy panties, his blood pulsed thickly, his cock throbbed.

Allie gasped when he touched her through her panties. The thin fabric was soaked. The scent of her arousal nearly tipped him over the edge.

He cupped her with his hand, rubbing her soft mound through the thin fabric. She gasped again and moved against him. Her wet pussy pressed against the palm of his hand.

He looked up at her and he had to smile. Her head was thrown back again, her hands grasping the edge of the bar. Her legs were spread wide for him. Her feet were propped up on the bar stools on either side of him.

Damn, he was going to miss her.

The image of Allie, wild and uninhibited, would be forever burned in his memory. And he'd guarantee she'd have one wild ride to remember when she was back home.

She was going to melt into a puddle on the bar. Mac kissed her stomach, gently, like feathers tickling her skin, teasing her senses. His breath was warm against her skin, his lips soft. She felt him grab her belly button ring with his teeth and gently tug on it. His hands stretched beneath her skirt, one hand grasping her ass, the other cupping her pussy.

She couldn't stop herself from rocking back and forth against his hands.

His kisses were soft and sweet, but right now she craved more.

She needed hard. She needed rough. The tension in her body was slowly building and there was only one way to scratch the itch that was driving her crazy.

"Mac," she gasped, not knowing how much longer she could stand it. "Please."

Mac grasped the edge of her panties and pulled down. She lifted her bottom a bit off the bar and he stripped them down her legs. They caught on the heel of one of her sandals. Mac yanked them over the heel and she kicked them into the darkness.

He looked up at her and his eyes were dark in the shadows. Silence throbbed around them. Her ragged breathing was all she could hear. The unscratched itch was all she could feel.

"Allie," he murmured, then bent his head to work his magic on her.

His tongue began to scratch the itch. Somehow he knew just how to touch her. He knew where. He knew how hard. His tongue circled her swollen clit, touching off prickles that shot through her body. She moaned and pressed harder against him. She grabbed the edge of the bar with one hand to steady herself, and with the other hand, tangled her fingers in his hair.

He brought her close to the edge, sensations spiraling. She was so close she could almost feel herself tumbling. Then he pulled away, pulling her back from the brink as well. She couldn't stop the whimper that escaped her lips.

Her entire body cried out. Her blood pounded wildly, her breath came out in gasps. He kissed her thighs again for a moment. He had to know he was driving her wild.

He straightened and pulled her head down to meet his. His hand on the back of her neck, he kissed her deeply, his mouth wet with her own juices. She tasted herself on his lips, his tongue. She started to rock against the bar, craving release.

"Easy," Mac murmured, grasping her hips with her hands. "I want it to last for you."

Couldn't he understand she was dying? "No, Mac. Please."

"Hey, we got all night."

She moaned. "No, I don't have all night. I need it now, Mac. I need it now."

He chuckled. "Addicted to my love already?"

She grabbed his head and pushed it back down between her open thighs. She felt the warm breath of his laughter on her thigh.

He started his assault again, gentle at first. He licked her pussy but didn't scratch the itch. His tongue made long strokes over and over again that stopped just short of her swollen clit. He plunged his tongue deep inside her, sucking her cunt, lapping her juices.

He caught her labia between his teeth and teased the sensitive folds. Teased her as well. She'd never craved anything the way she craved release right now. He'd made her crazy with desire, more sensitive to every touch than she'd ever been in her life.

When he finally swept his tongue across her clit, it was as if a jolt of pure electricity shot through her. Energy crackled through her body, sensations spiraled, the buzz within her built and grew. He pushed her closer and closer to the release she'd been craving. When he drove her over the edge, it was no mere tumble. It was a plunge. It was a high-flying dive into the waves that crashed over and over again, carrying her up and over again and again with them.

"Wow," she whispered when she could speak again. Her legs were weak and her arms shaking, how could she feel so awesome?

Once she could move, she swiveled around on the bar and lay down, stretching out on the length of it. Mac stood beside her, looking down on her. He was breathing as hard as she was.

"Hey, Mac," she said as soon as she could speak the words. She still sounded breathless. "You sure do know how to tend bar."

He laughed. "I'm not finished yet. Come on down and I'll show you some more."

She shook her head. "Oh, no. You come up here."

"What?"

"Come on up, the weather's fine."

"You want me to climb up on the bar?"

She remembered her fantasy the first night she walked in this place. "Oh, yeah."

"Well, I'd have to take my clothes off before I got up there."

And just when her heartbeat had started to get back to normal. "That's okay. I'd love to watch."

She could tell Mac was trying not to smile. Trying to look annoyed. She started to hum the stripper theme as he lifted an eyebrow and finished unbuttoning his shirt. He let the bright white shirt slide down his arms and fall to the floor behind him. Then she forgot to hum anymore. His hot gaze captured her as he slowly lowered his zipper. The raspy sound cut through the dark silence surrounding them. She held her breath until he stepped out of his pants.

Wow, his cock stood so tall and proud. The fact that she made him hard like that caused shivers to run through her body. How she wanted to touch it, to feel the velvety skin beneath her fingers. To hold that hard strength in her hand. She felt herself grow wet again as she thought about his cock sliding deep inside her. Filling her body. Filling her senses.

He pulled a condom out of the pocket of his pants before he dropped them to the floor. She shivered in anticipation as he smoothed their protection on his thick shaft.

She held out her arms to him. She couldn't help but smile when he actually climbed up on a bar stool just because she asked him to. Then he knelt astride her on the bar.

There was an intoxicating mixture of liquor scents in the air around them. But not as intoxicating as the sight of the man above her. She'd known it would be like this from the very beginning. But then again, she had never imagined it could be this wonderful.

She was wet and ready. She spread her thighs, opening herself to him. Wanting him, needing him in a way she'd never thought possible.

He slid his hard shaft into her ready body without a word. This was what she'd been waiting for. He fit her perfectly. He felt so good. The desire on his face, the slide of their bodies was the only communication they needed. She wrapped her shaky legs around him, pulling him deeper within her.

His eyes appeared dark with passion as he looked down at her. She held his gaze as he grasped her waist and rode her hard. The delicious friction started the wonderful tingles swirling again within her. When he brought her to the edge again, they both took the plunge, riding the waves together in each other's arms.

When she could breathe again, Allie opened her eyes. Mac was resting on his elbows over her. He was gazing down at her, a small smile on his face.

"Wow," she said.

He nodded. "You know, I have to serve drinks on this bar tonight." She laughed and gathered him to her. "I'm too heavy."

"You're fine," she whispered, savoring the weight of him. She wrapped her arms around him and rubbed the warm, bare skin on his back. "You're wonderful."

"I, uh, I had been planning to try to talk you into coming back to my place after we got done cleaning tonight," he told her.

"Really?" She tickled his ribs. "Did you think you were going to have a hard time convincing me?"

"Not really."

"Well, you were right, let's go."

"Go?"

"Well, yeah." She squirmed a little beneath him. "This bar is getting kind of hard."

Roger was waiting for them when they got home. The shaggy dog ran right past Mac and wagged his tail shamelessly at Allie. She threw her arms around his neck and he licked her face. He ignored Mac completely. What happened to loyalty? What happened to man's best friend? Mac took one look at Allie rolling around on the floor with Roger and forgave him. What male could resist her?

"Thirsty?" he asked. "Hungry?"

"No, thanks, I'm fine," she said, her face still buried in Roger's coat. Then she looked up at him from where she lay on the floor. Her tousled hair fanned out around her. "Which came first? The bar or the dog?"

"What?" Allie's skirt was bunched up against her hips and Mac could see her long, bare legs and a glimpse of her lacy panties. He could only think about ripping those panties off her and feeling those legs wrapped around him again. "What do you mean, which came first?"

"Well, they're both Jolly Rogers."

"Oh. Yeah, they are, but the bar came first," he said, sitting down beside her. He leaned back against the sofa and watched her charm the dog. "I thought up the pirate theme for the bar. Later I got Roger, and he had that smile, even as a puppy. As soon as I saw it, I knew what his name had to be."

She sat up and put her arms around her knees. The skirt covered her legs now, damn it. The buttons were once again neatly closed, even if the dress was a little wrinkled. She leaned her chin on top of her knees and smiled at Mac. "So how did you end up owning a bar?"

"I grew up around here," he said, before he had time to think about it. "About the time I wanted to move back, this bar came up for sale. I used to bartend back when I was in college, so it seemed to fit."

"And about as far away from writing as you can get."

"Exactly." He held his breath as he waited to see if she would continue the questioning.

She was quiet for a moment, then asked, "You got any more of those chocolate chip cookies?"

"Yeah, you want some?"

He started to get up from the floor, but Allie jumped to her feet and pushed him back down. "No, you stay there. I'll get them."

Roger bounded across the floor and followed her into the kitchen. Mac sat alone on the living room floor and stared after her. Could he convince Allie to stay here with him?

Did he really want her to?

Memories of Robyn flew unbidden into his head. Coming onto him at a cocktail party in New York City, rubbing up against him in that slinky blue dress. She fed him a line from the very beginning and he ate it up like the caviar she loved. She slept with him that night and moved in within a week. She said she loved him, but what she loved was the life he lived back then; the parties, the media, mixing with celebrities. She'd said whatever he wanted to hear and he believed every word.

But Allie was different. At least that's what he told himself. After trying to convince himself for days that she couldn't be trusted, now all he wanted was to believe in her.

Allie came back into the room, her hand deep in the bag of chocolate chip cookies. She sat down beside Mac, her back against the sofa, her leg pressed against his. Roger sat in front of her in classic beggar position.

"No chocolate, Roger," Mac said.

Allie grinned and broke off a piece of cookie with no chips in it. "Good boy," she crooned. Mac watched her feed the bit of cookie to the dog. Roger gazed at her with undying affection.

Allie turned to Mac then and fed him the rest of the cookie. She leaned into him until her lips brushed his ear. "Good boy," she whispered in a seductive tone and then sucked on his earlobe.

The erotic sensation made Mac suck in his breath, but in doing so, he choked on the cookie and started coughing. Allie laughed and pounded him on the back.

"Are you all right?" she asked between chuckles.

"Yeah," he croaked, then coughed some more.

She ran and got him a glass of water, then knelt before him and lifted the glass to his lips. Their eyes caught, and while Mac drank the water that soothed his throat, his eyes never left her face. The sight of her, so young and full of possibilities, embracing life as if it was a precious gift, soothed his cynical soul.

Could it work? Could he and Allie be happy together? Was real love out there somewhere? A love that wasn't selfish? Robyn had pretty much convinced him there was no such thing as real love. Convinced him that love wasn't worth the risk.

Allie had him wondering again.

He gathered her in his arms. "Allie," he murmured in her ear. She straddled his legs and settled on his lap. He closed his eyes. "Allie."

"Simon says... kiss me."

His eyes flew open. "What?"

She grinned. "Didn't you ever play Simon Says when you were growing up?"

"Well, sure. When your name is Simon, that game takes on a whole new meaning."

"Is that how you came up with the name for your column?"

The last thing he wanted to talk about was his column. "Yeah."

"I thought so." She winked. "So. Simon says, kiss me."

He captured her mouth with his, grabbing the back of her head to hold her close. Her wet lips slid against hers. He couldn't seem to get close enough to her. No matter how close, it wasn't enough. No matter how much he tasted her, he wanted more.

She pulled away from him and slowly unbuttoned the front of her dress. He nearly drooled as he watched her open every single button from neckline to hem. Every single button. The dress fell open, baring her full breasts, her flat belly with the little ring, her lacy panties. He moaned.

She smiled slyly. "Touch my breasts."

He eagerly reached out, but she pushed his hands away. "No, no. I didn't say Simon says."

His hands were still outstretched, his fingers tingling. "Allie."

She leaned back against the sofa and dropped her head back on the seat cushion. Her back arched and those lovely breasts jutted out, close enough to touch. "Simon says, suck my nipples."

He didn't have to be told twice. Those pink buds looked so sweet and tender. He latched onto one with eager lips. He rolled the tight bead with his tongue, then sucked it deeply into his mouth. Allie moaned and wriggled beneath him. Without releasing the treasure between his lips, he rose up onto his knees in order to relieve some of the pressure his cock was causing in his trousers.

She tasted so sweet. She smelled of musky sex. Her pussy had to be wet again. He ached to put his hand there and feel her slick folds beneath his fingers. But this was her game right now, and he would go along with it.

For now.

After he had lavished her other nipple with the same attention, his body pulsing with need, Allie sighed and sat up straight. "You do that very well."

"Thank you."

"Simon says, take your pants off."

"All right." He kicked off his shoes, then stood up on unsteady legs and quickly shed his trousers and briefs.

"Simon says, sit on the sofa."

He did as she ordered. Allie knelt in front of him, the open dress spread out behind her like wings.

But this was no angel. The wicked gleam in her eyes told him that.

"Remember the drink I ordered tonight?"

"The white wine?" he asked, knowing that wasn't what she was talking about.

"No, silly. When I first came in. Remember what I ordered?"

His cock twitched before the words came out of his mouth. "A blow job." His voice was even shaky.

She brushed one finger along the ridge of his cock and he nearly came right then. "Well, you didn't say Simon says, but I guess I can go along with it anyway."

She smiled and he was drawn to that wide mouth, the too-big-for-her-face mouth he'd been fantasizing about from the very first time he saw her. She opened those lips, all slick and polish, and took his cock deeply into her mouth.

Then he could no longer fantasize but only feel.

Her mouth was hot and wet. She came down on him in long, hard strokes, taking him so deeply he could have been choking her except she wasn't gagging. She was making yummy sounds, as if his cock was the most delicious thing she'd ever eaten in her life.

Her hands were all over him too. She ran a hand over his chest, raking her nails lightly over his nipples. Sparks shot through his body. Her other hand trailed over his thighs and her fingers teased his balls. Tremors rolled along his skin and crashed into the sparks.

He tried to make it last, man he'd have given anything to make it last all night long, but he was being overwhelmed by sensations. A man could only take so much pleasure before he exploded.

He came with a roar in his ears and a powerful surge into Allie's mouth. He seemed to pulse into her for ages, but she kept those magnificent lips around his cock and drank him in. Finally, she ran her tongue along the tip of his cock, as if she was trying to catch every drop. Then she sat back with a sigh, like she was the one who'd just been satisfied.

She looked up at him, her eyes wide. "Good?"

He nodded. "Oh, yeah. But now it's my turn."

"Oh?" He could tell she tried to sound annoyed, but he recognized the amusement in her voice.

"Yeah, Simon says, lie down on the carpet."

"Okay."

She gracefully fell backwards, her dress floating and spreading out around her. Her hair looked wild and tangled. Her eyes were half-hooded, her smile soft. Roger came over to play, but Mac sent him over to the corner.

"Aren't you going to join me?" she asked.

Mac shook his head. He had a perfect view from his seat on the sofa for what he had in mind. "Take off your panties."

She slowly slid her hands down across her breasts and along her flat stomach, but stopped when the tips of her fingers touched the lacy top of her panties. "You didn't say—"

"Yeah, yeah," he growled. "Simon says, take off your panties."

She grinned and lifted her ass off the carpet. She slid the panties off her hips, then lifted her legs and eased the panties off. They fell in a tiny pile beside her foot.

"Simon says, open your legs."

Without a word, she bent her knees and spread her legs. Her pussy was there in full view for him to enjoy, to admire. It was pink and wet and shiny.

His mouth went dry. He had to swallow several times before he could talk. "Simon says, touch yourself."

"What?"

"Touch yourself, Allie. It will feel so good. Stroke yourself. Pet that pussy."

He could tell she wasn't sure she wanted to do this in front of him, but she slowly brought her hands down between her legs. "Yes, sweetheart. Let me see you make yourself feel good."

She started to stroke the slick folds of flesh between her legs. Hesitantly at first, but then she gradually got into it. His cock grew rigid again as he watched her fingers tangle with her slick lips, then brush over her swollen clit. He could see how her fingers slid through flesh made slippery by her own juices. Her body began to move as her strokes became more sure and strong. She started breathing hard, a soft sheen of perspiration covering her body.

"That's it, baby," he said, his voice rough. He was breathing as hard as she was. "Now fuck yourself. Simon says fuck yourself, Allie. How many fingers will fit into you? Two? Three? Four?"

Her eyes were closed now. She slipped two fingers inside herself, dragging them back and forth against her flesh. Then she pushed three fingers inside. She bent her knees and lifted her ass off the floor with each thrust of her fingers.

"Harder, Allie. Fuck yourself harder. See how good it feels to be fucked. Oh, yeah. That's the way."

Mac didn't know how much more of this he was going to be able to take. His body felt as if it was on fire, flames licking his cock from within. But it was so amazing to watch Allie like this, uninhibited and giving herself pleasure as she had just given him.

"Let me see you come now, Allie. You're so close. So damn close. You know how to do it. Rub that clit. It's so ready for you. Come for me, Allie."

She spread her legs wide, exposing the swollen clit. She circled it with a wet finger, while she began to knead one of her breasts with her other hand. Her fingers began to pull at her nipple as the fingers of her other hand rubbed her clit.

She screamed as she came. Her body bucked and her fingers continued to move, brushing her tender clit. Finally her body slowed its movements, and then she stopped and her hands dropped to her sides.

Mac joined her on the floor. He knelt between her legs. "Open your eyes, sweetheart," he said. He rubbed his cock, now shielded with a condom, along her soft, wet pussy. "Let me in."

Allie opened her eyes and smiled. He slid easily into her sweet flesh. She put her legs around him, pulling him deep inside her. "Hard, Mac," she gasped. "Fuck me hard."

He slammed into her, driving her down into the carpet. He grabbed her soft ass with his hands and held on for the ride. She met him stroke for stroke, adding her energy, stoking the fire.

He should have been able to last longer, after all, she'd milked him dry only a few minutes ago. But the friction built. The flames spread. The pressure grew until there was no way he could hold it in.

He put one hand between their bodies and touched her clit. It was like putting a match to dynamite. She came apart around him and when he felt her muscles clench around his cock he was a goner.

He hoped he didn't blow off the condom. He hoped he didn't blow off the top of his head. When the energy left his body in a rush, he collapsed on top of Allie.

"I'm sorry. I'm sorry," he mumbled into the breast his face was lucky enough to land on. "I can't move."

She laughed. The sound was like musical rain falling around him. "That's okay. Neither can I."

"That's because you have a two hundred pound man on top of you."

"True."

In another minute, Mac pushed up and looked down at the woman he was in love with. She looked thoroughly loved. Her lips were slightly swollen, her eyes soft and hazy. Her beautiful red hair was a tangled mess. He liked her this way.

"No slow comfortable screw for you, I see."

She shook her head. "Never did like them all that much."

He kissed her nose. "I'll be right back."

She hadn't moved by the time he got back from the bathroom. He stretched out beside her and took her into his arms. She placed her head on his shoulder and snuggled closer. "I can't believe this is really happening," she said softly, almost as if to herself.

"To think I didn't even know you a week ago," Mac said, kissing her hair.

"I feel as if I've known you forever," she said. She tickled his neck with warm kisses, but a sudden chill ran through him. "You're every bit as wonderful as I always knew you would be."

"Allie."

The deep growl in his voice surprised him as much as it did Allie. She looked up at him with a frown on his face. "What?"

He shrugged her off his shoulder and sat up. "Do not say you knew me from those stupid 'Simon Says' columns."

She sat up in front of him. "But I did. I do." Her expression was so sincere Mac knew she believed what she was saying. That made it all the worse.

"You know as well as I do," she went on, "that a person's words are their most personal way of communicating. Of expressing what's inside them. Your words spoke to me, Mac. Your words drew me to you. Your words made me fall in love with you."

Mac pushed her away and stood up. He walked away from her before he said something he'd regret. She sat there, naked, on the floor, looking up at him with that awe-struck look on her face and he wanted to throw something across the room.

She'd never loved him, never loved Mac MacKenzie. It was Simon MacKenzie she loved. He was stupid to have thought otherwise. Why had he even dared hope it could be different this time?

"You don't know what you're talking about," Mac said. She stood up and came toward him. He looked out the window into the darkness, seeing instead her reflection behind him. He suddenly realized they were both standing naked in front of the open window. He picked up her dress and thrust it into her hands. "Simon MacKenzie doesn't exist."

She put the dress on, but didn't button it. "What are you talking about? You're Simon MacKenzie. You wrote those words." She took a step back, doubt marring her expression for the first time. "You did didn't you? You did write those columns."

He pulled his trousers up and zipped them. "Yeah, I wrote them."

"Then I don't understand what you're saying," she said. She came up behind him and placed her hands on his shoulders. He watched her in the window pane. "You wrote words that spoke to millions of people. You wrote words that stirred them and made them think. You wrote with such integrity."

Mac spun around. "I told you before not to make me into something I'm not."

"But, Mac."

"Allie, listen to me. I'm not who you think I am. Simon MacKenzie was not who you thought he was."

"I still don't understand."

Mac saw his dreams for the future blowing away like the smoke he used to blow in people's eyes. But he had to tell her the truth. "Simon MacKenzie was a fake."

Chapter 7

Allie stared at Mac, trying to decipher his expression and understand his words. What could he possibly mean? He stared at his feet and didn't meet her eyes for several long moments. When he finally raised his head to look at her, she was startled to see the tormented look in his eyes.

"When I started writing those columns," he said, "I was young and idealistic, just like you."

There was a sarcastic slur to his voice. "Why do you make that sound like a bad thing?" she asked.

"No, it's not a bad thing," he replied, his voice turning tired and sad. "It's a wonderful place to be, but you can only go there once. And once you've left it, you can never go back."

She wanted to wrap her arms around him and make the hurt go away. Instead, she started to button her dress. "What happened to your idealism, Mac?"

He sank down onto the sofa and looked down at his clasped hands. Allie dropped to the floor at his feet. Roger lay down beside her.

"I majored in journalism in college and wrote in the college paper," he told her. "During my senior year, one of the parents happened to see an issue his son brought home. Marv Lewis was an editor for a small town newspaper. He liked what he read and offered me a monthly column, writing about whatever in the world I wanted to write about."

Mac looked down at her, the expression on his face telling her he still couldn't believe someone had done that.

"Well, obviously, he recognized talent when he saw it," she said.

He shrugged. "Whatever the reason, I was in heaven. I did that monthly column until I graduated, then I went to the paper to work fulltime. I learned more in a few months under Marv Lewis than I did in four years of college.

"The years went by so fast. Before I knew it, my column had been picked up and was being syndicated all over the country. Who could imagine that?"

Allie could picture a young Mac, blown away by the fact that people all over the country were reading his words. She leaned against the sofa and put her arms around his leg. She felt the tension there before he began to speak again.

"Then before I knew it, they wanted one every week. And then they wanted a daily. And I said yes. Hell, who wouldn't say yes? But a person only has so many opinions. Only so many things he feels really strongly about. But they were willing to pay me a lot of money to write and to get people talking about what I wrote." He stared at Allie. "It was all to sell more of their newspapers."

He stood up and looked down on her. "So I gave them what they wanted. You go on and on about my so-called integrity, but I was merely writing for entertainment, Allie, not for the good of humanity."

She stood up and faced him. "No, Mac."

He went on as if she'd never spoken. "You talk about my daring opinions, but more times than not, I wrote whatever I thought would make good copy. I would even play devil's advocate, taking whatever side I thought would get people more riled up." He grasped her shoulders. "And I had a ball doing it, Allie, don't think I didn't. I was having fun! I wasn't thinking of any moral responsibility. I wasn't thinking about what it meant to my readers. Hell, it was only a stupid column."

He let go of her shoulders and spread his hands wide. "It was all for entertainment, Allie. It was all for making money. What do you think of all that talk about integrity now?"

"Mac."

"That's not all. Because, you see, the joke was on me after all. I was doing it for fun, but my readers were taking it seriously." He paced around the living room. "Do you remember the column I wrote on the problems in the public school system and parental responsibility?"

Allie nodded.

"Well, my daring opinion for that day was that parents should take matters into their own hands and take whatever bold steps were necessary to have a voice in what the schools were teaching their children. And one of my readers, a man named Sidney Barlow who had a son in first grade and a daughter in third, went into an elementary school in a small town in Ohio with a revolver and demanded changes in the school curriculum. He took the principal and several teachers and students hostage."

"Oh, Mac." She didn't want to hear any more, but she couldn't stop herself from asking, "Did he shoot anyone?"

"Yeah. Yeah, he did. He made his demands, he scared those little kids half to death, and when he saw he was going to be arrested, he shot himself in the head in front of all the hostages."

"Oh, no!" Allie cried. "Oh, Mac, that's awful, but I don't see why—"

"I didn't even know it had happened at the time. The day after, I got a letter in the mail signed by a Sidney Barlow. He said he was fired up by my column, that he wasn't going to put up with the apathetic school system any longer, and he was gong to take a bold step, exactly like I told him to. He said he didn't know what the outcome would be, but he wanted me to know that he was doing it because of me."

Oh God. Her heart cried out for Mac. He'd obviously been blaming himself for it ever since. "Oh, Mac, it wasn't your fault."

He stared at her, devastation on his face.

"There's nothing wrong with advocating that parents take an active role in their children's education."

"That man went into a school with a gun because he thought I told him he should. He killed himself because of me. I realized then that what I was making up off the top of my head was actually affecting peoples' lives." He turned away and stared out the window.

She wished she knew how to reach him. He was silent for a moment before he turned back to face her again.

"I didn't want that responsibility. So I quit. I walked away. Ran away, if that's the way you want to see it. I bought a bar in Buffalo and left New York City far behind. I haven't written anything since that day. And I never will again."

"Oh, Mac."

"So now you know the true story of Simon MacKenzie. Not so noble, was he? Not someone to fall in love with just because of his stupid words." He picked up her shoes and shoved them into her hands. "So get the hell out of here and write that article that means so much to you. Looks like you got your interview after all." He looked her up and down, disgust evident on his face. "And it only took a couple quick fucks. You were right. You are damned persuasive."

Allie gasped.

He simply turned and walked out of the room.

Tears streamed down her face, but whether they were from anger, hurt, or embarrassment, she didn't know. How could she feel such empathy for him at the same time that she wanted to wring his stupid neck?

He strode back into the living room, his eyes dark, his expression grim. "I called a cab."

She swiped at her tears with the back of her hand. "You're going to believe whatever you want to," Allie said, "but I never even thought about the interview tonight. That's not why I asked you about your idealism. And that's not why I made love with you. And it was making love, no matter what you call it."

She slid her sandals back on her feet. "Loving you was the best thing that ever happened to me, and I will never regret it. But right now, I don't want to be in the same room with you." She patted Roger on the head and then turned away. "I'll wait outside for the cab."

Mac waited until Allie left in the cab, then turned off all the lights. He sat on the sofa in the dark, Roger warming his feet. He rested his head in his hands. How could the most wonderful day turn into the most horrible day in only a few minutes? He'd never been on such an emotional roller coaster ride before in his life. Robyn had never made him feel like this.

That was probably because he had never felt for Robyn a fraction of what he felt for Allie. He'd thought Robyn would be supportive of him after what Barlow did. After all, she'd said she loved him. But Robyn hadn't wanted anything to do with his life after he quit writing.

Robyn left him for a best-selling novelist who would keep her in the lifestyle Mac no longer wanted. He thought he had been devastated then. But that had been nothing compared to the betrayal he felt when he realized that Allie was still hung up on the man she thought he was.

He laughed bitterly. Here he was, jealous of himself.

He stood up and made his way to the bedroom, but he only tossed and turned once he was in bed. She should have been here with him. He should have been tangled with her long legs, not with the twisted sheets.

She'd come to town singing his praises. He felt as if he'd let her down all those years ago. But what kind of relationship would they have had if he'd kept it all hidden? She'd still be thinking he was something he wasn't. And he'd be forever worried that someday she'd find out and hate him for lying to her.

Better that she hate him for telling her the truth.

Allie couldn't sleep. She tossed and turned on the hard motel mattress and played Mac's words over and over again in her mind. She knew he thought she would be appalled by his confession that he'd written sensational copy to sell newspapers, but she wasn't. When she heard him tell his story, she understood exactly what he had been going through. He'd been doing his job, the one he'd been paid to do.

She sat up in bed and switched on the lamp. She was tired of this motel room. Tired of the peach walls, the orange bedspread and the ugly paintings of flowers on the walls. It was obviously time to go home. She had no reason to stay any longer. She'd accomplished what she'd come here to do. But what good had it done her?

She'd gotten her elusive interview with Simon MacKenzie. She found out his deep, dark secret and now knew why he stopped writing. She should have been thrilled, but she was anything but happy.

Now that she had all the information she needed, she might as well finish the article right now. She couldn't sleep anyway. She turned on her laptop and called up the file called Simon MacKenzie, the one she'd started with such high hopes only a few days ago.

It didn't take her long to flesh out the article. She added the details Mac had given her, the ones that explained so much. When she got to the part where Mac felt so responsible for a reader's violent actions that he turned his back on his life as he knew it, Allie wiped away the tears. But as she wrote, she discovered a truth that Mac never admitted to. Maybe he didn't even realize it himself.

If he hadn't cared about what he wrote in his columns, if he hadn't been concerned about his readership, he wouldn't have stopped writing simply because one reader had interpreted Mac's words in his own way. If Mac hadn't cared what impact his words had on his readers, he would have continued writing whatever he thought would stir up the public and sell more newspapers.

Instead, he felt so personally responsible for his words, that rather than have them misinterpreted again, rather than have anyone else possibly be hurt by them, he stopped writing altogether. Stopped doing the one thing that made his heart beat, the one thing he lived for.

Allie was certain the words in the columns he wrote held more of Simon MacKenzie than he would ever admit. And she was just as certain that the sacrifice he had made was probably the hardest decision he'd ever had to make.

And she loved him all the more for it.

Her heart swelled with love for this man. For Mac. Not with the love she thought she felt for the man whose words had touched her heart. It was real love for the real man who had touched not only her heart, but her body and soul as well. Love so much stronger than she had ever imagined before today.

When she finished the article, Allie knew she'd accomplished one more of the goals she'd set for herself. She knew it was good. Hell, it was great. She knew all she had to do now was e-mail it to Marcia.

She knew she never would.

For the first time since her initial visit to the Jolly Roger, Allie had butterflies tickling her stomach when she walked inside. All the people she'd come to know and enjoy called out a greeting. Denise gave her a hug. Wally waved to her. Seth, sitting by himself at the other end of the bar, nodded at her. But her knees still shook as she walked over to the bar.

Mac was filling a drink order, but she knew the minute he glanced her way. Their eyes met, but his expression was blank. Then he quickly turned his attention back to the drinks. Her stomach clenched and she realized she hadn't smiled either.

Allie climbed up on the stool next to Wally and wished she knew what to say to Mac.

"Allie, I want you to meet someone," Wally said. For the first time, Allie noticed an attractive woman sitting on the other side of Wally. "This is my friend, Brenda. Brenda, this is Allie."

"Nice to meet you," Allie said. "Wally's a great guy."

Brenda smiled and took Wally's hand. "He sure is."

Allie made herself smile back. Would she ever hold Mac's hand again? Would she ever again feel as happy as Brenda looked?

"How's the mystery coming?"

Mac. Somehow he'd come closer when she wasn't watching. Her heart beat a little faster.

"It's coming along great." She looked up at him. He looked so sexy, even with that blank expression on his face. And while he wasn't smiling, at least he wasn't frowning. "I couldn't sleep last night so I got another couple chapters done."

"You couldn't sleep?"

She shook her head. "Too much on my mind."

"Yeah." He cleared his throat. "What can I get you?"

"Um, do you know how to make a Slippery Nipple?"

He just stared at her.

Wally started laughing. "Where do you find these drinks?"

"I look them up on the internet," she admitted. She held Mac's gaze. "Come on, Mac. A Slippery Nipple. I know you know how to make one."

"Are you sure you want one? Irish Crème and Peppermint Schnapps?"

"Um, yeah. That'll do for now," she said with a wink

He turned away to fill her order. She was certain he'd almost smiled. When he brought the glass to her, she caught his hand in hers. "We need to talk."

"I'm working."

"I know. I won't stop you from working. I think we need to clear up a few points."

"Such as?"

"Mac, I need a draft and a screwdriver," Denise said. She stood beside Allie while she waited. "How's everything?" The expression on her face said she was dying to know what happened last night.

"Fine," Allie said. She was aching to continue her conversation with Mac. If only they were somewhere more private. "How's that cute husband of yours?"

"Sexy as ever."

Mac finished the order in record time. He handed Denise the drinks and she left to deliver them, but not without a meaningful look over her shoulder.

"What points?" he asked Allie.

"Well, number one, no matter what you might think, I don't hate you for what you told me last night."

He was silent for a moment, his face still that expressionless mask. She wished she knew what was going on in that handsome, stubborn head of his.

She caught his hands in hers, ever conscious of Wally and Brenda sitting beside her. "You've made me love you even more."

He rolled his eyes. "Allie."

"I love you," she said, hoping he would get the meaning. "You."

"Hey, Mac," Seth called out. "I want something stronger. Scotch on the rocks."

Mac slipped out of her fingers. He frowned slightly, but poured the drink and delivered it to Seth.

"You think Seth's okay?" Wally asked when Mac came back.

Mac shook his head. "I don't know. He says there's nothing wrong."

"I'll go talk to him," Wally said. He told Brenda he'd be right back and walked down to Seth and sat down beside him.

"What's the matter with Seth?" Brenda asked.

"He's lonely," Mac told her. "He drinks more every night."

Wally was back in a matter of minutes. "He doesn't want to talk to me. Couldn't get him to tell me anything."

"You tried," Brenda said, patting his arm.

"Want another drink?" Wally asked her.

She shook her head. "No, I'm fine, but I'm really glad you brought me here tonight." She looked at Mac and Allie. "It was very nice meeting you all. I'm sure we'll be stopping by again."

"Ready for dinner and a movie?" Wally asked. She nodded and in another moment they were gone.

"I'm so glad Wally found someone," Allie said. "He looks really happy."

Mac nodded. He glanced down the bar to Seth. "And Seth is looking worse."

Allie caught his hand before he could wander off. At least he didn't pull out of her grasp. She lowered her voice and said, "I want you to know that I'm not doing the article for *Writer's World*."

His expression told her he wasn't sure if he believed her. "Why not?" he asked, his voice still cool. "That's what you came here for, wasn't it?"

He still didn't understand. "Yes." She squeezed his hand and he looked her in the eye. "But I happen to care more about you now than I do a stupid article."

Mac looked at Allie for a moment without saying a word. Then he glanced around as if to make sure no one was close enough to hear him. He leaned down to speak softly in her ear. "I didn't mean what I said about you having sex with me to get the story."

"I know."

"Having sex with you was wonderful." Finally, his voice was warm again.

She stroked her thumb over his hand. "I thought so too."

Denise came over and sat beside her. Mac stepped away. "Whew, my feet hurt tonight. That's what I get for breaking in a new pair of shoes without bringing the old pair for backup."

Allie yawned and rubbed her face with her hands. "Want me to get the next couple tables?"

Denise shook her head. "Thanks, but that's my job. And besides, you look tired."

"I didn't sleep well last night."

"Was that a good thing or a bad thing?" Denise asked with raised eyebrows.

"I'm not sure," Allie replied. She shot a glance at Mac. He was wiping down the far end of the bar. Where did they stand now? They'd apparently called a truce, but where did they go from here?

She couldn't help but remember what they'd done here last night. She swept her hands over the surface of the bar.

"Gee, Mac," she said, rubbing her fingers over the shiny wood in front of her. Wasn't this just about where her ass was lying last night? "I never noticed before how smooth and hard this bar is. Have you ever noticed how smooth and hard this bar is?"

She thought he was going to swallow his tongue. "I work at this bar every night," he said carefully. She swore she saw a smile trying to break through. "I've noticed."

"Oh, right," she said and slid him a small grin. She picked up her drink glass and licked the condensation off the edge. His eyes widened. He breathed a little harder. She still got to him. She still had a chance.

Mac looked at her, and the heat from his gaze must have raised her body temperature at least ten degrees. She fanned her face with a napkin and lifted her heavy hair off her neck. She held his gaze and recognized an urgent desire that met her own. She dropped her hair and let it fall back over her shoulders.

"Isn't it warm in here?" Allie asked Denise, but the soft and slow words were for Mac alone. "I swear I'm practically melting tonight."

Mac strode over to her. He leaned toward her, his strong hands spread over the surface of the bar. His gaze, hot with desire, swept over her body. She felt as if she was being drawn toward a flame. A hot flame, running over her face, along her neck, across her breasts that were already tingling with awareness, and down between her legs where she throbbed with arousal.

"Need some cooling off?" he whispered.

"Oh, yeah."

Mac straightened up. "Hey, Allie," he said in a low, smooth voice. "Would you want to give Denise's feet a break and run to the storage room and grab some more napkins? We're almost out."

"We are?" Denise asked with a frown. "I thought I set out plenty."

Mac stared at her. "We're almost out." He said the words slowly, then looked back to Allie. The heat from his gaze nearly melted the clothes off her body. She definitely needed cooling off. "Do you know where the storage room is?"

She tried not to let out the grin that was threatening to spread across her face. "Um, I'm not sure. Just down the hall, right? Somewhere down there?"

He glanced quickly to Denise. "I'd better show her where." He looked at Allie again and then grinned himself. "Come on."

She hopped off the stool and spurred by Mac's sense of urgency, dashed toward the hallway. When he reached the end of the bar, Mac grabbed her hand and pulled her along.

"Aw, Mac, just don't take too long, okay?" Denise called. "I don't mix drinks!"

Chapter 8

Mac heard Allie's laughter as he led her to the small storage room at the end of the hall. It rained over him as they ducked inside. The laughter bubbled up inside him as well.

What the hell had gotten into him? All he knew was he couldn't survive another minute without touching Allie. He was as hard as a horny teenager. Hell, he'd never even felt this much urgency back then. His hands were already underneath her T-shirt by the time they closed the door behind them.

Pitch dark. He fumbled for the light switch, then squinted in the harsh glare of the overhead light. He wanted to see her when he buried himself deep in her eager body. He wanted to see her eyes glazed with passion. He wanted her. Plain and simple.

He pushed her T-shirt up, his hands searching for her breasts, his lips already seared by hers. He found her firm breasts, this time captured in a lacy bra. The front clasp helped him release them easily from their bondage. He squeezed the firm flesh, kneading them with his hands. The nipples pebbled and he rolled them with his eager fingers.

She moaned into his mouth, arching her back to give him even better access to her beautiful breasts. Her tongue delved into his mouth, tangling with his tongue, sweeping, possessing. Her hands flew all over his body, grasping his hair, scratching his back, cupping his ass and drawing him closer to her.

She pressed her hips into his. The momentum pushed him back and he stumbled over something lying on the floor.

"Careful," she whispered.

"Damn peanuts."

She laughed again and grabbed his shoulders, keeping him from landing in a pile on the floor and taking her with him. He kicked the big box of peanuts out of the way. He needed a bigger storage room.

Allie rubbed her pussy against his heavy arousal. A wave of painful pleasure swept through him. The musky scent of sex drifted around him, sending him straight into overdrive. Without even giving it a conscious thought, his hands dropped to her shorts, unbuttoned them, and lowered the zipper. Their breathless panting sounded as raspy as the zipper in the close quarters of the tiny storage room. He slid his hand inside her shorts. She was already wet, her panties soaked.

She drew his lower lip into his mouth as he urgently pushed her shorts and panties over her hips. They slid silently to the floor. She sucked on the lip as she worked on his zipper. With her hands on his cock and his lip between her teeth, he was at her mercy. His body pulsed with need. All his blood had rushed from his brain to his cock, but somehow he did manage to remember to grab a condom out of the pocket before she pushed his pants and briefs down to his ankles.

He moaned when Allie took the condom packet out of his hands. She tore the packet open and let the plastic fly. As she began to gradually slide the condom over him, he gasped and closed his eyes. Her mischievous chuckle washed over him. She drew the condom so damn slowly over his throbbing cock, stroking the length of him over and over again, driving him quickly near the edge.

"Now," he whispered, his voice strained.

"Okay." The amusement in her voice might have irritated him if she wasn't breathing so hard he was afraid she might hyperventilate at any moment.

He slid into her as if he was made for her. His thrusts pushed her against the wall with a loud thud. He hoped the sound didn't carry out into the bar-room. She grabbed his shoulders and pushed back, meeting him thrust for thrust. The sweetest little noises came from the back of her throat, letting him know she was close to climaxing. He clenched his jaw as he tried to hold on, tried to bring her to her release before he lost it completely.

He swept a hand down over her breasts, across her stomach and down into the wet curls between her legs. He found her clit and brushed over it with one relentless finger. She laughed out loud when she came and her spasms tightened around him, squeezing his cock and sending him over the edge. Together they rode wave after wave, joining in the laughter and the ecstasy.

"Wow," she said, brushing his hair off his forehead. "I have a new appreciation for the quickie."

He laughed again. He'd never laughed so much as since he'd met Allie. He felt free. Free from the burden of secrecy he'd been shouldering for way too long. He had been right to trust her. She was what he needed in his life. Whether she stayed or left, she was worth the risk.

They straightened each other's clothes and hair before they opened the door. Mac knew he'd get a razzing when they came back out, but he wouldn't have missed it for all the kidding in the world. He started to lead the way, when Allie tapped him on the shoulder.

He turned and she placed a package in his hands.

"Napkins."

"Allie, go home."

She looked up at Mac through half-closed eyes and yawned again. "I'm too tired to drive to Pittsburgh tonight."

"Not Pittsburgh." Just the thought made his stomach turn over. "But I know you're tired. You're going to fall off that barstool in a minute."

She shook her head. "I'm okay. I thought I was getting used to these crazy hours. I don't know how you guys do it."

Those bedroom eyes were driving him crazy. He wished he could take her home right now. He fished into his pocket. "Here's my house key. Go crash there 'til I get out of here. Roger would love the company."

He could tell she was about to make an excuse, but then she yawned again. "Well, okay," she said, her voice soft and sleepy. She slid off the stool. "Just so Roger won't be lonely."

"Drive carefully," he said and watched her walk away. He could hardly bear to see her go and he knew she was simply going over to his place. How could he stand it when she left for Pittsburgh?

"She's going soon," Denise said, taking the stool Allie had so recently been sitting on. "You know that, don't you?"

He stared at the door. "Yeah."

"Unless, of course, she has a reason to stay."

He looked at Denise. He frowned at the gleam in her eye. "If you have something to say, say it."

"Oh, come on, Mac. Ask her to stay."

"Man, are you whipped!"

Mac and Denise turned to look at Seth, who had shouted his comment for the whole bar to hear. "You say something, Seth?" Mac asked.

"Look at you, moping over some piece of ass walking out of your bar. It's pathetic. The Mac I always knew was tough. What happened to you?"

Mac poured a cup of coffee and set it in front of Seth. "I think you've had enough to drink tonight."

"Yeah, well, the Mac I always knew didn't spout his opinions all over the place either. He was quiet and listened, like a bartender's supposed to do. Kept his mouth shut. Didn't tell Wally it was okay to start dating again. Didn't tell his customers they'd had enough to drink. What happened to you?"

Mac glanced around. The crowd was thinning out. Denise was starting to pick up. She threw a worried glance his way.

He poured himself a cup of coffee and sat on the stool next to Seth. "I guess I realized that when friends care about each other, they can't keep their opinions to themselves. I wouldn't be a friend if I didn't say I was worried about you."

Seth pushed the coffee away, spilling it over onto the bar. "You're not a friend, you're just a bartender. I don't have any friends."

"Of course, you do. I am your friend, Seth. Wally's your friend, he's worried about you too."

"Wally? Nah, he's got a woman now, he doesn't have any time for me. And you have Allie. Nobody has time for fat old Seth."

Mac sighed. He was no psychologist. He wasn't trained to give expert opinions to someone who was depressed. Maybe Seth was right. Maybe he should just stand behind the bar and keep his mouth shut like he used to.

But he could see Seth was lonely. And hurting. And he didn't have a clue what to do about it.

But he had to give it a try.

Allie used the key Mac gave her to let herself into his house. Roger greeted her with his usual smile and wag of the tail. She'd stopped at her hotel room and grabbed her laptop. She set it down on the sofa, then sat on the floor and put her arms around the dog.

Roger kissed her face, waking her up a little bit. She pulled the laptop off the sofa and opened it up on the floor in front of her. She pulled up the file for her mystery. Chapter five. How could she be on chapter five already? The words were flowing out of her. It was amazing.

She crossed her legs and leaned over the keyboard. Soon she was searching the dark streets of Pittsburgh with her intrepid heroine, looking for a ruthless killer, her tiredness forgotten.

She'd just begun chapter six when the telephone rang.

By reflex, she answered before she remembered it was Mac's phone. But it was him on the other end.

"Did I wake you?"

"No. I'm writing," she told him. "Pretty soon my sleuth is going to be in real danger from the killer." She laughed. "I can't wait."

"Great. I wanted to let you know I'm going to be a little late." She could hear the regret in his voice. "Seth and I have been talking. He just left and I still need to clean up."

"Is he okay?"

"I hope so. He's lonely and depressed. Jealous of Wally and me."

"Jealous? Why?"

"Because we have beautiful women and he has no one."

So did that mean Mac thought of her as his beautiful woman? A little shiver of delight ran through her. "What did you tell him?"

"That he had to go out and get involved in life again. That he couldn't hide away and expect love to come and find him."

Mac was talking about love? "That sounds like exactly the right thing to say."

"I miss you."

The soft whisper sent warm shivers along her skin. "I wish you were here right now so I could touch you," she said. Her breath came out on a ragged sigh. "I like touching you."

"You do?" She heard the clinking of glasses in the background. Mac was washing up.

"I love touching you."

"Where would you touch me?" His voice was deep and full of heat.

"I'd start with your face," she said, smiling as she pictured him. "I love your face."

"It's not a smooth, pretty boy face."

"That's why I like it so much," she said. "It has character. It's interesting. It has texture beneath my fingers."

Mac made a sound deep in his throat. "I can almost feel you touching me."

"I'd start with your forehead," she said, keeping her voice smooth and low. She dropped her head back against the sofa and closed her eyes, seeing him in her mind. "I'd stroke your brow and follow those sexy little lines by your eyes with my fingertips. Then I'd trace your lips with my fingers and you'd wet them with your tongue."

"Damn right, I would," Mac replied, his voice uneven. "I'd take one of them deep into my mouth and suck on it."

Allie curled her fingers into the carpet. "Then I'd unbutton that white shirt you have on and push it off your shoulders so I can feel your skin. So I can feel your muscles. You have great muscles."

"Allie," Mac said with a sigh.

"I'd massage your shoulders with my fingers, because you've been working hard and you're tense."

"I'm not tense."

"Okay, I'll skip the massage."

"Well, maybe a little tense."

She laughed, a soft chuckle into the phone. "Then I'd trail my fingers lightly down your chest. I love the soft dark hair sprinkled over your pecs.

I'd brush my hand over the hair on your chest and then I'd stop and play with your hard nipples for a minute."

There was nothing but hard breathing coming over the phone line.

"Then I'd slide my hands all the way down to the waistband of those tight black pants."

"My pants aren't tight."

"Oh, sure they are, and in all the right places, too."

"Well, I have to admit they do feel a little snug at the moment." She could hear the touch of amusement in his voice and she smiled in response.

"I'd slide down your zipper so they wouldn't be so tight, and then I'd take your hard cock in my hands."

"Oh, God, Allie, I can feel your hands on it right now."

"Then I'd sink down onto my knees in front of you, and I'd take that thick, hard cock into my mouth. I'd lick it 'til it's all shiny and wet. I like it that way."

"You do?" His voice sounded a little strangled.

"Oh, yeah. Then I'd suck it, Mac. Suck it hard and deep until you come in my mouth and I suck you dry."

He groaned. "You better stop or I'm going to come right now."

She chuckled and licked her lips from the image she'd painted. Now it was his turn. "So where will you touch me?"

"First I'd plunge my hands into your fiery hair," he said. "Your hair is so soft, it tickles my arms." He took a deep breath. She could almost feel the warmth through the phone. "Then I'd cup your face in my hands and kiss you until you couldn't think straight."

She already couldn't think straight. She closed the laptop and set it on the end table. No more writing tonight. She kicked off her sandals and closed her eyes again. "Then what would you do?"

"I'd—" Mac's voice cut off and then he cursed. "Sorry, tripped over the broom. You know, I think I may need that massage when I get home. I've got a crick in my neck from this cordless phone."

"Poor thing," she said. She knew she should hang up and let him finish the cleaning so he could get here sooner, but she couldn't stop herself from asking, "What would you do to me next, Mac?"

"I'd kiss your soft neck, right there where the pulse beats," he said. "Then I'd tear that shirt off you so I could get to your breasts. Did you know you have the most beautiful breasts I've ever seen?"

Allie couldn't say anything. She could only breathe hard and fast into the phone.

"I'd catch them in my hands and love them with my fingers. I'll roll your nipples around until they're hard and red and you're gasping beneath me. Then I'd love them with my mouth, sucking on them until you're wriggling beneath me. I could spend hours loving your breasts, Allie. Hours with your body under mine."

Allie tried to laugh lightly, but it came out sounding breathy and shaky. She could almost feel him touching her aching breasts. "You know, I'm getting quite warm. I think I may have to take my shirt off myself."

Mac cleared his throat. "Right now?"

"Oh, yeah. Hold on a sec." She put the receiver down on the sofa and pulled her T-shirt over her head. "That feels much better. I was getting so hot."

"Oh, God, Allie, I'm burning up."

"The bra needs to go too. It's too tight." Her fingers scrambled over the clasp and flicked it open. The air cooled her heated skin as the bra slipped off her arms and down to the floor. She tucked the phone back under her chin and squeezed her swollen breasts with her hands. "I'm touching my breasts and pretending it's you."

Mac groaned. "I need to touch you. After I finish with your breasts, I'll put my hand between your legs and feel your pussy. Is it wet, Allie?"

She unzipped her shorts and slid her fingers inside. "Oh, Mac, it's so wet. You've made it all wet and slippery."

"I want to plunge my fingers inside you, all hot and wet and coated with your juices. I want to play with your clit until you cry out my name."

Her fingers dipped in and out of her body, building on the frenzy their words had started. "Oh, yes, Mac."

"I want to feel my cock inside you. I want to see you ride it like a wild stallion. I want to feel you squeeze it when you come."

Her heart was pounding so hard she could barely hear him. Her entire body throbbed with need. She teased the swollen nub with her fingers and that was all it took. Waves of sensation swept over her, lifting her up and over, sending her soaring and swirling and screaming his name.

After a moment, Mac said, "Sounds like you got there ahead of me."

"Mmm." She settled back down the earth, warm and satisfied. "How much longer will you be?"

"Not long, I swear."

She slowly slid her hand out of her shorts. "Just remember, I'm waiting for you in nothing but a pair of unzipped shorts. Roger is getting quite an eyeful."

"Lucky dog."

He was going to ask her to stay. Beg her, if that's what it took. He'd driven this same route countless times, but this was the first time he drove home with a sense of anticipation. The first time he looked forward to going home.

How was it he had never realized he was lonely? It could easily have been him instead of Seth who needed the advice he so easily dished out tonight.

Get a life. Don't sit home by yourself. Go out and do something.

How had he convinced himself all these years that he liked being alone? Someone who believed in fate might say he had been just biding his time until he met Allie. They might have been right.

Raindrops began to spatter the windshield. It would be good to get inside and snuggle with Allie. The light was burning in the living room window. Roger looked out as Mac pulled his Jeep into the driveway. Tonight the house looked like more than just the place he slept and ate in. It looked like a home.

There was no call of welcome when he stepped inside, however. The whirlwind who had turned his life upside down didn't look like a troublemaker at the moment. She didn't even look like the sexy temptress he had talked to over the telephone.

She was the picture of youth and innocence as she slept on the sofa. She was lying on her stomach, her hair covering half her face and spreading over her shoulders like a veil, almost concealing the fact that she was naked above the waist.

Should he wake her? While his fingers itched to touch those bare arms, those shoulders, those breasts, he knew she needed her sleep. She wasn't used to the kind of hours he kept.

But, man, he wanted to touch her.

He was walking over to the sofa when he saw her laptop sitting on the end table. She was so excited about her mystery novel. But they hadn't had a chance to talk about it much. He gingerly picked up the computer and sat down in the armchair. It wouldn't hurt to take a peek.

He didn't own a computer anymore. He'd gotten rid of it the same time he'd turned his back on television, radio, newspapers and New York City. He may have been out of practice, but he didn't have any problem finding the word processing program on the desktop. Without a mouse, it took him a moment to find the correct button, but once he did he clicked on the icon. It quickly brought him up to a blank page. The list of recent documents showed up at the side. The top one said Mystery. He was about to click on that when he read the next one down.

Simon MacKenzie.

Frowning, Mac clicked on his name. The file came up and he started to read.

He is still a man of strong convictions, even if he doesn't put them into print any longer. Surrounded by loyal friends, he lives by night, dispensing drinks and lending an ear.

Mac scrolled through the entire article Allie had told him she wasn't going to write. It was well-written. It was a fair portrayal of his life.

It was what she sat on the barstool, looked him straight in the eye, and swore she wasn't going to do.

Bitterness churned in his stomach like acid. Hadn't his time with Robyn taught him anything? He glanced over at the sleeping woman beside him, but he couldn't bear to look at her for long. She'd used him just like Robyn had.

Why was he surprised? Allie told him at the very beginning that she'd get the interview. That she'd be very persuasive.

Rain pelted the house now. The sharp barrage rattled the window and the racket added to the pounding in his head.

Didn't he know life was always waiting to kick you in the teeth? This was why he lived alone and liked it that way.

The loud ring of the telephone startled him, but he didn't move. He couldn't drag his eyes away from the words on the screen in front of him. The proof that Allie didn't deserve his trust. The phone continued to ring and finally Allie stirred beside him. She reached for the phone, her eyes still half-closed. She'd already picked up the receiver when she saw Mac sitting there staring at her, the open laptop on his knees.

"I see you wrote the article after all," he said flatly.

"Mac, I—" She was interrupted by whoever was on the phone. "Denise? Wait a minute, you're talking too fast. What did you say? Yes, Mac is here." She looked up at Mac and he saw the color drain from her face. "Oh, my God, where are you? We'll be right there."

She hung up the phone and grabbed the T-shirt that had fallen to the floor. "Chuck was shot tonight. Denise doesn't know yet if he's alive or dead."

Chapter 9

Mac slammed shut the laptop cover, dropped it on the sofa, and lunged to his feet. "Where is he?"

"She said they took him to ECMC," Allie said as she pulled the T-shirt over her head and zipped up her shorts. "Do you know where that is?"

"Yeah." He headed for the door, keys in hand. "You better go back to your hotel now."

Meaning he didn't want to see her. Allie tried not to let him see how much that hurt her. "I'm going with you."

Mac stopped and glared at her.

She glared back. "I haven't known them as long as you, but they're my friends too."

She could tell from his expression that he didn't want to waste time arguing about this. His sigh was deep and loud. "Come on then."

He threw open the door without looking back to see if she followed him. She was nearly drenched by the time she got to the Jeep. She jumped in as he started it up.

Neither of them spoke for several minutes. The rain battered the Jeep. The windshield wipers ran at full speed, streaking the rain that battered the window.

Allie stole a glance at Mac. His expression was grim, his jaw clenched, his fingers white-knuckled on the steering wheel. He stared straight ahead. Tension radiated from him, and the waves crashed over her. Was it only his concern for Chuck and the horrible driving conditions, or was his anger at her adding to his stress?

"Mac, I can explain."

"Save it."

"But I didn't submit the article!"

"The last thing I want right now is to hear more of your lies." He took a corner so tightly, the tires squealed on the wet pavement.

She leaned forward to look into his face. "I have never lied to you."

"Shut up and let me drive."

She shivered, both from wet and from worry. Chuck could be dying. Denise was in anguish. It was selfish to be worried about losing Mac at a time like this.

But she couldn't help it. Once glance at his stony expression and Allie was afraid that she'd never be able to repair the damage caused when Mac saw that finished article.

�֍ﬞ)(ʗ֍)(ﬞ֍

Mac had always hated the smell of hospitals, the sharp scent of disinfectant and the sour odor of disease. He'd never associated a hospital with healing, only with death and dying. He hoped like hell it would change his opinion tonight.

He strode down the corridor of the Erie County Medical Center, hoping with every second he wasn't too late. Allie matched him stride for stride. They found Denise and her sister, Lisa, pacing in a waiting room. Their parents sat on a bench beside a blank television clutching each other's hands.

Denise fell into his arms. Her whole body shook. Mac sank down into a chair and helped Denise down to the seat beside him. Out of the corner of his eye, he saw Allie talking quietly with Lisa.

"Mac, I'm so scared," Denise whispered. "What if I never see him again? What if I never get the chance to tell him again that I love him?"

"Hush. You will," he said, gently rubbing her back. "What did they tell you?"

"He's in surgery. They won't know how much internal damage was done until they get in there." Her voice broke.

Allie came over and knelt down in front of Denise. She took Denise's hands.

"Chuck is a strong man," Allie said. "And Lisa tells me this hospital is the best place for him to be. Chuck has you and your love to live for. He has all these people praying for him. We just have to stay positive."

"It's so hard," Denise said with a sob. "All I can think of is all the things that could go wrong. He got shot by a guy he pulled over for speeding; how wrong is that?"

"But at that time of night, he was lucky someone saw what happened and got help right away."

Denise nodded.

It hurt Mac to look at Allie, her riot of red hair and those beautiful blue eyes. That erotic mouth that spoke lies. He wanted to yell at her and tell her to get the hell out of there.

But one look at Denise and he knew he couldn't do that. Right now it was about Denise and Chuck. His anger at Allie's betrayal would have to wait until later.

Allie glanced up at him, her expression tentative, a little hopeful. She looked away quickly when he stared back at her.

Denise caught the exchange and he was immediately sorry he hadn't kept his thoughts to himself, at least for the time being. Denise didn't need to have them to worry about on top of everything else.

Allie stood up and walked to the other side of the room. She stared out the window, her stance rigid. Tonight would have been so different if he hadn't opened that laptop. He would have been holding Allie and comforting her, as much as he would have been comforting Denise. He would have insisted Allie be part of the group. He would have thought she belonged here.

How could he have been so wrong about Allie? She'd blown into his life without warning and swept him away with her words. She'd twisted her way through his suspicions and made him trust her. He'd fallen for her pretty face, her firm body, her persuasive words.

It was like Robyn all over again. He should have known better.

He felt a hand on his shoulder. It was Denise.

"Mac, what's wrong?" There were dark circles under her eyes and he regretted adding to her stress tonight.

He took her hand and squeezed it. "I'm worried about Chuck."

She shook her head and frowned at him. "What's wrong between you and Allie?"

He lowered his voice to a whisper. "Don't worry about it."

Denise dropped her voice too. "Mac, did you do something stupid?"

Wasn't that just like a woman? "Me? Why do you think this is my fault?"

"Because I know Allie loves you."

"No, she doesn't," he said, forcing himself to keep his voice low. "She used me. She used all of us."

"What are you talking about?"

He was rescued by the arrival of Chuck's parents who'd had to drive in from Rochester. Denise left him to go over to them and he had to force himself not to turn and look for Allie.

He had to forget about ever again sinking into her warm embrace or burying himself in her hot body. He had to stop thinking about the way she kissed him senseless and made him laugh. The way she blew away the lonely cobwebs he'd been caught up in.

He looked for her anyway. He was still staring at her when she slowly turned around and looked at him. Her expression was grim, but she made no attempt to brush away the tears that ran down her cheeks. His gut reaction, the one he'd always trusted in the past, urged him to go to her, to comfort her, to support her.

But she didn't deserve his support.

And right now he couldn't even comfort himself.

At some point, Allie fell asleep in one of the hard and uncomfortable chairs. When she woke up, her back and neck ached and her eyes burned. Her clothing still felt damp and clung to her skin. Looking around the room, she saw Denise and Lisa sitting nearby with their parents. Mac was across the room with Chuck's parents. A few other people she didn't know had gathered as well.

Denise must have seen her straighten up, because she rose and walked over to her.

"No word yet?" Allie asked.

Denise shook her head.

Allie stood up gingerly and stretched. Her back screamed. She glanced across the room at Mac and her heart echoed the sentiment.

"What happened between you and Mac?" Denise asked.

Allie shrugged her shoulders. "Mac thinks I lied to him."

"But what happened?" Denise repeated.

"It really doesn't matter," Allie said with a sigh. "If he doesn't trust me, then nothing else matters."

"Go talk to him."

Allie shook her head. "He won't believe anything I tell him now." Her eyes felt tired and gritty, and she fought back new tears that threatened to spill. She'd cried all the tears she was going to cry over Simon MacKenzie.

Denise took her hands and they sat back down.

"I never should have come here," Allie said. "I was too damn sure of myself. I thought I could find Simon MacKenzie, talk him into an interview and make him fall in love with me. How pathetic is that?"

"But he did fall in love with you," Denise said. "I know he did."

"No, he just lusted after a young chick who fawned all over him."

"No, Allie."

"Hey, I'm the one who's supposed to be comforting you," Allie said. She tried to think of something to say, but her fuzzy brain went blank. "See, I guess I'm clean out of positive thoughts. What good are they anyway? I can think them all I want, but it's not going to help Chuck, is it?"

"Allie."

"No, Mac was right that first night. No matter what I set my mind to, the only one I can affect is myself."

Denise was about to say something, but at that moment, a tall, tired-looking man in scrubs walked into the room. She touched Allie's hand as if for luck and rushed over to him. They talked softly and then Denise turned, her face glowing through her tears.

"He's going to make it!"

Relief washed over Allie. She hadn't realized how truly frightened she had been. She hung back from the family celebration, not feeling she really belonged in that big group hug. She saw from the corner of her eye that Mac was hanging back too.

She ached to think that she'd never feel his arms around her again. That he didn't love her enough to trust her.

Mac started toward her, but then stopped. The hint of a beard threw shadows across his face. After the brief hesitation, he came all the way over to her. "Are you all right?" he asked, the tone of his voice formal, as if he were talking to a stranger he'd just met instead of someone he'd loved atop a bar.

No, she was dying inside. "I'm fine," she said, her voice a little shakier than she would have liked. "I'm so relieved Chuck's going to be okay."

Mac nodded. His expression was guarded, not at all relieved or happy.

But then, hers probably wasn't either.

They stood side by side, but they might as well have been miles apart. They silently watched Denise and her family laugh and cry and hug each other. Mac was so close she had to resist the desire to lean into him.

But she never would do that again.

Now that she knew Chuck was going to be okay, she had to get out of there. She yawned, big and loud. "Boy, I could really use some coffee."

"I'll get some," Mac said quickly, as if he were jumping at the chance to get away from her too.

"Thanks." She ran her hands over her tangled hair. "I'm going to run to the ladies' room and try to freshen up a little."

As soon as Mac was gone, she kissed Denise on the cheek and told her she'd call her later. Then she walked out the door without a backward glance.

❦

Wally and Brenda stopped by the bar to get news about Chuck. "I can't believe it," Wally said. "I heard the guy had a trunk full of drugs."

"I heard the guy had just knocked off a convenience store and was making a getaway," Seth said, walking in and sitting beside Wally.

"I don't know the real story," Mac said. "I'm just glad they caught the guy."

He was also really glad to see Seth sitting beside his old friend again.

"So Chuck's going to be okay?" Seth asked.

"He was lucky," Mac said. "I guess the bullet missed anything vital. The doctor had some patching up to do, but he predicts Chuck will make a full recovery."

"So what are you doing with this stuff?" Brenda asked, pointing to the papers Mac had spread out on the bar.

"I'm trying to come up with some fund-raising ideas. Denise isn't going to be able to work for a while. She's going to need to be with Chuck."

"I can help you with that," Seth said. He looked at Mac and his eyes twinkled. "Someone told me I needed to get involved in stuff. My brother plays in an oldies band. I bet I could get them to play at a benefit dance if we could find some place to hold it."

"I have some friends who own a restaurant with a big banquet room upstairs," Brenda said. "I'm sure they'd be willing to help. I'll talk to them."

Seth and Wally and Brenda started batting ideas back and forth. Dates and hours and themes, things Mac hadn't even begun to think about. He stepped back and let them talk, smiling at their enthusiasm. He knew it helped to be doing something productive in a situation you had no control over.

Lisa had offered to waitress until Mac could find a substitute. She came out of the store room with a can of peanuts and a package of napkins. Memories of Allie slammed into him like a tidal wave. She'd run off this morning while he went to get her some coffee. He should have been relieved, but he couldn't stop the disappointment that sank in his stomach when he realized she was gone.

"Hey, Mac, where's Allie?" Wally asked, as if he could read Mac's thoughts. "Is she helping out Denise?"

"Nah, she's gone," Mac said, trying for a light tone in his voice. "Back where she came from."

"Really?" Brenda replied. "You mean, for good? I thought you two really hit it off."

"She was a phony, guys," Mac told them. "She was just using us all to get the dope for that article of hers."

"Hell, Mac," Wally said. "We all knew that right from the beginning. She never made a secret of wanting to write that article on you."

Allie's words came back to haunt him. *I have never lied to you.*

"She wanted to write that article because she thought so highly of you, you know," Seth said. "She never wanted to cause trouble."

"But she knew I didn't want her to publish that article," Mac reminded them. "And she told me she wasn't going to."

"So what's the problem?" Wally asked.

"I found it"

"Found what?" Brenda asked.

"She wrote the article. I read it."

"In the magazine?" Seth asked.

"No, on her computer."

"How was it?" Wally asked.

"How was what?"

"Allie's article."

Mac's head was starting to hurt. "It was good, but don't you understand? She lied to me."

"Did she?" Brenda asked. "What did she tell you?"

He remembered that horrible ride to the hospital and the fist in Mac's stomach clenched a little tighter. "She said she didn't submit it."

"Don't you believe her?"

Mac had learned a lot of things about Allie in the short time that he knew her, and one of them was that she wasn't a quitter. If she'd made up her mind to write that article, she would have had to finish it, if only to prove to herself that she could.

Shit. He had to find her.

Chapter 10

Of course, this couldn't be easy. Mac called Allie's hotel, but the clerk confirmed that she'd checked out this morning. He called directory assistance and got her phone number in Pittsburgh. As he dialed, he planned what he was going to say.

First of all, he had to beg her forgiveness. He'd admit he was an idiot. He'd admit he'd jumped to conclusions and didn't give her a chance to explain. He hoped all that would be enough to at least stop her from hanging up on him. Then he'd admit he loved her and couldn't live without her.

But there was no answer, even though he called practically every five minutes all night long. She didn't even have an answering machine to leave a remorseful message. It was the middle of the night, where could she be?

"Shouldn't she have made it back by now?" Mac asked Lisa. She shrugged and handed him a couple of beer mugs to wash up. "What if she's had an accident? She didn't get much sleep last night. She could have fallen asleep at the wheel."

"Just chill," Lisa said. "I'm sure she's fine."

"Then why isn't she answering her phone?"

Lisa hiked herself up onto the stool in front of him. It was near closing time and the bar was deserted. "Number one," she said, holding up one highly manicured finger, "maybe she didn't go right back to Pittsburgh. Maybe she stopped somewhere on the way. Number two, maybe her phone is out of order. Number three, maybe she has caller ID and doesn't want to talk to you."

"You're a big help," Mac said with a frown. He ran his hand through his hair. He couldn't blame Allie if she didn't want to talk to him. After all, he'd told her in no uncertain terms that he didn't want to talk to her. "How can I apologize to her if she won't answer her phone?"

"Send her an e-mail," Lisa said, checking out her nails in the dim light of the bar.

"I don't have a computer and I don't know her e-mail address," Mac said.

Lisa looked up at him as if the possibility had never occurred to her. "Well, then I guess you could always write her a letter."

Write. Write?

Yeah, but not a letter. He had a better idea. He dug out his wallet. He hoped he still had the phone number.

Mac couldn't sleep when he got home. Words were whirling around in his head, things he needed to say, phrases he had to get just right. He had nothing to write on. He dug through his drawers but knew he wouldn't find any paper or pencils. He'd deliberately kept them out of his house.

Allie had taken her laptop and left his key. He picked up the key and ran it through his fingers. He threw himself down on the sofa. Roger curled up by his feet. Silence wrapped around him.

Not too long ago, this had been his life. The quiet. The solitude.

The boredom.

Mac didn't want this life anymore. He wanted Allie here to laugh with, to share his day with. And to share his nights.

He grabbed Roger's leash and they jogged the couple blocks to an all-night convenience store. He bought a couple of spiral notebooks and a package of pens. There were too many words fighting for space in his brain. He had to start writing them down.

He wrote and scratched out words and wrote again until well after dawn. He was waiting at the computer store when they opened their doors that morning. Writing by hand wasn't going to cut it. He couldn't even read his own handwriting. He let the salesman talk him into the most expensive laptop they had in stock. He wrote the check and hurried home with it.

He had to finish the column as soon as possible if he wanted it to run in tomorrow's edition.

When Allie woke up in the bright little guest room in Denise's house, the sun was streaming through the windows. She stretched and glanced at the clock on the nightstand. It was after noon. Never in her life had she slept that late or that long. She'd slept over twelve hours. After a long shower and a bite to eat, Allie settled in with her laptop. She knew she should head back to Pittsburgh, but first she told herself she wanted to make sure Chuck was okay, and then it was getting too late to take off now, and it was better to work on her book today and leave first thing in the morning.

She had to start making plans. She could rely on her savings for a while, but if she was going to have a chance of paying the bills writing fiction, she had to get this book finished. The thought scared her and excited her at the same time. None of her interviews and articles gave her the charge that writing this story did. Creating her own characters. Creating her own story. It was the best.

But it wouldn't pay the bills unless she could sell it. And before she could sell it, she had to finish it. She scrolled through the last chapter she had done, editing the spelling and grammar here and there. It bugged her not to have it right before she went on to the next chapter. An editor she interviewed once for *Writer's World* had told her—

Allie jumped to her feet, almost dumping the laptop on the floor. Of course, Gloria! The two of them had gotten along really well during the interview and even went out to dinner afterward. Gloria edited mysteries. She even told Allie that if she ever wanted to switch to fiction, to give her a call.

How could she have forgotten that? Probably because her mind and every other part of her body had been concentrating on Mac, on loving Mac, on winning Mac's heart, and there'd been little room for anything else.

Well, she was going to have lots of time for other things now. She ignored the empty feeling swirling in her stomach. She wasn't going to waste any more time feeling sorry for herself. She grabbed her purse and dumped the stack of business cards out of the case she carried. She hoped she still had the phone number.

It was late morning when she woke up. So much for leaving first thing. After a quick shower, she packed up all her things and brought them downstairs to take to her car. When she walked through the living room she saw the light blinking on the answering machine. Three messages. Probably friends checking on how Chuck was doing. They must have called while she was sleeping or in the shower.

She loaded the car and then walked back to the house to leave the key on the coffee table. She was going to miss the new friends she'd made here.

She was going to miss a lot of things.

The telephone rang just as she was going out the door. Allie hesitated. Should she answer Chuck and Denise's phone? She shrugged and decided against it. Whoever it was could leave a message.

The answering machine picked up and suddenly Denise's voice was coming through. "Allie? Where are you? Please don't tell me you've gone already!"

Allie ran back and picked up the receiver. "I'm here," she said. "I was just leaving."

"I've been calling all morning," Denise said with a hint of desperation in her voice.

"I'm a heavy sleeper." Now that she'd made her mind up to go, she had to get this over with. "Listen, I want to thank you for everything you've done, Denise, but I've really got to get going. I've got a long drive."

"Have you seen the paper this morning?"

"No, I haven't been out yet."

"Run down to the corner store and buy a copy of the Buffalo News."

"What?"

"Right now, Allie. Do it."

Denise hung up before Allie could ask any more questions. What could it be? If it was some kind of horrible news, why wouldn't Denise have told her what it was?

Allie sighed and left the house, shutting the door behind her. She'd stop and get a paper on the way out of town. She stopped at the nearest convenience store, poured herself a cup of coffee, grabbed a package of chocolate covered doughnuts and then stopped in front of the rack of newspapers. She set the coffee and doughnuts on the counter and grabbed the morning edition of the Buffalo News.

She scanned the headline. It was news on the political front, nothing for Denise to be so excited about. Then in boldface on the left side of the front page, she saw the heading "New Simon Says Column". The smaller print read, "Simon MacKenzie comes out of retirement" and directed the reader to the section and page number of the column.

Allie's hands shook as she paid for the newspaper. She was already back in her car before she realized she'd forgotten the coffee and doughnuts.

She opened the paper with trembling hands and found the page, honking the horn once as she tried to maneuver the newspaper in the small area of the driver's seat. The title read, "I'm Sorry, Allie."

For years I wrote a newspaper column where I talked about whatever I thought was important, and for some reason, people liked to read what I had to say. However, nothing I ever wrote about was more important than what has now brought me out of my self-imposed "retirement". Not what, in fact, but who. Alison Chandler is her name and I let her get away by being an idiot.

It's been said that you can't teach an old dog new tricks. Well, I have to admit I am an old dog and I was set in my ways. They were lonely ways. Boring ways. Allie invaded my privacy, crashed into my carefully guarded space, and dragged me kicking and screaming back into this business we call life.

I thought I was in love once before. What her name was doesn't matter, but she told me whatever I wanted to hear in order to get me to do whatever

*she wanted. And I believed her lies. By the time I found out about her decep-
tion, she had a lot more than my privacy to take along to the next guy. And
I felt like a fool.*

*None of this is Allie's fault, but I let my past influence my present and
dictate my future. I called her a liar and I never gave her a chance to explain.
I'd like to spend the rest of my life trying to make it up to her.*

*I don't know where she is. So if anyone knows Alison Chandler, a talented
writer from Pittsburgh, Pennsylvania, please ask her to give me another
chance. Tell her I'm a first class jerk. Tell her that I love her. Tell her that I
can't live without her.*

I don't want to go back to my old dog ways.

I'm sorry, Allie, please come back.

Suddenly there was a knock on the door of Allie's car. "Excuse me, miss?
Are you alright?

Allie looked up from the newspaper, tears streaming down her cheeks, and
turned to the concerned elderly woman. She nodded. "I'm wonderful."

Mac had hoped to hear from Allie before he went into work, but his phone
only rang once by the time he had to leave the house. It was Lisa.

"Mac, I'm really sorry," she said, sounding breathless, "but I can't work
for you tonight."

He cursed under his breath. He'd been afraid of this. He should have known
Lisa wouldn't be reliable help. "Well, that's just great."

"I got someone else to work for me," Lisa said quickly. "Don't worry, she's
an experienced waitress."

Right. Don't worry. Like he didn't do anything else but worry. Why hadn't
he heard from Allie? The column ran in the morning editions all over the
country. Maybe she hadn't read the paper, even though he knew she read it
every day.

But worse, maybe she had already read it and she didn't even care.

The substitute waitress still hadn't shown up half an hour before opening. Mac would never have a chance to show her where everything was if she
didn't get here soon. And if this one was as unreliable as Lisa, he was going
to wring somebody's neck.

He was checking the inventory in the store room when he heard the door
open and close. "It's about time," he called out.

"I agree," a familiar voice replied.

Mac froze. He turned and walked slowly down the hall to the doorway.

Allie stood beside the bar wearing a white blouse, black pants and walking shoes, her hair pulled back in a braid.

Dozens of thoughts whirled through his head. How wonderful she looked. What was she doing here? Had she read the column? Did she forgive him?

"I heard you need a waitress," she said, flashing that wide wonderful smile he thought he'd never see again.

It took a moment for her words to kick in. "You're my substitute?"

She nodded. "I think I've finally gotten used to these crazy hours. I've been writing all evening and sleeping all morning. I think I can handle the crowd for you for as long as you need me."

That would be for the rest of his life.

They stood half a room apart, unmoving, as if cemented to the floor. Mac wanted to take her into his arms, nestle his face in the cleavage peeking out from that starchy white shirt, lower her to the floor and bury himself in her soft body, but he couldn't do any of those things until he knew how things stood between them.

"Allie, I'm sorry."

She held up her hand to stop him. "Mac, I read your column. You apolo-gized to me in front of the whole world. You don't need to do it again."

"Yes, I do." Today and maybe for the rest of his life.

He crossed the floor to her and took her hands in his, finally touching her. "I thought I knew it all. I'm sorry I never gave you a chance to explain."

"I thought you didn't love me," Allie said, breaking his heart once again. She lifted her hand to his cheek and softly stroked his face. "I thought if you loved me, you'd believe in me."

"I should have," he told her. "And I should have told you about Robyn. But all I could think of was how much her lies had hurt, especially so soon after Barlow killed himself. I didn't think I could survive that again."

"I don't ever want to hurt you." She sighed, her breath warm against his face. "I love you, Mac."

"I love you, too. But I never realized how much until you were gone and I didn't know if I'd ever see you again." Mac stepped away from her then, but placed his hands on her shoulders. "Do you think we can make this work?"

"Of course we can. We're meant to be together." She laughed, the sound like music to his ears. "Don't you know that by now?"

"Yeah, I know that now." Man, he'd missed the laughter. He kissed her then, feeling the promise in her lips, the promise of a happy future together. The celebratory kiss soon heated up as Allie swept her tongue along his lips. He opened to her, eager to taste her once again. Customers would be coming in the door soon, but he couldn't resist. She tasted sweeter than he remembered, even sweeter since he thought he lost her forever.

She pressed her hips into his as he sucked on her tongue, drinking her in. His pants were getting tighter by the moment. He groaned. "I think I'm going to have to tend bar with a hard-on tonight."

She rubbed her hip against his straining zipper. "Oh, no, we can't have that."

He shrugged. "I've gotten used to it in the past few days."

A mischievous grin spread across her face and she tugged on the front of his shirt. "Come on."

Mac shot a glance at the clock. "Why do I get the feeling you're up to no good?"

Her grin grew wider. "Simon says... behind the bar, right now."

She'd started to unbutton her shirt even before they got behind the long bar. She wasn't wearing a bra and her nipples beaded under his gaze. He palmed each breast and rubbed the nipples with his thumbs.

"Perfect. You are perfect," he murmured. He gathered her in his arms and brought them down onto the floor. He wanted to spend all evening with Allie, stroking, licking, sucking, thrusting. He groaned. "Damn. We don't have much time."

"We have the rest of our lives," she reminded him.

"Yeah, well, tell that to my cock."

Kneeling before him, she reached out and grabbed the thick shaft through his trousers. "Poor boy, we'd better do something quick then, before someone comes in and catches us."

Mac noticed the gleam in her eyes. "I almost forgot about that wide exhibitionist streak you have."

She unzipped his trousers and slid them down over his hips. His cock sprang free. She stroked it with her soft hands while Mac reached out with shaky hands to unzip her pants. He slid his hand between her legs and found her already wet. He pushed her pants down her legs, but for the moment left her wet panties on. He began to stroke her through the thin fabric. He teased the soft flesh, feeling her juices drip around him. He pushed one knuckle up into her until it wouldn't go any further.

Allie rocked against his hand, pushing herself harder against his knuckle. At the same time, she squeezed his cock in long, torturous strokes that threatened to make him explode at any moment.

He knew time was short. With an impatient jerk, he pulled her panties down her legs. Then he gently laid her down on her back. He dug a condom out of the pocket of his trousers and slid it over his throbbing cock. He didn't even have to say "Simon Says" before she spread her knees for him. He plunged his cock into her waiting core, sliding into the wet, hot center of her.

This was where he belonged, he thought as he thrust into her over and over again. Maybe she was right when she said they were meant for each other.

Of course, she was right.

Her hips rose up to meet him, stroke for stroke, going faster and faster with each thrust. Her cries rose in rhythm with their bodies' dance. When she exploded, he felt her climax deep within him. Her muscles clenched around his cock, milking him. He grabbed her ass as he came, plunging deep into her, holding her tightly against him, riding her with all the passion and love and trust he'd come to experience, thanks to her.

He would have liked to have remained buried in her hot body for the rest of the night, but he knew a customer could be coming through the door any moment. He looked down at the lovely woman beneath him and brushed a stray hair out of her eyes.

"Later," he promised, reluctantly withdrawing from her body. "Later, we'll do this right."

She sat up and kissed him lightly on the lips. "Any time."

They stood up and quickly dressed, each straightening the other's clothing, as he heard the door open.

"You know, Mac, you really should think about hiring another bartender," she said as she finished buttoning his shirt. "When's the last time you took a vacation?"

"Vacation? Another bartender?" Hmm, it didn't sound like such a bad idea. He had the feeling he was going to want to do more than sleep and tend bar.

A lot more.

He gathered her into his arms once more as Seth gave him a thumb's up and settled on his regular stool. Life with Allie would never be boring. It was going to be hectic and fun-filled and a whole lot more trouble than it had ever been before.

He couldn't wait.

About the Author:

Natasha Moore fell in love with the written word as soon as she could read. As she grew up, she discovered romance and now enjoys the chance to add some extra sizzle to her stories. She lives in New York State with her real life hero who is happy to tell everyone that he's her inspiration. They travel in their RV whenever possible. The great thing about writing is she can take it anywhere. Find out more about Natasha at www.natashamoore.com *and feel free to drop her at note at* natasha@natashamoore.com.

Men you've been dreaming about!

Secrets

Satisfy your desire for more.

*F*eel the wild adventure, fierce passion and the power of love in every *Secrets* Collection story. Red Sage Publishing's romance authors create richly crafted, sexy, sensual, novella-length stories. Each one is just the right length for reading after a long and hectic day.

Each volume in the *Secrets* Collection has four diverse, ultra-sexy, romantic novellas brimming with adventure, passion and love. More adventurous tales for the adventurous reader. The *Secrets* Collection are a glorious mix of romance genre; numerous historical settings, contemporary, paranormal, science fiction and suspense. We are always looking for new adventures.

Reader response to the *Secrets* volumes has been great! Here's just a small sample:

> *"I loved the variety of settings. Four completely wonderful time periods, give you four completely wonderful reads."*

> *"Each story was a page-turning tale I hated to put down."*

> *"I love* Secrets*! When is the next volume coming out? This one was Hot! Loved the heroes!"*

Secrets have won raves and awards. We could go on, but why don't you find out for yourself—order your set of *Secrets* today! See the back for details.

Secrets, Volume 1

A Lady's Quest by Bonnie Hamre
Widowed Lady Antonia Blair-Sutworth searches for a
lover to save her from the handsome Duke of Suther-
land. The "auditions" may be shocking but utterly
tantalizing.

The Spinner's Dream by Alice Gaines
A seductive fantasy that leaves every woman wishing
for her own private love slave, desperate and running
for his life.

The Proposal by Ivy Landon
This tale is a walk on the wild side of love. *The
Proposal* will taunt you, tease you, and shock you. A
contemporary erotica for the adventurous woman.

The Gift by Jeanie LeGendre
Immerse yourself in this historic tale of exotic seduction, bondage and a concubine's
surrender to the Sultan's desire. Can Alessandra live the life and give the gift the
Sultan demands of her?

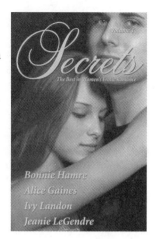

Secrets, Volume 2

Surrogate Lover by Doreen DeSalvo
Adrian Ross is a surrogate sex therapist who has all
the answers and control. He thought he'd seen and
done it all, but he'd never met Sarah.

Snowbound by Bonnie Hamre
A delicious, sensuous regency tale. The marriage-shy
Earl of Howden is teased and tortured by his own
desires and finds there is a woman who can equal his
overpowering sensuality.

Roarke's Prisoner by Angela Knight
Elise, a starship captain, remembers the eager animal
submission she'd known before at her captor's hands
and refuses to become his toy again. However, she has
no idea of the delights he's planned for her this time.

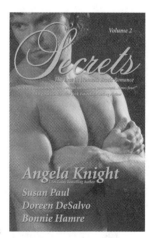

Savage Garden by Susan Paul
Raine's been captured by a mysterious and dangerous revolutionary leader in
Mexico. At first her only concern is survival, but she quickly finds lush erotic nights
in her captor's arms.

Winner of the Fallot Literary Award for Fiction!

Secrets, Volume 3

The Spy Who Loved Me by Jeanie Cesarini
Undercover FBI agent Paige Ellison's sexual appetites
rise to new levels when she works with leading man
Christopher Sharp, the cunning agent who uses all his
training to capture her body and heart.

The Barbarian by Ann Jacobs
Lady Brianna vows not to surrender to the barbaric
Giles, Earl of Harrow. He must use sexual arts
learned in the infidels' harem to conquer his bride. A
word of caution—this is not for the faint of heart.

Blood and Kisses by Angela Knight
A vampire assassin is after Beryl St. Cloud. Her only
hope lies with Decker, another vampire and ex-merce-
nary. Broke, she offers herself as payment for his services. Will his seductive powers
take her very soul?

Love Undercover by B.J. McCall
Amanda Forbes is the bait in a strip joint sting operation. While she performs, fellow
detective "Cowboy" Cooper gets to watch. Though he excites her, she must fight the
temptation to surrender to the passion.

Winner of the 1997 Under the Covers Readers Favorite Award

Secrets, Volume 4

An Act of Love by Jeanie Cesarini
Shelby Moran's past left her terrified of sex. International film star Jason Gage must gently coach the young
starlet in the ways of love. He wants more than an act—
he wants Shelby to feel true passion in his arms.

Enslaved by Desirée Lindsey
Lord Nicholas Summer's air of danger, dark passions,
and irresistible charm have brought Lady Crystal's
long-hidden desires to the surface. Will he be able to
give her the one thing she desires before it's too late?

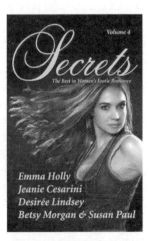

The Bodyguard by Betsy Morgan & Susan Paul
Kaki York is a bodyguard, but watching the wild,
erotic romps of her client's sexual conquests on the
security cameras is getting to her—and her partner, the ruggedly handsome James
Kulick. Can she resist his insistent desire to have her?

The Love Slave by Emma Holly
A woman's ultimate fantasy. For one year, Princess Lily will be attended to by three
delicious men of her choice. While she delights in playing with the first two, it's the
reluctant Grae, with his powerful chest, black eyes and hair, that stirs her desires.

Secrets, Volume 5

Beneath Two Moons by Sandy Fraser
Step into the future and find Conor, rough and masculine like frontiermen of old, on the prowl for a new conquest. In his sights, Dr. Eva Kelsey. She got away before, but this time Conor makes sure she begs for more.

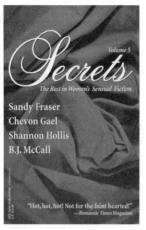

Insatiable by Chevon Gael
Marcus Remington photographs beautiful models for a living, but it's Ashlyn Fraser, a young exec having some glamour shots done, who has stolen his heart. It's up to Marcus to help her discover her inner sexual self.

Strictly Business by Shannon Hollis
Elizabeth Forrester knows it's tough enough for a woman to make it to the top in the corporate world. Garrett Hill, the most beautiful man in Silicon Valley, has to come along to stir up her wildest fantasies. Dare she give in to both their desires?

Alias Smith and Jones by B.J. McCall
Meredith Collins finds herself stranded at the airport. A handsome stranger by the name of Smith offers her sanctuary for the evening and she finds those mesmerizing, green-flecked eyes hard to resist. Are they to be just two ships passing in the night?

Secrets, Volume 6

Flint's Fuse by Sandy Fraser
Dana Madison's father has her "kidnapped" for her own safety. Flint, the tall, dark and dangerous mercenary, is hired for the job. But just which one is the prisoner—Dana will try *anything* to get away.

Love's Prisoner by MaryJanice Davidson
Trapped in an elevator, Jeannie Lawrence experienced unwilling rapture at Michael Windham's hands. She never expected the devilishly handsome man to show back up in her life—or turn out to be a werewolf!

The Education of Miss Felicity Wells by Alice Gaines
Felicity Wells wants to be sure she'll satisfy her soon-to-be husband but she needs a teacher. Dr. Marcus Slade, an experienced lover, agrees to take her on as a student, but can he stop short of taking her completely?

A Candidate for the Kiss by Angela Knight
Working on a story, reporter Dana Ivory stumbles onto a more amazing one—a sexy, secret agent who happens to be a vampire. She wants her story but Gabriel Archer wants more from her than just sex and blood.

Secrets, Volume 7

Amelia's Innocence by Julia Welles
Amelia didn't know her father bet her in a card game with Captain Quentin Hawke, so honor demands a compromise—three days of erotic foreplay, leaving her virginity and future intact.

The Woman of His Dreams by Jade Lawless
From the day artist Gray Avonaco moves in next door, Joanna Morgan is plagued by provocative dreams. But what she believes is unrequited lust, Gray sees as another chance to be with the woman he loves. He must persuade her that even death can't stop true love.

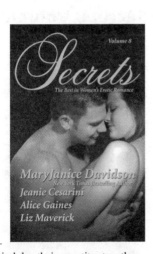

Surrender by Kathryn Anne Dubois
Free-spirited Lady Johanna wants no part of the binding strictures society imposes with her marriage to the powerful Duke. She doesn't know the dark Duke wants sensual adventure, and sexual satisfaction.

Kissing the Hunter by Angela Knight
Navy Seal Logan McLean hunts the vampires who murdered his wife. Virginia Hart is a sexy vampire searching for her lost soul-mate only to find him in a man determined to kill her. She must convince him all vampires aren't created equally.

Winner of the Venus Book Club Best Book of the Year

Secrets, Volume 8

Taming Kate by Jeanie Cesarini
Kathryn Roman inherits a legal brothel. Little does this city girl know the town wants her to be their new madam so they've charged Trey Holliday, one very dominant cowboy, with taming her.

Jared's Wolf by MaryJanice Davidson
Jared Rocke will do anything to avenge his sister's death, but ends up attracted to Moira Wolfbauer, the she-wolf sworn to protect her pack. Joining forces to stop a killer, they learn love defies all boundaries.

My Champion, My Lover by Alice Gaines
Celeste Broder is a woman committed for having a sexy appetite. Mayor Robert Albright may be her champion—if she can convince him her freedom will mean they can indulge their appetites together.

Kiss or Kill by Liz Maverick
In this post-apocalyptic world, Camille Kazinsky's military career rides on her ability to make a choice—whether the robo called Meat should live or die. Can he prove he's human enough to live, man enough… to make her feel like a woman.

Winner of the Venus Book Club Best Book of the Year

Secrets, Volume 9

Wild For You by Kathryn Anne Dubois
When college intern, Georgie, gets captured by a
Congo wildman, she discovers this specimen of male
virility has never seen a woman. The research possibilities are endless!

Wanted by Kimberly Dean
FBI Special Agent Jeff Reno wants Danielle Carver.
There's her body, brains—and that charge of treason
on her head. Dani goes on the run, but the sexy Fed is
hot on her trail.

Secluded by Lisa Marie Rice
Nicholas Lee's wealth and power came with a price—
his enemies will kill anyone he loves. When Isabelle
steals his heart, Nicholas secludes her in his palace for a lifetime of desire in only a
few days.

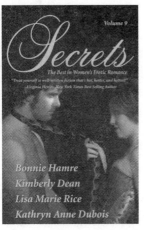

Flights of Fantasy by Bonnie Hamre
Chloe taught others to see the realities of life but she's never shared the intimate
world of her sensual yearnings. Given the chance, will she be woman enough to
fulfill her most secret erotic fantasy?

Secrets, Volume 10

Private Eyes by Dominique Sinclair
When a mystery man captivates P.I. Nicolla Black
during a stakeout, she discovers her no-seduction rule
bending under the pressure of long denied passion.
She agrees to the seduction, but he demands her total
surrender.

The Ruination of Lady Jane by Bonnie Hamre
To avoid her upcoming marriage, Lady Jane Ponson-
by-Maitland flees into the arms of Havyn Attercliffe.
She begs him to ruin her rather than turn her over to
her odious fiancé.

Code Name: Kiss by Jeanie Cesarini
Agent Lily Justiss is on a mission to defend her country
against terrorists that requires giving up her virginity as a sex slave. As her master
takes her body, desire for her commanding officer Seth Blackthorn fuels her mind.

The Sacrifice by Kathryn Anne Dubois
Lady Anastasia Bedovier is days from taking her vows as a Nun. Before she denies
her sensuality forever, she wants to experience pleasure. Count Maxwell is the perfect man to initiate her into erotic delight.

Secrets, Volume 11

Masquerade by Jennifer Probst
Hailey Ashton is determined to free herself from her
sexual restrictions. Four nights of erotic pleasures
without revealing her identity. A chance to explore her
secret desires without the fear of unmasking.

Ancient Pleasures by Jess Michaels
Isabella Winslow is obsessed with finding out what
caused her husband's death, but trapped in an Egyp-
tian concubine's tomb with a sexy American raider,
succumbing to the mummy's sensual curse takes over.

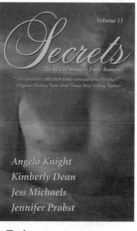

Manhunt by Kimberly Dean
Framed for murder, Michael Tucker takes Taryn
Swanson hostage—the one woman who can clear him.
Despite the evidence against him, the attraction is strong. Tucker resorts to uncon-
ventional, yet effective methods of persuasion to change the sexy ADA's mind.

Wake Me by Angela Knight
Chloe Hart received a sexy painting of a sleeping knight. Radolf of Varik has been
trapped there for centuries, cursed by a witch. His only hope is to visit the dreams of
women and make one of them fall in love with him so she can free him with a kiss.

Secrets, Volume 12

Good Girl Gone Bad by Dominique Sinclair
Setting out to do research for an article, nothing could
have prepared Reagan for Luke, or his offer to teach
her everything she needs to know about sex. Licen-
tious pleasures, forbidden desires… inspiring the best
writing she's ever done.

Aphrodite's Passion by Jess Michaels
When Selena flees Victorian London before her evil
stepchildren can institutionalize her for hysteria,
Gavin is asked to bring her back home. But when he
finds her living on the island of Cyprus, his need to
have her begins to block out every other impulse.

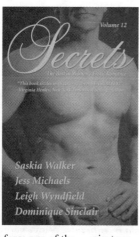

White Heat by Leigh Wyndfield
Raine is hiding in an icehouse in the middle of nowhere from one of the scariest men
in the universes. Walker escaped from a burning prison. Imagine their surprise when
they find out they have the same man to blame for their miseries. Passion, revenge
and love are in their future.

Summer Lightning by Saskia Walker
Sculptress Sally is enjoying an idyllic getaway on a secluded cove when she spots a
gorgeous man walking naked on the beach. When Julian finds an attractive woman
shacked up in his cove, he has to check her out. But what will he do when he finds
she's secretly been using him as a model?

Secrets, Volume 13

Out of Control by Rachelle Chase
Astrid's world revolves around her business and she's hoping to pick up wealthy Erik Santos as a client. He's hoping to pick up something entirely different. Will she give in to the seductive pull of his proposition?

Hawkmoor by Amber Green
Shape-shifters answer to Darien as he acts in the name of long-missing Lady Hawkmoor, their ruler. When she unexpectedly surfaces, Darien must deal with a scrappy individual whose wary eyes hold the other half of his soul, but who has the power to destroy his world.

Lessons in Pleasure by Charlotte Featherstone
A wicked bargain has Lily vowing never to yield to the
demands of the rake she once loved and lost. Unfortunately, Damian, the Earl of St. Croix, or Saint as he is infamously known, will not take 'no' for an answer.

In the Heat of the Night by Calista Fox
Haunted by a curse, Molina fears she won't live to see her 30th birthday. Nick, her former bodyguard, is re-hired to protect her from the fatal accidents that plague her family. Will his passion and love be enough to convince Molina they have a future together?

Secrets, Volume 14

Soul Kisses by Angela Knight
Beth's been kidnapped by Joaquin Ramirez, a sadistic vampire. Handsome vampire cousins, Morgan and Garret Axton, come to her rescue. Can she find happiness with two vampires?

Temptation in Time by Alexa Aames
Ariana escaped the Middle Ages after stealing a kiss of magic from sexy sorcerer, Marcus de Grey. When he brings her back, they begin a battle of wills and a sexual odyssey that could spell disaster for them both.

Ailis and the Beast by Jennifer Barlowe
When Ailis agreed to be her village's sacrifice to the mysterious Beast she was prepared to sacrifice her virtue, and possibly her life. But some things aren't what they seem. Ailis and the Beast are about to discover the greatest sacrifice may be the human heart.

Night Heat by Leigh Wynfield
When Rip Bowhite leads a revolt on the prison planet, he ends up struggling to survive against monsters that rule the night. Jemma, the prison's Healer, won't allow herself to be distracted by the instant attraction she feels for Rip. As the stakes are raised and death draws near, love seems doomed in the heat of the night.

Secrets, Volume 15

Simon Says by Jane Thompson
Simon Campbell is a newspaper columnist who panders to male fantasies. Georgina Kennedy is a respectable librarian. On the surface, these two have nothing in common... but don't judge a book by its cover.

Bite of the Wolf by Cynthia Eden
Gareth Morlet, alpha werewolf, has finally found his mate. All he has to do is convince Trinity to join with him, to give in to the pleasure of a werewolf's mating, and then she will be his... forever.

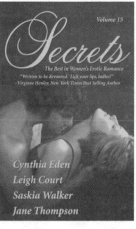

Falling for Trouble by Saskia Walker
With 48 hours to clear her brother's name, Sonia Harmond finds help from irresistible bad boy, Oliver Eaglestone. When the erotic tension between them hits fever pitch, securing evidence to thwart an international arms dealer isn't the only danger they face.

The Disciplinarian by Leigh Court
Headstrong Clarissa Babcock is sent for instruction in proper wifely obedience. Disciplinarian Jared Ashworth uses the tools of seduction to show her how to control a demanding husband, but her beauty, spirit, and uninhibited passion make Jared hunger to keep her—and their darkly erotic nights—all for himself!

Secrets, Volume 16

Never Enough by Cynthia Eden
Abby McGill has been playing with fire. Bad-boy Jake taught her the true meaning of desire, but she knows she has to end her relationship with him. But Jake isn't about to let the woman he wants walk away from him.

Bunko by Sheri Gilmoore
Tu Tran must decide between Jack, who promises to share every aspect of his life with her, or Dev, who hides behind a mask and only offers nights of erotic sex. Will she gamble on the man who can see behind her own mask and expose her true desires?

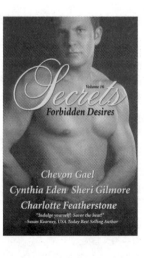

Hide and Seek by Chevon Gael
Kyle DeLaurier ditches his trophy-fiance in favor of a tropical paradise full of tall, tanned, topless females.
Private eye, Darcy McLeod, is on the trail of this runaway groom. Together they sizzle while playing Hide and Seek with their true identities.

Seduction of the Muse by Charlotte Featherstone
He's the Dark Lord, the mysterious author who pens the erotic tales of an innocent woman's seduction. She is his muse, the woman he watches from the dark shadows, the woman whose dreams he invades at night.

Secrets, Volume 17

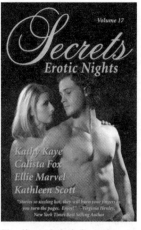

Rock Hard Candy by Kathy Kaye
Jessica Hennessy, descendent of a Voodoo priestess, decides it's time for the man of her dreams. A dose of her ancestor's aphrodisiac slipped into the gooey center of her homemade bon bons ought to do the trick.

Fatal Error by Kathleen Scott
Jesse Storm must make amends to humanity by destroying the software he helped design that's taken the government hostage. But he must also protect the woman he's loved in secret for nearly a decade.

Birthday by Ellie Marvel
Jasmine Templeton's been celibate long enough. Will a wild night at a hot new club with her two best friends ease the ache or just make it worse? Considering one is Charlie and she's been having strange notions about their relationship of late… It's definitely a birthday neither she nor Charlie will ever forget.

Intimate Rendezvous by Calista Fox
A thief causes trouble at Cassandra Kensington's nightclub and sexy P.I. Dean Hewitt arrives to help. One look at her sends his blood boiling, despite the fact that his keen instincts have him questioning the legitimacy of her business.

Secrets, Volume 18

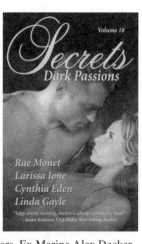

Lone Wolf Three by Rae Monet
Planetary politics and squabbling drain former rebel leader Taban Zias. But his anger quickly turns to desire when he meets, Lakota Blackson. She's Taban's perfect mate—now if he can just convince her.

Flesh to Fantasy by Larissa Ione
Kelsa Bradshaw is a loner happily immersed in a world of virtual reality. Trent Jordan is a paramedic who experiences the harsh realities of life. When their worlds collide in an erotic eruption can Trent convince Kelsa to turn the fantasy into something real?

Heart Full of Stars by Linda Gayle
Singer Fanta Rae finds herself stranded on a lonely Mars outpost with the first human male she's seen in years. Ex-Marine Alex Decker lost his family and guilt drove him into isolation, but when alien assassins come to enslave Fanta, she and Decker come together to fight for their lives.

The Wolf's Mate by Cynthia Eden
When Michael Morlet finds "Kat" Hardy fighting for her life, he instantly recognizes her as the mate he's been seeking all of his life, but someone's trying to kill her. With danger stalking them, will Kat trust him enough to become his mate?

Secrets, Volume 19

Affliction by Elisa Adams
Holly Aronson finally believes she's safe with sweet
Andrew. But when his life long friend, Shane, arrives, events begin to spiral out of control. She's
inexplicably drawn to Shane. As she runs for her life,
which one will protect her?

Falling Stars by Kathleen Scott
Daria is both a Primon fighter pilot and a Primon
princess. As a deadly new enemy faces appears, she
must choose between her duty to the fleet and the
desperate need to forge an alliance through her marriage to the enemy's General Raven.

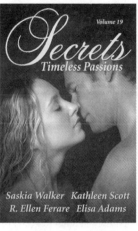

*Saskia Walker   Kathleen Scott
R. Ellen Ferare   Elisa Adams*

Toy in the Attic by R. Ellen Ferare
Gabrielle discovers a life-sized statue of a nude man. Her unexpected roommate
reveals himself to be a talented lover caught by a witch's curse. Can she help him
break free of the spell that holds him, without losing her heart along the way?

What You Wish For by Saskia Walker
Lucy Chambers is renovating her historic house. As her dreams about a stranger
become more intense, she wishes he were with her. Two hundred years in the past, the
man wishes for companionship. Suddenly they find themselves together—in his time.

Secrets, Volume 20

The Subject by Amber Green
One week Tyler is a game designer, signing the deal
of her life. The next, she's running for her life. Who
can she trust? Certainly not sexy, mysterious Esau,
who keeps showing up after the hoo-hah hits the fan!

Surrender by Dominique Sinclair
Agent Madeline Carter is in too deep. She's slipped
into Sebastian Maiocco's life to investigate his Sicil-
ian mafia family. He unearths desires Madeline's
unable to deny, conflicting the duty that honors her.
Madeline must surrender to Sebastian or risk being
exposed, leaving her target for a ruthless clan.

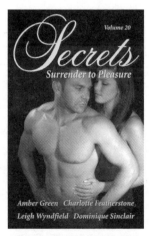

*Amber Green   Charlotte Featherstone,
Leigh Wyndfield   Dominique Sinclair*

Stasis by Leigh Wyndfield
Morgann Right's Commanding Officer's been drugged with Stasis, turning him into
a living statue she's forced to take care of for ten long days. As her hands tend to
him, she sees her CO in a totally different light. She wants him and, while she can
tell he wants her, touching him intimately might come back to haunt them both.

A Woman's Pleasure by Charlotte Featherstone
Widowed Isabella, Lady Langdon is yearning to discover all the pleasures denied her
in her marriage, she finds herself falling hard for the magnetic charms of the mysterious and exotic Julian Gresham—a man skilled in pleasures of the flesh.

Secrets, Volume 21

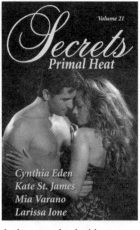

Caged Wolf by Cynthia Eden
Alerac La Morte has been drugged and kidnapped. He realizes his captor, Madison Langley, is actually his destined mate, but she hates his kind. Will Alerac convince her he's not the monster she thinks?

Wet Dreams by Larissa Ione
Injured and on the run, agent Brent Logan needs a miracle. What he gets is a boat owned by Marina Summers. Pursued by killers, ravaged by a storm, and plagued by engine troubles, they can do little but spend their final hours immersed in sensual pleasure.

Good Vibrations by Kate St. James
Lexi O'Brien vows to swear off sex while she attends grad school, so when her favorite out-of-town customer asks her out, she decides to indulge in an erotic fling. Little does she realize Gage Templeton is moving home, to her city, and has no intention of settling for a short-term affair..

Virgin of the Amazon by Mia Varano
Librarian Anna Winter gets lost on the Amazon and stumbles upon a tribe whose shaman wants a pale-skinned virgin to deflower. British adventurer Coop Daventry, the tribe's self-styled chief, wants to save her, but which man poses a greater threat?

Secrets, Volume 22

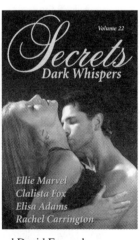

Heat by Ellie Marvel
Mild-mannered alien Tarkin is in heat and the only compatible female is a Terran. He courts her the old fashioned Terran way. Because if he can't seduce her before his cycle ends, he won't get a second chance.

Breathless by Rachel Carrington
Lark Hogan is a martial arts expert seeking vengeance for the death of her sister. She seeks help from Zac, a mercenary wizard. Confronting a common enemy, they battle their own demons as well as their powerful attraction, and will fight to the death to protect what they've found.

Midnight Rendezvous by Calista Fox
From New York to Cabo to Paris to Tokyo, Cat Hewitt and David Essex share decadent midnight rendezvous. But when the real world presses in on their erotic fantasies, and Cat's life is in danger, will their whirlwind romance stand a chance?

Birthday Wish by Elisa Adams
Anna Kelly had many goals before turning 30 and only one is left—to spend one night with sexy Dean Harrison. When Dean asks her what she wants for her birthday, she grabs at the opportunity to ask him for an experience she'll never forget.

Secrets, Volume 23

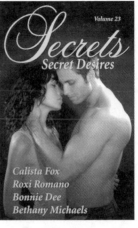

The Sex Slave by Roxi Romano
Jaci Coe needs a hero and the hard bodied man in
black meets all the criteria. Opportunistic Jaci takes
advantage of Lazarus Stone's commandingly protective nature, but together, they learn how to live free...
and love freely.

Forever My Love by Calista Fox
Professor Aja Woods is a 16th century witch... only
she doesn't know it. Christian St. James, her vampire
lover, has watched over her spirit for 500 years. When
her powers are recovered, so too are her memories of
Christian—and the love they once shared.

Reflection of Beauty by Bonnie Dee
Artist Christine Dawson is commissioned to paint a portrait of wealthy recluse, Eric
Leroux. It's up to her to reach the heart of this physically and emotionally scarred
man. Can love rescue Eric from isolation and restore his life?

Educating Eva by Bethany Lynn
Eva Blakely attends the infamous Ivy Hill houseparty to gather research for her book
Mating Rituals of the Human Male. But when she enlists the help of research "speci-
men" and notorious rake, Aidan Worthington, she gets some unexpected results.

Secrets, Volume 24

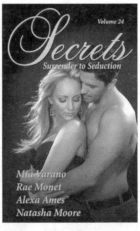

Hot on Her Heels by Mia Varano
Private investigator Jack Slater dons a g-string to
investigate the Lollipop Lounge, a male strip club.
He's not sure if the club's sexy owner, Vivica Steele,
is involved in the scam, but Jack figures he's just the
Lollipop to sweeten her life.

Shadow Wolf by Rae Monet
A half-breed Lupine challenges a high-ranking
Solarian Wolf Warrior. When Dia Nahiutras tries to
steal Roark D'Reincolt's wolf, does she get an enemy
forever or a mate for life?

Bad to the Bone by Natasha Moore
At her class reunion, Annie Shane sheds her good girl
reputation through one wild weekend with Luke Kendall. But Luke is done playing
the field and wants to settle down. What would a bad girl do?

War God by Alexa Ames
Estella Eaton, a lovely graduate student, is the unwitting carrier of the essence of
Aphrodite. But Ares, god of war, the ultimate alpha male, knows the truth and be-
comes obsessed with Estelle, pursuing her relentlessly. Can her modern sensibilities
and his ancient power coexist, or will their battle of wills destroy what matters most?

Secrets, Volume 25

Blood Hunt by Cynthia Eden
Vampiress Nema Alexander has a taste for bad boys.
Slade Brion has just been charged with tracking her
down. He won't stop until he catches her, and Nema
won't stop until she claims him, forever.

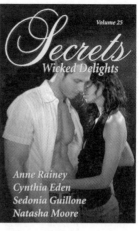

Scandalous Behavior by Anne Rainey
Tess Marley wants to take a walk on the wild side.
Who better to teach her about carnal pleasures than
her intriguing boss, Kevin Haines? But Tess makes
a major miscalculation when she crosses the line
between lust and love.

Enter the Hero by Sedonia Guillone
Kass and Lian are sentenced to sex slavery in the Con-
federation's pleasure district. Forced to make love for an audience, their hearts are
with each other while their bodies are on display. Now, in the midst of sexual slavery,
they have one more chance to escape to Paradise.

Up to No Good by Natasha Moore
Former syndicated columnist Simon "Mac" MacKenzie hides a tragic secret. When
freelance writer Alison Chandler tracks him down, he knows she's up to no good. Is
their attraction merely a distraction or the key to surviving their war of wills?

Secrets, Volume 26

Secret Rendezvous by Calista Fox
McCarthy Portman has seen enough happily-
ever-afters to long for one of her own, but when her
renowned matchmaking software pairs her with the
wild and wicked Josh Kensington, everything she's
always believed about love is turned upside down.

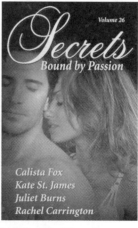

Enchanted Spell by Rachel Carrington
Witches and wizards don't mix. Every magical being
knows that. Yet, when a little mischievous magic
thrusts Ella and Kevlin together, they do so much
more than mix—they combust.

Exes and Ahhhs by Kate St. James
Former lovers Risa Haber and Eric Lange are partners
in a catering business, but Eric can't seem to remain a silent partner. Risa offers one
night of carnal delights if he'll sell her his share then disappear forever.

The Spy's Surrender by Juliet Burns
The famous courtesan Eva Werner is England's secret weapon against Napoleon. Her
orders are to attend a sadistic marquis' depraved house party and rescue a British spy
being held prisoner. As the weekend orgy begins, she's forced to make the spy her
love slave for the marquis' pleasure. But who is slave and who is master?

The Forever Kiss
by Angela Knight

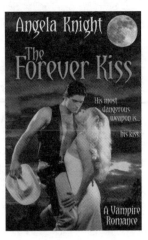

Listen to what reviewers say:

"*The Forever Kiss* flows well with good characters and an interesting plot. ... If you enjoy vampires and a lot of hot sex, you are sure to enjoy *The Forever Kiss*."

—*The Best Reviews*

"Battling vampires, a protective ghost and the ever present battle of good and evil keep excellent pace with the erotic delights in Angela Knight's *The Forever Kiss*—a book that absolutely bites with refreshing paranormal humor." **4½ Stars, Top Pick**

—*Romantic Times BOOKclub*

"I found *The Forever Kiss* to be an exceptionally written, refreshing book. ... I really enjoyed this book by Angela Knight. ... 5 angels!"

—*Fallen Angel Reviews*

"*The Forever Kiss* is the first single title released from Red Sage and if this is any indication of what we can expect, it won't be the last. ... The love scenes are hot enough to give a vampire a sunburn and the fight scenes will have you cheering for the good guys."

—*Really Bad Barb Reviews*

In *The Forever Kiss*:

For years, Valerie Chase has been haunted by dreams of a Texas Ranger she knows only as "Cowboy." As a child, he rescued her from the nightmare vampires who murdered her parents. As an adult, she still dreams of him—but now he's her seductive lover in nights of erotic pleasure.

Yet "Cowboy" is more than a dream—he's the real Cade McKinnon—and a vampire! For years, he's protected Valerie from Edward Ridgemont, the sadistic vampire who turned him. Now, Ridgmont wants Valerie for his own and Cade is the only one who can protect her.

When Val finds herself abducted by her handsome dream man, she's appalled to discover he's one of the vampires she fears. Now, caught in a web of fear and passion, she and Cade must learn to trust each other, even as an immortal monster stalks their every move.

Their only hope of survival is... *The Forever Kiss*.

Romantic Times Best Erotic Novel of the Year

Check out our hot eBook titles available online at eRedSage.com!

Visit the site regularly as we're always adding new eBook titles.

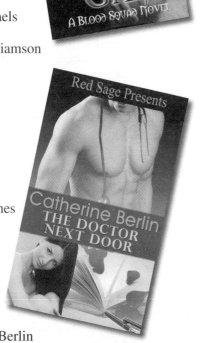

Here's just some of what you'll find:

A Christmas Cara by Bethany Michaels

A Damsel in Distress by Brenda Williamson

Blood Game by Rae Monet

Fires Within by Roxana Blaze

Forbidden Fruit by Anne Rainey

High Voltage by Calista Fox

Master of the Elements by Alice Gaines

One Wish by Calista Fox

Quinn's Curse by Natasha Moore

Rock My World by Caitlyn Willows

The Doctor Next Door by Catherine Berlin

Unclaimed by Nathalie Gray

It's not just reviewers raving about *Secrets*. See what readers have to say:

"When are you coming out with a new Volume? I want a new one next month!" via email from a reader.

"I loved the hot, wet sex without vulgar words being used to make it exciting." after *Volume 1*

"I loved the blend of sensuality and sexual intensity—HOT!" after *Volume 2*

"The best thing about *Secrets* is they're hot and brief! The least thing is you do not have enough of them!" after *Volume 3*

"I have been extremely satisfied with *Secrets*, keep up the good writing." after *Volume 4*

"Stories have plot and characters to support the erotica. They would be good strong stories without the heat." after *Volume 5*

"*Secrets* really knows how to push the envelop better than anyone else." after *Volume 6*

"These are the best sensual stories I have ever read!" after *Volume 7*

"I love, love, love the *Secrets* stories. I now have all of them, please have more books come out each year." after *Volume 8*

"These are the perfect sensual romance stories!" after *Volume 9*

"What I love about *Secrets Volume 10* is how I couldn't put it down!" after *Volume 10*

"All of the *Secrets* volumes are terrific! I have read all of them up to *Secrets Volume 11*. Please keep them coming! I will read every one you make!" after *Volume 11*

Finally, the men you've been dreaming about!

Give the Gift of Spicy Romantic Fiction

Don't want to wait? You can place a retail price ($12.99) order for any of the *Secrets* volumes from the following:

① online at **eRedSage.com**

② **Waldenbooks, Borders, and Books-a-Million Stores**

③ **Amazon.com** or **BarnesandNoble.com**

④ or buy them at your local bookstore or online book source.

Bookstores: Please contact Baker & Taylor Distributors, Ingram Book Distributor, or Red Sage Publishing, Inc. for bookstore sales.

Order by title or ISBN #:

Vol. 1: 0-9648942-0-3
ISBN #13 978-0-9648942-0-4

Vol. 2: 0-9648942-1-1
ISBN #13 978-0-9648942-1-1

Vol. 3: 0-9648942-2-X
ISBN #13 978-0-9648942-2-8

Vol. 4: 0-9648942-4-6
ISBN #13 978-0-9648942-4-2

Vol. 5: 0-9648942-5-4
ISBN #13 978-0-9648942-5-9

Vol. 6: 0-9648942-6-2
ISBN #13 978-0-9648942-6-6

Vol. 7: 0-9648942-7-0
ISBN #13 978-0-9648942-7-3

Vol. 8: 0-9648942-8-9
ISBN #13 978-0-9648942-9-7

Vol. 9: 0-9648942-9-7
ISBN #13 978-0-9648942-9-7

Vol. 10: 0-9754516-0-X
ISBN #13 978-0-9754516-0-1

Vol. 11: 0-9754516-1-8
ISBN #13 978-0-9754516-1-8

Vol. 12: 0-9754516-2-6
ISBN #13 978-0-9754516-2-5

Vol. 13: 0-9754516-3-4
ISBN #13 978-0-9754516-3-2

Vol. 14: 0-9754516-4-2
ISBN #13 978-0-9754516-4-9

Vol. 15: 0-9754516-5-0
ISBN #13 978-0-9754516-5-6

Vol. 16: 0-9754516-6-9
ISBN #13 978-0-9754516-6-3

Vol. 17: 0-9754516-7-7
ISBN #13 978-0-9754516-7-0

Vol. 18: 0-9754516-8-5
ISBN #13 978-0-9754516-8-7

Vol. 19: 0-9754516-9-3
ISBN #13 978-0-9754516-9-4

Vol. 20: 1-60310-000-8
ISBN #13 978-1-60310-000-7

Vol. 21: 1-60310-001-6
ISBN #13 978-1-60310-001-4

Vol. 22: 1-60310-002-4
ISBN #13 978-1-60310-002-1

Vol. 23: 1-60310-164-0
ISBN #13 978-1-60310-164-6

Vol. 24: 1-60310-165-9
ISBN #13 978-1-60310-165-3

Vol. 25: 1-60310-005-9
ISBN #13 978-1-60310-005-2

Vol. 26: 1-60310-006-7
ISBN #13 978-1-60310-006-9

The Forever Kiss:
0-9648942-3-8
ISBN #13
978-0-9648942-3-5 ($14.00)

Red Sage Publishing Order Form:

(Orders shipped in two to three days of receipt.)

Each volume of *Secrets* retails for $12.99, but you can get it direct via mail order for only $10.99 each. The novel *The Forever Kiss* retails for $14.00, but by direct mail order, you only pay $12.00. Use the order form below to place your direct mail order. Fill in the quantity you want for each book on the blanks beside the title.

—— *Secrets* Volume 1	—— *Secrets* Volume 10	—— *Secrets* Volume 19
—— *Secrets* Volume 2	—— *Secrets* Volume 11	—— *Secrets* Volume 20
—— *Secrets* Volume 3	—— *Secrets* Volume 12	—— *Secrets* Volume 21
—— *Secrets* Volume 4	—— *Secrets* Volume 13	—— *Secrets* Volume 22
—— *Secrets* Volume 5	—— *Secrets* Volume 14	—— *Secrets* Volume 23
—— *Secrets* Volume 6	—— *Secrets* Volume 15	—— *Secrets* Volume 24
—— *Secrets* Volume 7	—— *Secrets* Volume 16	—— *Secrets* Volume 25
—— *Secrets* Volume 8	—— *Secrets* Volume 17	—— *Secrets* Volume 26
—— *Secrets* Volume 9	—— *Secrets* Volume 18	—— *The Forever Kiss*

Total —— *Secrets* Volumes @ $10.99 each = $————————

Total —— *The Forever Kiss* @ $12.00 each = $————————

Shipping & handling (in the U.S.) $————————

US Priority Mail: UPS insured:

1–2 books .... $ 5.50   1–4 books $16.00
3–5 books .... $11.50   5–9 books $25.00
6–9 books................... $14.50   10–26 books $29.00
10–15 books $19.00
16–26 books .... $27.00   SUBTOTAL $————————

Florida 6% sales tax (if delivered in FL) $————————

TOTAL AMOUNT ENCLOSED $————————

Your personal information is kept private and not shared with anyone.

Name: (please print) ————————————————————————————

Address: (no P.O. Boxes) ————————————————————————

City/State/Zip: ——————————————————————————————

Phone or email: (only regarding order if necessary) ————————————————

You can order direct from **eRedSage.com** and use a credit card or you can use this form to send in your mail order with a check. Please make check payable to **Red Sage Publishing**. Check must be drawn on a U.S. bank in U.S. dollars. Mail your check and order form to:

Red Sage Publishing, Inc. Department S25 P.O. Box 4844 Seminole, FL 33775